CW01499408

*This novel is dedicated to the memory of my brother, Sandy Edwards.
Sandy was fascinated by history and found great pleasure in talking
about books... and talking.*

THE JACOBITE'S HEIR

MORAG EDWARDS

BLOODHOUND
— B O O K S —

Copyright © 2025 Morag Edwards

The right of Morag Edwards to be identified as the Author of the Work has been asserted by her in accordance with the Copyright, Designs and Patents Act 1988.

First published in 2025 by Bloodhound Books.

Apart from any use permitted under UK copyright law, this publication may only be reproduced, stored, or transmitted, in any form, or by any means, with prior permission in writing of the publisher or, in the case of reprographic production, in accordance with the terms of licences issued by the Copyright Licensing Agency.
All characters in this publication are fictitious and any resemblance to real persons, living or dead, is purely coincidental.

www.bloodhoundbooks.com

Print ISBN: 978-1-917705-27-1

PART ONE

CHAPTER I
1730

Henrietta fell in love with her mother's mother from the moment she was first enveloped in Lady Barbara Webb's vast bosom, barely contained within stays and frills of lace. Her brothers grimaced at Granny Webb's embrace but Henrietta felt only comfort to be held tight against yielding, pillowy skin, scented with violets. She also liked her grandmother's name, Barbara, finding the cadence soft and friendly.

The untimely death of Granny Waldegrave, the one she was named after, had meant leaving everything they had known at Navestock, to face an uncertain welcome from strangers, their grandparents living in Paris. Granny Webb's embrace had answered all Henrietta's fears. She would be safe here.

Her brothers remained at school in Britain and had to go back after the holidays. She didn't go to school, and would have lessons at home, leaving her free to accompany her grandmother to twice-weekly card games. Her role was to sit quietly, watch and listen, since her Scots governess, Miss Campbell, had reluctantly agreed to persuasion from Granny Webb that Henrietta could miss lessons.

3

Card games would improve Henrietta's limited mathematics, her grandmother argued, since Miss Campbell had already pointed out that these were woefully inadequate and quite neglected by her previous governess. She would be dealt a hand once she had studied the play, she was told; but Henrietta preferred to watch the aged friends, their shared complicity, their quirks, and mannerisms. It was funny how they called each other by their titles, but at thirteen she was old enough to guess this must have started as a joke but had become a habit.

Henrietta stared at her grandmother's lips, heavily rouged and framing rather large teeth, which made her attempts to mouth secrets to her companions, secrets which she believed were not for her granddaughter's ears, totally redundant.

As usual, the silent words were easily read. 'He let the side down,' was said, or at least not said, when one of Granny Webb's friends asked about Henrietta's father. Couldn't he look after his own children, instead of dropping them on his mother-in-law? Surely she'd done her bit by raising seven of her own.

Henrietta glanced between the women, their powdered hair and wrinkly necks no longer of interest, compared to the shifty glances between them, the nods they thought were hidden from her. She knew nothing about her father, in fact had never met him, at least not since her mother's death when she was only two.

The room felt stuffy, the fire tended too often by a maidservant. She stared at the gilded clock on the mantelpiece, wondering whether the muscular man holding the clock face on his broad shoulders was a god or an angel. The hands ticked towards four o'clock. If she ignored them, they jumped forward in bold steps but if she waited for them to move, the pause seemed interminable. Henrietta guessed it would soon be time to light the candles and take the carriage home to her grandparents' apartment in the Faubourg Saint-Germain. Before her grandmother fell asleep, as she always did in the carriage, Henrietta would find out exactly how her father had let everyone down.

'Henrietta,' Granny Webb interrupted her daydreaming, 'pass the Countess of Seaforth the marrons glacé and don't eat any more yourself.'

The women passed the sweetmeats between them and returned to their chat, any play becoming slow and disjointed.

The Countess of Melfort spoke to her directly. 'I was sorry to hear about the death of Lady Henrietta Waldegrave. Were you named after her?'

Henrietta tried to sit up straight from her low, wide-backed chair, surprised to be questioned about the death of her other grandmother. 'Yes, my father liked the name.'

'Henrietta Waldegrave was a FitzJames before she married,' Lady Webb interrupted, 'the daughter of the exiled king's father and Arabella Churchill.' Here, her lips went into action again, shaping the words, 'born on the other side of the blanket.'

Henrietta stored this away for further investigation. Her father's mother had not troubled herself with her grandchildren when they lived with her, their daily routine given over to nursemaids and governesses, but Henrietta could remember her boasting about being of royal descent.

History was another area her previous governess had neglected, according to Miss Campbell, so her grandmother's birth story made little sense. The women seated around this card table seemed to recognise a king called James, a different one from the kings she did know about, those of France or Great Britain. Perhaps if she had been allowed to go to school, she might have understood a bit more but one thing was already clear, Miss Campbell had plans to be more thorough.

Companions for decades, these titled ladies chose to play

cards in informal gowns, abandoning stays and hoops in favour of comfort, but the small, hot room still felt overstuffed with fabric and chairs squeezed around the Countess of Seaforth's folding table. Henrietta found it hard to breathe, the air thick with old-lady scent, not all of it pleasant. When the maidservant entered to light the candelabra, play came to an end and Henrietta gathered the scattered Cavagnole pieces back into their velvet pouch. Carriages were summoned and she helped the maids ease the stiff and slow moving ladies into their cloaks.

At her very first card game, the day after she arrived, she had watched Lady Webb's mouth signal to her friends that her new granddaughter was a 'lovely, helpful child' and was still keen to earn this approval.

From the nodding of Granny Webb's head, her chin slowly descending towards her chest in time with the rocking of the carriage, Henrietta knew she must act quickly. 'Granny, what did my father do, to let us all down?'

Her grandmother's head shot upright, as if jerked by a puppeteer. 'You mustn't listen to other people's conversations. Some things are private.'

The protest was bluster. Her grandmother loved sharing secrets. 'It's not private,' Henrietta replied. 'Your friends... they all know.'

'Oh well,' Lady Webb sighed, settling back into the leather seat, readying herself for a story, 'you have to be told sometime. Your father gave up his faith in order to inherit his title and estates. It's the law in Great Britain. The boys are being raised as Protestants but Lady Waldegrave insisted that you,

Henrietta, be raised in the faith of our family. With my complete approval, of course.'

Henrietta thought about lessons with her priest, how she had to keep her head averted from his breath that smelled of fish. Was it such a terrible thing her father had done, if he had no choice?

'Why was that wrong?' she asked. 'Of course he wanted his estates. If someone took something of mine, I'd try to get it back.'

Granny Webb's bosom began to heave under her cloak, a clue that she was about to speak about Henrietta's mother, her daughter Mary. It was one of the many things that Henrietta adored about her grandmother. She couldn't mention either of her dead daughters without first spilling tears, then memories. Only since living in Paris, her mother's home, had Henrietta learned about a young woman who had laughed and teased, a girl who had enjoyed animals, especially dogs and who could often be heard singing all through the apartment.

'Your mother would have hated it... she would have hated him for doing it. That's why he never visits. He would have to look into your eyes, your mother's eyes.'

'He doesn't visit me because he's ashamed of what he's done?'

Henrietta felt Granny Webb's head nod under her hood. 'You never see your father because your face reminds him of his decision. It's not your fault.'

She needed time to think about this. She thought her father's absence was because she had been born a girl but this new perspective, this betrayal of her mother's faith, meant it was personal. He didn't want to be with her, Henrietta, not just because she was a female child.

Granny Webb broke the silence. 'He waited until Mary was dead before swearing the oaths... that tells you everything. He not only let down your mother but our king, a man he had known from childhood.'

She reached out an arm and wrapped her cloak around Henrietta, bringing warmth and the scent of violets. 'He's not welcome in Paris amongst our people, sensible folk who want to restore a Stuart to the throne of Great Britain, but he's still your father and my son-in-law. Mary loved him, so he will always find a place at our table, if he ever chooses to visit.'

This was comforting. You could go wrong with this grandmother but never too far wrong, as long as you were family. Granny Webb hadn't even been angry when she found out that the boys called her 'Spider' behind her back. Henrietta could hardly remember if her brothers had ever been her friends. Since James went to Eton, he boasted about inheriting their father's title and twisted the skin on her arm if she didn't do what he wanted.

She had always ignored Johnny, her younger brother, because she had been told that his birth had killed their mother, but that wasn't true. Lip-reading words that passed between Granny Webb and her friends, she had learned that her mother died because of the next baby and not Johnny at all, 'born too soon after the last.'

Henrietta watched the ladies shake their heads and one of them murmured, 'He should have left her alone,' until she caught sight of Granny Webb's pursed lips and brief shake of her head. Henrietta felt sad for blaming her younger brother, for leaving him out for all their shared childhood, but as soon as she had forgiven him, he followed James to Eton and the Webb family estate at Odstock.

Granny Webb wasn't all that keen on the boys, although she hid it well. It was her idea to leave them in England, sending them to Odstock for most of the school holidays. Boys needed space to play, she explained to Grandpa Webb, after James and

Johnny had smashed her Saint-Cloud porcelain water pot playing handball in the vestibule. Saint-Cloud was expensive, as were all the pieces that cluttered the apartment. These pots, ewers, vases and jugs all had names and stories and to please Granny Webb, Henrietta tried to remember the provenance of every single one.

They travelled on in silence, enclosed within the family carriage that smelt of the leather chairs in Grandpa John's study. Her grandmother's breathing fell into the soft, whiffling sounds that preceded sleep.

Henrietta could not waste these precious seconds. 'What did you mean when you said that my father's mother was born on the wrong side of the blanket?'

Granny Webb gave a snort and smacked her lips. 'You ask too many questions, my girl. It means she was illegitimate. If you don't know what that means, ask Miss Campbell tomorrow. Now, let me sleep.'

'Miss Campbell, what does illegitimate mean?'

Her governess was a plain, dusty woman, who seemed to own only one grey dress, until Henrietta realised that she had several grey dresses, all the same.

At the question, Miss Campbell sniffed and set her mouth into a firm line. 'That's for Lady Webb to tell you. There's much you should know, a young woman of your age, but as an unmarried woman, it's not my place to discuss such matters.'

Whoever had decorated Henrietta's schoolroom had forgotten about gilt panelling, mirrors and swirling swags of cherubs and flowers. Instead there were plain walls with maps and shelves of books, that shared no claim to match the elegance of the library. This was where the younger Webb daughters had been taught and nothing had been moved or altered since.

Henrietta pretended to study the map that hung opposite their sturdy, oak table, her finger tracing fine cracks in the wood. 'What things do I need to know?'

Miss Campbell drew her thick eyebrows together, creating one bushy strip. 'Details about girls and women... long overdue, if you ask me. I'll remind your grandmother after lunch. Now, was there anything else you wanted to know? I do have a lesson planned.'

They were studying the kings and queens of England and Scotland and although Henrietta was bored, she wanted to impress, as a biddable young woman might. There was a question, one from the conversation yesterday, that her governess might be pleased to answer. 'Miss Campbell?' she asked. 'You will be surprised I don't know this, as well as all the woman things, but why did my other grandmother think she was related to a king? Who are these Jacobites anyway?'

CHAPTER 2

1731

Henrietta stared at Earl Waldegrave's face in the many mirrors glazing the walls of her grandparents' salon, hoping that by avoiding his eye, she might help him cope with the shame of betraying his wife's memory. She could see that any similarity she shared with her mother was a myth, a story spun from Granny Webb's loss. Only her father's features were reflected in her own, without a grain of her mother Mary.

Granny Webb was tolerating one of the two annual visits she allowed from James and Johnny, and Henrietta was in no doubt her father's unexpected appearance was to save him the trouble of visiting his sons in England. As for her, despite her grandmother's efforts to make her enchanting, a daughter any father would be proud of, she seemed to be invisible. His visit was a waste of time; from the first, he spoke only to her brothers.

It had been hard not to be drawn into her grandmother's excitement, the discussions about what they would eat, the music Henrietta would play for him on the spinet, how she must try to converse with him in French. Of course, there had to be a new gown.

'You must look your best for the Earl,' their family dressmaker mumbled through a mouthful of pins, peering at her so closely Henrietta could see dark hairs sprouting across her upper lip. 'He needs to meet a young woman, not a little girl.'

Henrietta defended herself. 'I don't meet any other girls. I've no idea how they dress.'

The dressmaker tugged at the folds of a gown that had once belonged to Henrietta's mother, dramatically slashing the front of the robe to pin a new rosebud silk petticoat underneath.

'I'm not saying your grandmother was wrong... I'd never say a word against Lady Webb, but she liked to dress you as a child. I said my bit last year but after that, I kept my counsel.'

Henrietta had grown, her body changing shape with the start of her monthly bleeds. The loose, back-fastening girls' dresses she had worn before were soon discarded in favour of stomachers and great folds of fabric at her backside.

'At least I could sit down in them,' she said, 'and run around after my brothers.'

'Well, there will be no more of that, not now you're a woman. You'll learn to walk and sit like a lady. Your father will expect nothing else. Now, *Lady* Waldegrave,' she added, emphasising the title, 'please turn around so I can pin up the back.'

Henrietta studied her reflection in the dressmaker's mirror, her waist drawn in tight and her tiny breasts forced upwards by the rigid boning of her stays.

Three days before the bleeds started, Granny Webb had puffed her way into Henrietta's bedchamber, followed by a young girl she introduced as Amelia.

Standing at the end of the bed, without any polite

preliminaries, her grandmother began her speech. 'This is Amelia, the girl who will wash your linen once you start bleeding.' Amelia held out a straw basket filled with folded cloths, like an offering.

'I'll start bleeding?'

'Yes, you will. All girls and women do. At least, I don't but that's another matter. You will bleed every few weeks, from between your legs. Amelia will show you how to wear your cloths and keep them in place. She'll show you how to keep clean.'

'Why has no one told me this before?'

'It's private,' Granny Webb said. 'You can talk to me about it and Amelia, but no one else.'

Amelia nodded, a whisper of pride sliding across her lips.

Henrietta protested. 'But this is so unfair, why does it have to happen?'

'It's so that you can bear a child. Without your monthly bleeds, you'll never have a baby.'

'I don't want to have a baby.'

'Your husband will want you to have a baby,' Granny Webb said firmly, allowing no argument. Henrietta was then forced to listen to the minutiae of how a baby was made, news clearly unfamiliar to Amelia, who looked as if she might faint. This terrible ordeal was only to happen, Granny stressed the word *only*, when a man and his wife wanted to make a baby.

It was ridiculous, of course. Henrietta had seen Johnny's private parts when he was a little boy and the act her grandmother described was simply impossible. Even if it were true, she would go into a convent well before any of this nonsense started.

Days later, Amelia stripped her bed and declared, '*les regles, les regles*', dancing around the room as if something wonderful had happened. Henrietta stared at the sheet, glaring at the faint smear of pink, then wound her nightdress around her legs to examine the huge stain on the back, blurred like red ink on a blotter. Granny Webb's chat had come in the nick of time.

Grandpa John was at lunch, in honour of their guest, sitting at one end of the long table, with his wife at the other. Earl Waldegrave sat between his sons, his back to the fireplace. Henrietta had been placed opposite him but when Granny Webb became distracted by the arrival of the soup tureen, lecturing their new servant about his awkward grip of the expensive porcelain, Henrietta inched her cutlery, napkin and glass closer to her grandmother's place. From further away, she could glance sideways at her father, instead of facing him across the table.

The Earl seemed comfortable, familiar even, with his sons. There were winks, whispers, cuffs at each other's shoulders but not even a smile in her direction. Henrietta felt a strange tightening in her throat and swallowed, exchanging a glance with her grandmother. No words were needed. Granny Webb's expressive lips twisted between dismay and determination.

'Earl Waldegrave... James,' she repeated, trying to draw his attention away from the adolescent crackle of the boys' laughter. 'Is not Henrietta the image of her mother? She will sing for us after lunch. She's a most accomplished young lady.'

Earl Waldegrave smiled at Lady Webb and dipped his head but angled his body to face his father-in-law. 'I'm so glad you are raising Henrietta,' he said. 'Her mother would have been proud. Thank you.'

John Webb waved his napkin in the general direction of Henrietta and his wife. 'All credit goes to the lady at the end of the table and your own mother, of course. I'm afraid I'm rather too busy with matters... matters at the court of King James in Rome, to spend time with children.' This unaccustomed speech from her grandfather ended with a frown at his grandsons, who were making faces into their spoons, so he would have missed the mottled blotches of colour rising up the new British Ambassador's throat.

Henrietta missed nothing, both the flush on her father's face and two bright pink spots glistening under the powder on Lady Webb's cheeks, a sure sign her grandmother was struggling with anger. Grandpa John had mentioned the Stuart court, embarrassing her father; and Granny Webb must be furious with her son-in-law because he couldn't put his feelings aside, even for five minutes, to glance at his own daughter. It was a relief when everyone examined their soup bowls and concentrated on spooning up mouthfuls, the men muttering that it was delicious. Watching her father sip from his spoon, she decided that he was quite handsome. They shared a mouth, where the top lip was narrower than the bottom and their eyes were the same shape and colour, but her father's darted around the room, as if reluctant to settle anywhere, especially on her.

The interminable meal dragged on, her grandparents asking the Earl polite questions about his new role in France, and Waldegrave steering the conversation away from any further mention of Jacobite politics. From her lessons with Miss Campbell, Henrietta understood that her grandparents and their friends were actually her father's enemies and it was his duty to report back on their activities to the British government. With the tight stays pressing onto her stomach and the atmosphere in the room thick with tension, Henrietta started to feel sick.

She leaned forward, touched her grandmother's arm, and whispered, 'I'm about to vomit.'

'Go, go,' her grandmother said, flapping her hand. 'Find Amelia and she'll help you. I'm afraid I must stay here.'

With a curt nod to her father, Henrietta fled from the room and ran down the passage to her bedchamber, shouting for her maidservant. 'Amelia, Amelia. I'm going to be sick!'

'I'm here!' Amelia called from the closet where the maids sorted linen. She hurried after her mistress, snatching a bowl from one of the lacquered consoles lining the long corridor. Henrietta pushed the proffered bowl aside, threw herself onto the bed and gave a loud, rumbling, belch.

Amelia unlaced the new dress, stripping Henrietta down to her loose undergarments. A friendship of sorts was growing between the girls, arising from the intimacy of Amelia's duties. They were able to gossip and share secrets, as long as these were Henrietta's secrets. Both understood the rules and boundaries. If Amelia went too far, she would lose her job, whereas Henrietta would only lose a friend, even if Amelia was her only friend.

'Thank goodness for that,' Henrietta said, rolling onto her back and rubbing her stomach.

Amelia laughed. 'So, that was the problem. It was only trapped wind. I'll put this bowl back.'

Henrietta pushed herself upright, swinging her legs over the side of the bed, and announced in her grandmother's voice, 'Meissen, 1726. Bought when we were visiting Lille.'

Amelia stared at the bowl she held in her hands, then back at Henrietta. A snort of laughter gurgled up from her throat and Henrietta joined in, both girls falling to their knees, gripping their stomachs as if they were in pain. Whenever one of them managed to control themselves, a single glance at the other started the whole cycle again.

Once the Meissen bowl was safely back in place, Amelia and

Henrietta lay side by side on the bed, cackling every time Henrietta belched or farted.

'Well, Hensy,' Amelia said. 'Your father has had a surprising effect on you. Not what I was expecting.'

'I hated him at first,' Henrietta said. 'He paid me no attention at all. It was as if I wasn't there. He knows my brothers well; they must see him often in England but he lives here, Amelia, so why doesn't he visit or invite me to his apartment?'

'I don't know,' Amelia replied, shaking her head. 'It doesn't make any sense.'

'He can't look at me, or my grandmother. She thinks he feels shame for giving up the Catholic faith but I think it's about love. In this apartment, he must see my mother everywhere. He misses her.'

'That's sad,' Amelia replied, clasping her hands to her chest. 'They must have been very happy together.'

'I think they were.' Henrietta sighed, her eyes stinging. She blinked, wiping tears from her cheeks with the back of her hand. 'I'm going to marry for love, only for love.'

Amelia turned onto her side and scooped Henrietta into an embrace. 'Me too. Love is everything, don't you think?'

Henrietta rested her head in the crook of Amelia's shoulder, smelling a sharp, oily scent where the maid's cap hid her hair. 'Perhaps if he knows I understand how he feels, he'll want to see more of me. I should write him a letter, tell him he is forgiven.'

Amelia drew back, allowing Henrietta to see her face. 'Of course you must. We'll make a start in the morning.'

CHAPTER 3

1732

A month after Henrietta turned fifteen, Granny Webb said she was old enough to enjoy a trip to the opera. She had chosen one suitable for a young girl, all about a Bible story, although not one she was personally familiar with.

When she heard this, Miss Campbell decided it wasn't helpful for both Henrietta and Lady Webb to be ignorant of the plot.

'It's based on the story of Jephtha,' Miss Campbell said, assuming an expression of triumph that Henrietta knew well. It was certain her governess had based at least a further two weeks of lessons on this topic.

'Is it a romance?' Henrietta asked. 'Will there be love?'

'Yes, yes, but that's not the point. What's unusual in this opera is the overlap between our Christian God and pagan gods. So interesting, don't you think? Our priest isn't happy with Lady Webb's choice and the Cardinal altogether disapproves of the opera. It's always fun to annoy the Cardinal,' Miss Campbell said, giving a hiccupping giggle. 'Listen carefully, while I tell you some of the story.'

Henrietta nodded, resting her forehead on her folded arms until the moment she had hoped for, a love scene. Miss Campbell tried to rush through it but Henrietta stopped her.

'Wait, wait... the prisoner Ammon and Iphise are in love, but how can they ever be together? Is this a tragedy which ends badly?'

Miss Campbell shook her head. 'I'm not going to spoil the end for you, Lady Waldegrave, but it would be helpful if you thought less about romance and more about learning. Here's your task for today. I want you to research the gods Apollo, Venus and Polyhymnia and write a profile of each one. You may use the library if we don't have the books you need in here, but I'm expecting a full page on each god. Tomorrow, we will consider the ethics of Jephtha's oath. Is it ever right to promise to take a life, even if the vow is made to our Christian God? Think about that overnight.'

In the afternoon, they played cards with Granny Webb's friends. Henrietta no longer tried to interpret the ladies' hidden signals in a futile attempt to work out whatever it was they were trying to hide because she was now a seasoned card player. Challenged by a young girl with a quick brain, the old women sharpened their play, sitting with their backs straight, small eyes peering at the cards on the table. Henrietta spent every game studying their moves and working out what cards they were holding back, not what they were gossiping about. She didn't like to lose and these elderly ladies weren't fools.

The maidservant, bringing in their tea and cakes, stepped on the paw of Lady Melfort's little dog, quietly resting on a cushion under the table, but hidden within the folds of her mistress' dress. The yelp of pain shocked everyone, then the dog nipped the servant's ankle. A porcelain cup was dropped and although it didn't break, the gamers declared play was over, mopping at their décolletages with scented handkerchiefs.

Once peace had been restored, Granny Webb admired Lady Melfort's new veneered cabinet, with ingenious drawers and cubby holes which allowed the ladies to serve themselves. There was even space for a bowl of water, where they could rinse their cups.

'So ingenious,' Lady Webb said. 'We should have one at home, don't you think, Henrietta?'

'It's perfect,' she agreed, and Lady Melfort dipped her head in pleasure at the compliment, resting a hand on Henrietta's bare arm. She glanced down, feeling the old woman's firm grip, her young skin shining taut and pale under the aged hand, speckled with brown spots.

'And what about a husband?' Lady Melfort whispered, her eyes bright. 'Any suitors?'

Lady Webb straightened her back and placed her cup and saucer on the table. 'We're not discussing that yet, Lady Melfort. Henrietta is still young and I'm too selfish. I enjoy her company. We'll leave it another year.'

Henrietta knew from Granny Webb's laugh, rather high and forced, that she wasn't pleased with the question, but this was intriguing. Who had her grandmother meant by *we*? Could it be Grandpa John or even her father? Earl Waldegrave hadn't replied to any of her letters but was it possible he was thinking about her, talking about her with Granny Webb?

That night, as Amelia brushed out her hair, Henrietta shared her secret. 'I'm getting married next year, when I'm sixteen. Don't tell anyone else, Lady Webb doesn't want it talked about.'

In the dressing table mirror, she watched Amelia roll her eyes. 'Rather you than me.'

Henrietta sighed. 'But he will court me, bring me presents, declare his love on bended knee.'

Amelia paused, placing the silver hairbrush next to its companion comb and Henrietta's night-time ribbons. 'He will, of course,' she mumbled through a mouthful of hair pins, twisting her mistresses hair into a knot. 'But what if he's too fat and old to get back up off the floor.'

'Oh, Amelia, don't be so unromantic. They won't choose someone fat and old for me. He'll be young and handsome, you'll see.'

'Has he already been selected, this treasure?'

'I asked Granny… Lady Webb… in the carriage. She says they've no one in mind and I've not to think about it for a moment longer.'

Amelia pulled the night-time cap over Henrietta's eyes, blinding her friend. 'Not much hope of that. Shall we draw up a list?'

With her thumb, Henrietta pushed the cap above her brows, allowing her eyes to meet Amelia's in the mirror. She leaned forward on her elbows, cupping her chin between upturned palms. 'Who shall we start with? You go first.'

Lord and Lady Webb had their own box at the Théâtre du Palais-Royal, directly opposite other families that Granny Webb seemed to know. Judging by her waving at them with her fan, they were her friends. Others, she seemed to know but dislike, from the twist of her full lips whenever they tried waving at her. Their manservant had trimmed and replaced the candles in their box several times already and the air was thick from the smoke of hundreds of them lighting the auditorium. Henrietta's eyes stung.

She leaned towards her grandmother, her voice hoarse from the dense fug created by guttering candles. 'When will it start?'

'Once everyone has arrived,' her grandmother whispered, although there was no chance her voice would carry over the rabble from the parterre below.

Henrietta glanced around. 'But they're so slow. Look at them all, chatting and dithering, instead of taking their seats.'

Granny Webb frowned. 'Not everyone is young and sprightly like you. Anyway, they want to see who's here, meet their friends, find out who's alive and who's dead.'

The orchestra filed into rows of chairs in front of the stage and the hubbub quietened when the instruments began tuning in a discordant muddle of sounds. Henrietta rested her arms on the padded rail encircling their box. A man in the crowd below noticed her and waved, calling out, '*Bonjour, ma beaute.*'

Granny Webb tugged at Henrietta's shoulder, gently pulling her backwards into her seat. 'Don't draw attention to yourself. The men below can be rowdy. We don't want to encourage them.'

Their manservant, whose name was Leo and Amelia's favourite, was already leaning over their balcony and making threatening gestures at someone in the audience below.

Henrietta folded her arms and slumped back as far as her extravagant, hooped petticoat would allow. 'It's so dull up here, I'd rather be down there with them.'

'Nonsense,' Granny Webb said, in a tone she usually reserved for her grandsons. 'Here, read the libretto, it won't be long now. Look, stagehands are beginning to lower the chandeliers from the ceiling.'

At last the auditorium was dark and the curtain rose to a magical scene of ancient Rome, shimmering through the haze of smoke. The standing patrons in the parterre fell silent. Music filled the auditorium and players crowded the stage with a throbbing chorus of men's voices. At last, the soloists drew the audience into the tragedy and Henrietta's heart raced with fear at the lovers' predicament. Sweat gathered under her breasts and at the nape of her neck. The audience held their collective breath... will Ammon lose Iphise to her father's rash promise. But wait... another collective sigh... a burst of flame from Heaven. The priests are satisfied with God's message. Iphise's life has been saved but is it too late?

Henrietta spun around towards her grandmother, biting her fist. 'Is Ammon dead?'

'Not at all,' Granny Webb whispered. 'Look at the stage, my darling, he lives. They are reunited in their love.'

Before Leo could lead them safely to their coach and horses, all the candles in the auditorium had to be lit. Henrietta was happy to wait, watching the stagehands lower them from the ceiling, each chandelier holding at least fifty. While the theatre emptied, she listened to the sound of the crowd, enjoying an unfamiliar buzzing sensation in her chest and from low in her stomach, something warm but exciting.

Granny Webb wrapped Henrietta's cape around her when they stood to leave, drawing her granddaughter close as she tied the neck. 'Well, did you enjoy that, my dear?'

Henrietta inhaled deeply, wondering how she could possibly describe feelings that were so pleasurable. 'I loved it,' she replied. 'Can we come again? I don't want to miss a single performance.'

The curtain that separated their box from the passage behind twitched to one side and Leo, who saw their visitor first, bowed low from the waist. A tall, older man peered around, distracted, as if he had accidentally entered the wrong box and from his lost, vacant stare, Henrietta thought he must be befuddled. On catching sight of Lady Webb, he gave a sharp backwards nod of recognition, almost losing his wig. After he had regained his balance, briefly sacrificed in the act of retrieving his hair piece, he reached out to grasp Lady Webb's hand in his.

Bowing low to allow his lips to brush her gloved hand, he said, 'I thought I might find you here. How wonderful to meet like this.'

The elderly pair sat down and Henrietta did the same, wondering who this man could be. Her grandmother didn't know any men.

'Henrietta, this is the Marquess of Powis,' Granny Webb introduced her. 'He is the most important Catholic peer in Great Britain and a man who loves opera.'

Henrietta felt the Marquess study her, holding her eyes for a fraction too long, and then, instead of bowing, or taking her hand, he gave a nod, as if he was satisfied about something. Abandoned at the edge of the conversation, she thought she heard her father's name and her own, before their voices rose again in the mannered exchange of a farewell. The Marquess bowed to her and to her grandmother when Leo held the curtain aside for him to leave. Before he ducked under the folds, the old man turned back and stared, his gaze tracking across Henrietta's face and body, as if he wanted to commit every bit of her to memory.

It was hard to imagine the streets of Paris could ever smell sweet, but after the thick stuffiness of the auditorium, the night air was sharp and clean. Henrietta was happy to wait by the horses, even though Leo had opened the door of the carriage and was standing next to it, his posture tense. She leaned her cheek against each horse in turn, touching their soft, trembling nostrils and breathing in their grassy breath, as she kissed them on the lips. The horses tossed her aside, jangling their harnesses but still she waited outside, even though she could see Leo was impatient. Granny Webb's infuriating habit was always to chat with the coachman, asking about his wife and family, even though Amelia told her Lady Webb hardly ever remembered his name.

Henrietta absorbed the Parisian nightscape. The shops were still trading, brightly lit from inside like a stage set. She watched the etiquette of purchase, pointing, smiling, nodding, bowing, an exchange of coins, the handing over of a parcel. The final scene was one where a door was held wide open by the shopkeeper for the triumphant departure of an elegant lady. One day, that would be her, leaving a Parisian boutique with her head held high. She would not send a servant out to buy everything for her, like Granny Webb.

In the carriage, as the rocking motion began, her grandmother gave every sign of falling into a deep sleep.

'Who was that man?' Henrietta asked, keen to keep her grandmother awake. 'He seemed interested in me but he was staring. I didn't enjoy his attention.'

Granny Webb made an impatient 'tsk' sound. 'You will have to get used to it, Henrietta, you are a beautiful young woman. Men stare at women, even old men, who ought to know better. Anyway, many years back, we shared a family tragedy. It was to do with our daughter, Anna Marie.'

This was a new story and keen to encourage her grandmother, Henrietta said, 'Tell me everything.'

Granny Webb paused, then sighed, as if deciding to take a risk. 'The Marquess has a much younger sister called Winifred. Her husband and Anna Maria's husband were both Jacobite peers. They were captured in a battle between the Jacobites and the British government's army. They were both supposed to be executed for treason, but only our daughter's husband was killed. It was twenty years ago but still seems like yesterday.'

'What happened to the other man, Winifred's husband?' Henrietta interrupted.

'He escaped from the Tower of London, with the help of his wife. Everyone said that my daughter's husband, James Radclyffe, was executed instead of William Maxwell because the British king felt so humiliated. We don't believe that story. Winifred was charged with treason and followed her husband into exile. Her brother, the elderly man you met, he helped her to flee from the king's men.'

Henrietta had to know, even though asking more questions might upset her grandmother. 'What happened to Anna Maria?'

'She exiled herself in Brussels, where she died a few years later. Her heart was broken.'

'That is so sad.' Henrietta sighed, piecing together some of the jigsaw of her grandparents' lives. 'Is that why you and Grandpa John live in Paris?'

'Of course. With our daughter's husband branded a traitor, we had to leave everything behind. We stayed near Anna Maria, to help her with the children, but after she died, we settled in Paris.'

Granny Webb's shoulders began to heave and Henrietta knew to stay silent and allow her grandmother to weep.

It was a surprise when Granny Webb spoke again. 'Your father visited King George and spoke up for our son-in-law, argued for a pardon. We'll always be grateful to him for that.'

Granny Webb's quiet sobbing slowed and then drifted into a soft snoring sound, signalling the rhythm of sleep. Henrietta drew up the blind. Tree-lined boulevards passed, branches silhouetted within the subtle glow from street lighting. She remembered another journey, the flight from Essex with her brothers. Days spent being tossed from side to side, terrifying hours in the bowels of a boat, the smell of vomit and shit. Johnny never stopped crying, their unsympathetic governess furious at having to accompany them. It felt as if no one would ever love them again.

Panic crept along Henrietta's insides and stroked at the back of her neck. Something about her grandmother's friend, the one at the opera, troubled her, the way he had examined her as if she were a possession, her worth being weighed against qualities she did not understand. She scrubbed at her gloved hands, tried to swallow, but gave in to fear, sliding from her bench seat and tucking her body close beside her grandmother's, as much as her hooped undergarments would allow. Granny Webb muttered and Henrietta felt a cloak wrap around her, a firm squeeze on her shoulders and the reassuring smell of violets.

She would not lose this grandmother, even if a man loved her as much as Ammon loved Iphise. Her grandparents wouldn't ask her to leave, not if she wasn't ready. They wouldn't agree to her marrying the Marquess, if that was his intention and not her imagination. They simply wouldn't do that to her.

CHAPTER 4

1733

I t was many months before Henrietta met the Marquess of Powis again, long enough for her to forget their strange encounter. She and Amelia had stopped talking about future husbands and had made a pact never to marry. Her letters to her father were now seen as an embarrassing folly, typical of young, inexperienced girls, something she would never have started without Amelia's encouragement.

Amelia's mother worked in the kitchens and was a useful source of information when Granny Webb was trying to keep secrets. Henrietta was well past her sixteenth birthday, and the gardens in the Tuileries were turning the yellow and bronze of early autumn, when Amelia told her that Lady Webb had left instructions to dress her mistress for an important guest.

Henrietta raised her arms for her linen shift. 'Who does your mother say is visiting?'

'There are four for lunch, your grandparents and two men. I'm afraid lunch doesn't seem to include you.'

Henrietta turned away to allow Amelia to thread a lace through the eyelet holes at the back of her stays. 'So I have to be at the meeting but I'm to have no lunch. What's going on?'

Amelia tugged at the laces. 'They're important men, judging by the fuss about the menu. Leo got a telling off from Lady Webb about the state of his uniform, so he's sulking.'

Henrietta was about to ask whether Leo was returning Amelia's interest but decided against it. Amelia's mother maintained an unfair surveillance of her daughter, considered by both girls to be unreasonable, but Henrietta wanted to keep her friend's attention on this puzzling gathering.

Amelia tied a hoop petticoat over Henrietta's hips and raised the new grey silk gown, lifting it over Henrietta's arms and fastening the front to reveal the embroidered stomacher. They both turned to face the mirror, side by side, as Amelia adjusted the lace at the sleeves and neckline.

'It's beautiful,' Amelia said. 'Who on earth is Lady Webb trying to impress?'

Henrietta frowned at her friend's reflection. 'Is this the dreaded husband meeting?'

'What else can it be? If your father was marrying again, or there was a matter of inheritance, Lady Webb wouldn't hide it from you. Their secrecy is making me worried.'

Henrietta needed to empty her bladder, a most inconvenient procedure now she was dressed. 'Me too,' she replied. 'If it was someone who would please me, someone perfect, I don't think my grandmother would be able to hide her delight. She's no good at keeping secrets. It feels as if a decision has already been made, behind my back.'

Amelia gestured towards the dressing table. 'We'd better do your hair or you'll be late. Remember what we talked about? You can say no.'

Henrietta sat down but still faced Amelia, lifting her hands, palms raised. 'How many times can I say no before I'm sent to a convent?'

Amelia spun Henrietta's chair around to face the mirror and

parted the lace drapes that blocked her view of her mistress' face. 'If you don't like the man,' she said, 'if he repulses you, you must refuse. Remember what you'll be expected to do with him. If you hate him on sight, you'll loathe him in bed.'

Henrietta watched Amelia's practised hands dress her hair but said nothing more. Her friend was only fourteen and not from a titled family. It was all very well for her to sound so certain, but what did she know? She was at no risk of being married off for money. Her own mother had given birth at fourteen and had never married, although in the household she was always referred to as Madame Laurent.

'There,' Amelia said, pinning Henrietta's cap to the back of her head, its lace lappets trailing down her back, a parody of a wedding veil.

Henrietta narrowed her eyes. 'Did you choose that one on purpose?'

Amelia grinned and held up earrings against Henrietta's earlobes. 'Would I do such a wicked thing? I think this jewellery looks best, don't you agree?'

Henrietta waited outside Grandpa John's study, listening to the low murmur of voices from inside. Who would the visitor be? Through this door might sit a young man, every bit as nervous as her, or even a mature but still desirable husband, perhaps recently widowed, a man who would be patient, kind and loving. She was about to tap again, when Louis, a servant subjected to excoriating ridicule behind his back from Amelia because of his unfortunate skin condition, swung open the door from inside and bowed low to let her pass.

She paused to scan the room. Opposite her, next to Grandpa John, was her father and on his left was the old man from the opera house. Henrietta held her breath to stop her protest, *No, no... not this one. He's too old.*

Granny Webb patted the chair beside her and Henrietta slumped down with little grace, her eyes lowered. She must not cry.

Their frivolous chatter flowed around her, enquiries about health, grandchildren, the difficulty of finding decent servants, but one voice was missing. Her father was not taking part. Lifting her eyes just enough to study him, Henrietta saw he had turned his body away from the group. One elbow rested on the back of his chair and he stroked his top lip, while his other hand betrayed impatience, tugging at the knee of his breeches.

Granny Webb touched her arm. 'Henrietta, the Marquess of Powis has asked you a question.'

The old man coughed to clear phlegm from his throat and fiddled with his cravat. His wig seemed impossibly high by modern French standards and she felt a desperate urge to laugh. This man was a joke, with his last century suit and ill-fitting shoes. Grandpa John was a picture of high fashion by comparison. Couldn't they see he was utterly wrong for her? She would refuse him.

The man rose and stretched out his hand to take hers, brushing the tips of her fingers with his lips. 'My dear,' he said, 'please call me William. I must say, you are a picture of youth and grace.'

Henrietta snatched back her hand and slid it under the folds of her new gown, trying to wipe her fingers against the fabric. She remembered to lift her eyes and say, 'Thank you.'

William Herbert sat down with the methodical care of an old man, rearranging his cane and gloves from their already quite satisfactory resting place. He spoke to her again. 'Henrietta, I know how much you enjoy the opera. I have tickets for *Hippolyte et Aricie* at the Palais Royal tonight, if you would give me the honour of your company. I believe it's the first work of its type composed by Rameau.'

Earl Waldegrave made a barely audible sound, something between a snort and a cough. Henrietta looked up and found he was staring at her, as if her answer mattered.

She did not look at the Marquess but held her father's gaze. 'I'm afraid we already have tickets,' she whispered, 'but thank you for your kind offer.'

'Henrietta, that's not a problem,' Granny Webb interrupted. 'I will accompany you tonight, if you'd be willing to go with the Marquess.'

'Why not?' Grandpa John spoke at last. 'Keep an old man company.' He looked around, as if he'd said something funny but no one laughed. In fact, her father glared at her grandfather with a look of pure hatred.

The sudden appearance of tears, the strength of their flow, was as much a surprise to Henrietta as everyone else. Louis chose the worst moment to back into the room with a tray of coffee and the adults hid their embarrassment by laying out Lady Webb's porcelain cups, admiring the fine silver coffee pot and pouring the coffee themselves. Robbed of his only task, Louis waited, twisting his hands around a linen cloth, staring at her. The moment he left, news of her embarrassing breach of etiquette would reach the kitchen, and Amelia.

Granny Webb passed her a cup of the dark, bitter liquid, which she knew Henrietta disliked. 'Here, sip this, you'll feel better. Now, what on earth is the matter?'

Henrietta found her voice, surprisingly high and clear. 'I refuse to marry him. He's too old.'

In the silence, the familiar room closed around her. She tracked its dark leather chairs, their frames studded with brass pins she liked to count if her grandfather kept her waiting, the repeating pattern on the wallpaper that reminded her of the shells of a hundred tortoises, the bookcases still taller than her, the sombre desk, the windows shrouded in deeply folded drapes. Why was it always dark in here?

The adults began to laugh. Henrietta stared, shocked. Even her father grinned, while the others seemed unable to control themselves, the two old men slapping their thighs and her grandmother using a tiny lace handkerchief to dab at tears in the corners of her eyes.

'Oh my goodness,' Granny Webb said, hiccupping, 'William doesn't want to marry you, my dear. He's here to advocate for his younger son, Lord Edward Herbert.'

Henrietta looked at her grandmother and back at William Herbert, who nodded confirmation, his efforts to control his laughter ending in a fit of coughing.

'You're as bad as my daughter Mary,' he said, shaking his head and wheezing between coughs. 'She thinks I should find another wife but there's no chance. I'm almost seventy for heaven's sake! No, I'll leave all that to the younger men. My son is keen to be wed and both families agree it would be a good match for you.'

'The very best we could hope for,' Grandpa John interrupted. 'The Herbert family are the most influential Catholics in England... after we left, of course.'

The room felt uncomfortably hot and stuffy and Henrietta's ears filled with a ringing sound. 'I'm so sorry,' she said. 'No one explained to me what this was all about. Of course I'll meet your son.'

Earl Waldegrave jumped to his feet as if stung and the surprise made everyone pull back, afraid he was going to hit them. He strode around the low table and knelt at Henrietta's side, grasping both her hands between his. She felt his skin dry and warm, slightly rough, like the table in the servants' dining room.

His voice sounded gruff and hoarse. 'Henrietta, you don't have to compromise. Edward Herbert is thirty-four and a very sick man. I can introduce you to many young men, here in Paris or in London, if you will renounce your faith.'

Granny Webb challenged him. 'James, that's not fair. Don't ask Henrietta to make that choice.'

Earl Waldegrave gripped her hands more tightly, her fingers crushed by his strength, his bright penetrating eyes searching her face. 'You do have a choice, Henrietta. Become a Protestant and you will find a new family with me and your brothers. No one will pressure you to marry, least of all me.'

Henrietta glanced at her grandmother's face, saw the trembling lips, the fear shining beneath her heavy eyelids and knew there was only one answer she could give. 'No, thank you, Father. I will meet the Marquess of Powis' son with a view to marriage.'

Waldegrave dropped her hands, allowing them to fall into her lap as if he found them no longer to his taste. He pushed against his knee to stand and bowed low, his gaze falling over no one in particular, least of all Henrietta. He turned sharply on his heel and strode from the room, slamming the door behind him.

Henrietta did not even own a small portrait of the man she was expected to marry and no one seemed to think it mattered. Weeks passed and it felt as if the dreadful meeting in her grandfather's study had never happened. Granny Webb dismissed her questions with the explanation that her jointure had to be settled between the Marquess and Grandpa John and both men were acting like stubborn old fools.

'The Marquess is a kind man,' her grandmother explained,

'but not always a wise one. Your grandfather has to take care, negotiating with him on your behalf.'

'Why do you say he's not wise?' Henrietta asked.

'Many said he should have let his sister be arrested but he was determined to save her, whatever the cost to himself and others. Perhaps he is a man who doesn't get the measure of things and risks promising too much.'

'Not like Grandpa John,' Henrietta added.

'Indeed, very unlike your grandfather but then, when Winifred had to go to Rome without her daughter Anne, the Marquess looked after the child and her maid. Your grandfather wouldn't have dreamed of agreeing to that.'

Henrietta considered her grandmother's words. 'It's hard to decide about people, isn't it?' she replied at last. 'They're never one thing or the other. My father is a good example. I could easily hate him but in Grandpa's study, he seemed upset, as if he cared about me.'

'Hold on to that wise thought,' Granny Webb replied. 'Your father cares about you deeply but he is a victim of his pride. We're all a puzzle to other people; the Marquess allows his kindness to blind him to the truth, your grandfather is a great leader of men but he can be hidebound by tradition and rules.'

'And what about you?' Henrietta interrupted. 'What are your two sides?'

'That, my dear, I will leave to you to decide for yourself.'

The night before Christmas, Amelia aired the clothes her mistress would wear to mass in front of the fire, while Henrietta watched from the bed.

'What do you think he looks like?' Amelia asked.

'I'm guessing a younger version of his father,' Henrietta said. 'The Marquess is still quite a handsome man.'

Amelia crossed the room to clear the bowl and washcloth from the dressing table. Without looking at Henrietta, she said,

'Why is it taking so long? You need to meet him, this Edward Herbert. Why hasn't he written to you?'

Henrietta didn't like this pointed out, even though she shared the same doubts. If Edward Herbert didn't want to be married, and this union was a duty for him, shouldn't he at least pretend?

She quoted her grandmother, as if Lady Webb had the answer to everything. 'They're quarrelling about the jointure, so nothing is settled. I might not marry after all.'

Amelia sat on the edge of the bed, holding the bowl close to her chest. 'What's a jointure?'

'When a couple marry, the groom's father has to give the bride a sum of money, in case she's widowed. It needs to be enough for me to live on if Edward dies... at least until I marry again. My grandmother says that the Marquess isn't offering enough.'

Amelia frowned and lowered her gaze. 'My mother's friend, who used to work for the Countess of Seaforth before she died last year, overheard some talk. The Marquess has no money. His daughter lost the family fortune through gambling.'

Henrietta pulled the bedclothes over her knees and sat up. 'That's not true, Amelia. You shouldn't spread gossip.'

'It's not gossip. The countess was the Marquess' older sister, so she would know.'

'Leave me,' Henrietta protested. 'I don't like what you're saying.'

Amelia waited, hesitant, but spoke again. 'Hensy, you can refuse to marry this man, you can refuse to become part of the Herbert family.'

'I'm Lady Waldegrave, soon to be Lady Herbert... and don't call me Hensy. I want to be alone.' Henrietta buried her head under the covers and felt Amelia draw the heavy drapes around her.

There was something final about Amelia's last tug of the hangings, an impatience in the action that left Henrietta in no doubt that she had hurt her friend, perhaps even lost her. It felt like her father's final slam of the study door, an echo of the pain in her heart that said, *I am no longer his daughter.*

Henrietta sat up, enclosed in her stuffy cage, and picked at some loose skin hanging from her thumbnail. She must try not to care. As a married woman there would be parties, friends, and perhaps even children. She would find new people, more interesting people and start again. Apart from Granny Webb, she would miss nobody here and especially not Amelia.

CHAPTER 5

1734

Amelia must have spoken to her mother, and the day after their row, Henrietta found her grandmother's personal maid attempting to care for her, in addition to her duties for Lady Webb. She was a tight-lipped woman Amelia called *The Bitch* but her name was actually Celine. Slamming down Henrietta's hairbrushes, tutting with impatience and sighing loudly, Celine made it clear that these extra demands were an imposition. At the same time, she was obsequiously polite, so Henrietta couldn't complain about her. She missed Amelia, the intimacy of their morning and evening routine and the hours they spent whispering in the linen room, gossiping about the household.

When the imminent marriage was announced to the household, Miss Campbell left, arguing that she had been employed to teach Henrietta until she was eighteen and where, tell me where, would she find another job at this late stage of her career? Although Henrietta had no regrets about the end of her schooling, and didn't miss her tutor at all, Granny Webb's plan to fill her days learning about the management duties of a wife had fallen flat.

There was only a month until they left for Odstock Manor, one of many Webb family properties in England, with a wedding planned for the seventeenth of July. Everything was strangely subdued. *Shouldn't there be a flurry of action, the choosing and packing of a bridal trousseau,* Henrietta thought. *Shouldn't there be some excitement?*

This week's lessons were about how to work with kitchen staff. As the woman of the house, she would be expected to plan food for each day and draw up a budget with the cook, who in turn would order and pay for the provisions. The whole thing seemed daunting and Henrietta secretly thought she would just let the cook do what she liked.

Granny Webb waited in her private salon. She tapped the chair next to her and Henrietta sat down, pushing her fingers through the mesh chairback, as she had done as a child but now she found there was space only for her smallest finger.

Granny Webb rebuked her. 'Henrietta, stop fiddling with the chair and concentrate.' Spread across the green baize of the card table were recipes and lists of ingredients in her grandmother's idiosyncratic handwriting, with spelling that would never have been tolerated by Miss Campbell.

Granny Webb pinched the bridge of her nose before lifting her pince-nez to the light from the window, checking whether the lenses were smudged.

She looks tired, Henrietta thought, *and much older than sixty-four.* 'Granny, are you well?' she asked.

'Another of my friends died this morning. This is a sad time of life. Every day, someone else is taken... and you are leaving us too. I know you have to marry but it's happening sooner than I'd have liked. This place will feel empty without you.'

'I don't have to leave,' Henrietta said. 'I haven't heard a word from Lord Edward, so he's unlikely to be heartbroken. Why don't we call it off?'

Granny Webb shook her head. 'The men have sorted all the details. The only person who could have stopped this union is your father and he has grudgingly given his consent, although he will not attend the ceremony. The Marquess and your father have both made a generous marriage settlement upon you and your future husband. It's a good match; I'm just being selfish.'

'Our fathers are giving us money?'

'No, not money, you silly girl. They're giving you the titles to properties and estates they already own and you're expected to live off the income. That's why you need to learn to budget.'

'Granny, did you have to learn all this before you married Grandpa John?'

'Of course I did, and my mother prepared me to expect little in the way of romance. Your grandfather was too busy fighting wars to bother with love letters. In those days, I'm not sure he would have known how to write one. Marriage is a business, Henrietta. We find romance in the arts and love in our children.'

It was Henrietta's turn to sigh. 'It all seems bleak. It's not what I expected to feel, as a bride. We haven't even talked about my wedding dress.'

Granny Webb seemed to rally. 'Of course we will, sweetheart. The ceremony will be a private affair at Odstock Manor, so you don't need anything too showy, but I do understand that you want to look beautiful. We'll visit Magoulet's boutique tomorrow and choose some fabrics, how about that?'

'Can Amelia come too?'

Granny Webb hesitated. 'I wondered when you would decide to make up with her. I've had my doubts about the friendship, thinking you might have become too close to a servant, but you are alone here and friendship is important, as I have learned to my cost this last year. Make amends with

Amelia... and if that means inviting her on our shopping trip, then go ahead.'

Amelia was delighted to be asked, although Henrietta suspected she was more enthusiastic about riding postilion with Leo, than choosing fabrics. At the boutique, a young woman, more a model than a sales assistant, showed them to a table set within the curve of a bay window, its panes as wide as they were deep, so that everyone passing by had the best view of the shop's aristocratic clientele. They were brought chocolate in miniscule cups while the assistant reached into drawers to find samples of fabric for inspection.

After instructing the sales woman that they needed fabric for a wedding gown and also three robes for daytime wear, Lady Webb fell asleep, snoring loudly. Amelia pretended not to notice and Henrietta tried to follow her example, but she was worried about her grandmother, her dwindling energy and strength.

'No, no, not that one,' Amelia said, shaking her head at the sales woman. 'It's a summer wedding, in England. That looks like something you would find in a Parisian brothel.'

'Amelia!' Henrietta protested, glancing at her grandmother, but Lady Webb slept on, her chin fallen to her chest.

Amelia winked, before addressing the sales assistant in an even more commanding voice. 'Lady Waldegrave is joining the most respected Catholic family in Great Britain. We need elegant fabrics suitable for summer, one which will inevitably be cooler than here. They must be light but warm enough for interiors that never see the sun.'

The assistant hurried away to search for more samples. 'Where on earth did all that come from?' Henrietta asked.

'My mother told me what to ask for, quoting the lovely Celine of course. That woman thinks she knows everything. By the way, I'm back on duty tonight, if you'll accept me.'

Henrietta leaned across the table and snatched at Amelia's hand. 'Thank goodness. I've missed you. Have you missed me?'

Amelia's face dropped, as if about to share bad news. 'There's a rumour The Bitch is about to resign because you're so demanding. Someone has to help with your toilette and they've insisted that person is me.' She squeezed Henrietta's fingers and grinned. 'Of course I've missed you, Hensy. I'm sure we'll quarrel again but not for a while, I hope.'

Granny Webb slept on, while Amelia rejected several fabrics and designs that Henrietta liked. 'They're all too Parisian,' she said, 'you'll make your English relatives seem dowdy by comparison.'

'But what about my wedding dress?' Henrietta protested. 'The bride is meant to outshine all the guests.'

'You heard Lady Webb,' Amelia argued. 'No one will see you except for family, but you're right, we need to make sure your husband thinks he's seen an angel.'

They compromised, Henrietta thinking that an angel was not the look she wanted. In the end, they chose a design that was almost at the height of Paris fashion, but not quite. Henrietta was measured behind a screen of green velvet drapes, and Amelia ordered more chocolate, using her most demanding tone. The young women chose not to wake Granny Webb and sipped from their dainty cups, in no hurry to return to the apartment.

Henrietta gazed through the window at adult women strolling along the pavement outside, parasols raised to protect their delicate skin from the sun. 'This is how I want to live, don't you?'

Amelia frowned. 'I'm not sure what you mean. You already live like this.'

'I can't easily explain,' Henrietta said. 'I want to be

independent, free. I'd like to walk out of this shop and hire a public carriage to take me home, to my handsome husband. I'd like to shop and stroll and chat every day, like those women over there.'

'You're hoping that marriage will bring you that?'

'Perhaps not straight away, but if my husband is distracted, or malleable, or both, it might be possible.'

Amelia drained her cup and stood, instructing the sales assistant to find their summer capes. 'Rather you than me. The answer is to stay single, like my mother. I'll find Leo and ask him to bring around the coach. Perhaps it's time to wake your grandmother?'

Henrietta woke to the slap of feet on tiles and someone calling her name, 'Henrietta, Henrietta!'

Amelia burst into the room and wrenched her bed hangings apart. 'You must come at once. It's Lady Webb. She can't walk or speak.'

Together, the girls fled to Lady Webb's chamber, Henrietta tugging her wrapping gown over her shoulders as she ran. At the open door, Henrietta hesitated, seeing Celine already at her grandmother's bedside. Amelia touched her elbow and whispered, 'Your grandmother needs you, not Celine. Don't worry, a physician has already been called.'

Granny Webb lay flat on the mattress, pale and sweating. Her face was almost unrecognisable, lips and eyes drooping on one side, a thin thread of saliva oozing from her mouth down to the bolster. Henrietta paused to look back at Amelia, who made an agitated gesture as if to say, *hurry up, what are you waiting for?*

Celine sat in the only chair and made no movement to vacate it, so Henrietta rested her bottom against the edge of the high bed, leaning against the embroidered drapes hanging from the frame. When she pressed her grandmother's hand, the fingers stayed lifeless and flaccid.

She spoke, to see if this brought some response. 'Granny, can you hear me? What has happened to you?'

Lady Webb's eyes opened wide, bright with tears but instead of words, she made a horrible moaning sound, like an animal in pain. Celine leaned over and wiped the saliva from the corner of Lady Webb's mouth.

'When is the doctor coming?' Henrietta asked. 'Has my grandfather been woken?'

'Lord Webb is waiting for the physician's carriage at the street entrance. He'll bring the doctor up here as soon as he arrives. It won't be long.'

Henrietta nodded, unusually glad of Celine's calm presence. She had no idea what to do and wanted her grandmother back, not this strange apparition.

'Try taking her other hand,' Celine suggested. Henrietta reached across and squeezed Granny Webb's hand, delighted to feel a response.

'She pressed my fingers, Celine, I felt her!'

Suddenly, the room was full of men. Grandpa John wore a dressing robe, his scalp visible through thinning hair, his old, mottled face still lined with pressure tracks from his bolster. Henrietta stared at her grandfather, another apparition, and then at the physician, fully wigged and dressed as if he had been called from a late-night party.

The physician bowed to Henrietta and held out his elbow to escort her out through the open door.

'Lady Waldegrave,' he said. 'Please leave us now. I will remain with your grandmother for several hours and would not want to keep you from your rest. I see there is a maidservant here who will bring me everything I need.'

The door closed softly behind her. Henrietta turned away and walked the long corridor back to her bedchamber, stroking her grandmother's treasured porcelain ornaments as she passed. There was still hope. Inside that broken shell of a woman, her grandmother had answered her touch. The physician would bring her back.

Amelia waited for her, dressed in her night shift. Together and without a word, they crawled under the bed clothes, her friend tucking the covers tightly around them both. Henrietta turned onto her side, dizzy with exhaustion, and fell into a deep sleep. Amelia's arm dropped across her shoulder.

The next morning, Granny Webb sat upright, propped against bolsters, her hair dressed and covered in a neat cap, with a fresh night-robe tied at her neck. Her face had returned to normal and she could speak. Within a week, she had regained the use of her left arm but still walked with a limp.

Henrietta shared the joy of the household at this miracle recovery but Granny Webb was not herself, a truth that everyone else preferred to ignore. Her grandmother forgot essential details and was often muddled. Worse, she was nearly always asleep. Only weeks remained before Henrietta was to leave Paris, when her life would change for ever and she would live amongst strangers. No one seemed to remember or care, least of all her grandmother.

The packing was left to Amelia, Henrietta and whichever of the housemaids had any time, for a wedding that still seemed more myth than reality. When her dresses arrived from Magoulet's, Henrietta modelled them for her grandmother, who soon tired and lost interest. Was it possible she would not come with them, might not be well enough to make the long journey to Wiltshire?

Two days before she was due to leave, Grandpa John called her to his study. Henrietta stood by his desk, just as she had when she was thirteen, always worried she might have done something wrong but hoping there was a sweetmeat hidden in one of his closed fists.

Grandpa John removed his pince-nez and rubbed at the pink groove across the bridge of his nose. 'I know you share my worries about your grandmother, Henrietta. We can both see she has improved but is far from well. The physician has advised that she should not attend your wedding, but when has your grandmother ever taken advice?'

Henrietta gasped. 'You mean, she's coming with me?'

'It would take a stronger man than me to stop her. She wants to see you married, Henrietta, but this is a chance for us to see our children. It may be her last.'

'But, Grandpa, that's wonderful...'

'A word of caution,' he interrupted. 'Our journey will be slower because of your grandmother's need to rest and she isn't going to be able to help with the wedding plans as much as she would have liked. Our son Thomas, the one who lives at Odstock, and his sister Barbara will assist you. She's married to Viscount Montague.' Grandpa John paused to allow this moment of pride to settle between them.

'I don't mind, I don't care,' Henrietta gasped. 'I just want you both at my wedding.'

'Thank you, my dear, as we want to be with you. One other thing... there's going to be a lot of extra work for Thomas and his servants, so I've arranged for the maidservant you're fond of to come with us. Her mother has agreed.'

Had she heard correctly? Amelia was coming too. A thank you was quite useless, would never capture her excitement and gratitude. Instead, she bent down and kissed her grandfather on his cheek, feeling her lips scratch against his coarse skin.

'Now, now,' he said, reaching for some papers and replacing his pince-nez. 'That's enough of that. Off you go and tell your maidservant, but remember, Henrietta, I'm expecting no nonsense from you two. In a few weeks, you'll be a married woman.'

CHAPTER 6

1734

This family were strangers to her. She did not belong. The Webbs clustered around the sturdy dining table with its straight, fat legs, chattering and laughing as if they had never been apart.

She sat at one end, next to her grandfather, with Granny Webb at the other end, flushed and excited. In between sat Thomas, a younger model of his father, his sister Barbara next to her trophy husband, Viscount Anthony Browne, another sister Winifred with her husband, not a trophy, and finally, opposite her, was the youngest sister Bridget, unmarried and solemn, although Henrietta couldn't be sure which state had come first. When Henrietta tried to catch her eye, Bridget gave a fleeting smile but quickly looked down at her hands.

There was no one here for her, not a single Waldegrave or anyone from the family she was about to join. Tomorrow she would meet her future husband for the first time, but not a single person in this room cared. They talked about the past, shared stories from their boisterous childhoods, recounted sad reminiscences of two sisters now gone, causing Granny Webb to break down into a muddle of grief and joy.

Henrietta's attention drifted and their voices became a background hum. Two days ago, when their carriage had finally turned into the drive for Odstock Manor, Henrietta had felt an immediate warmth towards the old brick house, with its steeply pitched roof, tall chimneys and small windows. She knew English country houses, had lived for years at Navestock with Granny Waldegrave, but that had been too imposing and formal, with miles of empty, dark corridors where children weren't allowed to run and a garden designed for adults to walk, not for children to play.

Her eyes roamed around the dining room and she decided that the interior didn't match the hopes raised by her first sight of the house. She missed the pastel swirls that embellished every wall of their Parisian apartment, the light thrown from tall windows, not these dark, panelled walls and looming family portraits. She didn't know where she would live with Edward, but if it was a place like this, as lady of the house she would be entitled to make some changes.

'Grandpa,' she whispered. 'I have a headache. I'm meeting my husband tomorrow and I'd like to be fresh. Please can I go to bed?'

Lord Webb was in full cry, calling down the table to his younger son and Henrietta had to shake his arm and repeat herself.

'What was that?' he said, leaning his good ear towards her.

'I want to go to bed,' Henrietta shouted. At the same moment, the table fell silent.

'She wants to go to bed,' Grandpa Webb bellowed down the table to his wife, who paused in mid-whisper to her daughter Barbara.

'Of course, my darling, off you go,' Granny Webb said, blowing Henrietta a kiss. 'I'll come and see you later.' Granny

Webb turned back to the expectant faces and mouthed, *big day tomorrow.*

A servant passed Henrietta a lit candle and she hurried up the staircase to her room, chased by unwelcome shadows beyond her pool of light. Most of all she hated the longcase clock and ran to her door when it began its warning click and whirr. Amelia had been absorbed into the lively household below stairs, evidently much more fun than the grand rooms where Henrietta was forced to spend her days, planning every detail of the wedding with her Aunt Barbara. Now, she only saw Amelia first thing in the morning and before bed.

'I wonder what he'll be like,' Amelia said, passing Henrietta warm cloths to wash her face and hands.

Henrietta scrubbed at her cheeks, smelling the lavender oil. 'I'm excited but scared too,' she replied. 'He's not been married before, so he could be a toad.'

There was no fancy, spinning chair set before the dressing table in this English country house, so Henrietta had to stand up when Amelia needed to turn her chair to face the plain mirror. She unpinned Henrietta's hair and brushed it out with firm, practised strokes.

'I keep saying this, Hensy, but you can say no.'

'What would they do with me? It would be a convent, no question.'

Amelia paused, holding Henrietta's eyes. 'I hope it goes well and you like what you see, I really do want that for you, but a convent isn't the end of the world. I heard downstairs that one of the Webb daughters entered a convent for a while but she came out and now she's found a husband.'

Henrietta snorted. 'Do you mean Winifred? Have you seen her husband?'

Their laughter had reached an unfortunate pitch of

breathless squeals when Lady Webb soundlessly entered the bedchamber.

'You seem to be over your headache, Henrietta. What are you two finding so funny?' Lady Webb's tone was rich with disapproval and laced with disappointment.

Amelia curtsied. 'Sorry, sorry... Lady Waldegrave is a bit over-tired, so I was trying to calm her with lavender water. She's worrying about tomorrow and has become a little hysterical.'

In the dressing table mirror, Henrietta glanced at her grandmother and saw the familiar twist of her rouged lips.

Granny Webb frowned at Amelia and said, 'That's enough for tonight, my girl. I will finish Lady Waldegrave's hair.'

The door closed but Henrietta knew Amelia would be listening outside.

Granny Webb gave her granddaughter's hair a few more strokes, unnecessarily tugging hard at a few tangled strands.

'Now listen to me, young lady. Tomorrow you will meet your future husband. He's expecting a woman, not a silly girl. Whatever you think of him, you talk to me, not Amelia, or your opinion will soon be all over the servants' quarters.'

'But what if I hate him? What if the sight of him makes me retch?'

'Don't be so dramatic, Henrietta, that's most unlikely. If you simply cannot bear to marry him, we will accept your decision, of course we will, but your future will not lie with us. If you disgrace your grandfather, he will not allow you to return to Paris.'

This was a harsh truth. Her throat tightened. 'What about Amelia?' she whispered. 'Would she be allowed back to Paris?'

'No, she would not. Her future is now bound up with yours. The decisions you make are for both of you. Remember that lesson, Henrietta.'

Henrietta chewed her lip, watching her grandmother limp to the door. She loved Granny Webb, more than anyone else, but right now, she hated her too, hated not quite deserving the love she gave to her daughters, hated being forced to face the reality of her duties within her grandparents' world. She hadn't realised there were boundaries and limits to their love for her, because she believed they had loved her mother unquestioningly and would love her every bit as deeply. What they really felt for her was responsibility and obligation, and in return, that was all they expected from her.

Henrietta walked across lawns to the orchard, where Edward Herbert waited. Bridget Webb, assigned chaperone duties, walked a short distance behind and Henrietta gave her shy aunt no encouragement to catch up or chat. Her new robe trailed along the grass, the hem wet from lingering dew. Despite the shade, the day promised to be hot, with a blue sky misted only by streaks of high cloud. She surprised a blackbird, who flew a short distance, protesting at her intrusion. He eyed her from a branch, his beak crammed with worms, and flew off into the edge of the woods, where his fledglings waited.

As she dressed Henrietta that morning, Amelia had been unusually silent and respectful. She must have heard everything, had understood Granny Webb's warning about their future. The girl had seemed watchful, afraid of making a mistake as she swept Henrietta's hair upwards from her face and pinned it under a neat cap with long lappets reaching to the waist, before applying only the smallest amount of make-up to enhance her mistress' cheekbones and long eyelashes.

Side by side, they admired the new robe in the dressing mirror, a blue silk, slashed at the front to reveal a white stomacher with a ladder of embroidery to match the blue. It was simple but elegant and the absence of a hoop emphasised Henrietta's slim figure. She was glad Amelia had insisted that Magoulet's designer reduce the folds of fabric at the back, because she wanted to be able to sit comfortably and focus on her lover, which in this moment, was what Edward might be.

Before she left to find her betrothed husband, Amelia took her hand and said, 'Henrietta, you look beautiful. He's a lucky man.'

On a sunny bench shaded by the branches of an apple tree, already heavy with tiny, green fruit, a man stood as she approached. He was not as tall as his father but still well grown. As Henrietta drew nearer, she noticed his modern wig, set well back on his head and tied at the back with a bow. His hairline had receded but this was covered by wig powder. Edward's coat and breeches were new and this pleased Henrietta. He had been nervous too, had wanted to look his best. Edward bowed low and when he raised his head she liked his face. It was kind, his brown eyes lined with friendship, his nose spread across with endearing freckles, his smile generous, showing even, clean teeth.

He held her hand for longer than was customary, his eyes tracking her face and body.

'Well, Lady Waldegrave,' he said. 'I think I've come off best in this arrangement, don't you agree? Perhaps my father's not so stupid after all.'

Henrietta followed Edward's gesture to sit down next to him on the bench. 'Your father is a kind man. Why do you say he is stupid?' she said.

Edward's expression lost its warmth. 'That's a conversation for another day. Right now, let's find out about each other. Ask me anything.'

'Well...' Henrietta hesitated. 'Why didn't you try to court me, write me any love letters, buy me gifts.'

'Ah, straight to the point... good. That was remiss of me, but I didn't believe the marriage would happen. My older brother will inherit the title but to my surprise, my father realised that any hope of the Herbert line continuing through his heir was a lost cause. He switched his attention to me, almost overnight, and discovered you in Paris. I didn't trust that the financial negotiations would be successful, given his–'

'So, you didn't want to be married?' Henrietta interrupted.

'To be truthful, not then but now I've met you, nothing would make me happier.' Edward started to cough, deep, wet hacks that left him red and breathless. 'I'm not a great catch, as you can see. Don't feel you have to say yes. My aunt is abbess of a convent in Bruges. If you need to escape, I'll get you there safely and I'll also make sure you won't be trapped. Your stay will only last a few weeks.'

The drama intrigued Henrietta, imagining herself taking the starring role in a midnight flight to escape a loveless marriage, but in truth, she already liked Edward. She would have him.

'Of course I won't do that,' she said. 'You're still attractive for a man of thirty-four and I enjoy the way you speak to me, as if I'm not a silly young girl.'

Edward raised his eyebrows. 'Who said I was thirty-four?'

Henrietta laughed. 'It was my father. I think he was trying to discourage me.'

'Ah, the esteemed Earl Waldegrave. Not a man to be trusted. Actually, I'm thirty, a wide enough age gap I know, but perhaps tolerable?'

Edward fell to his knees and Henrietta thought he'd had some sort of collapse or fainting fit. He steadied himself by reaching out for the seat of the bench, took her hand and kissed the tips of her fingers. 'Lady Henrietta Waldegrave,' he said. 'Will you honour me by agreeing to become my wife?'

A breeze rustled in the leaves above them and the repetitive tapping of a woodpecker echoed from a decayed pear tree. Henrietta was aware that Bridget, sitting at a discreet distance, had shifted in her seat, and was leaning forward, trying to catch their words.

'Thank you, Lord Edward Herbert, I agree to marriage,' Henrietta whispered.

Edward rolled onto the grass and could not speak for several minutes as a new bout of coughing racked his body. 'Thank goodness for that,' he wheezed, resting on his elbow, his back covered in grass seed. 'You can see I'm not a well man.'

Henrietta paused. Perhaps her next question was too personal. 'What is wrong with you, Edward? What do your physicians say?'

He pulled at a stalk of grass and started to chew the end. 'They've no idea. All I know is that my cough is usually worse in the winter but there's something about this bloody orchard that's not suiting me. Let's walk in the gardens.'

Edward knelt, only raising himself to stand by relying on the bench, his breathing an audible wheeze. He brushed grass from his coat and breeches and held out the crook of his elbow for Henrietta.

'Shall we try the rose garden?' he said. 'Let's take a look at the bower where we will be married. Speaking for myself, I'm not sure I can wait three days.'

CHAPTER 7

1734

Henrietta woke early. She wasn't sympathetic to birds trying to outdo lowing cows from the fields and woodland bordering the garden. The cacophony of the countryside was not something she could ever get used to. Today, she would ask Edward where they would live and hoped it would be in London. The family seat was Powis Castle in Wales but like the Webb family, the Herberts probably owned other houses where she and Edward could make their home.

The bedroom door clicked open and Henrietta sat up. Because of the heat, last night Amelia had not lowered the drapes from their ties at the window or pulled across the tapestry hangings around her bed frame. Her visitor was Granny Webb, still in her night shift. She limped around to Henrietta's side and sat down heavily on the feather mattress, her breathing audible in short rasps.

Taking Henrietta's hand, Granny Webb said, 'I hoped to catch you before Amelia came to dress you. I spoke harshly the other night and I wanted to say sorry. It is true that you won't be allowed to return to Paris if you refuse Lord Herbert, but we wouldn't abandon you. I hope you know that.'

Henrietta nodded and squeezed her grandmother's fingers, feeling the sharp scratch of rings sliding over bony knuckles. She didn't trust herself to speak.

'Anyway, that's enough,' Granny Webb continued. 'Bridget let slip that she thought your first meeting went rather well?'

'He's not... he's not what I expected,' Henrietta said. 'He talks to me as if I'm his equal. He won't go through with a marriage against my will but I said yes. I think we'll be happy together.'

Granny Webb enveloped her in a hug, bearing the fragrance of rosewater from her morning wash. 'I'm so glad. This has been a difficult time for you and I've been far too preoccupied with my own health. If there is anything you want to ask me about becoming a married woman...'

Henrietta pretended to consider this, one finger pressed against her cheek. 'I don't think so,' she replied. 'How can I ever forget what you told me the last time we had the marriage talk. You put Amelia off forever.'

Granny Webb laughed. 'I think her mother is rather more responsible for that decision but I agree, I was perhaps a little too factual in front of such a young child. I wanted you to know everything that my mother failed to tell me.'

Henrietta sat up further and wrapped her arms around her legs, resting her chin on her knees. 'Granny, I have one worry. Edward seems ill. I wonder if it's more serious than we were led to believe?'

Granny Webb nodded, but would not meet Henrietta's eyes. 'I haven't met Edward yet because he's living locally in rooms, as etiquette dictates, but Bridget said he was troubled by a deep cough. I hope his father has been honest with us.'

So, Bridget had reported everything back to her mother. It

felt as if she and Edward had been trailed by a spy, not a chaperone. 'I don't want her following me today when I meet Edward. We'll be married the day after tomorrow, so what impropriety could possibly occur?'

'We can't leave you unchaperoned, sweetheart. At breakfast, let's see if one of the other women will help you. Perhaps a married woman will be a little bit more discreet than poor Bridget.'

Granny Webb slid off the bed and patted Henrietta's arm. 'Amelia will be with you any moment, so I'll leave you to dress.'

Her grandmother limped across the polished floorboards to the window. 'What a fine day,' she said, without turning around. 'A beautiful new dress, a kind husband... you are a lucky girl, Henrietta.'

Amelia stopped at the door to pick up something from the floor. 'It's a letter, Henrietta, addressed to you. I'll disappear to fetch your hot water from the scullery and leave you alone to read it.'

Henrietta was already out of bed, standing just where Lady Webb had been only minutes before. She tapped Edward's letter against her lips, then held it up to read in the bright light, indifferent to the dew on the gardens and the woodland beyond, fading into a purple slash of low hills.

'Another strip wash I'm afraid,' Amelia said, heaving a jug and bowl onto the washstand, 'but on your wedding day your hosts have promised a bath.'

'Don't you miss Paris?' Henrietta said, turning from the window. 'The English are dirty... but don't repeat that downstairs.'

Amelia lifted Henrietta's night shift over her head and said, 'Was the letter from Lord Herbert?'

'It's exactly the sort of letter I yearned to receive in Paris. He writes so well, I can almost forgive his neglect.'

Amelia laughed. 'Not too quickly, I hope. His failure to properly court you deserves at least three days of sulking. I don't suppose you can keep it up once you're married. He looks nice, by the way. We watched him arrive from the dining room window yesterday and there was considerable discussion about his merits in the servants' hall afterwards.'

'Everything is so public,' Henrietta said. 'I hate being talked about.'

Amelia rolled her eyes. 'Enjoy the attention... it won't last. My mother says that at her age, she's become invisible. We'd better hurry, the Webbs have already gathered for breakfast.'

In the dining room, Henrietta saw no sign that Granny Webb had become invisible, her family hanging on every word, anxious eyes waiting their turn to be noticed by their mother. She thought about Amelia's mother and the unlikelihood that Madame Laurent had truly become invisible either. Henrietta resolved never to disappear, that would not be her fate. She and Edward would become the talk of London and Paris. Yes, Paris... they would go back to her home when the time was right. She had only met her future husband once, but he didn't seem to be the type of man who would refuse her.

On the side table there was a choice of potato cakes, served with butter and sugar, stewed pears, and eggs cooked with cream, ginger, and spinach. Henrietta picked at the unfamiliar food, putting a little of each on her plate, wondering if she dare ask for some bread. A servant approached, bearing a letter on a silver salver. Henrietta snatched at it, hiding the paper behind her back, but it was too late, the room fell silent and everyone turned to stare.

If they want a show, I'll give them one, Henrietta decided, slowly picking at the sealing wax, and unfolding the paper between two fingers, as if it were hot. She shook the letter out with a flourish but within seconds had crumpled the letter into the pocket under her robe. Her cheeks throbbed, burning with a rush of blood and she knew she was pink from her neck to her forehead. What was he thinking? How could he write such words!

'Is everything alright, Henrietta,' Granny Webb asked. 'There's not a problem is there?'

Henrietta left her plate on the sideboard and dipped a curtsy to the family. 'It's nothing at all,' she said. 'Only a note from Lord Herbert, asking me to meet him in the garden later this morning. If you will excuse me, I must leave.'

The door closed behind her to the sound of a ripple of laughter.

The rose garden was where they would be married and Edward had suggested they meet there again, to check how the wedding stage would look. The gardeners were already busy, creating a bower of late roses where they would exchange their vows.

Henrietta flounced onto a stone bench, next to the man who would soon be her husband. She refused to give him her hand.

Edward's brow creased with concern. 'What have I done? Have I offended you?'

'Such thoughts about me are best kept to yourself, not laid out for everyone to read.'

'Ah, my letter... my words were for your eyes only. I thought you would be pleased, given my earlier failings at courtship.'

'I had to read it in front of my whole family at breakfast. It was so embarrassing. They laughed at me.'

Edward pressed both sides of his nose between his fingers.

His shoulders started to shake and sounds like gulping hiccups escaped his mouth. He was laughing at her too.

Henrietta stared, waiting for him to stop, but his laughter grew until tears coursed down his cheeks.

'I'm so sorry, my darling,' Edward spluttered, 'but I can't rid myself of the image of Lady Webb slowly grasping what was in my letter.'

'It's not funny,' Henrietta said, but in that moment, she pictured Granny Webb's face. She started to laugh too, making the kind of sounds she only ever shared with Amelia.

Her aunt Barbara, Lady Montague, peered from behind a laurel hedge, where she was hiding.

'Is everything alright?' she called out. 'Shall I call a physician, Lord Herbert?'

'Oh gawd,' Edward muttered. 'Your family already think I'm degenerate and now I'm dying. It just gets worse. Come on, let's walk. I need to talk to you about my family.'

They strode past Aunt Barbara, staring straight ahead as if she wasn't there, and found the burgeoning crops of the kitchen garden, where they strolled up and down and around the formal paths. Whenever Edward made an important point, he stopped walking and stared into her eyes. The midday sun was hot and even the gardeners had sought shelter in the brick tool store. Henrietta wished she had a parasol.

She learned that Edward had no contact with his father, although the Marquess would attend the wedding. He communicated with his older brother only through lawyers about the lawsuit they had jointly taken out against their sister, Mary Herbert, who had gambled away the family's wealth and left them deeply in debt. Edward spat out her name as if the taste disgusted him. He had two other living sisters but neither of them spoke to their father or their brothers because the family had failed to honour their marriage settlements.

'It's a mess, I'm afraid, and I hesitate to bring you into it,' Edward concluded.

Henrietta paused beside some newly espaliered apple trees, feeling the heat of the day radiating from the brick walls. 'Are you saying there's no money?'

Edward shook his head. 'There's plenty of money. Look at how my brother lives. But my sister Mary behaves like a running tap and my father keeps being drawn into her plans, giving her more and more. Our lead mines are doing well. With proper management of the estates, we would prosper, but I'm third in line when it comes to making decisions. If you'll still have me, we could rebuild the family's wealth, after my father and brother die, of course.'

'How likely is that?' Henrietta asked.

'My brother... very likely. My father... hmm... unfortunately, he's very fit.'

Henrietta and Edward walked on, taking a path towards the herb garden. This was troubling news. She didn't have contact with her own father and brothers, so their families weren't so different but she'd never been short of material wealth, could not imagine how it must feel. But Edward had said there was plenty of money and he didn't look poor, with his expensive clothes and fine wig. There was no way she could refuse him now... anyway, she didn't want to refuse him, but had Grandpa John been deceived by the Marquess?

They paused and the scent of herbs, curling in the heat of the sun, permeated the thick air. 'Of course I will marry you, Edward,' Henrietta said, 'but how do you live? I feel my grandfather should have asked such a question, before accepting the marriage proposal.'

Edward nodded and bent to kiss her hand. 'I have an income from the estate, I borrow money like everyone else, I gamble sometimes. You won't feel the pinch of poverty,

Henrietta. It's just the family's wealth isn't on a sure footing, not like the Webbs' fortune. You've grown up in Paris, so you will be ignorant of how Catholic families are treated in this country. My father only had his title and estates restored twelve years ago and your father had to renounce his faith to regain his.'

Henrietta sighed and flapped at her face with her fan. 'I'm hot, and all this feels very businesslike. I'd like to go inside and rest now. Let's not talk about money, at least not until after the wedding. I'm already feeling like your wife and I've not yet enjoyed being a bride.'

Edward leaned forward and glancing around for sight of Lady Montague, kissed Henrietta on the lips. 'I'm so lucky to be marrying you, Henrietta. You will bring joy and fun back into my life. I have forgotten how that feels.'

CHAPTER 8

1734

Henrietta woke early and padded across to the door, where the white corner of another letter poked out from beneath the rush matting. Climbing back upon her high bed, she scanned Edward's words, aware that she was smiling.

Amelia burst into the room, followed by two male servants staggering under the weight of a bath. Behind them maidservants, trailing the scent of lavender, rosemary, and thyme, carried jugs of hot water. Henrietta crushed the letter under her bolster.

'So what did he say?' Amelia asked, pouring water over Henrietta's head, and scrubbing at her scalp. 'I saw you hiding it.'

Henrietta turned her face away, in case she blushed. 'Oh, much the same... all very embarrassing.'

'Let's hope he's not over-selling himself,' Amelia said. 'You'll find out tonight. No, not tonight, since we'll be travelling. Perhaps tomorrow night. Lucky you!'

She held out a towel and Henrietta stepped into it, trying not to leave puddles to drip through the wooden floorboards.

Henrietta dried herself, then smoothed her skin with rose oil, the precious liquid dripped into her open hand by Amelia. Covered in a light linen robe to absorb the excess, Henrietta sat in front of her dressing table mirror, while Amelia tugged at her hair with a brush to free it from tangles.

'You should see the chaos downstairs,' Amelia said, biting on her lower lip as she began applying rouge to Henrietta's cheeks. 'The cook can't cope with a wedding meal for twelve, never mind the gathering later. This place is so backward.'

Henrietta placed a hand on Amelia's. 'What gathering?' she asked.

'The cook says it's an English tradition. All the neighbours are invited to the manor this evening and even the servants can join in, once the food is served. There's music and dancing too. Trust us to be missing it.'

'My grandmother said nothing to me about a party.'

'You're not invited, that's why. The eldest Webb son has arrived and he and Thomas are taking charge. The cook says Lady Webb's not well enough for all that organising. Your father-in-law is here and is wandering around looking lost.'

Henrietta's shoulders slumped. 'It seems to me that this wedding has little to do with me. It's not what I expected.'

'I think it's true of most weddings. It's like a stage show: you're an essential prop but have no speaking lines.'

Both girls fell silent as Amelia worked on Henrietta's face.

Henrietta broke the silence. 'I met the priest yesterday. Both Edward and I had to talk to him alone, to prepare us for marriage. He didn't say anything about a party either. I bet he stays for it.'

'Did you learn anything new?' Amelia asked, tipping Henrietta's chin to brush her eyebrows.

'The family priest covered the whole thing with me in Paris; it's just an ordinary mass. Since it's in Latin, I'll probably drift off but the priest will prompt us when we need to sit down or stand up, or when we have to reply.'

Amelia pulled a chair to the open window. 'Come and sit here. I need the sun on your hair or it won't dry. The aunts are expected any minute with your headdress and the robe itself. I'll go and find out what's happened to your breakfast.'

'Amelia, please rescue Edward's father,' Henrietta called after her. 'Leave him with my aunt Bridget.'

Henrietta drew a brush through her hair. She loved the feeling of clean hair, free from tight ribbons and silly caps. In her new house, where she would be the mistress and entitled to dress however she liked, she would wear her hair loose. Edward had arranged for them to spend a few days at Powis House in London and promised to show her his city. He'd even agreed to an evening of music or theatre, if there was anything worth seeing.

Amelia returned with a tray of stewed plums, bread, and some wine. 'This is all I could find and I had to fight for it. I've brought enough for two.'

Henrietta protested, 'You would think the bride might have some priority on her wedding day.'

Amelia widened her eyes at this unlikely idea. 'Your grandmother caught me sneaking into the dining room. She said a bride doesn't need anything to eat but I won't let you stand for hours in the sun, the centre of attention, without any food.'

Henrietta dipped her bread into the plums and sucked on the juice. 'I bet Edward has been fed,' she said.

Amelia mumbled through a mouthful of crust. 'Of course he has.'

∾

The family gathered before the rose bower, the approaching paths flagged by garlands of flowers, the seats draped with crisp linen. Henrietta peered around the edge of the bower, catching sight of Edward waiting in front of the priest. He glanced around, tugging on his cravat, as if he felt panicked.

Edward's father, William Herbert, sat next to Lord and Lady Webb, chewing on a fingernail, one bony leg twisted around the ankle of the other. Henrietta noticed his awkward discomfort, his loneliness, and wished he and Edward could be friends. He stood out amongst the chattering Webbs, further enlivened by the arrival of John, the heir.

Bridget shifted behind to tug at her headdress and Henrietta took another chance to scan the waiting group for the presence of her father or brothers. They had been invited and there was still time.

Her aunt Barbara spun her around and gripped both of her hands. 'You look perfect, Henrietta, the most pleasing of brides. Are you ready to join your new husband? I think he's getting hot.'

Henrietta blinked away the unexpected sting of tears. 'There's no one here for me.'

Aunt Barbara frowned, puzzled. 'Don't be a silly girl, we're all here for you.'

Henrietta tried to explain. 'I mean, my father and brothers aren't coming.'

Aunt Barbara released one hand and rested it on her back, giving her a gentle push. 'All the more reason to get married and start your own family. Off you go.'

Grandpa John waited for her at the edge of the bower. When she saw him, Henrietta stopped walking. Seeing her hesitate, Grandpa John roughly scrubbed at his eyes with his wrists and tried to smile. He pointed his elbow towards her.

'Sorry, Henrietta, I'm a sentimental old fool. Ignore my tears. For a moment, I thought you were your mother.'

Henrietta knew she looked beautiful. She and Amelia had been stunned into silence when side by side, they had admired their handiwork in the bedroom mirror. The silk gown from Magoulet's rippled from soft pink to almost magenta whenever Henrietta turned in the sunlight. Granny Webb had ruled there were to be no hoops, since seating was limited, but the dress was gathered into deep, whipped cream folds at the back, with a matching bow flopping at her breast. The sleeves descended in tiers of lace and ruffled fabric, as far as her elbow. Fresh rosebuds picked from the garden only that morning, wound through the ropes of pearls Amelia had twisted into her hair. She was the image of a fantastical wood nymph, one who might fly away at any moment.

Grandpa John released his arm and she stepped forward to stand at Edward's side. His expression of disbelief, closely followed by joy, swept away her longing for her father, or her brothers. This man loved her and that would be enough. The ceremony passed in a murmur of liturgy. She spoke when asked, sat down, stood up, as a bee hummed purposefully above her head and a bird repeated the same few notes, over and over, from the orchard behind. Edward placed a ring on her finger and everyone clapped. He bent his head to kiss her, a light touch on the lips, and whispered in her ear, 'Welcome, Lady Herbert.'

Everyone else seemed to enjoy what followed, judging by the jangle of voices, the laughter, the clattering plates, and the strange mix of smells, onions, spices and over-heated bodies. Later came waves of breath heavy with wine exhaled from faces pushed too close and many wet kisses on her fingers or cheeks. Across the dining room, she caught sight of Edward and he winked. Amelia, drafted to help serve the food, squeezed her waist as she bustled past, arms laden with pewter trays.

Standing frozen in one corner, Henrietta picked at tiny portions of food brought to her by servants. Only the Marquess spoke to her at length, sharing too many details about his daughter's plan to acquire more mines in Spain. She felt disloyal even listening, knowing how the conversation would infuriate Edward.

Granny Webb limped across the room towards her, bending her head to speak in private. 'Your husband wants to leave in half an hour,' she whispered. 'His carriage is waiting. Amelia has laid out your travelling clothes and is expecting you in your bedchamber. Everything you need is packed.'

Henrietta felt the room tilt, the family portraits spin. She grasped her grandmother's arm, and when she trusted herself to speak, her voice sounded louder than intended. 'When will I see you again?'

'Dignity, Henrietta, dignity,' Granny Webb hissed.

An expectant silence fell and Granny Webb announced to the room, 'Lord and Lady Herbert will soon leave. Please join us outside the house to wish them farewell. You may rest in your rooms or walk in the gardens until the estate workers and servants arrive for a celebration feast tonight.'

The old hall clock chimed two o'clock. From the dining room, the sound of cheers settled into the hum of well-fed chatter. On the staircase, Henrietta paused to listen, clutching at the newel post on the turn of the stairs, the one that reminded her of a Parisian street lamp.

This was the moment when everything would change, when she would turn from a young bride into a wife. She wasn't ready.

CHAPTER 9

1734

Amelia was the last person Henrietta expected to be lying next to on her wedding night. After they left the manor house in a cloud of dried flower petals, Edward fell asleep in the carriage, only stirring when troubled by his cough. The journey felt long and treacherous, rolling along rutted tracks and it was almost dark before they stopped at an inn outside Farnborough.

Edward stirred and rubbed his eyes, turning to wink at her as he climbed down through the door held open by Gilbert, his manservant. Henrietta watched her husband cross the courtyard and disappear inside the inn, before stepping down from the carriage herself.

Amelia climbed gingerly from her seat at the rear of the coach, where she had travelled next to Gilbert, pulling off her thick cloak and gloves, and waited in the courtyard with Henrietta. The coachman stayed in his seat, staring straight ahead and idly flicking his whip. No one spoke and the quiet night echoed around them to the sound of an owl, calling from a tree behind the inn.

Edward strode back towards them, frowning. 'They only

have two rooms, so I'll sleep with the men, all boys together. The two woman can have the other room, of course.'

It made sense. There was no point arguing. After some bread, cheese and ale, Amelia and Henrietta left the men alone and began to climb the steep, dusty stairs to their shared bedroom. There was barely enough light from their single candle and Henrietta needed to grip the beams supporting the staircase for balance, feeling the heads of huge nails beneath her fingertips.

Edward called up to her from the bottom step. 'Henrietta!'

She paused and carefully stepped backwards down the steps, until she was level with her husband.

He pulled her close and pushed his lips onto hers, in a slow, searching kiss. 'I'm so sorry,' he said, drawing back to see her eyes. 'I should have warned you we wouldn't reach London tonight. I'll make it up to you tomorrow.'

Henrietta stroked his cheek, as if she didn't mind but actually, she did mind. Instead, she said, 'Goodnight, Edward,' and hurried up the dark staircase towards Amelia, waiting as a dark shadow in the open bedroom door, backlit by their candle.

Both girls were on their backs, trying to find a comfortable hollow in the lumpy mattress. There was an ominous rustling from the eaves.

'I bet that lot are snoring right now,' Amelia spoke into the dark. 'I'm exhausted but so tense after today, I can't sleep.'

Henrietta turned towards her friend, even though she couldn't see Amelia's face. 'I can't sleep because I'm furious. I do understand we had to stop, but I'm the last to know anything. It feels like I'm part of the luggage, just something to be humped around.'

'He's used to leading a man's life,' Amelia said. 'He's never had to consult anyone before, to share what he's doing. If it upsets you, you'll have to make things clear from the start. Tell him you expect to be included in future.'

Henrietta rolled back to face the wall and pushed her face into her pillow. 'Indeed, I will... I'll start tomorrow. Let's try and get some sleep, even if that stupid mouse has other plans.'

'What if it's a rat?' Amelia said.

'Be quiet, Amelia, it's not a rat. It's a squirrel.'

Amelia laughed and turned her body to face the door. 'Right, it's a squirrel. Goodnight, Hensy.'

If she closed her eyes, spun around three times, and opened them again, she could be in Paris. Edward led her into the hall of Powis House, explaining that the French Ambassador had burned the place down and his employer, the king, had rebuilt it from the ashes, using a French architect and designer.

'It's spectacular,' Henrietta said. 'It's the grandest house I've ever seen.'

'Not to my taste, I'm afraid,' Edward replied, handing his gloves and cloak to Gilbert. 'But I thought you'd like it. My older brother, Lord Montgomery, lives here, but he's away for a few days.'

Henrietta drew her eyes away from the sweep of stairs, with its open balustrade of twisted, gilt foliage. 'Where do you actually live, Edward?' she asked.

He hesitated, as if deciding whether to answer her question. 'Sometimes in Hendon, sometimes in Bath. I have rooms there, for my health.'

'Will we live in Bath or Hendon?' she asked.

'Why don't you pop upstairs to change and wash,' Edward replied. 'Amelia will have unpacked.'

Henrietta hesitated, her initial delight fading. 'Shall we meet for lunch?'

Edward frowned and rubbed his chin with his fist. 'My brother left rather a skeleton staff, but at least we have a cook. I'll ask Gilbert to speak to her, organise some food. Shall we say... in an hour?'

Henrietta waited at the bottom of the elegant staircase. 'Edward, I don't know where my... our... bedroom is.'

Edward tried to hoist her over his shoulder but dropped her on the third step, bending over to wheeze and cough. 'I will show you,' he laughed, once he was able to stand upright, 'but better to take my hand.' On the landing, he paused in front of an open door, lifted her chin and pressed his lips onto hers, his tongue searching between her teeth. Had Amelia not been waiting, their wedding night might have happened there and then, which would have been much more exciting and less frightening than the bedtime scene she was trying not to imagine. Seeing Henrietta's servant, Edward shrugged, turned on his heel and went in search of lunch.

The room was bathed in light from tall windows, with panels on the walls framing a multitude of cherubs, their faces picked out in gold leaf. Henrietta danced across the room to her large bed, draped in folded hangings of cream silk, and threw herself onto the mattress. This wasn't their home, but she could still pretend.

Amelia worked without energy and was unusually silent, laying out a clean dress and pouring scented oil into a bowl of warm water, set into the washstand. Henrietta splashed her hands and face, smelling roses and almonds, as Amelia picked up her discarded clothes. At the dressing table, robed as if for a French toilette, Henrietta waited for her hair to be brushed and styled.

'What beautiful fabric,' she said, lifting the toile lace skirt that wrapped around the legs of the dressing table. 'It's nicer than mine at home, don't you think?'

Amelia nodded and began to remove her mistresses' cap, her deft fingers fumbling with the pins. She dropped the hairbrush several times, cursing her own clumsiness, until Henrietta retrieved it for the final time and swung the chair around.

'What is it, Amelia, what's the matter?' she said, bending her head to catch Amelia's eye. 'Don't you like it here?'

Amelia looked away, biting her lip. 'It's nothing.'

'You can tell me. Please tell me. Are you homesick?'

Amelia glanced around the room. 'It may look fine in here,' she replied, speaking in a low voice that Henrietta could barely hear, 'but only a few rooms are furnished and there's no staff. A house of this size should be bustling with life downstairs but it's empty. It's dirty too... you should see my room.'

'Oh, Amelia, what a disappointment. It's not Edward's house. He's borrowing it from his brother, so that we can see London. In a few days, we'll move to our proper home. Can you manage until then?'

Amelia sat down on the bed, twisting Henrietta's cap between her hands. 'I'm worried that things aren't what they seem. I've thought and thought about whether I should tell you, but Gilbert and the coachman, Robert, said that Lord Herbert didn't share a room with them at the inn. There was a bed for him but he was gone all night.'

Henrietta felt something very cold grip her stomach. She didn't want to hear this, she couldn't be forced to know this, not before her wedding night.

When she spoke, she tried to sound unconcerned and formal, as Lady Henrietta Herbert should. 'I'm certain Lord Herbert had important business to attend to and the men simply fell asleep before he returned. Everything will be fine, Amelia, please don't worry.'

Amelia dipped Henrietta a brief curtsy and finished dressing her mistress. 'I'm sorry to have troubled you, my lady,' she said. 'I'm sure you're right. All will be well.'

Henrietta waited for Edward in their wide bed, washed and scented, wearing a new linen night shift, edged with Parisian lace. He was in his dressing room, taking an extraordinary time to prepare.

She wanted the thing that Granny Webb had described to be finished, to join the company of married women who knew what it was like, but she also wanted to linger, touching each other in the privacy of darkness. After much kissing, Edward would take his time over whatever came next, he would be patient and not hurt her.

She squeezed her hands and tried to shake out her nerves through her fingertips. Her stomach growled and a new fear crept into her thoughts. What if she needed to rush into her own dressing room and use the chamber pot, right in the middle of everything? How did other women manage this?

She had tried to forget the servants' spiteful gossip about Edward. This afternoon, he had been the perfect, attentive husband, taking her by boat to the Spring Gardens at Vauxhall. They had travelled by wherry, rowed by a waterman no older than herself, stripped to the waist, his taut body glistening with sweat. He stared, making no effort to disguise his lust, but Henrietta kept her eyes firmly on her new husband, a man obviously older but no less attractive.

She liked Edward's profile, his high forehead under a neat wig and a nose that seemed dignified without being too pointed. He turned to smile at her, his eyes crinkling at the corners against the sun's reflection on the water. He tried to point out a bridge crossing the Thames, heavy with houses, looking as if it might topple over, and the Palace of Westminster, the seat of the British government, but Henrietta wanted to stare at the crowded waterside, people no more than specks; stairs and landings lining the shore leading into small houses and secret alleys. The river seethed with crowded barges and sailing ships, everything busy, everything active, everything moving and shining, even the seabirds who dipped and cried.

It was a relief to reach the cool gardens, free at last from the powerful breeze of the river, and walk arm-in-arm along shaded walkways. She had enjoyed the attention of the waterman and thought Edward hadn't minded seeing a younger man admire his new wife. It pleased her to see the envious stares of men in these gardens too, their attention singling her out from dozens of other handsome couples.

Edward took her deep into the gardens, away from the main paths, seeking hidden arbours, where they could sit amongst the foliage, holding hands, occasionally risking a kiss if no other giggling couple strolled past. Everywhere there was the smell of food, the distant sound of music, cheering and clapping.

At the very centre of the gardens they found a circular room with a fountain. On every wall there were mirrors and she and Edward posed, nestling into each other and kissing, despite stares of barely concealed lust from men, as well as sounds of disapproval from older women. Edward disappeared to buy wine and cake and Henrietta waited, sitting on the edge of the fountain, trickling her fingers in the water to tease the scurrying, golden fish.

The sun dipped towards the horizon and Edward led Henrietta to a dining booth. It was a poor structure, held together more by climbing plants than wood and nails, but when a servant lit the candle at their table, the tendrils surrounded them with mysterious shadows. She drank two glassfuls of wine, more than was wise. Edward drank heavily, barely finishing one before signalling for another. A servant brought them a dish called hodgepodge, which had been simmering all afternoon, he said. After tasting the smallest mouthful, Henrietta hungrily swallowed the sweet and fragrant stew, scraping her platter clean. She had barely eaten since breakfast and the wine had made her almost faint with hunger.

They rose to leave, both staggering to find their balance against the rickety table and walked towards the riverside along paths made enticing by the light and shade cast from hundreds of lamps. Henrietta was not too drunk to notice other couples sneaking off down dark alleyways and felt a shiver of excitement. She hoped Edward would steer her into one of these secretive paths and take her right there, as if he couldn't wait a moment longer. Instead he strode ahead, tugging at her hand, blind to the fervour of lust preoccupying everyone else.

Henrietta startled from her daydream when Edward's dressing room door swung open, slamming against the opposite wall. He found his way to their bed by candlelight and lifted the bedcovers, climbing in beside her, his cold feet finding hers. Henrietta flinched and moved her legs but Edward reached out and pulled her towards him, wrapping an arm around her shoulders, so that her head lay on his chest.

'Ah, that's better,' he said, stroking her hair. 'Isn't it fine to lie here together, at last.'

Henrietta nodded, her face pressed into his chest, feeling something furry prickle against her nose. She waited but nothing more happened. Under her cheek, she could feel Edward's breath rise and fall, as if he were drifting into sleep.

She raised her head and shook his shoulder. 'Edward, this is our wedding night.'

Edward made a smacking sound with his lips. 'So it is,' he whispered. 'I'm rather tired, my darling, if you don't mind. I'll make it up to you tomorrow.'

He eased his body further down the bed and kissed her, ruffling the back of her head. 'Night, night, darling,' he said, and then began to snore.

Henrietta had spent only one night in bed with another human being and that was Amelia, at the inn. *She* had behaved with decorum but this was different. Edward stole the blankets, made snorting noises and regrettable sounds passed from his body all night, ones that anyone sensible would choose not to hear.

She must have slept eventually, because in the morning, Edward's side of the bed was empty but she had no recollection of him leaving. The drapes were pinned back and a bowl of steaming water stood on her dressing table.

'I thought I'd let you sleep,' Amelia said, bursting into the room with unnecessary energy. 'At breakfast, which I had to serve by the way, Lord Herbert said you'd had a bad night.'

Henrietta groaned and slung an arm across her eyes. 'It's not what you think.'

'Tell me what happened... but only if you want to.'

Henrietta paused. 'Amelia, have you ever heard anyone snore?'

'Yes, of course, my mother snores.'

'But have you heard someone snore on and on, and then stop and you think, at last, I can sleep now; and then they roar like a caged bear and start all over again.'

'I haven't heard that sort of snoring. Your husband is an unwell man. Is it something to do with his health?'

Henrietta tossed her pillow onto the floor. 'If it happens again, Amelia, he won't be an ill man, he'll be a dead man.'

CHAPTER 10

1734

H enrietta strode beside her husband, their arms linked, wishing he would slow his pace. He seemed to have no idea that women, not even Parisian women, walked so fast.

They had left the carriage at the entrance to the Tower of London, frustrated by the jam of vehicles, allowing their coachman to find somewhere to wait. She toiled up Tower Hill, feeling sweat gathering in the small of her back, glad Amelia had dressed her in an informal wrapping gown, a loose dress without the nuisance of a hoop or all the extra fabric at the back. She hoped people wouldn't stare at her unsuitable outfit but keeping up with Edward would have been impossible wearing anything else.

'Edward, wait,' she begged, 'can we sit down?'

He found a low wall where an older part of the ramparts had been allowed to fall into disrepair and they sat side by side. 'I wanted you to see this,' he said, waving an arm to include the tangle of tall buildings enclosing the green space before them. 'About twenty years ago my aunt rescued her husband from here, right out from under the nose of the guards, on the very night before his execution. Her name is Winifred Maxwell. Such an escape had never been done before... actually, has never happened since.'

'Oh, I think I know this story,' Henrietta replied. 'My aunt – my mother's sister – her husband was taken prisoner at the same time but he was executed. They were Jacobites, weren't they, fighting at somewhere called Preston?'

Edward frowned. 'Who told you?'

Henrietta hesitated, seeing his disappointment. It would have been better to pretend she knew nothing. Unsure of her motives, except that she wanted her husband to think well of Granny Webb, she lied. 'Your father did, when he first came to Paris to meet me. He didn't say much but my governess explained everything.'

'Might have known the old goat would have got in first, exploiting his sister's misery to make himself seem more interesting.'

'But she lives in Rome with her husband, doesn't she?' Henrietta interjected. 'She's free from persecution.'

'But never free to return to this country,' Edward added. 'They were thrown out of France and she had to leave my cousin Anne behind in Paris, when she was just a child. I think my aunt Winifred has had her fair share of misery.'

'I hope to meet her one day,' Henrietta said. 'Perhaps we can travel to Rome together. It could be our honeymoon?'

It was as if Edward had not heard. 'Did my father tell you this bit... his parents were prisoners in the Tower for years, both of them facing execution.'

Henrietta dabbed at her neck with a lace cloth, heavily scented with lavender, scanning the crowds for a pedlar selling small ale. She needed a drink, not to listen to more Herbert family history, but forced herself to ask, 'Why were they held prisoner?'

'My grandfather was accused of conspiring to kill King Charles, who was a Protestant. It never came to trial. My grandmother tried to gain his release and ended up being accused of treason herself. She did go to court but was acquitted. When King James ran off to France in 1688, they went with him.'

Henrietta's thoughts drifted to her own grandparents, what their lives would have been like, if they hadn't fled to safety in Paris. It all seemed so long ago but Edward was her new husband and she should try to take more interest.

'My governess said they didn't spare women, they *were* actually executed, so it can't have been a happy childhood for your father and his sisters, waiting for their mother to lose her head.'

Edward laughed and patted her knee. 'My goodness, we are gloomy this morning. If you like, we can visit the graves of three queens, all put to death on this very spot. It's just over there.' He indicated across the green.

'This is fascinating, Edward,' Henrietta said, 'but first, can we find something to drink?'

Edward tossed the last of his small ale onto the grass in front of the Chapel Royal. 'That tasted like piss,' he said, 'and cost me two pennies. Later, we'll drink some decent London beer.'

Henrietta sipped hers, glad to have found some shade under a tree. She regretted setting off without a parasol and after her bad night, longed for a cool, shady room, not more beer.

'Come on,' Edward said, holding out a hand to help her stand. 'Let's track down the menagerie.'

The animals were not difficult to find, the smell of rotting flesh and urine rising as they neared the cages. Henrietta held her scented cloth under her nose, flinching as a lion threw himself at the bars of the enclosure, making it rattle and shake as if the huge animal was barely contained.

'Here, miss,' a keeper called out to her. 'Three pennies to throw them a live dog or cat. Take your pick.'

Edward's expression darkened and he stepped forward to rebuke the man. Henrietta felt a familiar growl from her stomach and her throat squeezed tight. She was about to be sick. 'Can we go, Edward... please!'

He looked down at her, his eyebrows raised in surprise. 'You don't want to see the Crown Jewels?'

Henrietta steadied herself against his arm and shook her head. 'I'd like to go home. I'm afraid I might faint.'

They didn't go home. She slept as the carriage inched through traffic, the jolting of their frequent stops playing out a dream landscape, an endless journey where someone kept waking her. The carriage stopped outside an inn, and she opened one eye to read a sign that said the Cock Tavern. Gilbert helped her down, the balls of her feet burning with pain at every step.

Edward appeared from inside the tavern, holding out his arm to steady her. 'I've found us a decent corner at the back,' he whispered. 'The landlady will take you upstairs where you can refresh yourself. Not many women of your background are seen in London hostelries, so they're keen to make you comfortable.'

The room was dim, the single window dirty but Henrietta could make out the shape of a lumpen bed and ached to stretch out and sleep. She was grateful for a pot to use, clean water, and soap and stripped off her frayed stockings, lowering her bare feet into a bowl, sighing with relief. Outside the room, the landlady waited and when too much time had passed, she knocked on the door, reminding Henrietta that Lord Herbert was waiting. Of course, her husband was known here by name.

The landlady escorted Henrietta back down the narrow staircase and through a crowded room, lit only by small windows that faced the street. She caught sight of Robert, their coachman, sipping at a jar of ale, relaxed and at ease with only the horses for company. She pushed through the tables behind her host and the hubbub of male voices fell silent. The high-pitched laughter of the women took longer to ebb.

One woman spoke, loud enough for Henrietta to hear. 'You would think Lady Herbert could afford a better dress than that one. It looks like my second best.' Many others joined in with her cackling laugh.

Edward waited at a table in a panelled alcove, in front of two jars of ale and a plate of oysters. He stood when she entered and gestured for her to sit down next to him.

'Best oysters in London.' He grinned. 'Thought we might need them to set us up for tonight, at least I will.'

Henrietta sipped at the bitter ale and wiped her mouth, using the back of her hand, since there were no napkins. 'Why would we need oysters?'

Edward laughed. 'They get you in the mood, pep you up... for later, I mean. Come on, try one.'

Henrietta cautiously picked up an oyster, smelling the salty brine. She allowed it to slip over her tongue, just as Edward had shown her but her throat allowed it no further. She retched and spat the slimy mess into her hand. 'I'm sorry, I can't eat these.'

Edward winked. 'Then, all the more for me.'

She watched Edward tip the oysters into his mouth, each one followed by a deep draught of ale. He studied her as he ate, as if expecting a reaction, a comment. There would be no better time to question him about his family's finances.

'Why do you hate your father?' she asked.

Edward snapped his fingers for more ale. 'I hate all my family; he's nothing special.'

'But what have they done?'

'My brother is a gambler and a drunk. My sister Mary is escorted by a man called Gage but won't marry him. She borrowed a fortune to invest in a scheme called the Mississippi something or other and persuaded my father to be her guarantor. She's now running around in Spain like a madwoman, prospecting for mines of all things, yet my father still supports her. The family is bankrupt and we're pursued by some rather unpleasant debt collectors. My brother has already spent several nights in a debtors prison.'

Henrietta stayed silent, allowing his tirade to settle. Her first thought was for herself, the money she had been promised by the Marquess of Powis on marrying Edward. Was it all a deception? She wouldn't ask, not right now, not before they were properly man and wife.

'I know about Mary, but you mentioned other sisters?'

Edward shrugged. 'I don't even know where they live, so there's no point talking about them. They cut us off.'

Henrietta would have enjoyed having female relatives, women she could turn to, learn things from, even trust. Perhaps she could help to repair this family enmity, once she and Edward had settled into marriage.

He leaned back in his chair, surveying her. 'Enough about me. Why do you hate your father?'

Henrietta flinched. 'That's not true. I don't hate him,' she replied. 'He has nothing to do with me because I refused to disown the Catholic faith, yet it was his choice to leave me with my mother's Catholic family. My brothers don't think for themselves, they just copy their father and both have renounced their faith. One day I will be reconciled with my father, I want to believe it.'

Edward reached over the table for her hand. 'We must make a new family, my sweet Henrietta. We will be strong, we'll be successful, we'll show them.'

Henrietta wondered if the oysters had done their work. She would find out soon enough, but Edward was taking a long time in his dressing room, even longer than last night. At least she was feeling better, having rested for hours after they returned from their expedition. Amelia had stripped her of her sticky day clothes and dabbed her brow with cool water until she slept. She no longer felt nervous, only impatient.

How did her husband actually live, she wondered, if he was pursued by debtors? How much time did he spend in taverns? He was a mystery, a stranger, this man who was about to fulfil his marital duty. Without this essential step, they weren't properly married and she was tired of the burden.

Edward stumbled into the bedroom and sprinted towards the bed. Throwing back the covers, he pushed up her night shift and forced her limbs apart with his knees. Raising his own shirt, he fell onto her and thrust something between her legs. He grunted three times, rocking back and forth on his elbows, then collapsed onto her belly, wheezing.

'Thank Christ for that,' he murmured, rolling over onto his back. 'I managed.'

Henrietta dragged her shift down to cover her thighs and rolled onto her side. She could see Edward's reddened face, since there hadn't even been time to blow out the candle. 'What did you manage?'

'I'm sure you didn't notice,' he mumbled, 'but I've had my way with you.'

'That was it?'

Edward peered at Henrietta from under his eyelids. With a dismissive wave, he gestured towards his groin. 'You won't know this, being a nice, well-brought up girl, but men aren't all the same size. If your governess showed you drawings of Michelangelo's David, you're going to be disappointed when you see me. It does the business, or at least it used to... no complaints, anyway. But nowadays, I can't raise myself to action, at least not without studying drawings I keep in my dressing room. Would you like to see them?'

Henrietta shook her head. 'No, I wouldn't. The oysters didn't work?'

'I'm afraid not and the drawings took far longer than usual. It's this bloody illness, I'm afraid. It feels as if my strength is draining away.'

'What is wrong with you, Edward? I hope you aren't about to... to leave me.'

Edward reached for Henrietta's shoulders and turned her body to face him fully. 'Not with a beautiful new bride to live for.'

His hand slipped under her shift. 'You won't know this either, at least I hope you don't. There are many, many ways for a man to give a woman pleasure, even one as ill as me. Let me show you.'

Henrietta lay awake, listening to her husband snore. She didn't mind, she didn't want to sleep and lose this feeling, this warm, buzzing contentment. What did it matter if Edward couldn't perform like other men? She would settle for the rest, for her body to be played like a fine instrument, for her pleasure to be paramount, rather than his.

There was so much Granny Webb hadn't told her but perhaps her poor grandmother didn't even know. If women kept the sex act secret, the things she and Edward had just done were even more of a conspiracy, known only to a privileged group. Now, Lady Henrietta Herbert was one of them.

CHAPTER II
1734

In the morning, Edward was gone but Henrietta was learning he was an early riser and hoped there was still time to exchange complicit glances over the breakfast table.

Downstairs, only a solitary place was set, with no signs of crumbs or a crumpled napkin to suggest any other living being had passed through this room. Amelia shrugged when asked whether her master had breakfasted and when she returned with coffee, bread and fruit for Henrietta, she said the stable lad had overheard horses being harnessed before daylight. The carriage was gone and there was no sign of Gilbert or Robert.

There was nothing else to do but wait. Amelia showed her the withdrawing room, which was at least clean and furnished. Henrietta made a circuit, her finger tracing the flowing golden scrollwork that edged the wall panelling, then sat down in one of the upholstered chairs, stroking the padded armrests and swinging her legs.

In the corner, she noticed a writing table, much like her grandmother's, and crossed the room, tucking herself into the scribe's chair. She thought she would write a letter to her grandparents, but there was no paper, pen or inkstand.

The clock on the mantel struck ten and Henrietta walked over to the fireplace, hoping her reflection in the mirror would show how last night had changed her. No matter how many times she turned her head, or lifted her chin, she looked exactly the same, even a little weary about the eyes.

Henrietta sighed and slumped down again in another of the armchairs. She couldn't send for Amelia: the cook would have asked her to help prepare lunch. Where on earth was Edward?

A man's voice sounded from the hall, gruff and impatient. Henrietta stilled, holding her breath, waiting for the tap on the door.

'My lady, this is Lord Montgomery, your husband's brother. He needs to speak to you with some urgency,' Amelia said, swinging the door wide enough to allow a strange man to thrust his way past.

Henrietta rose and bit her knuckles. 'Edward is dead, isn't he?'

Lord Montgomery waved impatiently at her empty chair and fussed over spreading his coat before taking a seat opposite. 'Don't talk nonsense, Lady Herbert,' he said, his lips settling into what looked like a permanent sneer. 'If he's not here, that's Edward I'm afraid. Get used to it.'

Henrietta felt an immediate dislike for this man and with a lift of her finger, signalled for Amelia to wait. 'I'm delighted to meet you, Lord Montgomery,' Henrietta said, searching for a cold but regal tone. 'What a pity you couldn't find the time to come to our wedding.'

Montgomery tugged at his cravat. 'Look, I don't know how to say this nicely, so I'll be direct. I need my house. I need you gone,' he glanced at his timepiece, 'by this afternoon.'

Amelia was behind Lord Montgomery's back, mouthing the

very words Henrietta wanted to use herself but she was no longer Henrietta Waldegrave, she was Lady Edward Herbert, a married woman, who must not behave like a child. She would not be frightened by this bully.

'That is impossible,' she replied. 'I will wait for my husband's return. My maidservant and I have nowhere to go and are without a carriage.'

'You can use my carriage, as long as I get it back tomorrow. My coachman will take you to the Herbert manor house at Hendon. Now, I suggest your maid prepares for a departure, within two hours.'

Henrietta scanned Montgomery's face, so like Edward's but reddened with thread veins and disfigured by a bulbous nose. 'From what I've heard from my husband, I expected no less from you than this rudeness, this incivility.'

Montgomery snorted. 'From what I know of your husband, dear girl, I'm surprised it took him this long to disappear. Now, Lady Herbert, or may I call you Henrietta, go and change. Your carriage awaits.'

Lord Montgomery turned and snapped his fingers at Amelia. 'Tell the cook I'm staying for lunch.'

They arrived in darkness, met at the door by a dishevelled housekeeper in her night things, holding up a candle. She introduced herself as Mrs Adams and stared at Amelia with curiosity.

'This is Mademoiselle Laurent, my maidservant,' Henrietta explained, as the coachman carried in their trunks and dropped them in the hall behind them. 'I am Lady Henrietta Herbert,' she added, in case an introduction was necessary. 'I hope we were expected.'

Mrs Adams raised her candle, as if trying to see them better. The pool of light created heavy shadows below her eyes, etching deep lines down her cheeks. She looked terrifying.

'Lord Montgomery told me to expect you, Lady Herbert, but not when you might arrive. You must be tired. I will take you up to your room myself.'

Amelia was directed to a narrow staircase leading from the hall, where she would find the servants' quarters and Henrietta was shown to a bedroom, clean but damp, without hot water or cloths and only one stub of candle. Without a wash and stripped down to her undergarments, Henrietta slipped under bed covers that felt chilled and smelt musty. Outside her door, the floorboards creaked and something rustled behind the wainscoting. She would not blow out her candle until it guttered, would not draw the drapes around her bed. This place wasn't safe and she would fight her burning need to sleep until dawn reassured her otherwise.

'How could Edward abandon me like this?' she whispered aloud. 'What will happen to us?' Giving in to her disappointment, her fears, brought tears and once those had flowed, drenching her pillow, Henrietta slept.

'Well this place isn't what we expected,' Amelia said, drawing back the curtains at the window. 'If you thought Odstock was bad, it's a palace compared to here. There's the housekeeper, a cook, a general dogsbody, and a stable boy who's meant to be the gardener as well. I've been told to instruct you that there's a staff meeting at eleven.'

Henrietta sat up, frayed with lack of sleep. She guessed that Amelia was trying to be cheerful but also would have shed miserable tears, alone last night. They had to stay strong for each other, keep up the pretence.

'If this is to be our home,' Henrietta said, 'we have to make the best of it. You are my maid, paid for by my family. I'll try to make sure that the housekeeper doesn't take advantage of you.'

Amelia sat on the edge of Henrietta's mattress and picked at loose threads on the faded embroidery bedcover. 'The trouble is, I know how a house should be run. I can't stop myself from pointing things out and taking over. I've already put the cook's nose out, trying to find hot water and clean cloths.'

'Let's hope this is only temporary,' Henrietta said. 'Once my husband returns, I'm sure we'll find somewhere better to live.'

'Where do you think he is?' Amelia asked.

'You heard what his brother said. This is his normal behaviour, apparently.'

'Downstairs they're saying that the manor house has been in the Herbert family for generations but has always been let. Lord Edward only moved in last year and he's only ever here for a few days every month, to do his lord of the manor thing.'

'Where do they say he goes the rest of the time?'

'He doesn't announce it but the rumour is, he lives in Bath.'

Mrs Adams escorted Henrietta around the ancient manor house. It had a simple layout of rooms set around a cobbled courtyard, with small, latticed windows and heavy, wooden furniture, generations old, in every room. Ancestral portraits dotted the walls.

Henrietta pretended to be delighted with the house but everything seemed worn, with some furniture actually broken and clumsily repaired. After a breakfast of eggs, with potatoes and spinach, she asked if she might go outside and Mrs Adams showed her the way into the garden and orchard.

Henrietta made several tours of the garden, trying to fill the time before her meeting with the staff. She trailed through the formal beds at the side of the house, but they were overgrown with weeds and it was difficult to find the paths. In the orchard, the ancient trees were unpruned, tangled branches bowed with ripening fruit. Piles of rotting apples, left unused from the previous autumn, hummed with wasps.

The huge vegetable garden grew more weeds than food, but one rectangle seemed well-tended, with robust crops bursting from the tilled earth. She stared at these healthy plants, assuming this patch was all the household required. Looking back at the house, she saw it nested into the surrounding landscape, smug with centuries of history, like Odstock in every respect, except that Odstock lived and thrived, a family home for generations of people who took pride in their surroundings.

Amelia called to her from the gate and lifting her skirts, tiptoed through beds full of yellowing and decayed vegetation, collapsed at the end of their lives. She sat down next to Henrietta on the crumbling wall of what must once have been a pigsty.

'The house meeting is about to start, I thought I'd come and find you.'

Henrietta reached out and tucked a strand of Amelia's hair back under her cap. 'What are we doing here?'

'I've no idea what you're doing here,' Amelia replied, 'but I'm trying to help with the organisation of this place and I seem to have annoyed Mrs Adams as well as the cook, who is called Sarah by the way. She may have a second name but she's so sour-faced, I didn't ask. They all need a thorough rollicking from Lady Webb. Nobody had started on lunch an hour ago but at least we'll have some roasted vegetables, thanks to my intervention.'

Henrietta felt the throb of unshed tears from behind her eyes but couldn't risk the humiliation of openly crying in front of her brave friend, only fifteen years old and trying so hard. 'I miss my grandparents, Amelia. Do you think they ever wonder what I'm doing, or worry about me? They haven't written.'

Amelia tipped Henrietta's chin towards her and looked into her mistress' eyes. 'Hensy, they don't know where you are; we don't know where we are. Ask the housekeeper for writing materials and this afternoon, let's write some letters. Someone needs to be told that your new husband has abandoned you.'

Henrietta stood and dragged her shawl from the wall, the weave catching against the rough edges, and draped it over her shoulders. 'He hasn't abandoned me. There will be a simple explanation. Please take me to the meeting.'

Her staff waited in the dining room. Henrietta sat down in a straight-backed chair at the head of the table, with Mrs Adams to her right. It was hard to see much beyond the plain wood-panelled walls, which seemed to draw all the light from the single window.

Mrs Adams introduced each member of staff in turn, including Mademoiselle Laurent, said with such disdain that Henrietta knew Amelia had already made everything more complicated for them both.

There was a child, a little girl, who was being trained to become a housemaid. The gardener, a young man called Joseph, had followed his father into the role and a handyman, who looked as if he would be handy with very little. The door burst open and a red-faced man, sweating as if he had walked for many miles, slumped down into an empty place, his cap screwed between tense fists.

'Lady Herbert, this is Mr Lewis,' the housekeeper waved a

hand towards the latecomer. 'He manages the farms and the estate.'

Henrietta smiled and dipped her head. 'Pleased to meet you, Mr Lewis. I'd like to learn more about what we grow on our farms and the income we earn from our tenants.'

Lewis stood up again, forcing back his chair, his knuckles resting on the table. He glared at Henrietta, but addressed Mrs Adams. 'I am not wasting my time talking to a girl who looks younger than my own daughter. When his lordship returns, if he ever does, I'll speak to him.'

He strode past, his eyes fixed on the door, and slammed it behind him. In the silence, the gloom thickened. In front of Henrietta, the servants' faces blurred, their outline fading.

Mrs Adams stepped in, as if trying to rescue her mistress. 'Lady Herbert, you are tired. I suggest you go to the parlour and I'll bring you some chocolate. Once you are rested, I'll send Sarah to see you. Lunch is organised for today, thank you, Mademoiselle Laurent, but cook needs advice on the menu for this evening and the rest of the week.'

Amelia hurried around the table to Henrietta's side and spoke to her in French. This was a mistake but she couldn't stop herself from replying in the language that was so comfortable and natural for them both. Mrs Adams beckoned the staff out of the room, each one frowning at this stranger, this foreigner, little more than a child, who had burst into their simple and undemanding lives in the middle of the night. She was their worst nightmare.

Left alone in the parlour, to her surprise and delight, Henrietta discovered a spinet under a dust sheet. This was something she could do, practise her music, and surprise Edward when he returned. Her husband had never heard her play. Mrs Adams brought her chocolate in a porcelain jug, with matching cup and saucer, on a silver tray. Henrietta admired the set and asked if it had been made by Meissen, becoming the co-operative girl once valued by her grandmother to please a new older woman. When the origins of the cup, saucer and jug had been explored, Henrietta requested writing materials, ink and any sheet music that could be found.

'Of course, my lady,' Mrs Adams replied, but hesitated at the door.

'Is there anything else?' Henrietta asked.

Mrs Adams passed the empty tray from one hand to the other. 'Lady Herbert, I understand how hard this is for you but it's hard for the staff as well. They don't see your youth, your inexperience, in the same way as I do. I can help you, teach you, but you must ask.'

'Thank you, Mrs Adams, that is kind.'

The woman lingered, lifting the pretty jug to pour out a few more drops and shifting the cup and saucer from their already acceptable position.

'You have more to say, Mrs Adams?'

'Your maid, Mademoiselle Laurent, is causing problems. I admire her confidence and experience but she is a servant. She must speak to her elders with respect and not make what I guess to be offensive comments in French. She thinks we can't understand her meaning, but we can.'

Henrietta allowed herself to smile, but only inside. Amelia spoke to no one with respect, apart from Granny Webb and her own mother. She arranged her eyebrows into a solemn frown and nodded. 'I will talk to her. Thank you for telling me, Mrs Adams. I am grateful for any guidance you are willing to share.'

CHAPTER 12

1734

The days before Edward's return settled into a quiet, dull routine. Henrietta knew her husband would eventually come back and looked forward to being furious with him.

In the mornings, after breakfast, she met with Mrs Adams first and then with the cook. It did not take long to realise that household duties were the same every day and meals varied only by what was available in the kitchen garden or from the farms.

She wondered whether to stop these discussions altogether but Granny Webb had schooled her in a deep intuition about other people. Everyone, except her, would miss a conversation that gave importance to their otherwise routine tasks. After her meetings, she practised the spinet, wrote letters, wandered around the house, ate her meals, and went to bed.

Every single day, Henrietta walked through the orchard and gardens, saddened by the neglect of box hedges that threw out branches at random, like whips, the end of summer dandelions and groundsel crowding between flagstones and roses, now heavy with ripening hips, strangled by bindweed.

Whenever she met Joseph in the vegetable garden, she smiled and asked him questions about the crops, trying to learn what they were growing, so that menu planning with the cook made more sense. Always, he remained frozen, his ears burning red, never replying, but instead clutching his cap between his hands and nodding like a puppet.

Amelia still tended to all of Henrietta's needs, washing and repairing her clothes and bedding, cleaning her mistress' room and ensuring an adequate supply of oils, soap and cloths for Henrietta's personal toilette, but there was still time to walk into the village together twice a week, making a circuit of the local church, the rectory and the straggle of cottages. They rarely saw another person but once, as they passed the vicarage, the rector's wife hurried out of the gate with her daughters, ignoring Henrietta's greeting.

Henrietta turned to Amelia. 'That was rude.'

'No one will speak to us,' Amelia said. 'It's because we're recusant.'

'What on earth is that?'

'We're Catholics and we don't worship in the church. We haven't done the oath,' Amelia replied.

'How do you know this?'

'Mrs Adams told me. A priest comes every month on Sundays and we have a mass in the parlour. She says no one in the village will visit you, even though you are the lady of the manor. If you want to be accepted, you have to renounce your faith.'

Henrietta turned and walked on. 'Well, that's shocking,' she said, over her shoulder. 'My husband tried to explain what it was like for Catholics in this country, but until now, I hadn't understood.'

Amelia hooked her arm through Henrietta's. 'We knew nothing at all about this place, what it was we were coming to,' she replied. 'To me, being Catholic is the least of our worries.'

Henrietta ended the conversation in the way she almost always did. 'I miss Paris.'

'Me too,' Amelia said, and they continued back to the manor house in silence.

Henrietta heard Edward's coach but decided to wait in the parlour, as if she had too much to occupy her to be troubled by rushing out to meet her husband. She listened to his progress, the never-ending conversation with Mrs Adams in the hall, the fuss with boots, cape, hat.

He burst into the parlour and swept Henrietta into his arms. 'Here's my little girl,' he shouted. 'As beautiful as ever. You are coming to bed with me, right now.'

'Edward, it's the middle of the day, what will the—'

Any further words were smothered, as Edward covered her face and neck with kisses. He hurried Henrietta upstairs to their room, his hand pressing at the small of her back, and tossed her onto the bed, lifting her skirts and pulling down her stockings, before repeating his exhilarating repertoire of tricks.

Exhausted with pleasure, Henrietta dozed and woke to find Edward's side of the bed empty. He sat at her dressing table, studying some cards, his hand working vigorously at something under his shirt. Seeing she was awake, he grinned and returned to the bed. 'Sorry, but we've got to do the other bit. I'm as ready as I'm ever going to be.'

'What bit?' Henrietta replied.

Edward frowned, apologetic. 'The son and heir thing. I'm afraid it's expected. Let's get on with it.'

Afterwards, Edward fell asleep, after coughing deeply from the exertion, although the son and heir exertion had lasted only a few minutes.

Henrietta slipped from the bed and crept towards the dressing table, where the cards lay, face down. She turned them over, her face burning at every drawing, some of a man and a woman, some a man and a man, others of a woman with a woman, doing things to each other that seemed physically impossible but from their round, staring eyes and waggling tongues, was successful in giving them great pleasure. The women's stays were loose or on the floor, huge breasts lolling and the men's enormous private parts waved from their gaping breeches.

Henrietta felt raw with shame, seeing in these drawings things she had believed were special and private between her and Edward, drawn so crudely for everyone to purchase and leer at. Then she felt annoyed. Didn't her husband have a lovely young bride? Why did he have to look at crude pictures to be ready for her?

The bedroom door creaked open and Amelia slipped into the room, carrying a bowl of scented water and fresh cloths. Henrietta pointed at her snoring husband and put a finger to her lips. Amelia's eyes drifted to the cards and Henrietta spread them out, watching her friend's eyebrows lift as she exposed each new card.

Amelia giggled, bending double with the effort of keeping silent, her hand covering her mouth. Henrietta tried not to join in but once Amelia started, it was impossible. She crouched on the rush matting, her head resting on her knees, her shoulders shaking. Amelia dropped down beside her, the girls leaning shoulder to shoulder, their efforts to stay quiet making everything worse.

It only took one unexpected snort, before they both fell onto their backs, clutching at their ribs and silently screaming with laughter. Lord Edward Herbert slept on, innocent in his marital bed.

At dinner, in the formal dining room laid with linen napkins, silverware and solid, English candleholders, Henrietta waited until they had been served before dismissing the child servant back to the kitchen. Edward ate with relish, as if there was nothing to say, nothing to account for.

Henrietta picked at her roast lamb, horseradish sauce and leeks, then put down her fork. 'Where have you been?' she asked.

Edward wiped his mouth with his napkin. 'In Bath, of course. I have rooms there for my health.'

'Next time, please take me with you.'

He took her hand and leaned back in his chair, inspecting her fingers. 'No, that can't happen. In Bath, I need to be alone.'

'What am I supposed to do here, without you?'

'What ladies of the manor do. Run the household, bear children, visit the sick...'

'You didn't tell me you were going. You vanished into the night and your brother insulted me. That's not fair.'

Edward used his fork to pierce a potato from the dish and waved it at her. 'I'll ask my lawyer to speak to him about that. He promised me we could have another day at Powis House. It didn't matter in the end, did it? You had to come here sometime.'

'You said nothing about Hendon Manor and nor did your father, when he negotiated our marriage settlement with my grandparents. I feel... I feel I was misled.'

Edward sighed and bit deeply into his potato, speaking with his mouth full. 'Whatever my father said or didn't say, it wasn't on my instructions. This marriage was thrust upon me, as much as it was on you. Personally I'm delighted with you and our marriage, but I'm not going to change my habits. You, perhaps, drew the short straw marrying me.'

'Not at all, Edward. All I ask is that you tell me when you're leaving and let me know when you'll be back. That's not too much to ask.'

Edward cut into his lamb and spent several minutes chewing before he used his fingers to draw a lump of gristle from his teeth, wiping it onto his napkin. 'I'm here for the parish court,' he said. 'You can count on me returning for those. It's one of my responsibilities, to meet the tenants, listen to their grievances, settle disputes, that sort of thing. I'll try to keep you informed about my movements but I'm not used to being beholden.'

Henrietta hesitated, thinking how to frame her greatest fear into words. 'Amelia says you have another woman in Bath. You're beholden to her, your mistress, but not to me.'

Amelia had said no such thing, but Henrietta couldn't admit how frightened she had been by his absence, being abandoned with strangers. It was hard to trust anything he said.

'That girl should watch her step,' Edward said. 'I can send her back to France.'

Henrietta straightened her shoulders and stared hard into her husband's eyes. 'No you cannot. She is an employee of Lord and Lady Webb. She returns to Paris only on my instructions, or theirs.'

Edward raised his eyebrows. 'Well said, Henrietta. Serves me right for marrying someone so young and spoiled. I do like your spirit. You're not willing to settle for my nonsense. I should have held out for a faded widow, one that wasn't too bright but had plenty of money.'

'Stop making fun of me,' Henrietta interrupted. 'Is there any truth in Amelia's accusation? You haven't answered me properly.'

'And I will not. If I choose to keep a mistress that's my business. I will say this, however. If you want me to live and remain fit enough to give you many children, I must take the waters, see my physician, and clear my chest of whatever it is that ails me in every other place in this godforsaken land except for Bath. Because I have to avoid the harvest, all that dust, wagons kicking up soil, hay flying everywhere, I will disappear every August, for the entire month. You can be certain of that.'

The young housemaid crept back into the room, her eyes bright points of light, reflecting the candelabra and whispered to Henrietta whether they were ready for their pudding.

'Lady Herbert hasn't finished her meat and potatoes,' Edward roared. 'She has to clear her plate. She needs all her strength for later.'

'Edward!' Henrietta protested. 'Not in front of the child.'

'She doesn't know what I'm talking about.'

'That doesn't matter,' Henrietta said. 'Whatever you say will be all over the servants' quarters by the morning.'

She heard an unexpected tone in her voice. Edward didn't notice, but she was repeating words used by someone else, another person who had abandoned her, who had left her alone to survive in this confusing world. Of course, her words were an echo of her grandmother.

As she watched him scoop pears and cream into his mouth, she wondered if it was worse to be abandoned by death, the way her mother and Granny Waldegrave had, or was the most dreadful thing to be abandoned by those who still lived, those who were supposed to love you, someone like her husband.

Henrietta lay on the day bed in the parlour, carried in from the hall by their handyman and his cousin from the village. It had lain idle for years, an occasional bed for dogs and a more permanent repository for cloaks and hats, idly tossed aside by guests and family. As soon as Mrs Adams knew that Henrietta was expecting a child and was quite unable to retain a single mouthful of food, she gave instructions for its rescue.

It was November, every day dark, everyone shuttered in behind cold and fog. Even before the problems of early pregnancy had beset Henrietta in October, she had decided to stay in bed every morning until it was light and remain by a fire in the parlour until it was time for her solitary evening meal and empty bed. This ancient farmhouse still had a hearth which stretched almost the length of one wall in the parlour, framed above by a beam taken from a giant tree, the bark and knots still visible. The men placed her couch against the fireplace, where Henrietta lay at this moment, trying not to move, distracting herself from her nausea by staring into the flames or searching for faces in the hewn wood of the mantel.

Edward behaved exactly as he had promised. He had not visited Hendon at all in August but had returned for a few days in September and October. Henrietta hoped that when he learned of the success of their son and heir efforts, his delight would keep him at home but the lure of Bath was too powerful.

Mrs Adams was kind, gentler than Henrietta had ever expected, bringing her tiny cups of saffron cordial to sip all through the day and a spoonful of creamed pudding scented with nutmeg on a tray at mealtimes, always waiting for Henrietta to retch into the bowl at her side before clearing everything away. Amelia visited but rarely stayed for long, wrinkling her nose at the smell of vomit that must pervade the room, before finding an excuse, no matter how trivial, so that she could leave.

Henrietta heard from Granny Webb at last, a letter written in early August but had since travelled between Powis House, and Powis Castle, before finding her at Hendon Manor.

They were well, her grandmother wrote in her distinctive backward sloping handwriting, but very tired after the wedding and the days spent travelling home. How delighted they had been with the wedding itself and to see Henrietta and Edward so happy together. Henrietta was a lucky girl, Granny Webb added, not all marriages turn out so well. There followed a long list of the ailments her elderly friends were now suffering and how much she was missed at the card table.

Henrietta draped an arm over her eyes and closed them, wondering whether she had the energy to rise and throw the letter onto the fire. As she moved, the day bed released a smell of dog. She would not reply, at least not until her silence gave them a reason to worry about her, if that should ever happen. There was a tap on the door and Henrietta made a grunting sound that gave permission to enter, even if there were no words. It was Amelia.

'I wondered if you wanted to take a turn outside?' Amelia asked. 'It's been a clear day and there's probably about half an hour's daylight left. We could walk around the cedar tree.'

A huge cedar tree, with its remarkable circumference, stood at the side of the manor house and made a useful destination when they tired of their walks to St Mary's church in the village. It passed the time to walk three times around the trunk, brushing their hands against the bark or picking up small branches laden with young, undeveloped cones from the litter beneath. Henrietta agreed, surprising herself. Amelia rushed away to find their cloaks and hats.

It was embarrassing to stop every few yards to vomit into piles of rotting leaves and Henrietta felt Amelia's impatience.

'I'm so sorry,' she said. 'I had no idea this happened to women. If Mrs Adams hadn't told me I was with child and such sickness is expected, I might have thought I was dying.'

Amelia wrinkled her nose. 'You know I hate vomit, I always have. You must remember from Paris?'

Henrietta had no memory of this particular foible but nodded anyway, before bending over to retch.

'In the kitchen, Mrs Adams said that you're sicker than most women are in pregnancy. It's a good sign apparently, it means a strong baby, probably a boy.'

Henrietta leaned her back against the trunk of the cedar tree and breathed through her nose. 'Thank goodness,' she whispered. 'If it's a boy, I won't need to have any more children. If it's a boy, I'll have secured the heir. If it's a boy, everything will change for us.'

Amelia copied Henrietta and leaned against the tree, stretching out her arms to feel the girth, moving the backs of her hands up and down against the bark. 'What do you think will change?'

'A boy will bring continuity. Edward's older brother is unlikely ever to have a child so I will give birth to the heir. We can insist on moving to Powis Castle, since my husband and his son will inherit everything. Surely Edward will want to be at home with me once he has a son, to watch his child grow?'

Amelia frowned and dropped her head. Lifting it again, her eyes sought Henrietta's. 'We can hope. I'm not sure Lord Herbert will change his ways for a child, since he hasn't for a perfect young bride like you.'

Henrietta began to walk towards the house but turned back to wait for Amelia. The lamps were already lit inside and the manor looked inviting and warm rather than glowering and moody. 'Come on, I'm getting cold,' she said. 'There's a letter inside from my grandmother. You should read it and tell me what you think.'

Amelia hurried to catch up. 'Is there anything from my mother? Did she ask about me?'

Henrietta shook her head. 'I'm afraid not, there's nothing.'

CHAPTER 13

1734

Two weeks later, Henrietta woke from her afternoon doze, recognising a voice in the hall, but unable to remember where she had heard this whining, needling tone before. Something wasn't to this man's liking and Mrs Adams was becoming flustered and apologetic.

Henrietta tried to raise herself from the couch. She was the lady of the house and no one should speak to her staff like that, but her head started to spin, her belly began to heave, and her throat tightened.

Mrs Adams pushed open the parlour door without knocking. 'I'm sorry to trouble you, my lady, but Lord Montgomery is here to see you.'

Montgomery pushed past the housekeeper, waving his hands under his nose. 'What a stench in here,' he bellowed. 'What on earth is wrong?'

Henrietta struggled to stand and Mrs Adams ran to her side, grasping her elbow. 'Lady Herbert is with child, my lord. We're all delighted of course, but these early weeks are affecting her badly.'

Lord Montgomery flicked his coat tails aside and dropped

into an armchair on one side of the fire, tipping his head towards the other chair. Henrietta found her balance against a high-backed chair then made her way to join her brother-in-law at the fireside. 'Please bring us some warm quince wine, Mrs Adams,' she said.

'No, no, the housekeeper must stay. Lady Herbert... or can I call you Henrietta... you will need her here.'

The women waited, while Montgomery picked at his teeth, glowering at whatever he had extracted, before throwing it onto the fire.

'There's no way I can say this kindly, so I'll not bother. Your husband, my younger brother, is dead. Found in his rooms, in Bath. By the time I was alerted, he'd been gone for at least a week. Not a pleasant sight, I can tell you.'

Henrietta gripped her own hands and felt Mrs Adams wrap an arm around her shoulders. 'Edward is dead, Edward is dead, Edward is dead,' she repeated, dry-eyed.

'The thing is,' Lord Montgomery continued. 'He's on his way here. We have to bury him as soon as we can. We use the parish churchyard for family burials, somewhere you've not visited, I'm sure.'

'But we'll need a priest,' Mrs Adams interrupted, 'and someone to lay out the body.'

'Well, get on with it, woman,' Montgomery sneered. 'Take Lady Herbert upstairs but find another servant to sit with her. You will be too busy. I need a bed made up for tonight and a meal. Oh, and make sure my horse is stabled. Not too much trouble, is it?'

Outside, a slash of daylight split the darkening sky but her quiet bedroom was already dark and bitterly cold. Henrietta sat on the bed, fully dressed, waiting for the loss to hit her but finding nothing inside except shock. Amelia carried in a candle which created a pool of light around the bed but dark shadows lingered in the corners. She tried to draw the drapes at the window but Henrietta asked her to leave them open and to blow out the candle. Patting her husband's side of the bed, so rarely used, she asked Amelia to sit next to her, as they had done so often in Paris whenever something important needed to be discussed.

The little housemaid carried in a bundle of wood for a fire, blinking in surprise to see her mistress and a maidservant fully clothed on the bed. They waited for the child to finish, the smoke from burning applewood drifting through the room, until the twigs flamed and the logs began to hiss. Through the small panes of the window, the setting sun was caught briefly in the broken clouds, until this too disappeared.

At last, Henrietta reached for Amelia's hand. 'The thing is,' she said, 'I've only known him for a few days, even though we have been married for four months. I liked him, he was funny and cheerful but he had a secret life. I was excluded from that. How can I grieve for him?'

'You can pretend,' Amelia said, gripping her friend's fingers. 'Think about the good things, everything you enjoyed with him, in the days you spent together. Mourn those rare, special times, and regret that there will be no more. Your husband will always be with you, in your child.'

In the light from the fireplace, Henrietta glanced down at her belly. 'What will become of us, Amelia? I'm frightened.'

'While you carry an heir, you are a precious asset to this family. I promise I'll look after you, Henrietta, but you must look after the child. It matters... for both of us. Your only responsibility is to safely deliver a baby who will thrive. He is our passage to greater things, our security for the future. Come now, let me ready you for bed. It's going to be a long day tomorrow and you need to start sleeping and eating, if only for the sake of the child.'

~

Henrietta had woken when Amelia rose before dawn, loosening the hangings around the bed frame before she left. Resting on her back in the dark cocoon, she stared at the diamonds cut into the wooden canopy above and reached up to trace their patterns.

'Edward is dead,' she repeated in a whisper, allowing the shock, the loss of their future, to strike her anew. If she lay quite still, she could trick the sickness into staying away, keep the child safe. Amelia was right, this baby must be born alive and healthy if she was to become a person who mattered, a woman who wasn't tossed aside whenever it suited someone else. As the mother of the Herbert heir, it would not matter that she no longer had a husband.

The bedroom door scraped against the floor, followed by the creak of Amelia's characteristic footsteps on the boards. The curtains were pulled aside from the canopy and Amelia began muttering about Henrietta's clothes, lying discarded on the floor, and fussing about why a fire in her ladyship's bedroom had been forgotten.

'You seem rattled,' Henrietta said, swinging her legs down onto the floorboards from her high mattress. 'Is it still early or have I slept late?'

Amelia chewed on a fingernail. 'Lord Montgomery's waiting for you in the parlour. He harangued us at breakfast because he expected you to be there. Please hurry and dress, if we're all to be saved from his temper.'

Hurrying, or doing anything fast, was not within Henrietta's grasp. It was another hour, close to eleven in the morning, when she joined Edward's brother in the parlour.

'At last,' he said, pausing in his trajectory from the window to the fireplace. 'The grieving widow appears. Sit down, Henrietta, there are things I must tell you.'

Henrietta nodded, feeling dizzy and damp with sweat from her effort not to vomit. She sat down furthest from the fire, next to a card table. Mrs Adams entered, bearing a tray with a crust of dry bread and more saffron cordial.

'Not now, woman,' Montgomery barked.

'Lady Herbert must eat,' Mrs Adams argued, placing the tray in front of Henrietta.

Montague flapped his hands at both women, as if dispersing troublesome smoke. 'I haven't time for this,' he said. 'Leave the food on the table and go.'

Mrs Adams dropped a curtsy towards Henrietta but gave Lord Montgomery a fixed stare. 'I'll wait outside the door, my lady,' she said.

Montgomery slouched into a chair opposite Henrietta and fell silent, stroking his top lip, as if the urgency of his own demands had suddenly deserted him. She studied her brother-in-law, wondering how the kind and handsome Marquess she had met in Paris, this thug's father, had managed to sire such a brute. The mother's disposition must have been unfortunate.

'You are my ward,' Montgomery announced, causing Henrietta to choke on her cordial.

She shook her head, disbelieving. 'I am what?'

'You are not an adult, so you and the unborn child have become my wards.'

'But I am a married woman and now a widow.'

'Doesn't matter. Now your husband is dead, I am responsible for you. I don't like it any more than you do and will try to find you a more suitable guardian as quickly as I can. The Court of Chancery will make the decision but that might take months. In the meantime, you'll live here, not at Powis House or

Powis Castle. My guess is you'll be returned to your grandparents, once the child is born.'

'Why not Powis Castle...?' Henrietta felt a familiar growl from her belly, a warning tightening of her throat, and reached for her sick bowl.

'Adams, in here... now!' Montgomery bellowed.

Edward's body arrived the next day on the back of a cart and both man and horses were left to rest in the stables. Henrietta's memory of Edward's face was already fading and she wondered aloud if she might visit him, to look inside the coffin, but Mrs Adams shook her head.

'The Marquess of Powis paid for his son's laying out and found a carpenter with enough time to make a decent coffin. My lady, your father-in-law's generosity is a great relief to me, given Lord Montgomery's last-minute instructions yesterday, but I'm afraid the casket has arrived sealed.'

Henrietta leaned against the sideboard. 'My husband was presented to me unseen and leaves me unseen, both the actions of the Marquess.'

Mrs Adams frowned and reached out as if to comfort Henrietta but allowed her hand to drop.

'Perhaps it was for the best, my lady. Lord Powis may have been thinking of you... your condition. He will be present for the funeral tomorrow, perhaps you can ask him about his intention then?'

Henrietta excused herself, already exhausted from too much standing, and crept up the tight circle of the stairs, pausing to draw breath by allowing her fingers to grip the twisted beams that formed the bones of the staircase. Once her body found the relief of her mattress and pillows, she knew she would not rise again that day. As promised, Amelia would find her and care for her. All she had to do was sleep and grow this child.

In the morning, Henrietta heard footsteps, hushed voices and doors being closed quietly, as the household woke early for the funeral mass in the parlour, led by their priest. When a babble rose from below, she guessed it had ended, the noise of servants dispersing to their tasks and Lord Montgomery's harsh voice rising above everything else.

Henrietta had been excused the mass, Amelia forcefully arguing against Lord Montgomery's instructions. The presence of a vomiting woman was not conducive to a respectful service.

The burial was to take place at the parish church of St Mary, the village reluctantly accepting that the Herbert family still had the right to lie in the churchyard as lords of the manor, even if they were practising Catholics. A small procession formed to walk to the churchyard behind Edward's coffin, with Henrietta alone at the head, thinking only of how she could stop herself from retching into the bowl secreted underneath her cape. Money could not be found for a hearse, nor was there time to arrange for one. The priest stood beside the single horse that would lead the farmer's cart, undecorated and forlorn. He signalled to the waiting group, holding up five fingers, indicating they must remain a few more minutes, to allow time for the Marquess' coach to arrive. Henrietta pulled the hood of her cloak further over her head as a fresh wind whipped eddies of fallen leaves to spin around her ankles.

The sound of horses' hooves echoed down the long approach to the manor and a coach bearing the Herbert family crest threw up stones and turf as it jolted to a halt beside the procession.

William Herbert, the Marquess of Powis, stepped down to join the line, adjusting his three-cornered hat and bowing to Henrietta, before linking his arm through hers. Henrietta smiled at her father-in-law, last seen on her wedding day, relieved to have a friend to escort her – but was anyone in this family truly her friend? Edward had been an unexpected friend, but only when it suited him, and now he was dead.

Unlike everyone else, who wore whatever they had that was sombre but clean, William Herbert wore a well-tailored black coat and breeches. He leaned down and whispered into her ear, 'I am so sorry, my dear.'

Behind them stood Lord Montgomery, accompanying Mrs Adams. Henrietta heard him 'tsk' in irritation at the delay. Next in line followed the tenant farmers and their wives. As the procession began to shuffle forward, William raised a hand and asked them to wait.

He hurried back to his coach, as fast as his advancing years would allow, and brought out a folded bundle of purple cloth. He unfurled a flag for everyone to admire, gold threads from the family crest burning in the last of the daylight revealing two startled animals holding aloft a crown and a dragon. The Marquess of Powis stretched the flag over his son's coffin and with the help of the priest, straightened the edges.

Henrietta turned back towards Lord Montgomery, to gauge his reaction to his father's thoughtful gesture but he shook his head and scowled, muttering, 'For Christ's sake, it's time to leave. You're the widow. Tell them to get a move on!'

At the graveside, Henrietta shivered, relying on her father-in-law's arm to keep her steady. The walking and the bitterly cold air had settled her stomach and she no longer feared being sick. During the words of the interment, crows gathered in the trees around the churchyard. She raised her eyes above the stark boughs bare of leaves, Edward's life celebrated by the absence of birdsong and the dying afternoon light, foreshadowing darkness to come.

She tried to remember her husband but all she could bring

to mind was his collection of drawings, driving his desperate effort to produce an heir. Her cheeks reddened when she thought of their few nights together, how he had given her so much pleasure at some cost to himself. The memory was a fitting memorial for her husband, a lesson in how a woman's body should be loved, generously given by an experienced man to an innocent girl. She would carry his gift into her future.

The priest dusted soil from his palms and the party turned from the graveside to begin the short journey back to the house. The Marquess tugged at Henrietta's sleeve and asked if she would accompany him into the church, where there was a memorial to one of his ancestors.

Henrietta stood beside her father-in-law, both staring at the memorial to William's grandfather on the north wall of the chancel. She felt that some remark was expected but kept silent. What did this distant ancestor mean to her, a girl married only briefly to a second son? William replaced his hat and they walked down the aisle, back into the churchyard. It was almost dark, but Henrietta could hear a crunching sound, spades thrusting into earth, stones rattling onto the lid of her husband's coffin, as the gravediggers hurried to finish their day's work.

'How are you bearing up?' William asked, again linking his arm through the crook of her elbow as they took the short walk back to Hendon Manor. Henrietta had to pause before she answered, feeling a telltale clutch in her belly.

'I am with child, sir,' she replied. 'There is no worse time to lose a husband.'

'No... indeed. I was delighted to hear of the chance of a Herbert heir, at last. You were happy with my son, I believe, in the few months you had together?'

Henrietta paused, then decided to speak the truth. 'I hardly knew him but on the few days we lived together, he was kind, gentle and tried to amuse me. Edward didn't treat me as a wife, more like a friend. He lives... lived in Bath, as you well know. I will never be sure whether there was another woman but it is rumoured. My husband was not prepared for the duties of marriage and, as we have learned to our cost, was too ill to bear those responsibilities.'

They reached the cedar tree and her father-in-law steered her around its girth, as if he needed more time. 'I am truly sorry,' he said. 'You must feel misled. I was so delighted to find a wife for my younger son, I was perhaps too hasty in agreeing to the marriage. Lord and Lady Webb were particularly keen.'

Henrietta gazed into the interior of the manor, at the welcoming candles set in the windows, and drew her cloak tightly around her. There was more to say. 'I have become Lord Montgomery's ward. Why am I not your ward?'

This question seemed to perplex William and he looked everywhere except at her. 'I'm afraid I knew nothing about this. I assume my eldest son, being called to Bath, had to make some emergency arrangements. You're not going to live with him, are you?'

'I'll remain here at Hendon until the birth. The staff are kind and my maidservant from Paris is with me. Lord Montgomery said I would return eventually to my grandparents but why not to Powis Castle? Am I not part of your family?'

Henrietta saw Mrs Adams peering through a window, searching for her.

The Marquess coughed and with the toe of his boot, pushed at a deep mound of leaf litter. 'Well, my dear, that depends on the... depends on the...'

'Depends on what?' Henrietta asked.

'Depends on...' William spun his hand, as though winding a clock.

'It depends on whether I produce a male heir,' Henrietta answered for him.

'That's it, my dear, that's it.' William drew a timepiece from his waistcoat. 'Goodness me, is that the time? I must return to London. I'm staying in my rooms in Frith Street.'

'You will not sleep the night here?' Henrietta asked. 'We need more time to talk.'

Her father-in-law clicked his fingers at his waiting coachman. The horses tugged against their harnesses, keen to be away. 'No, no, thank you, Henrietta. I'm afraid I cannot be in the same room as my eldest son. We are bitterly estranged.'

'Please wait, Lord Powis.' Henrietta touched his arm. 'I have one more thing to say.'

William lifted his hat and paused on the first step of the carriage. 'Yes, what is it?'

'If my husband died, I was promised six hundred pounds a year, to be paid by you, his father. It was part of my marriage settlement, the one apparently rushed through by my grandparents.'

Now it was fully dark, Henrietta could not see William's face but heard him mutter, 'Ward of court, Henrietta, you are a ward of court. Everything will be decided after the child is born.'

CHAPTER 14

1735

They survived the winter, its days short, the sky forever leaden and dark. For all of January, their world became trapped within snow and ice. To stay warm, Henrietta spent all of the coldest months in the kitchen, curled up in a rocking chair that had been dragged from the parlour. She had rarely visited this end of the house, where the servants' quarters above were reached by a separate staircase, no more than a ladder.

Sarah, the cook, shared a room with the little housemaid and Amelia squeezed into a cot bed behind a curtain on the landing. Mrs Adams had a home in the village, although it seemed as if she never left the manor house.

Henrietta knew she wasn't welcome. The servants regarded these rooms as their own, but no matter how deep and high their handyman stacked the fire in the parlour, icy draughts from outside crept down the chimney, circled the edges of the room, and sought her out wherever she took refuge.

Here, in the kitchen, the entire wall was given over to a fireplace and a separate bread oven produced fragrant loaves throughout the day.

Whenever she stretched the cook's patience with her presence, Henrietta sought the scullery, where there was endless hot water from a copper heated from below by another fire. Ignominy and humiliation were worthwhile if she could stay warm.

When her eyes tired from stitching clothes for an infant in poor light, Henrietta watched the red-faced and tireless miracle of Sarah's ability to turn unpromising ingredients into meals. With an end to her sickness, she had discovered a new, panicky hunger, and if her pride would allow, she begged the cook for a slice of warm bread and some cheese from the pantry.

During these months, Henrietta refused to eat alone in the icy dining room, despite Mrs Adams' attempts to encourage her. She shared the servants' table in the kitchen, ignoring the awkward silence.

Only at the end of April was Henrietta persuaded to give up the kitchen and she and Amelia began to walk again in the garden. Joseph had started to reveal paths and box hedges in the knot garden and had already planted this year's seeds for vegetables. If they chose a slow, ungainly walk to the village, which was rare given Henrietta's size, the staccato bleating of lambs in the fields around the manor reminded her of what was to come.

Henrietta knew nothing about childbirth, something the sheep had apparently achieved with great ease, even recklessly giving birth to two at once. She was frightened to raise with Mrs Adams what might happen at the actual birth. Would anyone help her or was this another thing she was expected to manage alone? Amelia was also ignorant, threatening Henrietta that there was no more fabric left in the seams of her dresses, as if growing so huge was something she could help.

The baby was due in June, and at the beginning of the month, as Henrietta lay beached on the day bed in the parlour,

Mrs Adams brought her a tray with chocolate to drink, and a plate of potato cakes. Instead of leaving these on the low table at Henrietta's side, she sat down in a chair, facing her mistress.

'My lady, we are to say a funeral mass here next week for Baroness Bellew of Dulek, followed by her burial in the churchyard. The Marquess of Powis has sent us instructions by messenger.'

Henrietta struggled to sit up and Mrs Adams assisted her, piling cushions at her back. 'Who on earth is Baroness Bellew of Dulek?'

'My lady, she's Anne Maxwell, the Marquess' niece. Her mother and father are the Earl and Countess of Nithsdale. They live in Rome, part of the exiled Jacobite court. I believe the Marquess was very fond of Anne.'

Henrietta paused, remembering the story. 'Anne's mother, Winifred, is the Marquess' youngest sister and my husband's aunt, the one who saved her husband from the Tower of London?'

Mrs Adams nodded. 'Yes, that's her. Anne lived in Paris for her education but later joined her parents in Rome. That's where she met Lord Bellew. They have a little girl, Frances, but I believe there's another child.'

Henrietta paused, already guessing at the truth behind Anne's untimely death. 'What do you mean by "another child"?'

Mrs Adams touched her knee. 'I can't hide this from you, Lady Herbert, but you must try not to worry. I'm afraid Anne died in childbirth.'

This funeral was not like Edward's, which seemed shameful, as if he had been in disgrace, which he probably was.

Henrietta had learned nothing about where Edward had been found or who he was with.

Lord Bellew arrived with a small child in his arms, Anne's little girl, left behind in the care of Mrs Adams for the mass. Henrietta stared at Bellew, who seemed furious and agitated rather than heartbroken.

It was obvious he had little to say to her father-in-law, the Marquess of Powis, and wondered about the row that must have occurred between these two powerful men, probably over where his wife should be buried. The Bellews must certainly have their own burial plot but William would have argued for Hendon, the churchyard that waited for him.

Through the drone of the priest's voice, Henrietta imagined Anne's parents, traitors to the crown and banned from their daughter's funeral. She raised herself from her chair, adjusting her wrapping gown across her huge belly, and straightened her shoulders. *As Anne's cousin by marriage,* Henrietta thought, *I will stand here for Winifred and by letter, I will share with her poor mother every detail of her beloved daughter's farewell.*

William Herbert had not arrived alone. At his side stood a pale-faced woman, her dark hair pulled back tightly under her cap, the few visible wisps showing signs of grey. She looked haggard, as if she had wrung every drop of sorrow from her body and was simply trying to stay alive. The Marquess did not introduce his companion to anyone and by the curl on Lord Bellew's lip as the woman was hurried past him, she was not a welcome presence. Henrietta noticed that the woman wore a dress that was much washed and darned and guessed she must be a servant, but why was she present for the funeral?

There was no farmer's cart for Anne. Lord Bellew had paid for a splendid funeral carriage, led by two black horses, with plumes set with jet stones, but the roof of the coach was strewn with white flowers. He led the procession to the churchyard, jerking at his child's hand as she tried to swing around his legs.

Standing immediately behind him, Henrietta saw the muscles in his cheeks clench and unclench. Once again, she walked beside her father-in-law, with the unknown visitor accompanied by Mrs Adams. Blossom from a wild cherry tree in the churchyard rained down onto their heads and shoulders, falling into the grave as Anne's coffin was lowered.

This is not right, Henrietta thought, feeling the baby somersaulting in her belly, *this should be a christening, not a funeral.*

When Frances began to cry, Lord Bellew lifted the child into his arms, turned sharply on his heels and stalked out of the churchyard, as if he had borne enough of this tragedy.

On the slow walk back to the manor, William because of his age and Henrietta because of her size, the mystery of their visitor was revealed.

'Henrietta, I need to leave her with you. Her name is Alice Douglas and she has cared for my sister's children since she was ten years old. She spent all of her life as Anne's nurse and then cared for Anne's daughter Frances. She has nowhere else to go.'

Henrietta thought of the fierce, angry man at Anne's funeral. 'Surely she's Lord Bellew's responsibility. Isn't there a baby to be nursed?'

'Bellew blames Alice for his wife's death and has thrown her out onto the street. She had nowhere else to turn, except to her friend Grace Evans, who alerted me. Grace is a remarkable, brave woman who remained at my sister's side throughout all her troubles but now enjoys a peaceful life in a cottage near me. You are about to give birth and Alice will assist you with everything. She is greatly experienced.'

'We cannot pay her. You know how frugally we live... there is nothing spare.'

'That is taken care of. I will send Mrs Adams extra to cover Alice's expenses and will provide enough for the services of a local midwife when your time comes. Until your guardianship is settled, you are a member of this family, Henrietta, about to bear my grandson. Anne's death and Bellew's unfair rage with Alice may be a sign that you and your child will thrive, because you will now have the benefit of Alice's wisdom and experience. If I were a religious man, I might be inclined to believe in God's grace. You will have the best of care in your confinement.'

Henrietta stopped walking and turned to glance up into William's reddened eyelids and bloodshot eyes. 'Thank you, my lord, for your foresight... for your protection. My grandmother told me how you once cared for Anne, when there was no one else. I am so sorry you have lost her.'

William turned away, his shoulders slumped. When he faced her again, the powder that had drifted from his wig onto his cheeks, was streaked with trails of damp. 'I must leave you now,' he said, wiping at his face with the ends of his cravat. 'Alice is inside with Mrs Adams. She is heartbroken, as you have seen, but I think it will help her to have a new purpose. Once she has settled, I am sure she will tell you her remarkable story but for now, just allow her to look after you and the baby.'

William reached for Henrietta's hand and bent low to kiss her fingers. 'Women endure so much,' he murmured, 'more than any man could cope with. But you, Henrietta, are strong. I have no fears for your future.'

Alice took to walking in the afternoons with Amelia and Henrietta and the three women sat together in the parlour in the morning, sewing baby clothes. Since Alice was not quite a lady, yet not a servant, Henrietta decided that companionship was worth more than status and made sure Amelia was included too. If this caused problems with the other servants, what did it matter? She was the lady of this house and could do what she liked.

The only person likely to complain was Mrs Adams and she didn't seem to mind, sometimes joining them to play whist on wet afternoons. Henrietta was reminded of the solace of her grandmother's salon, of quiet afternoons spent with women friends, and wished her life could continue like this, without the burden of having a baby.

The burden of a baby was not a matter she could avoid, with Alice around. The woman seemed to come alive, her drawn face lifting into a smile, whenever they talked about the early stages of labour, how the baby would be born and what was needed afterwards.

Amelia would suddenly remember a more pressing task elsewhere, even when Alice encouraged her to stay. It would be wise to book a midwife, Alice reminded Henrietta, even if they couldn't be sure of the date. Mrs Adams helped by identifying two local women, who they interviewed in the parlour.

The first was the farm manager's wife, Mrs Lewis. Henrietta tried not to let prejudice affect her judgement but the woman seemed every bit as rude as her husband.

The second, Mrs Wright, was a small, square woman, whose face looked as if it had been squashed by something heavy. Henrietta thought she brought with her the smell of farmyards, but her hands, cap and apron were clean and Alice seemed impressed by her experience. Mrs Wright left happily with a bag of coins, promising to be available for the next ten days. After the birth she would remain close by, in case there were problems.

Once Henrietta and Alice were alone, Alice disclosed that Anne Bellew had easily given birth to a baby boy but developed a fever so severe it killed her within days. She had tried to help, but Lord Bellew blamed her for his wife's death. This news was no comfort to Henrietta, who had believed that once the baby was born, her troubles would be over.

There was also the matter of feeding the child, which she had been surprised to learn was her responsibility. No matter how competent Alice seemed, it was unlikely that milk would magically appear from her breasts and no one was willing to talk about a wet nurse.

A huge chair with a hole in the seat appeared in Henrietta's bedroom one morning, carried by her midwife's husband and son, both bulky men who filled the small space with the smell of sweat and deep voices. The following day, when she returned upstairs to collect her shawl, logs had been stacked beside the empty fireplace, and a cot, ready for a baby, stood by her bed. Henrietta blinked, as if these objects were a trick of the light. What did everyone else know that she didn't?

That night, Henrietta felt hot and restless. There was a low ache in her belly that travelled to her back, where it lay festering and growing until she could stand the pain no more. Swinging her legs over the side of her bed, she gripped the twisted wood of her bedpost to help her stand. A flood of pink fluid rushed from between her legs and trickled through the gaps in the floorboards, dripping down into the hall below. The baby was coming, exactly as Alice had described.

Henrietta decided to lie down and get some rest, since the ache had disappeared but without warning, Mrs Wright bustled into the room, rolling up her sleeves. Dragged out of bed and made to march up and down, with Alice and the midwife each clinging to an elbow, the pain returned in deepening waves, and Henrietta had to bend double to roar in agony.

Even Amelia was forced to take a turn as the other women

took breaks but where was her break from this torture? She pushed aside another sip of water just as her body went into spasm. Her legs began to shake uncontrollably and she cried out in a wavering appeal for help. The women dropped her onto the birthing chair and Mrs Wright disappeared underneath, only to emerge red-faced and shouting, 'It's there. I can see the head!'

Henrietta's body was no longer her own. She squeezed both armrests and bellowed. Waves of agony crushed her body, as if something huge was being birthed through her backside. Mrs Wright's hands reached under the chair and brought out a bundle wrapped in clean linen, cutting at something bloody with huge scissors retrieved from the pocket of her apron.

'Let me see him, let me see him,' Henrietta croaked, holding out her hand.

'Stay where you are,' Mrs Wright barked, handing the parcel to Alice, 'you must deliver all the afterbirth.'

Alice carried the child to a table, readied for this moment with a fleece covered by more crisp linen. She fiercely rubbed at the child's back, blowing gently into his nose, until a cry, not unlike the lambs in the field, filled the room.

Henrietta called out, 'He's here. He's alive. I've done it!'

No one brought her the child, but she saw Amelia and Alice unwrap the baby and whisper. There was something wrong. Perhaps he had a hare lip like that child in the village.

'Let me see him,' she begged.

'Sit still, Lady Herbert,' the midwife commanded. 'I can't see all the afterbirth. You must wait.'

Another look passed between Alice and Amelia, then Henrietta caught them nod, as if something had been agreed. Alice wrapped the baby in a clean shawl and passed the child to Amelia. Placing the baby in Henrietta's outstretched arms, Amelia pulled back the covers.

'Hensy, it's a girl. You have a beautiful daughter.'

CHAPTER 15

1735

Henrietta did not need to be told, or at least not so often, that she was being irrational. Alice was tolerant but Mrs Wright, who still visited every day, lectured her about how lucky she was to have had such an easy birth, to have delivered a well-developed, healthy baby and there was plenty of time for sons, despite Henrietta's argument that she didn't have a husband.

'Well, marry the other brother, then,' was Mrs Wright's solution. 'Keep it in the family, if that's what you want. Now, let's get this baby fed. You don't want the expense of a wet nurse.'

'She doesn't like me,' Henrietta complained. 'She turns her head away, all the time.'

Henrietta's small breasts had refused to comply, only proving her suspicion about breastfeeding. Perhaps it was something that only women of the lower classes were able to do.

When she explained this to Mrs Wright, the midwife reddened with temper and roughly pinched Henrietta's bare nipple between her fingers, forcing it into the baby's open mouth. To her surprise, the child she had named Barbara nuzzled fiercely, and then started to suckle.

Mrs Wright was triumphant. 'Not so difficult is it, even for someone of your breeding. Keep it up, Lady Herbert, as often as you can manage and don't forget, it's through the night as well. I'll be back in the morning.'

'Through the night...' Henrietta stammered.

The midwife rolled her eyes. 'Young lady, you have Alice to change the baby's cloths and bring her to you whenever she cries. The one thing Alice can't do is feed this child. That's all we expect of you. Tomorrow morning, I want to see you out of bed and dressed, no more of this lazing about in bed. Keep the contents of your chamber pot, so I can check everything's working again... down below.'

Henrietta didn't like Mrs Wright but she did trust her. She would risk asking the question that had troubled her since learning about Anne's death. 'Why did Lady Bellew die several days after the birth?'

The words caused her voice to catch and suddenly she felt weak and frightened. 'Will that happen to me?'

Mrs Wright folded her arms and sat down, wiping her brow with the edge of a clean apron. It was hard to tell from the midwife's squashed features but Henrietta thought the older woman looked at her with something like fondness. 'It must have been retained afterbirth,' she replied. 'There's no need to worry, yours was intact.'

Mrs Wright eyes flashed in a moment of anger. 'It could easily have been sorted if they'd called a midwife, instead of blaming poor Alice. Now, drop these silly notions and get on with feeding your baby.'

The next morning, Henrietta's nipples were sore and cracked but Barbara's enthusiasm only seemed to increase with her mother's pain. Every time Alice brought the child, Henrietta winced as the baby latched on, but to her surprise, milk began to flow. Even Amelia seemed relieved. Henrietta could not see why she deserved their praise, achieving something a wet nurse manages every day, feeding a child that has nothing to do with them.

With the baby at her breast, Henrietta could see that she was pretty, quite similar to Edward in fact. She smelt Barbara's head, stroked the curve of her pouchy cheeks, and smiled at the grunting, greedy noises the baby made as she fed, but these were feelings of interest, not love. Henrietta waited for love to come but all she felt was boredom. It was a waste of time, raising a girl who would be palmed off in marriage to someone quite unsuitable, whereas a boy would have guaranteed her a position in the Herbert household for all time.

Before the birth, Lord Montgomery had informed her by letter that she and the child were now wards of her grandparents. Soon after the birth of his niece, he advised Mrs Adams that Henrietta and all the other women being maintained at the Herbert family's expense at Hendon Manor must leave as soon as possible, since he needed to let the house to tenants. There was no word at all from Barbara's grandfather, the Marquess of Powis.

One month after the birth, Alice also received a letter, one from Lord Bellew. She was to collect his daughter Frances from the Bellew house in London and return her to the care of the child's grandparents in Rome. Alice and Frances would remain as residents of the Muti Palace, until he chose to send for his daughter.

The women gathered in the parlour to discuss these directives, Barbara asleep in a crib beside a roaring fire, even though it was July. Henrietta cared for all of her companions, but her own shamefully selfish motive was to keep Alice at her side for as long as possible. This sweet, kind woman only had to lift Barbara from her crib for the endless crying to stop. Once they were in Paris, and settled, Granny Webb could take over.

'Since we have been instructed to leave Hendon,' Henrietta announced, 'I think we should all leave together. It makes sense to travel as a group to Paris, where Alice and Frances can rest, before they travel on to Rome. I'm sure Lord Bellew will provide the safest of coaches and extra guards to protect his daughter. Why don't we all take advantage of his generosity?'

Alice nodded in fervent assent. 'I have been so grateful to find refuge here, but I can't pretend I'm not desperate to see Frances again and for both of us to live with Winifred, I mean the Countess of Nithsdale. Frances will thrive with her grandparents. To have a chance to return to Rome, it feels like a miracle.'

Amelia interrupted her. '...and I can't wait to be back in Paris.'

Henrietta glanced across at Mrs Adams, the older woman's face furrowed with sorrow, hearing everyone blurting out that they couldn't wait to leave.

Amelia grimaced, realising her blunder. 'I'm sorry to be so rude... we are settled here. It didn't seem possible at the start but Hendon Manor has felt like a home to me.'

Mrs Adams nodded, as if she had made up her mind to speak. 'But why don't you stay? Lord Bellew could bring Frances here, at least for a while. This house would live again with two little girls running around. Perhaps Lord Montgomery would wait, if we explained that travelling such a distance with a baby and a small child is too much to ask?'

'That makes sense,' Henrietta replied. 'It's a fair proposal.' A delay would allow time for her father-in-law, the Marquess, to fall in love with his granddaughter, something easily achieved by everyone who held the baby, everyone except her. Once delighted by the child, he might be persuaded to move them into Powis Castle. One glance at Amelia's bereft expression persuaded Henrietta that no matter how reasonable Mrs Adams offer was, they must leave Hendon. She had been blind to how much her friend missed her mother and Paris, trapped here in the countryside with a mistress struggling with new motherhood.

'I'm sorry,' Alice said, 'I cannot stay any longer. Lord Bellew is only demanding this because he's tired of Frances. She must not be left for a moment longer with a father who doesn't want her. Also, I cannot deprive Winifred of the chance to raise her granddaughter. Since I read his letter, I have imagined Winifred's delight a thousand times over. Frances is the only person who can heal Winifred's pain.'

'What about you, Amelia?' Henrietta asked, helping her friend to speak the truth.

'I will remain with you, wherever you are,' Amelia replied, 'but it would be wonderful to go home, to see my mother.'

The baby started to cry and Alice hurried to lift her, bringing the damp, pink-cheeked child to Henrietta, who loosened her wrapping gown and set Barbara to suckle at her breast. Her companions waited, alert for her decision. In Hendon, she had authority, the respect bestowed by her position as the lady of this household, if not by her own limited qualities. How would she cope in Paris? Her grandparents knew she was a widow and may have learned she was a new mother, but they were ignorant of the tribulations life had brought since leaving them. She was no longer a biddable child but they would expect the old Henrietta to return.

'Mrs Adams, I'm afraid we must go,' she said, reaching across the table for the housekeeper's hand. 'Please inform Lord Montgomery that we will set off at the end of August. Alice, write to Lord Bellew and ask him to send Frances here by coach, with her nursemaid. Let him know we will all require the use of his carriage for travel to Dover, so it must be of a suitable size. Amelia, you must assist Mrs Adams in preparing our clothes for departure. I will write to my grandparents and warn them of our arrival.'

Frances Bellew arrived with her nurse within days of Lord Bellew receiving Alice's letter, confirming their suspicions that he had tired of his child. Amelia muttered, 'He has another woman, most likely,' and Henrietta nodded, lifting her eyebrows in condemnation.

Suddenly, the ancient manor house echoed with the sound of a child's footsteps, her surprisingly loud voice and toys ranked in order on the stairs or lined up across every surface. Even the baby stopped crying for a few minutes, her eyes wide and startled, whenever Frances leapt up and down at the side of the crib.

Mrs Adams is right, Henrietta thought, *a house is meant for children, but perhaps not a house I would choose to live in.*

Henrietta didn't take to Frances, finding her conversation limited and her games dull, but Alice was transformed. It helped everyone's mood to see Alice's natural energy restored, to hear her unexpected laughter and to see her dull eyes brighten. Even the cook smiled, when Frances invaded her kitchen demanding pieces of apple.

The youngest servant, no more than a child herself, hovered in corners watching Frances play, until she was released from her duties to relieve the exhausted adults. Since Alice was distracted with Frances, it was a considerable consolation for Henrietta when the nurse from the Bellew household offered to take over Barbara's care.

This idyll lasted only a few weeks. In early September, Lord

Bellew's grand coach, with two coachmen and an armed postilion, waited at the gates of Hendon Manor, the roof loaded with all their possessions, the adults and children tucked inside, apart from Henrietta, who lingered over her farewell with Mrs Adams.

'Lady Herbert,' Mrs Adams said, clasping both of Henrietta's hands in her own, 'I had no idea what to expect when you arrived that night, a year ago. You arrived a child and you leave as a young woman, a mother. I am proud of you, as if you were my own daughter. Your grandparents are lucky. I will miss you.'

'I couldn't have survived without you,' Henrietta replied. 'You led me without instruction, taught me through patience, tolerated my failings. If I had my way, I would stay here forever but I have learned that I have little control over my own destiny. I will always remember your kindness.'

Mrs Adams pulled Henrietta into her arms and held her there until drawing back, then she turned Henrietta around by the shoulders and pushed her firmly from behind. 'Leave now, Lady Herbert,' she said. 'Pull your shoulders back and face whatever comes next. Your strength will stay with you.'

The chatter from within Lord Bellew's well-built Berline carriage reminded Henrietta that she was the only one sad to be leaving. Everyone else was looking forward to Paris, to Rome and even little Frances couldn't sit still, catching the adults' excitement. Yet Frances was the only one who could expect a future like Henrietta's, a child rejected by her father, yet one who might still be useful if a suitable marriage came into view.

She carried a letter from her father, crushed into her purse. It had arrived by courier the day before. Too late, he offered his heartfelt regret at Edward's untimely death but expressed great pleasure at the birth of a granddaughter, while suggesting no immediate plan to meet the source of his delight. Earl Waldegrave repeated the same offer he had made in Paris; renounce her faith and she could have free access to all his properties in London, where she was welcome to make a home with her daughter. As her father, he would use his connections to find her a more suitable husband.

Suitable in what way, Henrietta thought, *a man who won't drop down dead?* She stared through the carriage window, imagining stepping off the coach in London and finding her own way to her father's house, clutching her baby. Her mind formed a picture of her companions' distraught faces, as she said farewell to them, but she shook the fantasy away. She reached for Barbara, taking the child from the young nursemaid's arms, and loosened her bodice to feed the baby, admiring the long eyelashes resting on the child's cheeks. Granny Webb would love her namesake and would teach Henrietta how to love her too.

The women dined in Rochester, and spent the night in an inn in Canterbury, one of a higher standard than the miserable hovel Edward had paid for on their wedding night.

Amelia said aloud at dinner that Lord Bellew must have another woman, because this expensive journey was being paid for by guilt. Frances asked everyone what 'guilt' meant. In the tangle of conflicting explanations, the little girl seemed satisfied with reassurance from Alice that her generous father had paid for everything with gilt coins.

The nursemaid slept with Barbara but Henrietta could not rest, despite the reassuring sound of Amelia's rhythmic breathing beside her. Memories of her husband, that other inn, his absence throughout the night on the day they were married. So much of his life had been hidden from her and in death, as in life, his secrets remained his own. Exhausted from imagining pretend confrontations with Edward about his deceit, where he always explained and apologised, she had not slept at all when the nurse brought Barbara for her early morning feed. Henrietta was glad to be rid of the curse of her imagination and when the baby was removed to be washed and dressed for her onward journey, with comforting sounds arising from below as the inn's staff woke to their duties, Henrietta rolled over into Amelia's back and fell asleep at last.

At the port, their luggage was carried onto the waiting schooner by their two coachmen, other passengers crowding around to stare at the uniform of the surly postilion, the Bellew crest marking the carriage out as belonging to people of rank. Henrietta and her party started towards the gangway, the ship's sails already unfurled and its prow tugging at the quayside. The crowd parted to allow them access, some even dropping a bow or a curtsy, just in case.

The three women lined up against the rail to wave farewell to the Bellew's nursemaid, watching her climb aboard their grand coach for her solitary journey back to London. She spread her hands wide to show her former companions that she was free from children and babies but her gesture brought a brief round of applause from passengers still admiring the coach. The horses, already restless from the harassment of diving seagulls and the worry of sneaking cats, tossed their heads and pulled on their harnesses when the coachman lightly touched their flanks with his whip.

The Bellew carriage climbed away from the port, only Henrietta resisting the sharp breeze to watch its departure, until it was indistinguishable in the landscape and the white cliffs became a smudge on the horizon. With a fair wind, in only a few hours they would sail into Calais where her grandfather's coach would be waiting. It was impossible to ignore a gnawing dread about her future, an uncertainty of her grandparents' welcome. She felt ashamed to be returning like this, a widow thrown out by her husband's family, bearing an unwelcome child. It felt as if she had let them down.

The wind rose, filling the sails, and waves slapped across the deck, soaking her feet. She escaped below to join the others, already tucked into their comfortable cabin and Frances asleep. Alice told them the story of sailing from Gravesend to Bruges with Winifred, her friend Grace Evans, and poor Anne, only six years old, fleeing from the king's men.

'The weather was so foul, the storm so great, we were all terrified,' Alice recounted. 'The Countess was expecting a baby and her body couldn't cope, tossed around from one side of the cabin to the other and constantly heaving with sickness. In the end, she spilled the baby into a bucket. I tried to hide it from Anne but I think she saw everything. That girl witnessed too much.'

Henrietta glanced at Frances, still fast asleep, and her eyes drifted to the pail in the corner. 'What happened then?' she asked.

'The storm didn't stop. We couldn't fetch any water or clean ourselves and my mistress, she...' Alice stopped and covered her mouth, turning her face away from her companions.

Henrietta had heard some of this from Edward and encouraged Alice to continue. 'The captain managed to steer the ship into a port on the Belgian coast?'

Alice nodded. 'We didn't think Winifred would live. She was carried onto the dock by the sailors but was so grey and lifeless. Grace said she was breathing and found a farmer on the quay willing to take us to the convent in his cart. Grace is like that, always practical, and able to take charge. I'm hopeless in a crisis. Anne clung to her mother's body for the entire journey... we couldn't peel her away.'

'You took her to St Augustine's Convent in Bruges,' Henrietta interrupted, 'to her sister, my husband's aunt Lucy?'

Alice nodded. 'Yes, we made it to safety and the Countess recovered with the care of the nuns, but it was slow. Winifred's sister, the Abbess, was so patient. We couldn't pay her anything for our care.'

'My goodness,' Amelia said. 'I thought things were bad for us, having to rely on the generosity of Lord Bellew, but we've been so lucky compared with Winifred... and you as well, Alice.'

'I will miss you,' Alice said, gently rocking Barbara in time with the rolling of the ship, 'but my home is with Winifred. I only hope she will be able to forgive me for neglecting Anne. I want to see her, but I'm scared too.'

Henrietta stretched out her arms for her baby and said, 'You didn't neglect Anne, you did your best. Winifred will welcome you, I'm certain of it.'

This was said as much for her own benefit, as for poor Alice. The Winifred who had replied to her letter about Anne's funeral had sounded like a person who would be fair and kind, but only a year ago, that had also felt true of Granny Webb. Perhaps Amelia was the only one amongst them truly confident of her welcome home.

CHAPTER 16

1736

Everything was the same but everything had changed. Granny Webb didn't seem to understand, or care, that she wasn't the seventeen-year-old bride who had left Paris two years before. Her grandparents welcomed her and there had been no blame for her widowed state, or her failure to produce a grandson, so her worst fears were not realised, but there wasn't much interest either.

The anniversary of her husband's death passed without comment and no one asked about her life at Hendon Manor. Henrietta tried to tell Granny Webb stories about Mrs Adams and how she hadn't liked Amelia at first. She explained about the garden and the crops they grew, described the way Catholic families were treated by their neighbours. At first, her grandmother tried to show interest, but then her eyes darted around the room, as if something else was on her mind.

Henrietta's excitement at the city's sophistication and the light streaming everywhere in the apartment soon passed and she missed her walks around the garden, the card games, the weary, downtrodden comfort of the old house at Hendon. She hadn't noticed, it had been so subtle, but under Mrs Adam's guidance she had become used to being noticed, consulted, even deferred to. She offered to help organise the household, but Granny Webb laughed as if a child was pretending to be an adult.

Granny Webb was even slower in her movements and her thinking than Henrietta remembered, so there were no gaming afternoons with her diminishing band of friends and no energy for evenings of opera either.

By contrast, her grandfather seemed energised by news from the Jacobite court in Rome, and made regular trips to the Muti Palace, which lasted for several weeks at a time. From there, he brought news of Alice and Lady Winifred, which pleased Henrietta and almost justified his frequent absences.

Alice left Paris after a month, keen to be in Rome before the autumn weather made travelling treacherous. Granny Webb had spent little time with Frances, and even less with Barbara, delegating both children to the nursery. In the afternoons, Henrietta was invited to sit with her grandmother to play two-handed card games or sew some clothes for the baby. Within half an hour, Granny Webb always fell asleep, her head lolling against the deep wings of her favourite chair.

'Granny?' Henrietta asked, seeing her grandmother's head begin to nod. 'Did I go wrong with the Marquess? I can't understand why he's shown no interest in the baby, why he didn't ask us to live with him at Powis Castle. He has shown no kindness to me but Alice Douglas, who is a servant, has seen no limit to his care.'

Granny Webb smacked her lips and peered at Henrietta from under her eyelids. 'Your husband was estranged from his father, which may have caused William to be a little wary of you, but that's not the real reason. With men like the Marquess of Powis, it's all about inheritance. You will marry again and everything that is yours will belong to your husband. The same is true of Barbara. He's trying to avoid anyone laying claim to his estates. I expect that Lord Montgomery is under considerable pressure to produce an heir.'

'If Barbara had been a boy, do you think we would be living at Powis Castle?'

Granny Webb sighed and nestled her head deeper into the folds of the chair. 'That is true, my dear, but there is nothing to be done. It's the way of the world. Now, please call Celine. I think I'll take to my bed for an hour or two.'

After Alice left, Henrietta expected to be asked to look after the child herself, overhearing whispering between her grandparents that the Marquess of Powis had again failed to pay her widow's jointure, but her grandmother didn't hesitate to find another nursemaid.

The baby no longer needed nursing at her breast and with this task complete, Henrietta was relieved to rid herself of her stained wrapping gowns but there didn't seem to be anything else to do, apart from asking Leo to take her in the coach to be measured for new gowns. She wandered the empty rooms of an apartment that now felt sterile and too formal, quickly bored by reading or practicing on the spinet. When she went in search of Amelia, whose time was now measured by her mother's new promotion to housekeeper, her friend was too busy even to whisper her dissatisfaction.

Henrietta visited the nursery every day and tried to help with the messy task of feeding Barbara, but the nursemaid became impatient and snatched the spoon out of her hand. If she tried to play with the crawling infant, her boredom was so profound she felt only relief when the nurse said it was time for Barbara to have her cloths changed or take a nap.

On Barbara's first birthday, a day unremarked in the Webb household, Henrietta went in search of her daughter. Now that she was walking and with blonde curls, Barbara had lost any resemblance to her father, a likeness that had owed much to being a baby with round cheeks and only a few wisps of hair.

Henrietta tried to interest the child in a new wooden horse that could be pulled along by a string, but the infant stared, glowered, and tossed the horse aside. Henrietta tried stacking some bricks, or rolling a ball but Barbara threw these, with surprising force, to clatter against the parquet floor. The nurse, whose name was Adele, raised her eyes from her sewing and tipped her head towards Barbara.

'She always does that, Lady Herbert. It drives me mad. Anyway, I'm about to dress her, take her out for a walk. There's a market garden nearby and she likes the flowers and animals.'

'Can I help dress her?' Henrietta asked.

The nurse stared, as if Henrietta had asked for something ridiculous, but passed over some tiny shoes, suitable for outside, and an outdoor cape with lengths of fabric attached, meant to catch a toddling child who might fall. Barbara arched her back and wailed as Henrietta struggled to place an outdoor cap on top of the light cap she already wore and it was impossible to lace shoes onto the baby's kicking feet.

'Oh, give her to me, my lady,' the nurse said, holding out her hands. Henrietta's skin prickled with humiliation as her daughter scrambled down from her lap and walked unsteadily to her nursemaid. When she reached the preferred knee, the child looked back at her mother and frowned, one finger in her mouth.

Henrietta watched the nurse efficiently dress her daughter in outdoor clothes, trying to find the courage to ask if she might accompany them on their walk. Instead, she said, 'Do you walk alone? Is it safe?'

The nurse gave a high laugh and then ducked her head, pretending to adjust the child's shoes. 'My lady, I walk with Louis,' she muttered.

Ah, Louis... how much that boy had changed in her absence, Henrietta thought. His skin had healed and he had gained several inches in height. She would not be welcome on this walk.

The nurse placed Barbara on the floor, the baby's dress and cape reaching only to mid-calf, as was expected for a newly walking child. 'Is that alright, my lady? We're very safe with a manservant to accompany us and he helps carry the child when she tires.'

'Of course,' Henrietta said. 'I was just worried about you walking alone. I will leave you now to your plants and animals.'

'Mainly goats and chickens, Lady Herbert.'

Henrietta paused at the door. 'At Hendon, we had lambs,' she said. 'I wish Barbara could see spring lambs, the way they leap and jump, as if they can't contain their joy at being alive.'

Adele picked Barbara up from the floor, where she arched her back in temper at the delay. 'Yes, my lady,' she said, as if giving serious consideration to Henrietta's words. 'Lambs would indeed be a special sight in the middle of Paris.'

Amelia still had responsibility for Henrietta's evening toilette and these were times when they could speak in private and grumble about their circumstances.

'I'm surprised my grandmother has so little interest in Barbara,' Henrietta confided in Amelia one night, as they lay side by side on the bed.

'Perhaps she doesn't like babies, or small children,' Amelia said.

'But she loved me and the boys when we landed on her so unexpectedly, and that was only six years ago. My younger brother was eleven.'

'My mother says...'

This would be important. Madame Laurent knew everything. Henrietta sat up, to pay more attention.

'My mother says,' Amelia continued, 'that Lady Webb left the care of her brood to nursemaids when they were little. Maybe she's one of those women who prefer older children.'

Henrietta felt some hope. Perhaps she wasn't a bad mother after all. It would come with time. 'Is that common?' she asked.

'Sometimes. But rich women never look after their own and remember, Lady Webb's not that well. The baby must tire her.'

Henrietta hesitated, unsure whether to confess. Some words could never be taken back, once they had been spoken. 'Amelia... Barbara tires me too, even though I hardly ever see her. But without my baby, I've nothing to fill my days. I can't meet anyone my own age, because I have no introductions. My grandparents are kind but this is not the life I want.'

Amelia folded her arms and dropped her chin, as if she too was weighing her words. 'It's not right for me either, Hensy. My mother works me like a slave, in fact I must go right now and help her with your grandmother's bedtime. I have an idea... think about it overnight... why don't you ask your grandfather if he'll take you to Rome with him? I will have to accompany you, of course.'

There was barely time to consider Amelia's plan before Henrietta was summoned to her grandfather's study. She decided not to arrive too soon or Grandpa John might think the idea of a visit to Rome was important. It was best to let him invite her, believe it was his idea and of no consequence to Henrietta, either way. Taking her time, she ambled down a long corridor lit by deep windows framed by floor-length drapes embroidered with tangled vines. She recalled the dark wood-panelled walls at Hendon, relieved only by portraits of unfriendly ancestors and monstrous fireplaces.

Grandpa Webb glanced up as she entered, removing his new spectacles from the end of his nose, and holding them up to the light to clean them of smudges. Henrietta guessed he wanted her to notice, since they were only recently arrived from a London optician. She sat down in the armchair at the side of his desk and waited, admiring the new wallpaper, a design that reminded her of Edward, and their day at Vauxhall Gardens, when he had shown her shimmering, golden fish darting to catch dragonflies skimming over the surface of the pond.

'I hope you can see better,' she said. 'It looks as if they're more secure than your old pair, with those clever arms that sit so neatly on your ears.'

Grandpa Webb adjusted his wig, one set low on his head, with tight curls on each side. This was a recent fashion, one adopted by most younger men but since her grandfather's frequent visits to Rome, he had abandoned his tall old-man wigs. Henrietta did not dare ask if he copied the style worn by the young princes, the two boys Winifred wrote about with such love, or whether he was trying to impress a woman, someone younger than himself.

'Yes, indeed, they're very comfortable,' he replied, 'which means I can wear them for longer.' He waved a hand at the stack of documents on his desk. 'Helps with this.'

'You asked to see me?' Henrietta asked.

'This is awkward,' Grandpa John said, 'but there's no point in pretending we're not disappointed with the Marquess of Powis, your father-in-law. I met Viscount Bolingbroke recently... he's just retired to France. Without wishing to gossip, he said he'd spoken to your father-in-law at his club before he left London and the Marquess complained that he'd never seen his granddaughter. I assume you gave him every chance, made him feel welcome to visit Hendon.'

'Of course,' Henrietta said, ignoring a needling doubt that

she might be to blame for William Herbert's neglect. 'I wrote to him when Barbara was born. He didn't even acknowledge her birth. It was up to him to arrange to see her.'

Grandpa John fell silent, fiddling with his precious spectacles. 'I'm asking because we've taken him to court for failure to pay your jointure and I don't want him to use lack of access to Barbara as his excuse. We will hear the outcome very soon, so I thought you should know.'

Henrietta looked down at her hands before speaking. 'Grandpa, the Herbert family have no money. It was obvious as soon as I met them and throughout the year I spent at Hendon Manor. I'm afraid we won't see a penny.'

Grandpa Webb sighed and returned to cleaning his glasses. 'Had Edward lived, things might have been different but the Marquess should have known how ill his son was. We were blinded by his generous settlement... perhaps hurried you into an unsuitable marriage. He has paid some of what is owed but it's sporadic and you need a steady sum to rely on, once you're an adult and bringing up a child alone.'

'Thank you, Grandfather, for fighting for me,' Henrietta said. 'My husband told me that his sister Mary constantly demands money to fund her mines in Spain, and his older brother is drinking away any profit from the lead mines on the family estate. There are other sisters too, whose husbands haven't seen a penny of their marriage settlements. I'm afraid we're at the end of a long queue.'

Grandpa Webb rubbed his eyes and placed his spectacles on the desk. At last, he turned to face her. 'He's a man who promises much and delivers little. He might not be able to find any ready cash but he hasn't tried to sell anything or raise a mortgage, things he could do to make everything right for his granddaughter. Perhaps he will listen to a direction from the court, instead of making excuses.'

Henrietta rested a hand on her grandfather's arm. 'I think you'll find that everything that can be sold from that family's estate has already gone and everything that can be mortgaged has been mortgaged. Lord Montgomery hurried us out of Hendon Manor because he needed income from tenants. You have no idea, Grandpa, how they live. Not everyone has the sense to manage money like you.'

'My goodness, Henrietta, perhaps I am learning a little about how life was for you in Hendon. You have come back changed, and not for the worse.'

'Thank you, Grandfather, I try to learn from experience, however bad, and not allow myself to be crushed. One more thing, I am aware that you frequently visit Rome and wondered if you might take me with you? I would like to meet the Countess of Nithsdale and her husband, and see Alice again.'

Grandpa Webb blinked and the colour drained from his cheeks, leaving only two pink spots below his eyes. Henrietta knew she had made a mistake by asking, but she wasn't sure why.

'Leave me now,' he said, pulling a document towards him and placing his spectacles back on his nose, easing the arms over his ears. 'I will let you know as soon as I have heard from the court. As for your request, we will discuss it then.'

That night, Granny Webb summoned Henrietta to her bedchamber. Amelia and her mother were dismissed.

Henrietta stood by her grandmother's bed, prepared for a scolding. 'I must speak to you about your request to visit Rome with your grandfather. You have put him in a difficult situation.'

He only has to say no, Henrietta thought. *What's difficult about that?* 'I'm sorry, Grandmother. I would not have asked unless I was desperate.'

'What on earth is making you desperate?'

Henrietta spread her arms, then let them fall. 'I'm trapped here. I'm bored. I meet no one my age. I want to marry again, live with a husband.'

Granny Webb made an impatient gesture towards the chair next to her bed and Henrietta sat down. 'And you think you will meet someone at King James' court, is that it? The princes are both younger than you and the men who gather around them are of a similar age. You are a widow and a mother. What young man will consider you?'

Henrietta felt a shiver of shame. 'I'd like to meet the Countess of Nithsdale. We have corresponded since her daughter's funeral.'

Granny Webb snorted, as if Henrietta had made a stupid joke. 'That woman is guilty of treason against the British monarch,' she growled. 'For goodness' sake, Henrietta, think of your father's position. We may not see eye to eye with him but he is the British Ambassador to France. Remember what happened to us, when our daughter Anna Maria was caught up in Jacobite conspiracy. We had to flee the country.'

'Grandfather is up to his neck in Jacobite treachery,' Henrietta muttered. 'Why else does he spend so much time in Rome?'

Granny Webb raised her hands in a gesture of frustration. 'Your grandfather is careful who he mixes with and goes nowhere near the Earl and Countess of Nithsdale. He consults with the king and his advisers, and then leaves. Anyway, your grandfather is not looking for a husband, but you are. You must guard your reputation, especially if you are planning to return to London once you reach your majority. Take my advice and forget about finding a husband your own age. Your best bet is to look out for an older man, newly widowed, with children who have lost their mother.'

Henrietta stared at her grandmother's aged face, without

powder or rouge, showing deep lines around her full mouth and dark pouches below the eyes. After this lengthy speech, so unusual since her stroke, Granny Webb's lips trembled and her hands plucked at the sleeves of her night shift.

I am second-hand goods, Henrietta thought, *only suitable for an older man, one even older than the first man you saddled me with.* She bit back these sharp, bitter words. They would satisfy in the moment but only lead to hours of tortured regret.

'I am sorry, Grandmother, you are right of course. I need to learn more about our Jacobite past and how it still matters. It's complex and I don't fully understand, but I trust you to guide me. Your advice about my future husband is sound.'

Granny Webb's expression softened and she stretched out an arm to pull Henrietta's head into her neck. 'We love you, Henrietta, and only want what's best for you,' she whispered. 'Your grandfather has noticed how you have matured but there are still things you need to learn. Leave me now. I need to sleep. You may be grown up but you can still wear me out.'

Henrietta pulled back from her grandmother's old lady smell, a scent that had once carried reassurance and comfort but now the violets were masked by a faint mildewy odour, redolent of autumn. All she could feel was resentment but tried to return Granny Webb's soft smile. 'Of course, Grandmother,' she said. 'I hope you feel more rested in the morning.'

Only a few weeks later, Grandpa Webb asked her to meet with him. Henrietta sat next to his desk as before and waited, with growing impatience, through the ritual of puffing on the lenses of his glasses, vigorously cleaning them with a linen cloth and taking too long adjusting the arms above each ear. He pulled a document towards him and pretended to read it through, as if it had just been delivered.

'You won your case against the Marquess of Powis,' he said, lifting his eyes to gauge her reaction. 'No surprise there, Henrietta, but the good news is that the court decreed he should pay another one hundred and fifty pounds a year to Barbara. The money will come to me, of course.'

Henrietta shrugged. 'There won't be any, at least not enough, so it doesn't matter who it comes to. You can't force him to pay, whatever the court says.'

'Well, there are bailiffs, but I hope it won't come to that. I feel more confident he might honour his debts, now that we have a favourable judgement, a judgement that will not have gone unnoticed in the Marquess' social circle.'

'I'm afraid I don't share your confidence,' Henrietta said. 'You will have to support me and my child, at least until I find another husband. We have to face reality.'

'We will always support you, Henrietta, I hope you believe that, but I will fight for what you're owed.'

Henrietta rose and smoothed her robe. 'Thank you, Grandfather. As for the other matter, let's not discuss a visit to Rome. I understand.'

What she understood was that her grandfather was lying. Granny Webb might believe her husband advised the exiled king but that was fantasy, a misguided belief that she was married to someone who was still useful. Grandpa Webb had another woman in Rome, Henrietta was certain of it, but for now she would keep this to herself.

CHAPTER 17

1738

Henrietta was twenty-one and it had been decided by her grandparents, without consultation, that she would live with John Webb, their heir, at the Webb family property in London. As Granny Webb became frailer and more short-tempered, their rows had become frequent and Henrietta flushed with shame remembering how she had provoked these quarrels. The final row with Granny Webb was one she would never forget. It was a relief when her grandparents gave her no choice but to leave, but winning had felt like a disgrace.

'You will not abandon your child to live with us,' Granny Webb argued, when Henrietta admitted her intention to leave without Barbara.

This particular refusal was unexpected. The Granny Webb she loved was a woman who had once welcomed children in need of a home. 'I must leave her,' Henrietta argued. 'Surely you can see that. She's settled here with Adele. I can't separate them and Adele doesn't want to live in London. The child is happy here. She hardly knows me.'

Granny Webb's voice rose to a screech and her eyes blazed. 'Whose fault is that! You spend no time with her.'

'I was too young for a baby. My husband had just died. The child didn't like me, right from the start.' Henrietta hated to hear the whine in her own voice.

Granny Webb growled from deep within her throat. 'Eighteen is not too young to have a baby. The fault lies with you. You were always a selfish girl.'

Henrietta felt bands of rage tighten across her chest but fought an instinct to shout. Instead, she whispered, 'You spend no time with the child either. Admit it, Granny, you don't even like her, the great-granddaughter who bears your name. If we're talking about who's selfish, you abandoned me after my marriage. You simply didn't care once I was off your hands.'

Granny Webb slumped into a chair, resting her elbows on a side table, her brow in her palms. She shook her head. 'You have made yourself clear, Henrietta, and will have your way, as you always do. We must trust that you will send for Barbara as soon as you are settled in London. Promise me that.'

Shocked to see a strange sheen gathering on her grandmother's grey skin, she summoned Madame Laurent, who tutted at Henrietta before helping Lady Webb to stand. As her grandmother was led from the parlour, the housekeeper insisting that bed was the only option, Henrietta reached out a hand in a final appeal for understanding. Granny Webb flapped at her, as if to brush away a nuisance fly.

On Henrietta's last visit to three-year-old Barbara before her escape from Paris, the child dropped a doll into her mother's lap and asked for help with the buttons on the tiny dress. Once this practical task was complete, the child had no further use for her and strode purposefully to the corner where her other dolls waited in a circle.

Henrietta watched the child play, hearing Adele's scolding voice mimicked in the little girl's game. As with Frances at the same age, Henrietta could not imagine how it was possible for an adult to enter this world of make-believe and felt only relief that she was leaving. There was nothing she could offer her daughter and the child would not miss her. She had promised to send for Barbara and perhaps she would, but no date had been set. That suited her well.

Henrietta raised herself from her chair in the rather dark parlour at Great Marlborough Street, although it was bathed in natural light compared to the parlour at Hendon. There was no point worrying about her grandparents or the child she had left behind. Such feelings belonged in the past. She shook her shoulders, keen for her day to begin.

What did suit her very well indeed was living in London, with Amelia for company, in her uncle's home. The houses on this street were newly completed but not grand. The builders tried to satisfy families like hers, those who needed a city address but had many other options if they tired of the proximity of neighbours and the mess of building works everywhere in London. Her Uncle John was spending the spring and summer with his wife Anne and their children at Hatherop Castle, leaving Henrietta in charge of the house, with a carriage for her sole use, a cook, a senior manservant and housemaids, all there to help her.

This city was not Paris; the carriages blocking every thoroughfare made walking unpleasant, not helped by the stinking mounds of horse dung everywhere. Beyond newly constructed streets lay dereliction, ancient buildings ripe for redevelopment, with unexpected patches of rough pasture beyond, still clinging to the boundaries of the city landscape.

Amelia tapped on the parlour door, already dressed for the outdoors, and helped Henrietta fasten her cape and find her gloves, since it was a chilly April day. They left her uncle's house to walk a few yards to an identical town house, with an identical hall and layout of rooms, except in mirror image. At the door, Amelia introduced Henrietta to a manservant and left as soon as her mistress stepped inside.

This unfamiliar world worried Henrietta, a society of married women who passed their time in each other's houses, one that her grandmother would have recognised and negotiated with confidence. Taking her turn to ask these new friends to her home would be expected but was something to be dreaded, in case she made a social error.

The host this afternoon was Frances, Baroness Byron, a woman Henrietta had only met once before at a different neighbour's house. Frances clapped her hands with delight to learn that they were both widows and both had married at seventeen, a coincidence that must surely mean they would be good friends.

Lady Byron sat alone in the parlour when Henrietta was introduced, a side table set with porcelain plates and glasses for six. Henrietta relaxed, she hadn't misread the invitation, others were expected.

'Lady Herbert, please sit down.' Frances indicated a sofa angled next to her armchair. 'I asked you to come earlier than the rest, because I wanted a chance to get to know you better. Please call me Frances. May I address you as Henrietta?'

'Of course,' Henrietta said, her eyes scanning the drawing room, noticing that Frances had chosen fashionable green wallpaper for her walls but the high, corniced ceilings and deep shuttered windows were the same as Uncle John's. She liked these houses, feeling comfortable in a home that avoided the opulence of her grandparents' apartment in Paris and the shabby gloom of the manor house at Hendon.

'Henrietta, I wanted to ask if you have any children? The question might seem as if I'm prying, but I have a good reason to ask.'

There was no point in lying. The woman was prying but she would have to answer. 'I have a little girl, Barbara, she's only three. She's in Paris with my grandparents but will join me once we're more settled.'

Frances nodded. 'I'm looking for women from good families to help with a cause that is dear to my heart, friends with a child or children but who have time to spare. My daughter is about to be married and my sons are away at school, so my days are my own. Since my husband died, I have been glad to have a project and I hope you might feel the same.'

'I am intrigued,' Henrietta said. 'Please tell me more.'

'As a newcomer to London, you will not have noticed, or I hope you haven't, the bodies of dead children lying on the street, or the state of the little children you see begging, many the same age as your daughter. I have joined a group of women petitioning the king to support the building of a Foundling Hospital, somewhere where impoverished women can bring their babies or children, to be cared for. We're a lively group and you'll make new friends.'

Henrietta felt uncertain. The idea of meeting a group of educated, opinionated women, mostly older than herself, was not appealing, but she had no choice. What possible excuse could she give?

'That sounds interesting,' she said. 'I'd be happy to join.'

Frances grinned widely, revealing slightly prominent front teeth, which only made her seem more naturally beautiful. The sound of women's high-pitched voices clamoured from the hall, shrieks of laughter announcing the arrival of the other players.

Frances reached across and grasped her hand. 'Welcome, Henrietta,' she whispered. 'You've made a good decision. We will benefit from your youth and intelligence and I will make sure you have every entrance you need to London society.'

Henrietta had been so well-schooled by her grandmother and her elderly friends, she had to concentrate hard not to win every game. She caught the other women glancing at her, trying to judge her place in their society, her right to be amongst them. Learning that she was a Webb, raised in Paris, seemed to satisfy their curiosity about her pedigree and resolved the puzzle of her skill at card games. One of the women, Lady Anne Blackwell, had brought along a sullen boy, who looked about seven years old. He was ignored and left to play alone with his toy soldiers in a corner of the room.

At the break for wine and cake, Anne Blackwell told the group about her visit to Drury Lane theatre to see *The Beggar's Opera.*

'Has anyone else been?' she asked. 'The tenor, who sings the role of Macheath, is rather... rather...'

'I think you're trying to say, Lady Blackwell,' one of the others interrupted, 'that those of us who have seen John Beard sing have – how shall I put this politely? – used the image of him for the benefit of our husbands.'

The women glanced across at the child, who appeared preoccupied with lining up his soldiers along the edge of a console table. Frances winked at Henrietta and said, 'Those of us without husbands can think about John Beard as much as we like.'

The women laughed, a deep cackling rumble that made Henrietta uncomfortable. Surely these women weren't joking about having sex with their husbands?'

Frances turned to Henrietta, coughing to suppress her mirth. 'I'm sorry, you must think us shockingly impolite. We've known each other a long time.'

'Not at all,' Henrietta replied, hot from the memory of Edward's skilful attention to her body. 'I love opera and went often with my grandmother.'

'You should try to see this one,' Anne interrupted. 'It's not really opera as you know it, in fact it makes fun of the operatic tradition.'

'It's really about politics and fighting society's ills, the same causes we're campaigning for with the Foundling Hospital,' Frances said. 'But you should go just to hear John Beard sing.'

Anne narrowed her eyes. 'You haven't roped the poor girl in to your charitable works already, have you, Frances?'

Frances smiled at Henrietta. 'Why would I waste any time? This young woman is exactly what we need. By the way, I've heard that John Beard gives private music lessons when he has the time. Anyone interested?'

Henrietta's curiosity was roused. She asked their butler to book tickets for her and Amelia to see *The Beggar's Opera,* as soon as it was showing again at Drury Lane and asked him to find her a box close to the stage. Amelia enjoyed singing along to well-known tunes and laughing at characters familiar to her from life below stairs but the play was not to Henrietta's liking. She knew nothing of London society or politics and felt puzzled when the rest of the audience bellowed and cheered in recognition. The smoke from the hundreds of candles hurt her eyes and the crowd in the parterre below were noisy and badly behaved, with frequent fights and throwing food.

Despite the mayhem, a tall young man, sturdy in build,

brought the crowd to an awed silence whenever he sang, the audience heaving a joint sigh of appreciation when he turned his face upwards towards Henrietta and sang to her as if he knew her intimately. Henrietta turned her face away, trying to hide her blush from the audience. Amelia grinned and shook her head. 'I'm guessing someone will be keen to take up the spinet again?'

They waited at the theatre door for their coach, the crowd thinning around them. Henrietta felt a tap on her shoulder and looked up into the eyes of John Beard, the man who had serenaded her. The remaining theatre-goers turned to stare, some edging towards Henrietta, keen to be noticed, to distract him from this woman, this interloper, who had caught their hero's interest.

Amelia stepped in. 'Mr Beard, may I introduce Lady Henrietta Herbert, recently arrived in London and a widow.'

'So young and already a widow,' John Beard said to Henrietta, bowing low and lifting her fingers to brush them with his lips. His eyes never left her face, nor did he release her hand. She felt blood thrum in her ears.

'We're looking for a music teacher,' Amelia continued. 'My mistress has sadly neglected her playing. She's really rather good on the spinet if she practices.'

John Beard's eyes still held Henrietta's. 'I am very busy,' he whispered, 'but I will make space for Lady Herbert. When would you like me to start?'

'Tomorrow,' Henrietta said. 'Can you come tomorrow?'

There was no need to explain to Amelia that a first music lesson required a bath, scented oils, and her best gown from Paris. It was also unspoken that Amelia would sit outside the door of the music room, not as a chaperone but to prevent the rest of the servants from intruding. John's gaze tracked her face, her throat, and the plunging neckline of her robe as they were introduced, but he was prepared to teach and carried a leather wallet full of suitable sheet music.

He sat at a discreet distance behind Henrietta, watching as she fumbled with the keys. She hated making mistakes, feeling his eyes prickling against the back of her neck, but when she struggled, again and again, to play anything close to the right notes, he moved across the room to stand close behind her, placing both hands over hers to guide her fingers. Her hands burned under his dry, warm palms and she stared at the fine, dark hairs on his knuckles. On impulse, Henrietta turned her head to look up into his face and he made a small unintended movement, as if to kiss her. She kept her face upturned, waiting, and John bent to kiss her with his full, soft lips. He led her by the hand to the sofa, where between many more kisses, they shared each other's story.

Henrietta learned she had no rival for John's heart, that he was a boy taken from his childhood home to sing in the Chapel Royal Choir and had few family ties. Henrietta told John about her dead husband, her young child left behind in Paris, the neglect she had suffered from the Herbert family, her rejection by her father. She couldn't find the words to talk about her grandparents, because that relationship felt unfinished and shameful.

In the months before the new theatre season began in September, John and Henrietta met every few days. He divided his time between his two employers, Charles Fleetwood at Drury Lane and George Frederic Handel at the King's Theatre, for singing lessons, rehearsals and work with Handel on new oratorio, but despite this demanding schedule, John spent every spare moment with Henrietta.

Music lessons were abandoned, each kiss followed by searching looks into each other's eyes, barely able to hide their desire. When John dropped to his knees to declare his love for her, it seemed inevitable when his hands found her ankles and strayed beneath her petticoat to trace the skin on her calves and inner thighs. Henrietta lay back on the sofa and welcomed him, desire and love igniting together in her body for the first time. His need for her was something he couldn't hide and she only wanted more and more of him, a young, strong man, smelling of earth and tasting of salt. Allowing her body to rise to his touch was as simple as breathing.

In early September, as Henrietta waited for John, dreamily tapping the keys on her spinet, Amelia knocked on the door. Lady Byron pushed past her into the music room and Harriet jumped, as if caught by an angry wife in adultery with a straying husband. Frances still wore her cloak and gloves, signalling her intention not to stay and refused Henrietta's offer of a chair. It was certain this was not an invitation to the next meeting of the Foundling Hospital working group.

'People are talking, Lady Herbert,' Frances said, without any courteous preamble. 'I hear that John Beard visits you almost every day and remains for too long. I understand you have no chaperone.'

This is no one's business but mine, Henrietta thought but said, 'Our time is spent innocently. John is teaching me to play the spinet. You recommended him for music lessons.'

Frances' reply came, guttural with scorn. 'It was a joke, Henrietta, not an instruction. Drop this liaison now, or you will find yourself exiled from decent society. I have informed your uncle, who will let your grandparents know. This is a respectable neighbourhood.'

'I do have a chaperone,' Henrietta stammered.

'Don't be ridiculous,' Frances snorted. 'That rude girl, the one who let me in? You must stop this or marry him at once. The choice is yours.' Lady Byron's lips twisted in disdain. 'I'm sure you understand, Lady Herbert, there is no longer a place for you on the Foundling Hospital committee. Our job is to deal with weak women with no morals. We must set an example.'

After Lady Byron swept from the room, Amelia scurrying behind, Henrietta dropped onto the music stool, aware of the Webb ancestors scowling at her from the walls. She was trembling, but with resentment and rage, rather than shame. As she waited for John, she thought of all the clever, scathing things she should have said to Frances Byron, a woman who suppressed her sexual desire into petty committee work and card games. When he arrived, John kissed her but pulled away, as if through his arms he sensed her tension.

His eyes scanned her face. 'What has happened, Henrietta?' he asked. 'Have I done something wrong?'

'I've been foolish,' Henrietta replied, 'believing we could keep this secret. Lady Byron has recently left, threatening me with telling my family about us.'

John flopped onto a sofa and pulled her onto his knee. She smelt his familiar odour of theatre changing rooms and the soap he used to shave.

'What can I do to put this right?' he asked.

'We must marry,' she said, 'as soon as a wedding can be arranged.'

It could not have been a coincidence that her younger brother was shown into the parlour after dinner, without prior arrangement or an invitation. Had he not been announced by the butler, Henrietta would not have recognised him. Johnny bristled with indignation, a posture which was laughable in a man so young, almost a boy.

'You have disgraced our family,' he shouted, without sitting down. 'You disgust me.'

Henrietta remained standing, even though her legs were trembling. 'I don't have any family, apart from our grandparents. My father has made that clear. How I choose to behave is my choice, my responsibility. I am a widow.'

'Yes and a merry one too, from what I've heard. You've lost any chance of a respectable marriage, Henrietta. You are the talk of London.'

'John Beard and I intend to marry, that will stop any gossip. Very soon, my behaviour will be forgotten.'

Her brother laughed, his voice a juvenile sneer. 'You'll marry for pleasure, my dear sister, your heart led by your groin, but will spend a lifetime of regret, tying yourself to a man so beneath your status.'

'It is my turn to be disgusted by you, little brother. I fear you know nothing of pleasure, whether in the groin or anywhere else. Now go from this house and never return. This is a Webb property and you are not welcome.'

After Waldegrave slammed his way out of the front door and the sound of his departing carriage rattled the open shutters, Amelia joined Henrietta in the parlour, pretending to light lamps for the evening.

'I thought you might want to talk,' she said, 'instead of sitting here in the dark. I was listening at the door. I heard what he said.'

'Did you know that everyone was watching me, what the gossips were saying? It seems as if I'm guilty of some transgression I wasn't even aware of.'

Amelia hesitated before replying. 'There was talk

downstairs, but then, there always is. I'm sorry, I should have paid more attention and warned you.'

'Do you think I've been wrong to find love with John Beard?'

'Not at all,' Amelia said, 'but I don't know how this society works. Neither of us do. How could we learn, since we were kept apart from all of that? Are you really going to marry John Beard?'

Henrietta nodded. 'As soon as we can find a priest, but that will be difficult. In a few weeks, John will be rushing from performance to performance, with no time to arrange a wedding. I can't see how it can be made to happen soon, but it must, if only to stop London society prying into my business.'

Amelia sat down, her hand resting on Henrietta's shoulder, her eyes creased with telltale humour.

'What's so funny, Amelia?' Henrietta snapped. 'This isn't a joke.'

'If you marry him, you'll become Mrs Beard.'

Henrietta pushed at her friend's shoulder. 'Don't laugh about this, Amelia. If we do manage to marry, I expect to be known as Lady Henrietta Beard but if I become as poor and low in status as my brother predicts, how on earth will I afford *you*.'

Amelia frowned, her lips downturned. 'Hensy, that's not funny either.'

The next morning, Henrietta eased open the wooden blinds and tugged back the drapes covering the music room window. A carriage bearing the Webb coat of arms drew up outside and a man dressed in black climbed down from the postilion's bench, drawing a letter from inside his cape.

Henrietta selected a high-backed wooden chair and waited, her hands resting in her lap, certain of what would come next.

The butler carried her grandfather's letter into the room on a silver platter and waited for a response, staring over her shoulder at a distant point beyond the window.

'Please ask Mademoiselle Laurent to join me,' she asked him. 'How long do we have?'

'You must leave in half an hour,' the butler said, his expression blank, as if throwing a woman out of her home was an everyday experience.

Amelia arrived, her face mottled with pink blotches and they crushed together into one of her uncle's generous armchairs to study Lord Webb's judgement. Her uncle needed to repossess the house, they read, but his family did not feel able to do so while Henrietta and her maidservant remained. They must leave immediately, using the carriage provided, and would be taken to a relative's house in Holborn.

If Henrietta insisted on marrying John Beard, the letter continued, where she chose to live would be the responsibility of her husband. Barbara must remain in Paris, even if she remarried, and the child's great-grandparents would continue as her legal guardians. Henrietta must have no further contact with her grandparents or her daughter. Mademoiselle Laurent should decide whether to stay or leave but would be welcome to return to the Webb household in Paris.

'What do you think, Amelia?' Henrietta asked, folding up the letter.

Amelia chewed her bottom lip, fighting tears. 'What choice do we have? We must start packing... right now. I'm getting a little tired of being thrown out of other people's houses, at such short notice.'

'Yes, me too,' Henrietta said, 'but once I'm married, John and I will have a home of our own. No one will dare to toss me aside then.'

'Yesterday you said you couldn't afford to employ me. Should I go back to Paris, return to my mother?'

'I'm sorry, Amelia, I shouldn't have made that cruel joke. John Beard is well paid and always in demand. He may not have a title but what's the point of that, if the title brings no money. You will always have a place at my side, if that's what you want. The choice is yours, Amelia, but for now,' Henrietta scanned the letter to check for their new address, 'let's head off to Red Lion Square in Holborn.'

CHAPTER 18

1739

The year Henrietta turned twenty-two, there had been no marriage to John but she didn't care. At last, she was living a different life, one that was right for her. Every day, from wherever he was playing, John sent a carriage and she spent all of her time at the theatre, whether it was the afternoon or the evening, watching him rehearse or perform.

After the last performance, there was always a party, the actors fired up and buzzing with unspent energy. She learned to drink beer and wine, enjoying the company of John's circle, men and women who laughed raucously. These friends teased each other, wore their hair loose and shirts or bodices unbuttoned. After sharp-eyed scrutiny from actresses who resented losing the attention of a man who may have been their lover, she was accepted and included.

Her relative, the lawyer Edward Webb, had chambers in Gray's Inn, close to his new home in Red Lion Square and was an easy-going bachelor who paid little attention to Henrietta or Amelia.

What had escaped her grandfather, in his pathetic attempt to control her from Paris, was that John Beard had a home of his own, only a few streets from Red Lion Square, allowing Henrietta to sleep there overnight whenever she chose.

Thoughts of her grandparents led to feelings of shame and a reluctant acceptance that her behaviour defied everything society expected from a woman of her class. She tried to block such thoughts, to wipe them from her memory. If she ever considered her daughter, it was only to marvel that actors could enter an imaginary world, just like Barbara did, as if they were still children.

Henrietta hated the dark mornings of early January and found great comfort in waking to John's warmth and generous bulk, her unfocused anxiety soothed by the rhythm of his sonorous breathing. This morning, he rolled over and scooped her towards his chest, kissing her hair. 'We mustn't forget to marry,' he murmured.

It seemed too early to be having such a conversation and Henrietta struggled to understand. 'Does it matter?' she whispered.

'I think it does. My friends may not care but my employers, my benefactors, mix with people who pretend to be scandalised by us. If a peer of the realm has an actress for a mistress, nobody cares but when Lady Henrietta Herbert takes an actor for a lover, it's not acceptable. I can't risk losing my position.'

This was fair. John's reputation as England's most admired tenor was beyond argument. Henrietta eased out from under John and rested on her elbow, trying to gauge her lover's mood. His expression was invisible but his pupils reflected a faint glimmer of light from the window, suggesting his eyes were damp.

'But, John,' she said, 'we have to find a priest willing to marry us and they will have heard the rumours too.'

'I might have found a solution. Have you heard of the Fleet Prison?'

'We'll marry in a prison?'

'You sound aghast, Henrietta, and I'm not surprised. If only it weren't so, but I'm told the marriages are legal, conducted by clergy who have been imprisoned there for debt. A wedding has to happen soon, before Handel is pressurised by his aristocratic friends to drop me. At the Fleet, there is no need for banns or a marriage licence.'

'It won't be a Catholic wedding?'

Henrietta felt John's head rock against the pillow. 'I'm afraid not, my darling, but we will have a marriage certificate. That's all that matters.'

They married the next day, only a week after her birthday, the ceremony squeezed in between John's morning rehearsal for Handel's new oratorio, *Saul*, and his evening pantomime at Drury Lane theatre. A carriage took them to Fleet Street but they walked its length to find the Fountain Tavern, where they would be married. Low shopfronts were hung with rough signs, painted to depict the hands of a man and woman joined together.

Men dressed as priests, with filthy surplices, leered as they passed, inviting them to enter within and marry. These false priests charged less than one guinea and Henrietta guessed that most would have settled for a bottle of gin. Right in front of them, a man carried a girl half his age into one of the shops, her drunken head lolling, her stays unlaced. Henrietta would have run, had John not tightly gripped her hand.

'We cannot marry here,' she whispered. 'These places exist so that men can exploit women. It's a trick. How could you have brought me to this place?'

John shook his head, scanning the street, a place riddled

with drunkenness and debauchery. 'I didn't know this was here and wish you hadn't seen it. An industry has grown up around the prison's reputation, and I can see it is replete with vice but we are marrying in the tavern, not in one of these squalid caves. I can promise you, Henrietta, the ceremony will be conducted by a legitimate member of the clergy.'

John drew a timepiece from his pocket. 'We must hurry. It's already four and I've to be back at six for the performance.'

They approached the only passerby who appeared sober, asking for directions to the tavern. In a dark room at the back of The Fountain, Henrietta stood next to John, facing an elderly reverend, who draped his silk stole over their joined hands and mumbled his way through the marriage vows. Her mind drifted to another tavern, a different back room, drinking beer and eating oysters with Edward Herbert, a lifetime ago.

Then, inexplicably, she thought of her father, imagining his scorn as his daughter abandoned her faith after all, in a place such as this. The only witness was the clerk and registrar, whose humble but dignified presence comforted her. Signing the register afterwards, her name next to John's, she felt reassured. This was a real wedding. She was married to John Beard and they would live a good life.

The following morning, Henrietta walked with Amelia to the garden at the centre of Red Lion Square. It was bitterly cold, their breath drifting in the remnants of the night's fog. Nothing moved amongst the bare branches of the garden's newly planted trees but sounds of carts, of working men's voices, rang out from the street, as if close by.

Her companion, her maidservant, her friend, had been neglected, left to occupy herself for most of the day and for many nights since they had been forced to live with Edward Webb. Amelia resided in his house as Henrietta lady's maid but her mistress was absent more than she was present and Edward did not want, or need, another servant.

Now Henrietta and John had married, without a word of warning, Amelia would be angry with her and rightly so. They would move permanently to John's house in New North Street but without any consideration of her loyal companion's future. In truth, Henrietta had no idea whether they could afford the luxury of a lady's maid.

Amelia chattered as they walked, as if nothing was wrong, sharing a story with Henrietta about armed lawyers fighting with the builders of Red Lion Square, to prevent a development so near to the Inns of Court. The railings around the square where they walked prevented farmers, evicted from this very land, returning to graze their sheep and rebuild their hovels.

Amelia is nervous, thought Henrietta, as her friend chattered. *We both are.* Avoiding the single, pressing topic that ought to be aired, she asked, 'Where have you learned such interesting stories?'

Amelia stopped walking and stared hard at Henrietta, her expression defying her friend to take issue with what she was about to reveal. 'Your cousin, if that is what he is, talks to me in the evenings, after we've had dinner,' she said. 'He likes my company.'

Henrietta paused, taking great care with her next words. 'Amelia, are you and Edward becoming close?'

Amelia glanced at the bushes by her side, her heavy brows knitted. 'I have something to confess. We are to be married.'

'You're marrying?' Henrietta gasped. She led Amelia by the hand to sit side by side on a nearby bench, feeling as cold as ice, despite her warm cloak. 'You hardly know him. As you have advised me many times, you are a young woman, you have choices.'

'It hasn't been the same for me, not from the first day you met John Beard,' Amelia replied. 'Since we moved out here, I never see you. You have no need of a companion now you have John and you don't need a lady's maid either. You are managing for yourself, although perhaps not all that well.'

They both glanced down at Henrietta's robe, hidden underneath her cloak, searching for somewhere to look, rather than face each other.

'Why didn't you tell me?' Henrietta protested. 'I can't believe this.'

Amelia sighed, her exhaled breath the only sound in the empty gardens. 'I don't want to go back to Paris, when you marry John. Edward works so hard, he's never been able to find a wife and I suppose he... finding me in his house and liking what he saw... he took his chance. He's funny and kind. Accepting his proposal is right for me.'

Henrietta hesitated, frightened that her fear for Amelia, risking a loveless marriage, would find a voice in anger. She breathed several times into her gloved hands, pretending to warm them, aware of her friend's face, wretched with anxiety, turned towards her.

'I haven't heard you speak a word about loving him,' she said.

'Hensy, it is a good marriage, the best I can hope for. You have found love with John, but for most women, that rarely happens. I will make sure I'm useful to Edward in his work and will do my best to be a loving wife. He will treat me well, I'm sure of it.'

An image of John came to Henrietta, fresh from this morning's embrace, his scratchy beard, his familiar, comforting smell. They were married, she had a new husband, one who loved her, had chosen her. She must find, somewhere deep within her selfish heart, a way to be generous.

'I also have some news,' Henrietta said. 'Yesterday, I married John. I'm sorry I couldn't tell you, but it was very sudden for me too. There were no guests.'

She reached for her friend and drew her into an embrace. Amelia did not resist, allowing herself to be held. 'Of course you must marry Edward,' Henrietta whispered. 'I am so sorry to have neglected you. I've taken you for granted. Thank you for choosing to marry into my family. We will not be strangers, Mrs Webb.'

News of Henrietta and John's wedding was reported in several newspapers, given her husband's fame, but no one – not her grandparents or her father – wrote to acknowledge her new position as a married woman. Once they became a boring, married couple, society gossip moved on to find other salacious miscreants, exactly as John had hoped.

Henrietta settled into her home in New North Street, using her experience from Hendon to take charge of the household servants, a surly group used to the relaxed regime of a single man who was rarely at home. This led to disagreements with the cook and the housekeeper, but if Granny Webb was no longer present in her life, her tone and manner lived on in Henrietta.

The houses in these newly built streets, each one identical, were soundly constructed, with attractive keystones over the windows, servants' quarters in the basement and light, spacious rooms on the floors above. Henrietta loved to walk through her neighbourhood, enjoying the regularity of the doors, the porches, the chimneys, each house quite indifferent to the social status of the human beings hidden beyond the front door. The local residents were artists, merchants and lawyers and Henrietta and John's disparate backgrounds meant nothing. They were accepted as a couple, without judgement, and entertained freely, seeing much of Edward and Amelia, who had married in the only way open to practising Catholics, a ceremony at home led by a priest, with John and Henrietta the only guests.

Marriage did not change her lifestyle. Henrietta spent all her days and evenings with John, watching him perform and celebrating with the cast afterwards.

Only gradually did she become aware that her husband was too quick to settle the account at whatever tavern or ale house the company had chosen for their party. She did not challenge him, knowing how much John needed to be the hospitable heart of the evening's fun. In turn, he did not question her pride in her appearance, encouraging her to spend on dressmakers, complimenting each new robe, her newly styled hair or headdress. John enjoyed seeing her feet and ankles in exquisite, handmade shoes but he was ignorant of how much her master shoemaker charged.

As a married woman, she had no idea how much John earned, and never questioned whether the Marquess of Powis was paying her jointure, since this now passed directly to John. She simply trusted there was enough.

The inevitable day came when regular suppliers and merchants began to refuse Henrietta's business. The best place for difficult conversations was in bed, after they had enjoyed each other's bodies, and were lying side by side, content with a deep sense of well-being and good fortune. Early one morning, in late October, Henrietta eased herself from under John, collapsed in satisfied exhaustion.

'We're spending too much,' she whispered in his ear. 'We

can't pay our accounts. The dressmaker refused to make anything more for me, until I've settled up.'

John snorted and moved his head to rest on her chest, where he could breathe more easily. 'I'll ask for more money,' he muttered.

'What about my widow's jointure, from my ex-husband's father? Is it being paid?'

John rolled onto his back and linked his fingers beneath his head. 'I haven't checked. I'm a singer, Henrietta. It's what I do best. What if you took charge of our money? We can always pretend it's me making the decisions, since that's what's expected.'

'If it helps, I will,' Henrietta replied, propping herself up on her elbow. 'Do you have a singing lesson, or any students, this morning?'

John shook his head. 'I'm free until this afternoon.'

'After we've eaten breakfast, we'll sit down with our accounts. We need to balance what's coming in against what's going out, and set some limits on our spending.'

John groaned and closed his eyes. 'It sounds as if you're going to enjoy this.'

This was true, Henrietta thought. Managing their finances would suit her. 'Yes,' she agreed, 'I think I will, as long as it's not already a disaster. After being a member of the Herbert family, I fear the uncertainty of debt.'

John fell silent and for a moment, she thought he had dropped back to sleep. 'Since we're speaking honestly,' he said, his voice so quiet she struggled to hear, 'I don't think I can keep up this pace for much longer. I'm weary. If we're not too much in debt, do you think it might be possible to cut back on my engagements? It wouldn't be for long, you know I live for my voice, but perhaps we might soon inherit something from your father, or we could ask Edward Webb to chase up your jointure, just to tide us over.'

Her strong, talented husband, at the peak of his career, wanted to take a break? Many thoughts came, so tangled, she couldn't begin to form a reply. If John left his singing roles, other men would easily be found to replace him. Her father may well leave her a little money, if he did not recover from his recent illness, but John had no idea how broken her relationship was with the Earl. Had he even been listening, during the many, many times she had explained this. And why wasn't he checking whether her jointure had been paid, if it was so essential to their future?

Finding no other way to deal with her frustration, she tried to joke. 'So, John Beard, you thought you were marrying a rich heiress? The truth is out: your ambition is to be a kept man.'

John must have heard the snag in her voice, because he didn't laugh. He swung his legs over the side of the bed and stood to pull down his night shirt. 'Not at all, Henrietta. The truth only became clear to me as I spoke. I feel exhausted and if I am expected to sing for the rest of my life, I may need to pause. You are right, we should check our finances and if it's possible for me to rest, I'd like to take the chance.'

'But your career, John, you can't throw it away!' Henrietta argued. 'If audiences don't see your face, they'll forget about you.'

John sighed and sat down again on the edge of the bed, angling his body to face her. 'If I continue as I am, I may have no career.'

The household stirred and Henrietta listened to sounds from below. Soon a servant would bring lit coals to start their fire, followed by another with hot water and cloths. She stepped across the bare floorboards to the window and eased back the heavy drapes. The sky was lightening over the rooftops opposite, the street below already busy with merchant's carts.

She felt a wash of loneliness, missing Amelia. How simple it would be to talk over this dilemma during her toilette and later, bring a proper, well thought out answer to her husband. Right now, all she wanted was a row. This was the first test of their relationship, one that had always seemed light and easy. If she made a mistake, it would hang like a pall over the rest of their marriage.

Henrietta turned back to face the room and smiled at John, who lifted his eyebrows.

'Of course you must take a break from your ridiculous pace,' she said. 'Let's work out the money situation and check the agreements you're already committed to for next year. A complete break might be something we have to work towards, in small steps, but if you need some time off, you must have it. I'm afraid we can't count on my father for any help but we should definitely chase the Marquess of Powis, if he's not paying what I'm owed.'

John's shoulders relaxed. 'I knew I could count on you, my darling wife. Now, come back to bed.' He patted the sheet next to him. 'I think there's enough time before the day begins.'

CHAPTER 19
1740

Name: Lady Barbara Herbert

Age: 5

Class: 1

Guardian: Sir John Webb, Paris

Father: Lord Edward Herbert (deceased)

Mother: Lady Henrietta Beard, London

By signing this form, parents/guardians agree to send their child with the correct uniform and clothing as identified in the attached list. Fees must be paid in advance of each term. No arrangements can be made for late payment. Parents/guardians must take note of school holidays, as specified on the list of term dates. The nuns of St Augustine's Convent are unable to look after any child who is not collected. They will be removed to the neighbouring poor house, also managed by the convent.

Henrietta signed the form, tossing down the quill in front of the Abbess, who was Edward Herbert's aunt Lucy, in a manner that must look like petulance but in fact was a mess of other emotions, the most awful being her deep shame.

Adele screaming and clinging to Barbara in the nursery, the child's face, frozen and pale when she had been left behind in her dormitory, and now this tall woman with her severe, lined face, so obviously disapproving.

'A favour to the family,' she had sniffed. 'We don't usually take boarders until they are seven.' This was the famous Aunt Lucy, a woman with a reputation for fierce intelligence but also kindness, a woman Alice had spoken about with admiration during their long journey from Hendon Manor to Paris. Henrietta hated her on sight, sensing judgement for placing a child so young into the convent's boarding school.

The day Granny Webb died, her Uncle John's servant banged on their door well before dawn, the coach already waiting. Her husband stood in his night shirt, bare feet set wide apart on the freezing tiles, as he wrapped a warm cloak around her. Henrietta refused John's insistence to come with her, knowing he was committed that night to a sold-out performance at Drury Lane.

She begged her uncle for a chance to wake Amelia, to bring her with them but he argued there wasn't time, if she wanted to see her grandmother alive. Throughout the journey he maintained a menacing silence made more frightening by his sneer, whenever the jolting of the carriage forced him to look at her. She longed for her friend, someone who had loved Granny Webb almost as much as she had.

They reached Paris in time to witness Granny Webb's final breath. Already, the grandmother she remembered was no longer present. Instead, only an aged face, mouth wide open, making embarrassing, gurgling sounds.

Amelia's mother encouraged her to hold Lady Webb's hand, to try some words and there had indeed been an imperceptible squeeze in response. At this remarkable sign of forgiveness, every emotion she had tried to suppress tumbled out; tears, explanations, regrets, declarations of love, until she rested her head on her grandmother's chest, exhausted. Then she felt a hand stroke her ear, before it fell away onto the mattress, heavy in death.

Ragged with exhaustion and her fresh grief, she stumbled into a dreadful row with her grandfather. He shouted at her across Granny Webb's still warm body, his bloodshot eyes brimming with tears.

'You will take your daughter home with you,' he bellowed. 'I cannot look after a child on my own.'

'You never go near Barbara as it is,' Henrietta yelled back. 'How does your wife's death make any difference? Keep Adele in your employ and the child will be cared for exactly as she is now.'

Grandpa Webb shook his head and lowered his voice, his tone hissing with venom. 'I cannot understand why you won't take the child, Henrietta. She is your daughter. Since you took up with this, this... singer, I no longer recognise you.'

'The singer, as you refer to him, is the most talented man of his generation in London. He earns more in a year than the entire Herbert household have seen in a lifetime, yet you were more than keen to palm me off on them. John and I have chosen a life that will not accommodate a child. He shares his days between clients, in different theatres, and I am always with him. I trusted that Barbara would be safe and happy here, for all of her childhood.'

It was easier to fight back, to pretend she truly had a choice rather than admit that despite John's success, there was no money to support a child.

'It is you who does not understand, Henrietta. I spend much of my time in Rome and I cannot leave the child alone, without a family member present. You stretch my already thin patience if you think I will support you and your husband's self-indulgent lifestyle.'

Henrietta tried to laugh but the sound she made was harsh, mocking. 'Ha! Of course you spend all your time in Rome. I wonder why that is?'

Grandpa Webb stared at her with disgust. 'I hope you do not mean that, Henrietta. Lust has driven you mad. I have heard this from your brothers. Do not assume that everyone is driven by the demands of the flesh, like you.'

Henrietta cruelly mimicked her grandfather's words. '*Demands of the flesh*,' she repeated. 'You sound like our priest. I am a married woman and will not tolerate such vile accusations.'

Madame Laurent stared with horror at each twisted, angry face and interrupted their argument, her own voice raised. 'Enough! Have some respect for the recently departed. Her soul may still be in this room!'

Both fell silent, shocked at the thought that Granny Webb might be listening. Henrietta spoke first. 'So what is the solution, Grandfather, since we will never agree.'

Grandpa Webb wiped a hand across his face, dragging at his lips, and shook his head. 'I had expected this, Henrietta, although I prayed that your mothering instinct would reveal itself in time. I regret I was mistaken in this hope. You will send Barbara to the Convent of St Augustine in Bruges, where your first husband's aunt is the Abbess. If it helps, I will pay the fees, since the child is my ward.'

That night, Madame Laurent sought Henrietta in her

bedchamber. She leaned back against the closed door, her arms folded across her chest. 'I have laid out Lady Webb's body. You may wish to see her, since I understand you are not taking part in the funeral mass and will not be expected to remain for the burial.'

Henrietta followed behind Amelia's mother and in the light from a single candle, she stared at a parody of Granny Webb, a woman whose expression was never still, her eyes always dancing. There were no violets here. She inched towards the body and bending to kiss her grandmother's brow, quickly drew back from the chilled, waxen texture against her lips.

'Madame Laurent,' she said, turning towards the housekeeper. 'I am sure you are concerned about Amelia but she is well, happily married and sends her best wishes. Please bring some writing paper and ink to my room, whenever you are free.'

Madame Laurent permitted the briefest smile. 'Thank you, Lady Beard. I would have asked about my daughter but I feared intruding on your grief. You should know how sad I am that you are no longer part of this family.'

That night, her candle burning low, Henrietta scratched out a letter to her father. It was the perfect opportunity to try and restore their relationship, since he was in Paris, beyond the malign influence of her brothers. His health was failing and given the chance, he might wish for a reconciliation with her, his only daughter, a woman who was reputed to look so like his dear wife.

What did the Catholic faith mean to her now, if abandoning it meant they could find some common ground before he died? Granny Webb had exerted the strongest influence on her to keep the faith of her birth, but she was gone and Henrietta had already been married by an Anglican priest.

These were not the words she wrote. Instead, she pleaded

her father's forgiveness for sins she did not repent and believed required no forgiveness, but this was not the moment to argue. After blotting her words, she added a postscript begging for a meeting before she left Paris.

Henrietta remained in the Webb apartments, delaying her return to London to wait for a reply from her father. Avoiding her grandfather and Uncle John, who stayed closeted together in Lord Webb's study, every morning she scanned the silver platter on the hall table. No letter arrived for her, amongst the many messages of condolence for her grandfather. The strain of eating alone, the hushed rooms and corridors, the hollow absence of Granny Webb, all became intolerable. She decided to leave at once and return to the only place where she was loved, the only place where her grandmother had never existed.

The Webb carriage took Henrietta to Calais, accompanied by a footman as escort. She would be met at Dover by a new carriage with a different escort, sent by John.

After their conversation last autumn, John had found it impossible to interrupt his remaining responsibilities before Christmas but since Charles Fleetwood had been persuaded to release John through the easier months of January and February, his schedule had been less frenetic. Henrietta learned it was possible to live frugally on what John could earn as a freelance singer but he still dreamed about stopping work altogether at the end of May. She hoped her husband might see the sense in accepting only the engagements he enjoyed, rather than withdrawing from the stage altogether. She imagined Granny Webb's scorn, had she known about Henrietta's husband failing in his duties to maintain his wife, a man she already disapproved of because he didn't have a title.

Watching the French shoreline become a dark smudge on the horizon, Henrietta tossed aside the hood of her travelling cape and allowed the breeze to tug strands of hair from her pins.

The shock of her grandmother's death crushed her anew, as if she had only just heard the news. Bending forward, she clutched the ship's rail, weeping freely into her elbow. When her throat and chest could find no more tears, Henrietta raised herself and used a handkerchief to wipe her eyes. Feeling her grandmother close, she acknowledged her own unwelcome feelings about John's decision, how every day she fought with her resentment. Yet his schedule for the coming months *was* impossible, tearing across the city from one theatre to another, barely in time to drag on a costume and rush onto the stage at the very moment he was expected to sing. It couldn't go on.

A man came to stand at her side. She turned towards him, her first instinct to be welcoming but she immediately regretted her smile.

He placed a hand on her arm and eased himself closer. She could smell brandy on his breath. 'I saw you were distressed.' He asked, 'Do you need any help?'

Henrietta shook her head, sliding her arm out from under his hand. 'I'm fine, thank you. My husband is meeting me in Dover.'

The stranger draped his arm loosely across her shoulder. 'It's cold out here. Why don't we go to my cabin for a drink?'

Henrietta snatched at the folds of her cape and the sudden movement forced his arm from her back. Lifting her hood, she glowered at this man and his delusion that a woman, any woman, would enjoy his intrusion.

'I am expected in the captain's cabin,' she said, struggling to remain polite. 'My grandfather, Sir John Webb, has arranged for me to be chaperoned there.'

The man leaned both arms on the rail and laughed. 'The captain's a lucky man,' he said, giving her a wink.

The housemaid crashed serving plates onto the sideboard, intending to show her displeasure that her master and mistress were breakfasting late again, but Henrietta pretended not to notice and the maid left the room with the empty platters, making sure to slam the door behind her.

Henrietta tossed her letter onto the table and said aloud, 'That's no surprise.'

John looked up from his bread and eggs, lifting his eyebrows in curiosity but still too busy chewing to speak.

'I was talking to my grandfather,' Henrietta said. 'He's married again and can't have Barbara for the school holidays.'

John swallowed and took a draught of ale. 'That's sudden. Your grandmother can't have been dead two months.'

Henrietta rolled her eyes. 'Not so sudden if you remember he's been meeting a woman for years, probably in Rome.'

John wiped the corner of his mouth with a napkin. 'Who is she?'

'Her name is Helen Moore... much too young for him of course. He's seventy, for heaven's sake.'

'If he met her in Rome, then she's likely to be a Jacobite.'

Henrietta weighted her tone with resigned patience. 'That's hardly the most important thing, is it, John? We have to find someone to look after Barbara in the summer, since Helen is apparently too precious to care for a child.'

'Actually, the Jacobite thing is important. Remember that Handel is the royal composer and the king isn't keen on Jacobites. He asked me about it the other day, about your loyalties. I was able to reassure him, of course, but was a bit taken aback by his line of questioning.'

Henrietta frowned. 'He has a nerve, asking you about my politics, my loyalty to the king. But what should we do about Barbara? I need to let my grandfather know.'

'We will look after her ourselves,' John said, throwing down his napkin. 'Now that I've stopped working, what's to stop us going over to France for the summer. It's time I met your daughter.'

'That's all very well,' Henrietta said, enunciating her words carefully to mask her frustration. Why did he never think things through? 'I'm delighted you're keen to meet Barbara but where will we find the money for a jaunt to France for eight weeks? We'll have to find accommodation in Lille... I'm not staying in Paris with my grandfather and *her*. Anyway, we wouldn't be welcome.'

The effort to save money due to John's absence from the stage, had made her irritable. Being cold, hungry and pregnant through the winter at Hendon was a hateful memory. She eked out what little they had to cover their costs but wasn't ready to allow money to dominate her life for a second time. On the other hand, John had reined in his spending and enjoyed being frugal, setting himself daily challenges to save money and boasting about these in a manner that was annoying.

The solution to their dilemma came from Granny Webb. A few days later, Henrietta wept with gratitude and relief when their solicitor and friend Edward Webb travelled the few streets between their homes to bring the news that Lady Barbara Webb had left her one hundred pounds in her will. It was a fortune, one that would cover all their expenses in Lille and would allow Henrietta to pay enough of her dressmaker's account so that he would agree make her a new robe, one that would not disgrace her in front of royalty.

On the eighth of May, she was to accompany John to the wedding of Princess Mary, the king's fourth daughter, where he had been invited to sing. This was one performance he could not refuse.

Listening to her husband's magnificent voice, Henrietta's temper flared at the waste of his talent. Why was he giving up, instead of simply choosing contracts with greater care? He had cheerfully handed over responsibility to her for managing their finances yet had never given a satisfactory explanation for his withdrawal from the theatre, their only reliable source of income. John had been overspending for years, despite his recent efforts and she had no natural instinct for saving. Without the income owed from her jointure, their finances were a mess.

In Lille, they found simple rooms on the second floor of a tall, narrow redbrick town house in the parish of Saint-Andre, its regular street plan reminding her of their neighbourhood in London.

John's energy and cheerful nature made him a natural playmate for her daughter but being with the child every day troubled Henrietta. It was like watching two puppies romp together in perpetual activity. Barbara and John shared a natural language and understanding, which they easily communicated to each other but excluded her. She did her share of childcare, putting Barbara to bed at night and reading her stories, but the child's obvious preference for John was a daily reminder that she was a useless mother.

Barbara lived in the present, unaware of time passing and her inevitable return to St Augustine's but from the little she said about the school, Henrietta could tell the child was unhappy. There was mention of smacking by nuns and a girl who had taken her doll, but nothing about friends, or even schoolwork. When asked to tell them about her school day, Barbara spread her hands in a resigned gesture and said, 'Bells, bells, bells, pray, pray, pray,' which made John roar with laughter. The person the child spoke of most was Adele, always asking when her nurse would come for her.

John never suggested they should take Barbara home. This was strange, given the fun he had with the child but if he had asked her, she might have agreed out of a sense of obligation, when she really wanted to refuse. It was best to leave this dilemma unspoken.

Instead, Henrietta wrote to her grandfather, laying out her terms. It wasn't that she didn't care for the child, she drafted, but other people were better placed to do this. Her husband would soon return to the stage, so frequent travel abroad would be impossible, particularly with the uncertainty over war with France. With regret, they would not be available to cover any future school holidays. The child should be with her nursemaid Adele, who could easily be employed to cover those weeks when Barbara was at home. Since Lord Webb remained the child's guardian and legally responsible for her, this arrangement would surely not inconvenience him or his new wife.

Taking the child back to St Augustine's was worse than Henrietta's memory of her little brother screaming, the day he learned of his mother's death. Barbara had to be dragged from John's arms and carried bodily into the convent by a grim faced nun, the echo of her cries drifting back to them from beyond the heavy door that gave access to the school.

The Abbess, Edward's aunt, had recently died and Henrietta was glad they didn't have to face her disapproval. They stood together, frozen, in the reception area of the convent, a statue of St Augustine herself smiling down at them with an expression that said, don't make a fuss, just go, the child will settle. There was no choice but to leave, John crying, and Henrietta furious with everyone who had put her in this ghastly situation. If only John had found the courage to say, 'let's take the child home', she might have agreed and then if things went wrong, it would be his fault. For once, she wouldn't have to carry all the blame.

Before they left Lille, energised by resentment, she wrote again to her father, suggesting he should try to meet her husband and his granddaughter, before it was too late. She made sure her London address was clearly visible and underlined. As a postscript, furious that dishonesty was necessary, she again begged his forgiveness.

It was a relief to be back in London but without John's career, their days were aimless. Money was so tight, they had to release household staff apart from the cook and one housemaid and it felt strange to visit Amelia, comfortably managing a large staff and so distracted by visits from neighbours and clients, she barely had time to sit in her own parlour for even half an hour. Henrietta keenly felt the difference in their financial circumstances and rarely issued an invitation for her friend to join her for chocolate or coffee at New North Street. Their lives were no longer entwined, their paths too separate, so there was little to share. Henrietta sensed disapproval of her decisions about Barbara and the awkwardness of owing Edward Webb so much money, made it easier to avoid Amelia. This wasn't a decision made by Henrietta but more the drift of inaction.

One evening, after dinner, John told Henrietta that Handel had been in touch. 'He's going to Ireland for the autumn and winter season and wanted me to come with him. We were rehearsing his new work *Messiah* before I left for Lille, but now he'll have to ask someone else to sing for the premiere in Dublin. I'm sure there are great tenors in Ireland but it's disappointing. The work was written for me.'

'Oh, John!' Henrietta allowed her hands to flop into her lap, the back of one hand slapping into the palm of the other. 'Why can't you go with him? Surely it makes sense.'

'I can't, Henrietta, I need to stay here with you, help with our money troubles, be beside you when your father dies. I don't want you to face these things alone. I don't want to be like him... like Edward Herbert.'

'But you would be earning money in Dublin, a lot of money. That would be the greatest help for us.'

John's mouth set into a stubborn line and his open, warm face shuttered, freezing her out. 'When did our lives become all about money, Henrietta?' he whispered, his eyes narrowing. 'My mind is made up. I will return to work when I'm ready. Anyway, I'm glad to have a break from Handel, he's not easy to work with.'

'I thought he liked you,' Henrietta said. 'You're his favourite tenor.'

'He might like me,' John replied, 'but I don't like him, so the matter is closed.'

Henrietta did not dare to test John further. Her habitual restraint had allowed them to float across many fissures in their relationship but he was acting like a man she hardly knew, his lack of direction, his hesitancy about decisions. She was scared by how close she had come to angering John but at last, he had admitted to hidden fears about behaving like her first husband through abandoning her for work.

Tomorrow, she would take the practical step to see what could be done about her jointure. She was owed so much money, it was time her ex-husband's family paid her what she was due. There must be another way to solve this, a way that might save her marriage and John's career.

PART TWO

CHAPTER 20

1745

Lady Barbara Herbert, Age 10, St Augustine's Convent

Sister Agathe has given me a book to write in. She said it was a journal, so that's what I'm going to call it. We like Sister Agathe and everyone in my class hopes she'll be our teacher again next year. Sister Agathe says that so much has been going on I need to write it all down. My great-grandfather has died but I couldn't go to the ~~funereal~~ funeral because it was too far away. My mother came here on her way to Paris but I didn't know who she was at first. She had on a new black dress. Her friend Amelia was with her and she said she knew me when I was a baby. I have to have another ~~guradian~~ guardian. My grandfather died too, in October, the same month as my great-grandfather. He was the Marquess of Powis. I am not sad because I never met him. I never met my father either. A prince has gone to fight in Scotland. My great-aunt Winifred looked after him in Rome, like Adele looks after me but Winifred is a Countess and Adele isn't. It has been a busy time for everyone.

HENRIETTA

hank goodness John has plenty of work, Henrietta thought, as the expensive carriage bearing her and Amelia to Paris sped through the northern French countryside. The Webb family heir, Thomas, had asked her to help his sisters close up the Paris apartment and she had immediately asked Amelia to accompany her. The pretext given was to allow Amelia to see her mother but Henrietta hoped they could find a way back to friendship.

In the end, John stayed away from the theatre for only a few months, his return hastened by the demands of creditors and their humiliation at her father's funeral. Her brother James, the new Earl Waldegrave, asked a servant to escort them to the back of the family chapel at Navestock, far away from the rest of the family. They walked the length of the chapel, pretending to ignore the turned heads and whispers as other guests recognised the disgraced daughter. Having her husband at her side mattered and would have been impossible if he had been expected to perform on stage that night.

From distant family members and estate managers, the only people who were willing to speak to her, she learned that her father had been in Britain for months before he died. Despite her pleading letters, he had not chosen to see her.

At the reading of the will, the solicitor stumbled and reddened when he read aloud Earl Waldegrave's hurtful words, 'to my worthless daughter I leave only five shillings'.

Henrietta dropped her gaze, hiding her face from the shocked stares of family and staff seated around the lawyer's desk. She understood the depths of her father's hatred, a man who in his dying months, had planned this cruelty. If he left her nothing, she would not have been obliged to attend, but by leaving her a paltry sum, he had publicly stabbed her from his grave.

Henrietta hoped that his loving marriage to her mother had been a sham. Mary had been raised a Webb and wouldn't have stood for his controlling ways. Like his daughter, her mother would have despised him and this was no more than he deserved.

Amelia woke from her doze and sat up straight to watch their slow progress through the outskirts of Paris, the streets not yet lit by public lamps. 'Henrietta,' she asked. 'Why is Thomas the heir?'

'You remember my Uncle John, the one who threw us out of Great Marlborough Street? Well he died last year,' Henrietta answered. 'Thomas never expected to inherit but I think he's very well suited. He's like his mother, sensible, well-organised and a countryman, through and through.'

Amelia sniffed and pursed her lips. 'I didn't like the way John treated us but I wouldn't have wished him dead, not with a wife and young family. Have you found out how your grandfather died?'

Henrietta shook her head. 'When I heard the news, I was terrified he'd got himself involved in this Jacobite uprising, but I think he was hunting in Aix-en-Provence. Perhaps he was offended when young Charles Edward Stuart didn't ask him to join the campaign, so he rode off in the opposite direction, in a huff. There won't be a funeral in Paris, he was buried almost immediately in Aix.'

'It was lovely to see Barbara,' Amelia said. 'She's so bright and funny and looks like you, not Edward Herbert.'

Henrietta shook her head. 'That's a relief. My grandfather's death leaves Barbara without a guardian, so for now, Edward's brother, the new Marquess of Powis, has stepped in again. You will remember him as that odious man, Lord Montgomery.'

Amelia grimaced. 'Oh no, not him. I can't think of anyone more unsuitable. I hope you don't mind me asking, Hensy, but why can't you be Barbara's guardian?'

Henrietta hesitated. She could not say, even to her childhood friend, that she did not feel any connection with her daughter. 'John and I are broke, Amelia, that's the truth, even though he's working. I want my daughter forever linked to the wealth of the Webbs or to have the aristocratic status of the Herberts. That's her due. What about you, Amelia? You're twenty-six now. Are you hoping for babies?'

Henrietta thought she saw a pink blotch on Amelia's neck, always a sign she was hiding something.

'I think I am with child,' Amelia said, 'but it's too early to be sure.'

'That's wonderful,' Henrietta gasped. 'Are you feeling well? I hope the rocking of the carriage hasn't made you sick.'

'Hmmm...' Amelia said, giving Henrietta a glance that said, *not like some people.* 'I don't feel any different, because I've only missed one bleed. We have tried to catch a baby but so far, no success. I didn't mind. I think I was a little put off by... you know, a fear of making a mistake. Are you bothered no more babies have come along with John?'

'Not at all,' Henrietta said. 'It's a relief. You'll be a good mother, I'm sure of it. I never took to it but you will be different.'

The women fell silent, reassured by confident words spoken aloud but their own experience of being mothered had been a lottery and there was nothing to suggest that Amelia would be any more a natural mother than Henrietta.

They arrived at the Webb apartments after dark, learning from Amelia's mother that Helen, her grandfather's wife, had packed up her own and Lord Webb's possessions and had already left for Wiltshire. Only Lady Webb's clothing, ornaments and personal items of furniture remained. Thomas Webb and his sister Bridget were out, visiting family friends for the evening.

Amelia disappeared with her mother and Henrietta ate a light meal, alone in the cavernous dining room. It was served by a man whose name she remembered just in time so she could thank him personally.

She wondered about the servants and where they would go once the apartment was closed up. Amelia's mother already had many offers from wealthy Parisian families, but might she choose to move to London, to be with her daughter, especially if Amelia was expecting a baby?

Henrietta tired of staring at her own reflection in the mirrored walls and thought about exploring the empty rooms but lamps had only been lit in the narrow passage from the dining room to her bedchamber. The echo of her footsteps in the shadowed, silent corridor hurried her towards the familiarity of her chamber.

Someone had made sure that candles were lit, warm water and cloths awaited her, and her night things lay on the bed, but Amelia would not come to undress her. She was now a married woman, with a lady's maid of her own at home and Amelia's mother would insist this boundary was respected.

Henrietta slumped onto her bed and rocked back onto the mattress, wondering what her husband was singing tonight. She missed his weight, his warmth and wanted to feel enclosed by his bulk, his arms circled tightly around her shoulders. After only a few months of absence, John's best singing roles were indeed lost to other men, but now he seemed to be recovering favour, performing Handel's operas and oratorios at Covent

Garden. The only threat to his career was the fear that London theatres might fall dark, if the Jacobite force reached London, as they had promised, but for now, patriotic ballads, which suited John's voice, were much in demand.

As she undressed and washed, Henrietta's thoughts drifted to money, as they did so often these days. With John earning, it was hard to understand why they never had enough but since neither of them limited their spending, recovering from her husband's disappearance from the stage had been almost impossible. She had borrowed from Edward Webb against her jointure and that income had saved them from hunger or from freezing to death through the winter but the debt still had to be paid back.

From her father's estate, she should have received the settlement promised when she first married, but her brother was proving to be as negligent as his father. She didn't relish starting a new legal battle against Lord Montgomery, now the Marquess of Powis, for what she was owed, but it had to be done. Lawyers cost a fortune, even if a family member was fighting on your behalf. There would be nothing for her in Sir John Webb's will. Granny Webb had been right about her husband, he was a principled man but uncompromising once his mind was made up.

In the morning, Henrietta sat with Amelia and Adele in Granny Webb's parlour to sew some new dresses for Barbara, using the drab, itchy cloth that the convent expected. The door opened and Thomas entered, bowing to her.

'I wondered if we might speak alone, Lady Beard,' he said. Amelia and Adele lifted their sewing and dropped the new Sir Thomas Webb a curtsy, before leaving Henrietta alone with her uncle.

'It is so lovely to see you,' Thomas said, pulling up a chair beside her and spreading his coat wide before plumping his large body onto the rather delicate cane seat. 'Such a pity that fine fellow John Beard isn't with you. I saw him sing *The Messiah* a couple of years ago at Covent Garden. What a voice!'

Henrietta thought about the cool reception she had received from Bridget, only this morning, as they packed away Granny Webb's clothing and jewellery.

'Thank you, Thomas. The rest of the family are less forgiving. I never resolved my quarrel with my grandfather, although I think in her final days, my grandmother pardoned me.'

'Yes, the Webb clan certainly weren't happy about what happened when you were living at my brother John's house, but it's all water under the bridge now.' Thomas emphasised his point by slapping his thigh. 'My mother was a wonderful woman before her stroke. I've discovered she made a legal arrangement to retain her marriage settlement, if my father died before her. She was from a rich family and brought much wealth to the marriage. She wasn't about to hand over her financial interests to a mere man.'

'I wish she were here to guide me,' Henrietta said but added no more, not wishing to spill her worries about debt to this kind uncle.

'My father wasn't so astute,' Thomas continued. 'The reason our wealth has been so well-managed is largely due to my mother. Do you know he bought Helen Moore properties before they were even married?'

'I'm not surprised,' Henrietta said. 'I suspected he had another woman but made him very angry when I raised it. We quarrelled, bitterly, on the day my grandmother died.'

'Before you leave,' Thomas said, 'I'd like you to choose something from my mother's porcelain collection, to remember her by. Everything else will be going to my sisters I'm afraid, but they don't need to know about this.'

'Thank you, Thomas, that is most kind,' Henrietta said. 'On another matter, what will happen to my daughter and Adele?'

'It will take several months to make this legal but my sister Barbara and her husband, Viscount Montague, have agreed to be her guardians. Their duties will start from today, so you have nothing to worry about. They've agreed to employ Adele within their household, since there are other children and she will continue as Lady Herbert's maidservant in the school holidays. Your daughter is a Webb,' Thomas boomed the word *Webb* and slapped his thigh again, making Henrietta jump. 'We couldn't risk that Herbert shower trying to take control of her.'

Henrietta felt her shoulders slump with relief. 'I am confident Lord Montgomery will not fight this. He has no interest in Barbara.'

Thomas stood up, beginning his parting gestures but he hovered, as if there was more to say.

'Is there anything else, Thomas?' she asked.

'Bit awkward,' Thomas said, 'but do be careful in London, Henrietta, in case there's an invasion. There was an attempt to implicate my father in the Stuart campaign. Someone found a letter lying on a road in Dorset.' Thomas allowed his voice to show contempt for the word *found*.

'They pretended it was in my father's hand, expressing his support for Charles Edward Stuart,' Thomas continued. 'It was all nonsense of course, my father was in France, so it went no further but it shows how petty some people can be. Don't forget that you are Bonnie Prince Charlie's kin, through your Waldegrave grandmother and it might suit some people to regard you as a traitor.'

Oh for goodness' sake, Henrietta thought, *first a whore and now a traitor.* 'Thank you for the warning, Uncle,' she said. 'I will maintain my guard.'

Before they left for home, Amelia helped Henrietta choose

her porcelain. Like children, they touched each piece and mimicked Granny Webb's voice, trying to name each one and teasing each other if they forgot where it was bought. Henrietta chose a recently purchased piece of Sevres and it was only when she held it high, to catch the afternoon light filtering through the delicate rim, she realised she was crying.

CHAPTER 21

1746

BARBARA

It is the school holidays but I still write in this journal because Sister Agathe says I should keep it up. I'm staying in Paris with my guardians.

The Viscountess is my great-aunt and her name is Barbara, just like mine. My great-grandmother was called Barbara as well. My great-aunt calls my great-grandmother Barbara One, herself Barbara Two and I am Barbara Three. It's supposed to stop us getting muddled over who we're talking about but I don't like being Barbara Three.

They have a grown-up daughter and a son, Anthony, who is sixteen. He's at boarding school like me and is teaching me to play cricket in the holidays. My guardians did have other children but Adele says they all died. The nuns say it's God's will but Adele said that's not true, then asked me not to tell anyone, which I haven't.

My great-aunt says I did well at school last year but I don't enjoy Latin. I'm good with numbers because my great-grandmother used to play cards with me. I was eleven in June, so I'm in senior school next term. That means I only share a dormitory with four other girls. We wear a different dress too, one that doesn't fasten at the back. It will still be grey and itchy. Sister Catherine will be my teacher next year and everyone says she's a bit strict.

I like staying with my guardians in Paris and don't want to go back to school. My great-aunt says I have to because the prince hasn't invaded England and they might want to visit their house in Essex. I haven't been there yet but Anthony says it's huge. Barbara Two said that whenever they're in Paris, they will come and take me out, even in term time. I don't know what the Abbess will say about that. I have to stop now because Adele says my lunch is ready.

HENRIETTA

London theatre breathed a sigh of relief as the invading Jacobite force was defeated at Culloden and the threat of invasion passed. Winifred Maxwell wrote to say that her dear prince was safe but someone known to the Webb family, a man called Charles Radclyffe, had been executed.

Henrietta struggled to remember the story of Anna Maria's marriage to James Radclyffe, it all seemed so long ago, but to Winifred, trapped in Rome, this tragedy mattered because Charles Radclyffe was their friend. The defeat of the Jacobite army would have shaken her grandparents, so perhaps it was best they hadn't lived to see it. As for herself, she only felt relief to be rid of unnecessary worry, gifted to her by her uncle, that other people might believe she shared Jacobite sympathies.

Henrietta and John were happy. Since returning from Paris, she had turned her back on everything a wealthy, aristocratic background had once promised and fully embraced her life with a loving husband and his talented, vibrant group of friends. She no longer followed him to his afternoon and evening performances, wherever they might be, and they had both given up late-night, after-performance parties, where friendships were fleeting and fuelled by alcohol.

Henrietta had enjoyed the risk and excitement, as if she had suddenly become alive to everything her former, suffocating life had forbidden, both as a woman and a titled member of her social class, but now she was content with their neat, terraced house, and her own interests, their three cats, and practising the spinet. John often invited friends home and she found pleasure in devising a menu with their cook, as Mrs Adams had taught her at Hendon.

Amelia had recently given birth to a baby girl, but apart from visiting to deliver a gift, Henrietta had no desire to spend time admiring a newborn or to sit for long in a parlour that reeked of milk and soiled cloths. Amelia described the delivery in detail, mistaken in her belief that since she had witnessed Barbara's birth, Henrietta might be interested. She was not and left as soon as courtesy would allow.

Their financial problems continued, although they both tried to avoid thinking about money. This was only possible because Edward Webb lent them even more against Henrietta's jointure, in the hope that he would be paid back some day.

John was earning well and still tried hard to rein in his spending but what on earth could Henrietta do? To support her husband, she had to attend performances at the royal court, as well as at John Rich's new theatre, Covent Garden. Robes and headdresses suitable for mixing with royalty were not cheap. In fact, she was collecting another gown later today, a mantua of rust-coloured silk, from her dressmaker.

She had recently been measured for new stays and was

shocked at the price. Her stay-maker had blamed the increase on a possibility of war with France, but would the prices come down once the threat was over? Of course they wouldn't! Having a content life at home and no longer rushing about London meant that she had gained weight. John was broader too but because of his height, he actually looked better. His girth suited the roles he played but Henrietta's girth did not suit her in any way at all.

Henrietta sat in the morning room, which overlooked their small garden, sipping coffee that Mrs Mills served with hot milk and sugar. Thinking of money made Henrietta irritable. The new Earl Waldegrave had eventually paid her what she was owed in South Sea Company shares, which were worthless.

The equally new Marquess of Powis denied he owed her anything, claiming he had not been party to her marriage settlement but her solicitor had found copies signed by Lord Montgomery. True to form, he had been too drunk to remember which documents he had put his name to.

Worse, he had recently written to Edward Webb arguing that he was owed money by Henrietta because of his brother's debts and the cost of the funeral. This was nonsense, she was only a child when her future husband was living on borrowed income and was Lord Montgomery's ward after Edward died. No one could sue a minor for debts, even a child married to the debtor. Everyone knew the Herbert family were in deep financial trouble. All their estates had been mortgaged, including Hendon Manor and the magnificent Powis House in London, everything other than the family seat, Powis Castle. Thank goodness her daughter was safe, secure within the care of the wealthy Webb family.

Henrietta stroked their ginger cat, curled on her lap, his rhythmic thrum of purring soothing her mood. His claws kneaded at her silk dress, catching on threads of fabric and she lifted him down before the dress was destroyed. Finding himself on the rug, Mr Peachum stalked away a few paces, and began washing the fur she had touched, keeping his back turned.

Henrietta smiled, enjoying the comfortable complicity of a happy marriage, where both of them still found it funny to name their pets after characters from *The Beggar's Opera*. Neither she nor John had the heart for more litigation, or the money to fund their costs but she would not allow such dreary thoughts to spoil her dinner party tonight with their friends from the theatre.

It was time to go down to the kitchen and see how Mrs Mills and the kitchen maid were progressing with the preparations. The servants were used to her lending a hand with cooking, although she wondered if they sometimes found her a nuisance.

Henrietta walked the length of the long tiled corridor from the morning room, down the stairs to the servants' quarters and retraced her steps along a narrow, slabbed passage to the dark kitchen at the back of the house. Conversation stopped as she entered the hot kitchen, a fire blazing in the wide hearth. Sensing she had interrupted a story about someone she knew, or even about herself or John, she paused to stroke Filch, resting on the cook's chair with his front paws neatly tucked under his chest.

'Is there anything for me to do?' she asked.

'You can chop the onions for the onion soup, my lady,' Mrs Mills answered, tossing her head towards a mound of onions on the kitchen table.

Henrietta washed her hands in the scullery and sat down to begin her task, picking up the sharp knife lying alongside the onions. She noticed Mrs Mills quickly turn away to reach for a platter from the sideboard, one that ran the entire length of the kitchen, in an attempt to hide what looked like a grin of satisfaction. Henrietta shrugged. If Mrs Mills thought she was discouraged by onions, she didn't know her mistress at all.

It was dark by the time the guests arrived and the house was dressed to perfection, with fires in the library and dining room and candles blazing on every surface, to best show off the fine panelling and cornices that lent their builder his reputation for quality. Henrietta and John had no manservant, like most of their friends. John was content to show his friends into the library for a glass of wine before dinner, as Henrietta was to serve the food left for them in the servery by the cook.

Henrietta told the story of the onion soup, apologising for her red-rimmed eyes. William Havard's wife Anne said it tasted even better for Henrietta's suffering. Before she served the jugged hare, allowing John to circle the table and refill their glasses from another bottle of French wine, the conversation turned to the summer season just passed.

They had all sung at Ranelagh and Vauxhall Gardens and together had revived *The Beggar's Opera* at the new suburban theatres in Twickenham and Richmond. Henrietta had avoided Vauxhall, the memories of being there with Edward as an anxious bride were still too painful. Ranelagh seemed respectable somehow, being more expensive and cleaner than Vauxhall. There wasn't the atmosphere of everything being about sex, although perhaps that had been down to her own understandable pre-occupation as a new bride with a reluctant husband.

'Wouldn't you like to live further out of London, where the air is clean?' John Dunstall asked, coughing theatrically as if to make his point. 'The houses they're building along the banks of the Thames are splendid.'

Henrietta laughed. 'We couldn't afford it. Anyway, how would you all get to your performances during the winter season, which are always in the city.'

'Ah, the winter season.' James Bencroft turned to John. 'What can we look forward to at Covent Garden from Handel's favourite?'

'We're rehearsing a new work, *Judas Maccabaeus*,' John replied, 'but talking of health, Handel isn't too well. I'm contracted for another two years, but I'm not sure he's up to it.'

'If it doesn't work out, we could stage *The Beggar's Opera* again through the winter season,' William interrupted. 'That work is turning out to be our bread and butter. The London audience never seems to tire of it.'

Henrietta stood to serve their main course, pausing to study her friends before carrying the dishes to the table. In the fug of candlelight, and through a haze of alcohol, she thought how beautiful they were, how interesting, how special. This was her family now, people she had chosen. How right she had been, to give up everything for John. In fact, she had given up nothing except another forced marriage to an old man.

After the apple pudding and cream, everyone stayed at the table for brandy, feeding bits from their plates to the cats weaving between their legs. Mr Peachum and Filch had been joined by Twitcher, their most nervous cat, who showed unusual temerity by jumping onto the table. No one seemed to care, but Henrietta decided enough was enough. Scooping up the protesting animals under her arms, she deposited them behind the door that led downstairs to the servants' area. When she returned, Kitty Clive was questioning John about the performances he shared with the tenor Thomas Lowe at both Drury Lane and Covent Garden.

'I thought you'd given up that place,' she said, raising her eyebrows. 'You told me you were committed to Covent Garden, like I am. You said you were trying to simplify your schedule.'

John pretended to look repentant and Henrietta smiled, waiting to see how he would placate Kitty. 'I've sung for many years with Thomas. Besides, I want to help out the new manager at Drury Lane, after Fleetwood skimmed off all the profits on his gambling habit. His name is David Garrick, do you know him?'

Kitty sniffed. 'Of course I know him, he was a great actor long before he started meddling in theatre management. I didn't expect you to support the opposition, that's all.'

'The arrangement suits us all, Kitty,' John replied, his tone intended to soothe but his eyes dancing with humour. 'Crowds are gathering at both theatres, hours before the performance. Tickets sell out within minutes. We all win.'

Kitty's voice rose, along with her colour. 'Well, I think it's disloyal,' she argued.

Her husband George placed a hand on Kitty's arm and said, 'My dear, we should go home, I sense you are tired. Henrietta and John, thank you for a lovely evening, as always.'

He looked around the table, his face bright in anticipation of hearty agreement. 'Our place next time?'

CHAPTER 22
1747

BARBARA

I don't write much in this book any more but I am so angry I need to tell someone how I feel. Anthony doesn't want me hanging around him anymore. He says that boys of seventeen don't spend their time with girls who are twelve. He didn't say 'boys', he said 'men' which is a joke because no one is further from being a man than Anthony. My great-aunt always takes his side because she's his mother. She says I should try to find out where my friends from the convent live in the holidays and she'll speak to their mothers about going to visit. Doesn't she realise I hate all the girls from school?

If I had a mother, it might be different. I know I do have a mother, she's called Henrietta Beard, but she just writes silly letters about her cats and her husband John, who's a singer. No one in the Montague family ever talks about Henrietta and if I bring her up, I just get looks and everyone goes quiet. I mean to write to my mother but I can't think of anything to say.

Anyway, Adele says that the Montague family will marry

me off when I'm thirteen, so I'll soon get away from Anthony. She thinks she avoided marriage because she was so busy looking after me but I think there are other reasons Adele doesn't have a husband. I wanted to tell her but stopped myself, which I think means I'm growing up. I won't write the reasons here because I don't trust Adele not to read this journal. Adele, you are not married because... ha, ha.

HENRIETTA

Henrietta and John met with their solicitor in his office at Gray's Inn, an instruction that showed the seriousness of the meeting. With his growing family of one baby girl and another on the way, Edward Webb needed to be paid back and this meant winning her legal action against the Herbert family. In fact, it wasn't her case, it was John's, since he was nominally responsible for all their financial affairs, including the embarrassing scale of her debt.

They sat in a circle around a low table, spread with documents that evidenced the work that her relative had already given to the case. The legal clerk brought them tea, which he poured before returning to a desk set at the side of the room, his pen poised over the inkwell.

Edward paused to read the documents, allowing time for Henrietta to study his neat wig, set far back on his head to reveal his powdered forehead. John rarely wore a wig, preferring a theatrical hat more suitable for Covent Garden's most dramatic hero.

The solicitor stroked his upper lip and looked from Henrietta to John before speaking. 'I recommend we tackle this on two fronts. Firstly, we demand that the Herbert family pay Henrietta what she's owed. That's not a surprise for either of you, I'm sure.'

'What is the surprise?' Henrietta asked.

Edward drank deeply from his tea cup and the clerk hurried over to refill it, tipping the teapot towards Henrietta and John, who both refused. 'It's twelve years since Lord Herbert died, without making a will.'

John gave a gasp. 'Goodness, twelve years,' he said.

Edward nodded. 'Indeed... twelve years where Henrietta has had no access to Lord Herbert's estate. Now, there may be nothing to inherit but it is something we should have pursued. Are you in agreement that we apply for access now?'

'Of course,' Henrietta replied. 'I assumed he owned nothing and it wasn't worth the cost or the effort.'

'That may be true,' Edward continued, 'but few men of his rank own nothing. What about his rooms in Bath, his carriage, the horses, his share of the income from his father's lead mines?'

Henrietta frowned, then laughed without mirth. 'Between his older sister Mary Herbert and his brother's spending, I suspect everything is gone. What's the risk?'

Edward paused. 'The risk is the cost, and it may be a fruitless cost. The litigation will also be lengthy. I will work for free until the case is resolved but these will be my charges, should we be successful.'

The solicitor slid a document across the polished table towards Henrietta, who passed it to John. They exchanged a glance, each communicating the same thought... *so much!* No wonder Amelia was always so expensively dressed.

Henrietta looked at John, expecting him to speak for them both, since the action would be in his name. He had already cut back on his performances this season, anticipating the legal meetings and court appearances that lay ahead. At Covent Garden, he had promised to abide by all contracted appearances but Handel had not been pleased to learn he was no longer available for anything else.

'You have done a thorough piece of work here, my friend,' John said. 'Since there is no way we can pay you the considerable sum you are already owed, we have no option. This is a lifetime's work. Who knows if any of us will live to see its outcome. I agree we should proceed.'

They walked home from Gray's Inn, both feeling the warmth of the summer afternoon. Henrietta paused to unwrap the lappets she wore like a loose scarf around her neck and flapped at her face with the ends, before pinning them back onto the crown of her cap. It was more than the heat of the day. She was hot and weary after the meeting, of course, but more than she ought to be, more than even a year ago. The most important thing was that John shouldn't notice. Fiddling with her hair gave her time to stop and breathe, even though her chest didn't seem to fill properly with air. It was the shock, she explained to herself, talking about her first husband and his funeral, after all this time.

She linked arms with John and they walked on, both silent in their own private thoughts about what had been agreed. For the first time, she saw her life as a chain of litigation that would outlive her. She wasn't happy with this picture but what else was there? She and John had no children, she was a stranger to her only daughter, her family had disowned her. Was her life to amount to no more than legal battles won or lost, being paid back money she was owed but had already spent?

Henrietta shook herself and spoke to John, keen to return to the here and now, the routine of the everyday. 'What are you singing tonight, my darling?'

'It's *Judas Maccabaeus* tonight. Since the defeat of the Jacobite army at Culloden, the London audience can't hear it often enough. Everyone seems to think it's about the Duke of Cumberland's success over the insurgents, our plucky battle against an invading army. The king is delighted and Handel is quite happy to play along... he'll give the public what they want, for as long as they want it. I'm not complaining, I enjoy singing Judas.'

'Let me know when you're next in the role,' Henrietta replied. 'I'd like to hear it again. I'm afraid I'm rather tired tonight and will stay at home. Do you want Mrs Mills to make you something to eat later? I think I'll have something on a tray and retire early.'

John stopped walking and looked down at his wife, gripping her elbows. 'Are you unwell?'

Henrietta shook her head and gave a forced, high-pitched laugh. 'Not at all. I found the meeting uncomfortable, that's all. I remember you asked me once why everything had to be about money and that's what I felt today. We're doing the right thing, but it feels a bit sad and pointless.'

John linked his arm through hers and walked on, tugging at her elbow to bring her steps into line with his. 'Then we must make sure that the wonderful life we share isn't all about money, Henrietta. I will try not to mention ever again how much you spend.'

Henrietta pretended to slap his arm. 'You never do, John. It's one of the things I love about you.'

At their door, John searched in his coat pocket for the key. 'To finish our conversation about my meal, in case you want to catch Mrs Mills before she leaves, I'm eating with John Rich at the Beefsteak Club tonight.' John raised his voice and spoke in a squeaky, aristocratic tone, 'Or should I call it the Sublime Society of Beefsteaks.'

Henrietta stepped into the welcome cool of the hall and slid her shawl from her shoulders, grinning at his mockery of the upper classes. She was pleased when Rich had invited her husband to join the Beefsteak Club. The membership were theatre folk, writers and artists and it was at these meetings when the real business of the theatre happened, as well as friendship, laughter and good food.

'You'll enjoy that,' she said. 'Don't forget to ask him about next season, what sort of contract he's thinking of offering. Tell him about the legal action... you'll need time off for meetings and court appearances.'

'Yes, of course, Lady Beard,' John said, giving her a small bow. 'I'll tell him if I remember but actually, my darling, I think I'd prefer to relax and enjoy myself.'

The following Sunday, Henrietta and John met friends at a regular evening salon hosted by the contralto singer Susannah Cibber and her husband Theo. Thomas Arne and his wife Cecilia were often guests, since Susannah and Thomas were siblings. John Beard and Thomas had been friends for many years, since their early days at Drury Lane theatre and Henrietta liked Cecilia, although she was more wary of Susannah. Her reputation on the stage matched John's, but she didn't share his easy-going nature.

Susannah and Theo were more comfortable financially than she and John. Their house was larger and they had a manservant, who now accepted their capes before escorting them into the drawing room.

Since the meeting with their lawyer, Henrietta had been

unable to rid herself of a feeling of dread, waking in the morning to a sense of darkness hovering at the edge of her vision. She usually felt better as the day passed but this evening, she was glad to see that neither Handel nor David Garrick were present. Handel was never unkind to her, but he ignored her, driving the conversation with his own preoccupations and looking to John and Susannah for encouragement. David, on the other hand, was too flirtatious, but Henrietta suspected that the attention he paid her was for Cecilia's benefit.

It was a chilly evening, despite the heat of the day and Henrietta was glad to be offered a seat by the fire, where she could lean back in a generous armchair and absorb the chat. The air was heavy with the mingled scent of the women and the tantalising smell of good wine. The friends were already joking about Handel in his absence, arguing that he let Susannah make constant mistakes in her singing but picked John up on the slightest error. Cecilia said the irascible composer was secretly in love with Susannah but Thomas interrupted, joking that Handel was actually in love with John but had been rebuffed for years.

As a servant filled their wine glasses and passed around a platter of delicate sweetmeats, the group fell silent. Henrietta studied Thomas' long nose and sharp chin, in contrast to John's broad and pleasant features. Her husband was stroking his beard, a smile playing on his lips and she waited for his reply to their teasing.

'Handel expects so much of me because he watched me sing in the Chapel Royal Choir as a boy and liked what he heard. Within a year or two of leaving the choir, I was singing important parts written only for me. He knew I had a sound background in music but risked a lot to promote me... his choice must have annoyed many established singers. He's always been harder on me than anyone else in the company, because he expects so much.'

'Whereas with me,' Susannah said, 'he expects nothing, except the gift of my voice. He knew I couldn't read music and has given up believing I'll ever learn. He teaches me the arias note by note. Luckily, I've a good memory for a tune.'

'Well I think it's a disgrace you can't read music,' Thomas interrupted, 'given what our parents spent on your education.'

Henrietta knew that Susannah and Thomas had inherited wealth from a father who was a master upholsterer, and both had been encouraged to lead artistic lives beyond the family business. She envied their friendship and wondered what it would have been like, to be close to her brothers, to have a family who wanted nothing for their children except to be happy in their chosen field. These two had grown up with so much choice, so much freedom.

The conversation paused again, to allow servants to rebuild the fire, trim the candles and circle again with wine and food.

John bit into his sweetmeat and leaned towards his friend, still chewing. 'Thomas, tell them about writing the national anthem.'

Thomas looked around the group. 'I'm sure you've all heard this before?'

Everyone shook their heads, although Henrietta guessed that she and perhaps Theo were the only ones in ignorance.

Thomas loosened his cravat and relaxed into his tale. 'With the threat from the Jacobite invasion, I was asked to compose an anthem that would rally the nation behind the king. The irony is that my family are recusant Catholics and some might believe we would be happy to see a Catholic as monarch. That's not the case, but I did take great pleasure in modifying an old Catholic tune as the basis for *God Save the King*.'

'I knew about his treachery,' John added, a smile softening his words. 'I was the first to sing the anthem on stage.'

'And now we can't close a single performance without it,' said Susannah. 'I always smile inside whenever I hear it but wouldn't want to appear disloyal.'

'My dear wife is the very apex of disloyalty.' John grinned, his eyes scanning his friends' faces. 'Charles Edward Stuart, the bonnie young prince, is her cousin.'

Everyone turned to stare at Henrietta. Into the silence, she blustered, 'John, that's not funny! It's just one of those accidents of birth. I've never met the man, nor do I share his sympathies, although there are some in my birth family who do. As you all know, I am estranged from both of my families but I was also brought up in the Catholic faith.'

Cecilia reached across and touched Henrietta's knee. 'Where do you worship, if you don't mind me asking?'

Henrietta shrugged. 'I don't. We can't pay a visiting priest and any other form of Catholic worship is banned.'

Cecilia looked at her husband. 'Thomas, Henrietta must come with us to the Sardinian chapel.'

Henrietta frowned, drawing her brows together. 'The Sardinian chapel?'

'Yes,' Cecilia continued, 'they're allowed to have a Catholic chapel behind the Sardinian embassy, so that employees can attend mass. Thomas directs the music.'

All other conversation stopped and Thomas addressed the group. 'It's one of those ridiculous anomalies which makes a mockery of the lack of religious freedom we Catholics suffer in this country. The embassies are outside British law, so the staff are free to worship as they choose. These chapels are all over London and anyone local, of the Catholic faith, can join them for mass. The government sometimes harasses visitors but the raids are half-hearted and usually known about well in advance. The Sardinian embassy is in Lincoln's Inn Fields, so very close to you, Henrietta. You are most welcome to join us.'

Henrietta glanced across at John before she replied. 'Thank you both, I would be delighted to come with you.'

Susannah clapped her hands and stood up. 'Well, that's settled. Now, let's play cards. This evening has become far too serious.'

CHAPTER 23
1748

MARY

Lady Mary Herbert decided to walk from the suburb of La Roule, where she lived, to her lawyer's new office on the fashionable Rue du Faubourg Saint-Honoré. Her maid Lucille had told her that walking was good exercise, especially for women over sixty, and she decided to take this advice, while wondering why a servant thought it was acceptable to speak to her as if they were friends. Mary had no friends, or any family to speak of now that her father, her aunt, and both of her brothers were dead. Her lawyer had tracked down two living sisters, which had been a surprise, since she had not been able to remember their names.

Mary had received nothing from the pitiful allowance her father left her in his will because of her brother's ridiculous accusation that she was solely responsible for the family's debt. It was of vital importance to settle this matter of inheritance, particularly due to the discovery of an unexpected rival, her brother Edward's daughter, Lady Barbara Herbert, a child forgotten by her and the rest of the family.

The path Mary followed out of La Roule was dusty and the verges grey with dried mud thrown up by passing coaches. As she walked, she regretted wearing her black dress and leaving her parasol behind. Although it was only nine o'clock on a May morning, the day would be hot.

She arrived breathless and sweaty, grateful for the cool of the shady office, a window flung open to let in a breeze and a drink of lemon cordial offered by the clerk. Once she had settled, dabbing her face and neck with a handkerchief, Mary glanced around the room, noting with disapproval that her lawyer had moved all his sturdy, solid-wood furniture from his humble room in La Roule, in a misjudged attempt to attract the business of Paris' nouveau riche. She had advised him of his mistake, but he had taken no notice.

Monsieur Moreau studied her with drooping, red-rimmed eyes, the lower lids forming pockets where liquid gathered, as if he had just shed tears. He always looked sad, which he had no reason to be, given his fees.

'Lady Herbert, I have found the child who was a temporary ward of your brother William. She is now living within the family of the Viscount Montague, here in Paris. Her name is Barbara and she attends the English convent, the Augustine Convent, in Bruges. I believe you once had some family connections there?'

'Yes indeed, my aunt was the Abbess. I've never met these people, these Montagues. Who are they?'

'They are an important, Catholic family here in Paris and also in Britain. Their family seat is Cowdray in Essex. Have you heard of it?'

Mary shook her head, pursing her lips in disdain. 'Please continue.'

'The Viscountess, also Barbara, was a Webb before marriage. The Webbs are a family of great wealth and loyal supporters of the Jacobite cause. Sir John Webb, who was your niece's guardian, died in the same month as your own father. From my inquiries, the child's mother Henrietta is out of the picture. She seems to have disgraced herself in some way.'

Mary stayed quiet, her mind turning over these facts. She had lived for years in Paris with her aunt Anne, who played cards with a group of elderly Jacobite women, including Barbara Webb's mother. After one of these games, her aunt said that for all their airs and graces, the Webbs were no better than farmers, not aristocrats like their family. As for Henrietta, her younger brother's unfortunate widow, in her experience it helped to have the mother rendered powerless, since mothers had a habit of fighting for their daughters. At least most mothers did, although that hadn't been true of her own. A cloud passed over the sun and the already gloomy room darkened.

'I need to meet this child. Please would you write to her guardians and arrange it. Write to the mother, not the father. All you need to say is that I'm the girl's aunt and keen to make her acquaintance.'

The lawyer nodded to his clerk, seated at a smaller desk facing the wall, who started to draft the letter. Moreau turned back to Mary. 'My lady, I'm surprised you haven't brought up the other matter. Did you read all of the letter I sent you, summarising your brother's last wishes?'

Mary remembered that night, two months ago, throwing the letter on the fire. There had been something about a distant cousin inheriting, but surely that wasn't possible, not when she and her niece had more legitimate claims.

'Aren't the Montagues fighting this, on Barbara's behalf?' she asked, allowing her tone to convey her contempt. 'Surely they wouldn't permit their ward to be disinherited in this way.'

The lawyer sighed. 'Not everyone has your appetite for

litigation, Lady Herbert. It would take years to resolve and without wishing to denigrate my own profession, most of the inheritance would end up lining our pockets. No, it has been agreed: Lord Henry Arthur Herbert of Chirbury will inherit. It makes far more sense for the Montagues to find Barbara a wealthy husband.'

'Read me the bit again, where my brother leaves everything to this stranger,' Mary asked, still doubting that this slap in the face for both her niece and herself was being quietly accepted by everyone.

The lawyer read aloud, emphasising that as a condition of the inheritance, Chirbury had promised to maintain the castle, all of the estate, the mines and the farms, and to retain all of the servants. The lawyer looked at Mary from under his brows, with an expression that was hard to read. 'Not something that either you or the young Lady Herbert could guarantee, don't you agree?'

The bastard agrees with my brother, she thought. *My own lawyer thinks it was right to disinherit me.* 'Tell me the rest,' she said, fighting a strong desire to walk out.

Moreau continued. 'In his will your brother stated that he had been asked to pay Lady Henrietta Beard, and her daughter, the sum of twenty-thousand pounds. He questions the amount and by passing the estate to Lord Chirbury, he has neatly sidestepped the matter of the disputed money being taken from his estate after his death. The Beards and your niece will have to start again and pursue Lord Chirbury for their claim.'

Mary breathed out slowly between pursed lips and clenched and unclenched her fists. 'They'd worked it out between them,' she said. 'Those two have been communicating for years. Chirbury was no stranger to my brother. Who is he anyway, this manipulative schemer?' she asked.

The solicitor rubbed his chin. 'He's a politician, he's dabbled in the army but the most important thing for the remaining Herbert family, including your niece Barbara, is that he's a Protestant. For the first time in its history, Powis Castle will no longer be a Catholic stronghold.'

Mary rose slowly, feeling the ache of her sixty-two years in her knees and accepted her cape from the clerk. She would walk home slowly and think about her conniving brother, a man who had stayed cunning enough to avoid his responsibilities, despite his fondness for alcohol. Grudgingly, Mary felt a degree of respect for his plan. She had little interest in Powis Castle or the religion of its incumbent but she needed to think carefully about how to turn this situation to her own advantage.

'I am wondering about your fee,' she asked the lawyer, turning at the door to face him. 'Since I am from a noble Jacobite family, as are you, will you consider a reduction? My grandfather fled to France with James II.'

The lawyer shook his head. 'If I had a livre for every Jacobite family in this city who claim their grandfather escaped from Britain with the exiled king's father, I would be a rich man. No, Lady Herbert, you cannot have a discount. May I remind you that your last invoice remains outstanding.'

Mary walked towards the Pont Neuf and her mind flitted towards Joseph, her former lover and business partner, who now lived on the left bank of the Seine, somewhere near St Germain-des-Pres. Since the unfortunate death of his young wife Catherine Caryll, only two months after their wedding, Joseph had been in deep hiding, preferring to spend his nights gambling in salons that didn't investigate their clients' backgrounds.

Their final row had been tumultuous, almost violent, cruel

words and hostile accusations spitting between them. They had fought many times before, but this rift felt permanent and they were no longer in contact. The scandal attached to him had tainted her own reputation, since she had arranged the match but she was a public figure, a business woman... *she* didn't have the luxury of hiding.

The bridge was busier than usual, with carriages, sedan chairs and single riders on horseback, hawkers dipping between the almost stationary traffic for the chance of a sale. She was glad to weave between the vehicles towards the raised walkway for pedestrians and push through the crowds towards the viewpoint in the centre of the bridge, where the statue of Henri IV stood. From her vantage point, she was able to enjoy a view of the city skyline, her temper soothed by the breeze from the river and the sun on her skin. She raised herself on tiptoe to watch the boats below and the wide streets beyond, lined with elegant town houses, threading out from the bridge, then closed her eyes, resting her elbows on the parapet.

'Think, Mary, think,' she chided herself aloud. Her brother had been clever but she was every bit as capable. Good luck to this distant relative Henry Arthur, who would now be pursued through the courts by Henrietta Beard. Twenty-thousand pounds was a vast sum of money. No, it was better not to fight for her rightful inheritance but to befriend this usurper, and make sure he not only acknowledged her status but paid back everything she was owed from her father's will.

The lawyer hadn't mentioned a wife, or children, so if Chirbury died without remedying this situation, the young Barbara Herbert would be his heir. She had to get to know her niece and use her matchmaking skills to find the girl a suitable husband. Influence was everything in Paris these days and this way, she might be able to restore her reputation as a woman of importance and keep the young couple forever in her debt.

Mary opened her eyes to check the time on the huge clock face of the Samaritaine building and became aware of a man staring. Her heart gave an unexpected skip and she wondered whether it was Joseph. Returning his stare, she recognised her mistake but every Parisian knew about the threat from thieves and pickpockets on this bridge, men and women often dressed to impersonate the aristocrats they robbed.

She decided to walk back to the point where she could find a carriage home. The Parisian public transport system reached every corner of the city, like a spider's web and everyone who could afford the fares, women as well as men, rode in these coaches. If she were protected by a coachman and fellow passengers returning from the city, her observer would not try to follow.

The coach was full of women returning from selling vegetables or flowers in central marketplaces, their baskets stacked on empty seats. Mary gestured impatiently to free a space but once she was seated, she ignored the hostile stares from the passenger next to her, who had been forced to pile her baskets onto her lap.

The situation was urgent, she thought, since the Montagues must already be searching for a suitable match for their ward. She could no longer easily read or write unless she was in the brightest of sunshine. Once home, she would ask Lucille to carry a table and her writing materials into the garden and write some letters before the light faded for the day.

Her old friend Fanny Oglethorpe, sadly now deceased, had a grandson who was at court. This young man, Charles Jules, Prince of Rochefort, should now be nineteen and would surely impress Viscount Montague with his pedigree. She would write to the French king, stressing her personal contacts and suggest a betrothal between Lady Barbara Herbert, a descendent of Jacobite nobility, and Fanny's grandson. Payment for her role could be arranged between them at a later date. This wasn't the time to make a fuss about money.

Her next step must be to meet her niece, to persuade the child that only her Herbert aunt knew what was best. If she travelled to the convent, she could meet the child there, far away from the influence of her guardians. She would write to the Abbess at once, making much of her family links with the convent and ask her to organise the meeting. Of course, the Montagues must be kept in the dark. If she hurried, Lucille could take both letters to the courier tonight. Satisfied with her plans, Mary's head lolled onto her chest and she fell asleep.

CHAPTER 24

1749

HENRIETTA

Henrietta and John walked slowly, hand in hand, to the Gray's Inn office of Edward Webb. They were answering an urgent summons from him, sent by courier the day before.

It was a year since the death of the Marquess of Powis, once Lord Montgomery and brother of her former husband Edward. She anticipated a discussion about the progress of their claim against his heir, the mysterious Lord Henry Arthur of Chirbury.

After a few days of warmth that hinted at spring, it was one of those chilly March days, where fires were lit in every grate, in every single room, to shake off the damp. Henrietta was finding it hard to breathe and John kept his pace steady, to match hers. They had talked about moving out to Chelsea, where the air was cleaner but John needed to stay near central London.

Late last year, he had renewed his contract with Drury Lane but was rarely asked to sing for Handel, even on rest days. She had not asked but wondered if he was keeping his engagements to the minimum because he was worried about her health.

Her lawyer avoided her gaze as he directed them into chairs opposite the desk and asked his clerk to bring coffee with sugar and cream. The fuss of serving, pouring, spooning, and stirring gave Henrietta a chance to study him and saw his hands shake as he lifted the small jug of cream. This was not going to be a day for good news.

'Henrietta and John,' he said, shuffling documents. 'The Earl of Powis has replied saying he has no knowledge of your claims against him and since he was not a signatory to your marriage settlement, he believes the matter has nothing to do with him.'

John raised a hand. 'Wait, wait, who is the Earl of Powis?'

'Sorry, I should have explained,' Edward Webb replied. 'He's been granted that title by the king but it's the same man, Henry Arthur of Chirbury.'

Henrietta felt her brow tighten, as if someone had squeezed a tourniquet around her skull. How easy life was for some... the right word here, join the best club, drop a letter there, a new title... all sorted.

'My daughter will be fourteen in June,' she said. 'A legal age where she can make her own decisions. What are our options? Should we continue to pursue this or allow her to fight her own battle, supported by my aunt and her husband? I'm weary and don't believe I will ever see a penny from the Herbert estate.'

The lawyer coughed and shook his head. 'I'm sorry, Henrietta, but have you forgotten my considerable investment, one that has allowed you to live the lifestyle you choose? You must continue to fight; there is no other option, if I am ever to be repaid. What Lady Barbara Herbert will do is for her to decide, guided by the Montagues.'

Henrietta nodded and reached for John's hand. 'But it's up

to my husband. All our legal actions are in his name. His career must come first, it is our only income.'

Edward Webb glanced at John, raising his eyebrows, searching for an answer.

John sighed and held both of Henrietta's hands between his. 'Of course we must continue. It's not just about money. I want to see the Herbert family in court, humiliated, just as we have been, however long it takes.'

Too long for me, Henrietta thought but said nothing, her tight throat blocking any chance of speaking.

John studied her, holding her gaze, his eyes forced wide open to prevent any unfortunate show of emotion. She returned his grip and dropped her head. *John knows,* she thought. *He knows he'll be fighting this alone.*

Before he left for the theatre, John settled Henrietta in front of a fire in the library, and asked Mrs Mills to bring her mistress a tray of tea. The cats sought out the warmth, their only other option being the conflagration of the kitchen range, where they ran the risk of singing their fur if they sat too close.

A cat occupied either side of Henrietta's fireplace, their eyes forming slits, while Filch sat on her lap, lifting his head to butt her fingers with his skull whenever she dozed enough to stop stroking.

It would have helped to talk to Amelia but the Webbs had two small children, with another expected and Henrietta found them exhausting. Amelia didn't seem to notice and never sent them out of the room with their nurse, so conversation was impossible.

The door rattled and Henrietta woke from a restless sleep, curled within a deeply upholstered armchair. The housemaid crept into the room and placed a letter on the side table next to her mistress.

The white document with its ominous red seal shone with menace in a room that had darkened through the short afternoon. She would not open it, not until the candles had been lit. There was nothing she wanted to read, nothing she wanted to know, except perhaps a few words from her daughter, and those never came.

Once pools of candlelight broke through the grey shadows of twilight and a discussion was had with Mrs Mills about what she would eat that night, Henrietta snapped the unfamiliar seal. The letter was from her aunt, Viscountess Montague, a woman who had never once written, in all the time she had assumed legal care of Barbara.

There was worrying news from the convent, her aunt wrote. Lady Mary Herbert, Barbara's aunt, had been pestering the Abbess with letters, demanding a secret meeting with the child.

Fortunately, the Abbess had refused all such approaches and had written to Viscount Montague for advice. What did Henrietta think, as the child's mother? The Montagues were convinced that Lady Mary Herbert was not a suitable person for young Barbara to meet, given her history of living with a man she had never married and her reputation for gambling, but if Henrietta wanted the visit to happen, they would agree, as long as it was supervised.

Remembering everything her first husband had told her about his sister, the bitterness and resentment he felt, energised Henrietta. How dare this Mary Herbert woman try to worm her way into her daughter's life. She carried a candle across to the writing desk and pulled down the lid to search for the writing materials stored inside.

Barbara's father hated Mary, she scrawled in haste to her aunt. *He would never have allowed them to meet and we must respect his views. I forbid any contact between Lady Mary Herbert and my daughter.*

Henrietta signed the letter and sealed it, wondering whether her aunt's comment about Mary Herbert's unmarried state and her affair was intended as a snide reflection on her own behaviour. Even if this was the case, the Montagues must be deeply concerned to have broken their silence and written to her. She must make sure she was included in whatever was happening in future, whatever decisions were being made about her daughter. Unsealing the letter, beneath her signature she added a long sentence of grateful thanks and blotted the fresh ink, hoping these humble words would be enough to satisfy the Montagues.

It was growing dark outside, the air thick with particles from neighbourhood fires, but Henrietta was determined to post the letter herself, to exchange coins for its safe passage and witness it pass directly into the hand of the courier's clerk. Covering her face with a scarf, she pulled her cape tightly around her shoulders and set off through the familiar streets, windows alight with lamps not yet hidden behind shutters. The courier's office would still be trading. All being well, her letter would reach Paris tomorrow.

BARBARA

Everyone has gone quite mad, even the nuns, and it takes a lot to rattle them, given their easy access to God. First the sisters hovered over me, wherever I went, saying you couldn't be too careful, someone might want to snatch you, which is nonsense because no one has ever come to see me in all the time I've been kept prisoner at this school, except to pick me up for holidays.

The next thing, Barbara Two turned up, all hot and red-faced and said she's taking me back to Paris for a while. I'm bundled into the embarrassing Montague coach, with all the girls in my form staring, but there's still no explanation. She said I'd find out soon enough, whatever that means.

Anthony is in his last year at school but hardly ever bothers to go because he already has a place at university. He was staying with a friend in a place called La Roule but then he fell ill. His mother was worried about him and decided to take the carriage to visit. Of course, I had to go too, even though Adele was in the middle of teaching me how to play quadrille.

The street where Anthony's friend lived was not the sort of place we usually visit. The road surface was pressed down dirt and the houses small and shabby. The carriage looked ridiculous parked outside and I felt so ashamed, I wanted to get inside the house as soon as possible, because people were gathering, as if we were some sort of show. While Barbara Two spoke to the boy's mother, I climbed the narrow staircase to Anthony's room. The ceiling hovered just above my head, and the window was small, so there wasn't much light but when I saw Anthony lying on a narrow strip of bed pressed against the wall, he really did look ill, his skin a bit green and his hair greasy.

'Anthony,' I whispered. 'We've come to take you home.'

He opened his eyes and stared at me as if he'd never met me before, then he seemed to understand and shook his head. 'I'm too ill to be moved. Where is my mother? Is she downstairs?'

In case I was expected to touch him or offer some words of comfort, I said I would go down and fetch her. There was also a smell that reminded me of the aged nuns at my convent and I'd stayed in his bedchamber as long as I could manage. On the landing, before I even reached the top of the stairs, I could hear shouting from below, two women screaming at each other like the washerwomen who work in St Augustine's laundry. The woman of the house stared up at me and raised both hands, palm upwards, as if I might be able to help. The front door stood open and I hurried down to stand next to her, judging whether it was safe to go outside.

My great-aunt had her hands on her hips, body tilted forward, screaming at an older woman with greying hair, tangled bits escaping from under her cap.

'How dare you spy on us, you vile woman,' Barbara Two yelled.

This was shocking, I had never heard her raise her voice, never mind shout.

'I wasn't spying,' the other woman spat back. 'I thought there must be a problem, because of this.' She waved a hand to take in the coach, as if only an emergency would explain its odd presence in this lowly street.

My great-aunt, blind to how she and her almost royal coach might look to others, protested, 'You could have knocked on the door. You climbed onto a chair and were spying through the window. I saw you!'

The offending chair stood below the sill, its presence undeniable. The older woman changed tack. 'I know who you are, I asked your coachman. You have my niece with you and I have every right to see her.'

I dipped back inside the door, aware that this quarrel was all about me. The door was still ajar, so I heard what followed.

'Her mother has left instructions. You cannot meet your niece. The girl's father, your brother, would not have allowed it. Now leave us alone.' Barbara Two was no longer shouting and had folded her arms in victory.

I guessed this woman must be my aunt. She wagged a finger right into my great-aunt's face, almost touching her nose. Her next words were spoken in a hiss but I managed to hear most of them. 'I know what you're up to. You're scheming to give Barbara to your son in marriage. That's illegal in this country, in case you haven't checked. I will block this all the way. I will write to the king.'

Our postilion, a tall man standing at my great-aunt's side, surely an unfair advantage, gave the other woman a push before dragging her by the elbow towards her own house, which was right next door.

Barbara Two hurried back through the front garden gate and joined us in the hall, red-faced and sweating.

Breathless, she spoke so rapidly, I could hardly make it out. 'I do apologise, Madame Lavigne, we must leave now. I will send the carriage back later to collect my son. This has been a most unfortunate encounter.'

Chaotic thoughts tumbled through my mind as we rolled through the unpaved streets of La Roule, before the view beyond the window at last reassured me we had reached the Paris I knew and were safe. My great-aunt's breathing slowed and once her hands stopped fidgeting with the edge of her cloak, I dared to ask the question that surfaced above all the others.

'Is it true what she said? Are you hoping that Anthony and I will marry?'

Barbara Two's eyes sought mine and slowly gained some focus. 'Of course not, that woman's just trying to make trouble. Let her write to the king; she's not the only one with friends at court.'

'Who is she?'

'Her name is Lady Mary Herbert. She's your father's sister. There was no love lost between them.'

'Why does she want to meet me? She's never tried before.'

'I have no idea. Knowing her reputation, it will be about money. With the Herbert family, it always is. The important thing to keep in mind, Barbara, is that she has shown no interest in you until now. We wouldn't keep you from an aunt who had always held good intentions towards you and nor would your mother. Now you're almost fourteen, and of marriageable age, unsuitable people will try to gain your trust.'

I hesitated before speaking again, uncertain how my words would be received. 'Why is my mother involved, all of a sudden?'

My great-aunt gave a sigh and stared out of the window. Turning back, she said, 'Perhaps that has been my error. We should try to involve her more in future. This is a turning point in your life, and I have been rather caught unawares. One thing is certain, you cannot return to St Augustine's. We'll try to find you another school. I've heard there's a good convent in Paris.'

My next thoughts could not be spoken aloud. Why should I go to another school? My great-aunt and her sisters had all been educated at home by a governess. Her mother, Barbara One, had been very proud of this. Why am I always the one sent out of the family when Anthony gets to loll around at home?

'I don't want to go to another school,' I said.

'Well that's not your choice, my dear, is it,' my great-aunt replied, her eyebrows raised and lips set into an unyielding line. The conversation was over.

CHAPTER 25

1749

MARY

There wasn't a moment to lose. Mary had to release her niece from the grip of those awful people before the child was betrothed to their son. She only had Barbara's best interests at heart, wanted to give the girl a chance to make her own choice of guardian. Mary was the best choice, of course, but she would not force herself upon her niece. All she wanted was to meet her.

That scene in the street had been so humiliating, she was forced to move, to leave behind her own little house and her maid Lucille, who had refused to come with her. It was no loss. The Prince de Conti owed her a favour and had found her an apartment in the Hotel de Boisbodron, closer to central Paris. Her rooms were dark, being at the back of the precinct, and smelled of mice, but Mary didn't care as long as she had enough light to write her letters.

She found a decent woman from Montgomeryshire, Anne Griffiths, to be her maid, a woman who was impressed by her employer's links with Wales. Despite Mary's honesty, admitting she had never visited Wales, Miss Griffiths endlessly told stories about people they might possibly have in common.

There had been no reply from the king about her proposal to marry her niece to the Prince of Rochefort, which was perhaps for the best given her letter had been written in a panic, before she had committed herself to Barbara's right to make her own choice.

Mary wrote another letter, this time to the British Ambassador for France, the Earl of Albemarle. As she scratched out the letter, using ink drier than she would have liked, it crossed her mind that not too long ago, her niece's grandfather had held this very position. How different things might have been if he had lived but there was always the girl's uncle, the new Earl Waldegrave, a man who might prove useful in the future if Mary's plans didn't work out.

Adding James Waldegrave's name to her list of important people to contact, Mary returned to her letter, explaining to the ambassador that a British subject, a girl of not yet fourteen, was about to be forced to marry the son of her guardians. Her family representative, Lady Mary Herbert, was being forbidden to even speak to the child. To be helpful, since the Earl of Albemarle must be a busy man, Mary added her opinion that her niece must be removed from the Montagues and returned to Great Britain, where the courts should decide on a more suitable guardian. Of course, the ambassador might hold a different view, which she would respect.

Mary blotted the ink and gave the letter to Miss Griffiths to take to the courier, hoping to find an hour's peace and quiet, away from the woman's yapping, to snatch some sleep.

The ambassador replied immediately and Mary was ordered to meet him at the official residence the following day. The room spoke of a gentleman's club in London, rather than a Parisian palace. Over the fireplace, there was a portrait of King George, a man who had once been a friend of her father and on the other walls, hung earlier monarchs, staring at her with wistful envy that she lived while they were dead.

There was a smell of leather and men, the room revealed in shades of sepia, the atmosphere gloomy with dark wood furniture of the best quality and deep armchairs studded with brass buttons.

The ambassador's servant brought wine and after pouring them both a glass, left the decanter on the small side table set between their two chairs. The Earl studied her as he sipped his wine and Mary returned his gaze, noticing a chin settling to fat and lips that gave the impression he found something about her amusing. His wig was set back, revealing a high forehead, without a dusting of powder.

'Thank you for your letter, Lady Herbert, I am concerned about the situation you describe, but first, is there truth in the rumour that you met Prince Charles Edward Stuart in Paris, on his way to invade Scotland?'

Mary shifted in her seat. Why had this unfortunate event been brought up? Was it a trap, a feeble attempt to test her loyalty? 'He turned up at my house. I've no idea why. It was an awkward meeting and I'd rather not be reminded of it.'

Albemarle's wide-set eyes and arched brows again conveyed the impression that something was funny. Had there been gossip about how she had been forced to entertain the exiled prince from her bed? Is this what the ambassador had found out when he asked his staff about her?

'But why did he seek you out, Lady Mary? That's what I'm interested in.'

Mary shrugged. 'My family have had Jacobite connections for generations. I gave him some refreshments and sent him on his way.'

The Earl sighed and his eyes settled on a distant point beyond Mary's shoulder. 'I chased him, you know, after Culloden. Never caught the bugger. He led my men a merry dance, I can tell you. I thought you might be interested to hear the story, since you knew him personally.'

Mary was not interested but had long ago learned to humour old soldiers, even though this one was considerably younger than most of the men who bored her with tales of battles lost and won. He was clearly jealous of her contact with his prey, the young man he had promised to capture on behalf of the British people... well, the English anyway.

'Do tell me more,' she said, smiling in a manner she hoped might pass for encouragement and settled into her chair. 'It all sounds fascinating.'

An hour later, the wine bottle empty, Mary felt she had paid her dues and decided to interrupt her host. 'Thank you for explaining to me the military strategy behind searching for the prince. It was a most complicated endeavour. I'm so sorry you weren't successful. Less complicated, I hope, is the matter of my niece. Have you come to a decision?'

The Earl leaned towards her, steadying himself on the armrest of his chair. Mary had allowed him to drink most of the wine by sipping her own and placing her hand above her glass whenever more was offered.

'I have indeed,' he said. 'I will instruct Viscount Montague to bring Lady Barbara Herbert back to Great Britain as soon as she is fourteen and present her to the Chancery Court. It's the only way this matter can be resolved. He's a Freemason, you know, Viscount Montague. Never got on with that lot.'

'Will you also instruct him to give me a chance to meet my niece, here in Paris?'

'Of course, Lady Herbert. I will include that in my letter, which I will write later on today, after I've had my afternoon nap.'

Mary felt a sharp tug on her arm and was dragged into a doorway at the entrance to the Hotel Boisbodron. She was rarely off her guard in Paris, given the problem with pickpockets and thieves, but she was not used to alcohol in the afternoon, even two small glasses, and her attention had slipped. She did not feel any immediate fear, since the man was well-dressed, although he was clearly not of the aristocracy. He did smell of cheap brandy, however, and Mary snatched her arm out of his grip.

'How dare you,' she shouted. 'Leave me alone.' Passers-by began to gather, since it was unusual to hear a woman's raised voice above the normal background hubbub of the streets.

The man swept a wide-brimmed hat from his head, his hair tied back in the ponytail younger men preferred. He gave a deep bow from the waist. 'I do apologise, Lady Herbert, I have been searching for you everywhere and was directed to your apartment. I have been sent to find you by the Earl of Powis. He wishes to communicate with you.'

Mary narrowed her eyes. 'Where's your proof?'

From inside his coat, the man pulled out a letter, and Mary felt a flutter of remorse when she saw the Powis seal. It could have been a letter from her father. She scanned the letter from the latest Powis incumbent, introducing his agent, a certain Mr Shirley, who would explain everything. Because of the sensitive nature of the discussion, he was unwilling to commit his thoughts to paper.

Mary would not have invited Mr Shirley up to her rooms but Miss Griffiths was at home and able to act as chaperone. Visitors were so rare, the maidservant had to ask Mary where the best tea service was kept and after some searching by them both, it was found in a side console in the narrow hall. After pouring tea, Miss Griffiths settled herself in a chair just outside the parlour, where Mary was certain she was listening to every word.

'So, Mr Shirley,' Mary began, 'this is a surprise. What does your lord and master want with me, apart from robbing me of my inheritance.'

The agent shook his head, as if Mary's scornful tone could not be taken seriously by any sensible person. 'You are quite mistaken, Lady Herbert, he only has your best interests at heart. He is shocked to have discovered that you are living on charity.'

'Duchesse d'Herbert,' Mary corrected him, using the Jacobite title she deserved. Whatever this rude man thought, she was not impoverished, nor was she living on charity, not like she had been in Spain. Her remaining Spanish mine still brought in some revenue and she had invested wisely in a mine at Poullaouen. The qualities of efficiency and business acumen she held in abundance allowed her to recognise the same strengths in others and she was now receiving a useful income from her early investment. Those fools who dithered had regretted their indecision at their leisure.

'Tell me, Mr Shirley,' she said. 'How is he planning to address my best interests, those he apparently holds close to his heart?'

'My apologies, Duchesse. I understand that you are owed a considerable sum from the Powis estate. The Earl will make sure you are paid, if you agree to assist him.'

Mary hesitated. This was exactly what she wanted to hear but would the price he tried to extract be too high?

'Tell me more,' she said.

'My employer wishes to marry Lady Barbara Herbert. He needs your help to make it happen.'

So, so clever, Mary thought. *He owes the girl a fortune, marries her and wipes out the debt in a stroke.* If this had been worked out, years ago, with her brother, she had met her match in Chirbury.

She did not give any sign of approval, because she was unsure whether she did actually approve. 'The child is not yet fourteen,' she said, 'and Henry Arthur is a man in his forties. Most respectable people would take against such a match, myself included.'

'It's not so unusual these days,' Shirley argued in his master's defence. 'I can promise you, your niece will be well looked after in such a marriage and will regain the titles and position in society which are her right by birth.'

Mine too, Mary thought, *but the Earl is not offering to marry me.* Instead, she murmured, 'He will be debt-free and in time, there will be an heir. I can only admire his foresight.'

'You will not help us, Duchesse d'Herbert?'

Mary chewed her lower lip. 'I didn't say that.'

The invitation, which read more like a summons, arrived within two weeks. The Earl of Albemarle was a man of his word, worth the investment of two hours of her time listening to his rambling reminiscences.

A manservant showed her into a formal sitting room in the Montagues' elegant apartment in the Faubourg Saint-Germain, a room clearly designed for audiences such as these, one where a member of the family was forced to spend time with someone they were obliged to meet but comfort was kept to a minimum, so the visitor would not overstay their welcome.

It was years since Mary had visited a Parisian apartment owned by the ridiculously wealthy, but these rooms were no surprise to her. The mirrors, the panelling, the swirls of flowers, cherubs and nymphs, the gilding; it all made her head hurt. She sat alone for longer than any fourteen-year-old should keep an aunt waiting and was about to put her head out into the corridor and shout for help, when a girl entered, accompanied by a young woman.

Introductions were made. The girl was obviously Barbara, the woman the eldest daughter of the Montagues. Barbara seemed to find it funny that they were both called Mary.

'Mary One and Mary Two,' the girl said, giggling through a challenging stare directed at her aunt.

'You can refer to me as the Duchesse d'Herbert,' Mary said, having taken an instant dislike to her niece. Yet it was disconcerting: she could have been looking at her brother Edward. It ought to have been impossible to bring his face to mind, but somewhere in her memory, she had stored an image of him as a child. The blonde, fine hair, pale eyes, and rounded cheeks, finished by a soft chin. He was here, in front of her, carried forward in the body of his daughter.

Mary searched for something to say, since she had no acquaintance with young girls and their lives. 'How is your new school?' she asked.

Barbara shrugged and her lips toyed with a smirk. 'I hardly started at my new convent before I had to be removed, thanks to you. My guardians have been told to take me to Britain, to their estate at Cowdray and then I have to go before the courts. My cousin Anthony will be coming too, he always spends the summer in England.'

Mary straightened her back, glancing at herself in the mirrored wall and disliking what she saw. 'Ah, that young man, the one they're planning you should marry. I'm here to tell you that you have options. You have choice. Don't allow anyone to force you into an unsuitable match.'

Barbara's irritating smirk widened into a grin. 'From what I've heard, Aunt Mary, no one managed to push you into any match at all. This idea of a union between myself and Anthony exists only in your over-excitable imagination. I would never marry him and he would refuse to marry me. He is my brother in all but name and he has a shocking complexion.'

Mary felt a surge of temper, as if the girl had slapped her. Where had she learned to speak to her elders with such impertinence? It didn't help that the Montagues' daughter had sniggered when Barbara accused her aunt of being over-excitable. What sort of family was this? Neither of the child's guardians could be bothered to attend an important meeting about their ward and had sent a barely grown woman in their stead. It was time her niece was removed, before more harm was done to her nature and she became unmarriageable.

Mary no longer held any desire to be Barbara's guardian and felt not an ounce of guilt about conniving with the Earl of Powis to snare the child into a marriage. From what she could see, as an experienced matchmaker, they were made for each other.

Mary sniffed. 'My only ambition was to assist with your difficult transition into adulthood, to behave as an aunt should, without any regard for my personal gain. The Earl of Powis has inherited all of the Herbert estates and wishes to embrace you into the Herbert family, as his heir. Of course that cannot happen, while you are in the clutches of the Montagues. I can arrange for you to meet him, once you are living at Cowdray.'

After dropping this unexpected gambit into their one-sided

conversation, Mary had the pleasure of watching the girl's cheeks drain of colour, her eyes scanning the companion's face for help. *This pert little madam has met her equal in me,* she thought.

Barbara chewed on her lip, as if she might cry but then her eyes hardened. She glared at Mary. 'So you came to offer me options, to protect me, but if the Earl of Powis becomes my new guardian, that will no doubt benefit you as well as him. Please remember this, I am fourteen and will make my own decisions without guidance from you, or anyone else.'

The Montagues' eldest daughter stood and tipped her chin at Barbara, hinting she should follow her to the door. 'My cousin is happy living within my family,' she said, using her height to intimidate their guest. 'Changing her guardians is far from her thoughts, as is marriage to anyone, least of all my brother Anthony. Her education has been interrupted by your interference and we will have to find her another school in England. My family has been caused a great deal of distress by your thoughtless accusations about our care of Barbara. Please do not wait to hear from us; we will deal directly with the Chancery Court.'

Mary also stood, reluctant to remain at a disadvantage. 'You will indeed hear from the court,' Mary hissed. 'I am not alone in worrying about your family's guardianship of my niece and from what I have seen today of her attitude, their fears are justified. The next step will not be to your liking.'

The other Mary answered in a tone which carried everything of her taken-for-granted titles, wealth, and privilege, everything Mary Herbert had been denied. 'Since our sources inform us you have no right to style yourself as a Duchess, I will address you as Lady Herbert. Please do not threaten us, Lady Herbert.'

Lady Mary Montague flicked a hand in a gesture of dismissal before Mary could muster a suitable response and continued. 'A woman of your age must tire easily. Please remain seated and a servant will escort you from the building.'

CHAPTER 26

1749

HENRIETTA

It was only a short walk to the Sardinian chapel but Henrietta paced her footsteps to conserve energy, feeling angry that her chest wasn't trying hard enough to breathe, while her heart worked hard enough for them both, pattering and thumping despite all her efforts to keep it steady.

On this day, a Wednesday morning in June, the clandestine church wrapped her in still, damp air, its habitual smell of incense mixed with the odour of clothes left too long without washing. The small organ played softly as she slipped into a chair below the galleried balcony. She rested, breathing in short gasps, until she was able to inhale more deeply. A priest paused to adjust the position of a candlestick on the altar before stopping to whisper to two women, praying side by side on the steps.

Henrietta came to this church whenever she could manage the distance, sometimes to sit alone and empty her head of any thoughts, at other times to speak to the priest about death.

John would be impatient with her if he knew, the charade they both maintained was that her health problem would pass, but even if it did, trying to find her faith by taxing the priest with difficult questions, did her no harm. Her grandparents were dead and so was her father. Her mother died years ago. Where were they now? If there was nothing after death, then why was life so short?

A worrying letter had arrived by courier this morning from Barbara Montague. They were returning at once to their estate at Cowdray to face the Chancery Court in late July, since their guardianship of her daughter was being challenged by the Earl of Powis. Spiteful people were saying they had ambitions to marry their son Anthony to Barbara but Henrietta must have faith. There was no truth in this. It was certain the court would settle in their favour and life would return to normal but it was important to prepare for the worst. If they lost custody of Barbara, the chancellor would expect an interim guardian to remove the child from the court, until a permanent decision could be made about her future. Henrietta should make these arrangements, since the Montagues would not be allowed this privilege. There was a risk that no one else in court would think of the child, left alone without a guardian, apart from themselves and her mother. Henrietta must write to Lord Hardwicke with her instructions, as soon as possible. Could she possibly consider acting as interim guardian for her own daughter?

Henrietta pulled the letter out from a pocket sewn inside her robe and in the half light, screwed up her eyes to reread her aunt's words. Once she was home, she would write to the Lord High Chancellor and take the letter to the meeting with her solicitor tomorrow, where she and John had been asked to meet the Earl of Powis' London agent.

She raised her eyes to the domed ceiling over the altar and thought about who she could ask to look after the child. She and John were not short of friends who would take her daughter for a few weeks. The difficult part was explaining why this could not be her, Barbara's mother.

The priest weaved between chairs scattered through the nave and dragged one across to sit next to her, leaning his elbows on his knees and looking up at her with concern. She was glad it was the younger of the two Sardinian priests. He was a good listener who gave the impression of having all the time in the world to spend with his parishioners. The older priest seemed distracted, his eyes flitting from your face if anyone new entered, or if there was an unexpected sound. Guards were known to have raided the chapel, arresting anyone who was not an embassy employee, so his lack of attention was perhaps forgivable.

'Lady Beard, I'm glad to see you. We have missed you at our services. There was a rumour that you were unwell.'

'Thank you, father,' Henrietta replied. 'I have not been myself and find the walk too far. We are moving to Chelsea for John's summer season, so I will not be able to return until the winter. John is singing at Ranelagh Gardens and I will benefit from the country air.'

The priest straightened his back and frowned. 'I'm sorry we will lose you from the congregation but it's only for the summer. Is there anything you need to talk over with me today?'

'My daughter is being brought from Paris to face the Chancery Court, as an accusation has been made against her present guardians, my aunt and her husband.'

The priest frowned. 'I have to ask you, is there any truth in the accusation?'

Henrietta shook her head. 'Not at all. Barbara is happy with

252

the Montagues and was making good progress at her convent school in Bruges. Her whole life has been unsettled and the worst thing is, she may end up with strangers, without warning. I fear the outcome, father, something inside is warning me that I cannot rely on the courts to make a fair decision.'

'This is awful, Lady Beard. I cannot begin to imagine how you are feeling. Who is pursuing this action?'

'The new Earl of Powis, for motives I cannot yet fathom. He is supported by Barbara's aunt, Lady Mary Herbert, I fear out of sheer vindictiveness. My child's father hated her.'

'We will pray together, Lady Beard. It may not change the outcome but will help you to bear your suffering.'

'The thing is, father, the thing is–' Henrietta began to weep, a sobbing she could not control, horrible noises gurgling from her throat as she fought for air.

The priest hurried away and returned with a small glass of wine. 'Drink this,' he said. 'Take small sips.'

Henrietta did as she was instructed, aware of his eyes holding hers, waiting to hear her shameful confession.

'The thing is,' she continued, 'I should take her. I could offer to be Barbara's interim guardian and fight for her to live with me and John, as her parents. But I cannot, father, I cannot.'

'I am guessing,' the priest said, his tone gentle, 'that you believe it is too late for you.'

Henrietta nodded. 'It is too late, in every way. We cannot have her in Chelsea, we have only taken two rooms but I must live there if there is any chance of regaining my health. If I do not recover, the child will return only to watch her mother die.'

The priest's expression shifted from concern to sorrow. 'That is sad.'

'Even if I live,' Henrietta gulped, 'we cannot afford school fees, or music lessons, or new dresses, everything she is used to.

I no longer know her, the life she has led. She will not want... she will not choose me.'

'Can I call you Henrietta?' the priest asked.

Henrietta nodded and tried to stifle any tears, aware of the other two woman staring.

'As your priest, I am duty bound to say that God will forgive you, but I think the problem is you cannot forgive yourself?'

Hearing these kind words, Henrietta could only look down at her hands, wringing at a sodden handkerchief.

'From what you have told me,' the priest continued, 'you made a decision about your daughter when you were barely an adult, a very different person from the woman you are now. You must try to understand the young woman you were and accept that things cannot now be changed.'

The sound from the organ rose to fill the small chapel, as the music reached its crescendo. Henrietta wondered if their friend Thomas Arne was playing but she could only see the organist's hunched shoulders. 'What shall I do about my daughter? She will be here soon.'

The priest frowned and stroked his neat beard. 'You must tell her what you have told me. If you cannot meet her, write a letter. Even if she has no sympathy towards you at present, she may find comfort in your words, later in her life.'

Henrietta rose to leave, to begin the slow walk back to Great North Street. 'Thank you, father, I will.'

The priest also rose, his chair scraping against the flagstones. 'I will give you the name of a convent in Hammersmith, a nursing order who will care for you when you feel it is time. If I write to them today, they will be prepared to accept you, however many months or years you have ahead of you.'

'You think I am dying, father?'

He shook his head. 'I am not a physician but I can see that

John may need some help, even if your visits to the convent are only temporary. The nuns will restore you and assist you with any doubts you may have about your faith.'

Henrietta turned her face away, feeling her throat tighten. 'I hope I will see you in the autumn,' she whispered, 'with my health restored.'

'I will pray for that moment, Henrietta,' he said.

On her slow walk home, Henrietta passed the end of Amelia and Edward's street and considered whether she had enough strength left for a visit. Her friend would welcome her, invite her to rest but as she reached the turning, Henrietta realised her remaining energy would only take her as far as New North Street. Amelia was expecting another child and this pregnancy was proving more troublesome than her previous two. Perhaps it was best, for them both, not to try.

Lord Powis' agent waited for them in Edward Webb's office and stood as they entered, to tip a small bow in Henrietta's direction. He ignored John's outstretched hand. The man was neat in stature, and without his tall wig, only reached to John's shoulder. His otherwise pleasant face was spoiled by prominent teeth that would not have disgraced a rabbit. Henrietta tried not to stare and forced her gaze towards her cousin, who began formal introductions.

The agent, Corbyn Morris, impatient with such formalities, swept away the offer of coffee, dripping lace from the sleeve of his coat. 'We are all busy people,' he interrupted the lawyer, directing his attention for the first time to John. 'As you are aware, your wife's daughter is facing the Chancery Court in a matter of weeks. The Earl of Powis is proposing that his mother,

Lady Chirbury, become the child's guardian and is seeking your support.'

John's voice rose; shocking to witness from a man who was never angry. 'On what grounds?'

'I am not at liberty to discuss our arguments before the hearing but they are compelling. We will win this without you but if you and your wife would agree, we will pay your wife's debts and find you a position in the army or the government, something more suited for the husband of Lady Henrietta.'

'My husband has a job,' Henrietta interrupted, feeling heat rising from her neckline. 'He is the most feted tenor in this country. What is behind Powis' sudden and unwanted interference in my daughter's life?'

Morris cleared his throat. 'The Earl of Powis is the head of your daughter's family and has concerns about the way she is being raised.'

'My daughter is a Waldegrave and a Webb,' Henrietta argued, 'as am I. The Herberts lost any interest in her the day she was born.'

Edward Webb, so far ignored in this exchange, stepped in. 'Mr Morris, please put any proposals in writing to me before the hearing. The Herbert family owe Lady Beard a considerable sum and I would expect payment of those arrears to be the Earl's priority, not her current debts or unwarranted offers of jobs for her husband.'

Henrietta smiled at her cousin, Amelia's husband. What a good man he was, how much help he had given her and John, how generous he had been with his advice and time, for which he never charged. She must remember to thank him, before it was too late. She felt her chest squeeze; the room was stifling. 'Please can I have that coffee after all?' she asked.

Morris drummed his fingers on the arm of his chair as coffee was served, his attention directed at the lawyer. 'Am I to assume that my master's offer has been refused?'

Edward looked at Henrietta, then at John and both nodded their assent. Henrietta pulled a letter from her robe pocket. 'I have written to the Lord Chancellor with instructions for my daughter's care, should the Montagues lose custody of her.'

'Wait, wait, wait,' Morris interrupted, holding up a hand. 'The court will decide who will be her guardian. You gave up any influence over your daughter's future years ago, Lady Beard.'

From a stranger, this harsh observation felt like a slap and she pulled back from Morris' raised hand. John jumped to his feet, as if he wanted to hit the man. A shocked hush fell across the combatants; even the clerk turned around from his desk, his face white with fear.

Only Edward Webb appeared calm, but he also rose from behind his desk to show his authority. 'Lady Beard is right. God forbid the Montagues lose custody of Barbara, but if they do, guardianship will be decided at a second hearing. Lady Beard is wise to have suggested a plan for a temporary guardian, unless your master has already done so?'

Morris shook his head. 'I will leave you now. There is no more to be done. If you pass me your letter, Lady Beard, I will deliver it by hand to the Lord Chancellor. I am meeting him later today.'

Henrietta hesitated, almost handing the letter to the agent but her cousin leaned over his desk, his palm upwards and took the letter from her. 'Thank you, Mr Morris, but I will take charge of this letter and ensure it reaches its destination. My clerk will deliver it.'

Morris waited for his cloak and when it arrived, made a fuss of fastening the neck, despite the humidity of the day. 'I will walk with you a short way, if you don't mind,' he said, directing this invitation to Henrietta. 'I need to reassure the Earl that your mind is made up about his offer.'

Edward Webb stepped around his desk and opened the door for Corbyn Morris. 'Henrietta and John must stay here,' he said, bowing to the agent. 'We need to discuss what will happen at the court, since my clients have no experience of such a hearing. It can be daunting, for the unprepared. I'm sure you understand.'

CHAPTER 27

1749

BARBARA

I didn't expect to lose my family. The adults, all except my mother, had reassured me that everything would be well. I just had to get through the day and we would all settle back into life as it was before.

I'm not someone who scares easily, but I hated sitting by myself in the cave they call Westminster Hall, where every sound, footstep or even papers shuffling, echoed upwards to the bones of the roof. Voices boomed or were too quiet, depending on where the person was seated and sometimes I struggled to hear. No matter how often my great-aunt waved at me from where she sat with Viscount Montague, I was alone. There was no one else there for me, with my mother in a nursing convent and John singing that very afternoon at Ranelagh.

There was no doubt about my mother's poor health. I didn't choose to spend last night with her but Barbara Two insisted, as if there was some urgency. I know about convents but this one was different. There were no children or bells, or nuns shouting, only quiet, the smell of cooking and sisters gliding between rows of beds with pans, cloths and drinking vessels. My mother was in a room of her own, with a small cot squeezed in for me. I wouldn't have recognised her, not only because it was years since we last met, but she was so thin and weary, only a few straggling strands of hair unrestrained by her cap. She hugged me but I hated feeling her bones through her thin shift and I think I might have pulled away. I wish I hadn't.

She struggled to talk because of her problem with breathing and she kept on crying. I really would have preferred not to be there. I thought of what my last night at Cowdray would have been like, instead of this torment, playing cricket with Anthony in the Long Gallery and cards with my great-aunt in the parlour while Anthony and his father shared manly thoughts about the estate. Barbara Two had explained very little about the hearing, I think she didn't expect things to turn out the way they did, but at least my mother tried to help me understand.

Facing each other across our two cots, she took my hands between hers. 'Tomorrow, you will hear some unpleasant things about your family and perhaps about me. The adults will lie because you are important to them, not because they care about you but because only you can make something else happen in their lives, something they want. This is hard to fathom but try to hold on to what you believe to be true. When Lord Hardwicke asks you for your views, do not be afraid to tell him.'

As she spoke, it hit me like a blow to the chest that I might not go home with the Montagues. I struggled to keep my voice steady. One of us crying was enough.

'What will happen to me?' I said.

My mother paused to cough, clearing phlegm from her throat. 'If the Montagues are discharged, I'm afraid you will have no further contact with them. The Earl of Powis will argue that his mother should be your guardian, but that will be decided at a later hearing. I have arranged that you will leave the court with trusted friends of mine. My husband will visit you there. I am afraid I cannot, because of what you see before you.'

A kitchen girl entered, bringing us bread and soup. I ate everything my mother left. Our platters were cleared, and a nursing sister took my mother away to clean her and make her ready for bed. Once I was alone, a different sister peered around the door and told me not to worry. Lady Beard was very ill, she said, but some recovery was still possible. This would not be our last night together.

We lay in our beds, pushed side by side, but not touching. The candles were snuffed out and in the safety of darkness my mother whispered that she regretted leaving me behind in France when I was a young child. She hoped I might understand one day, even if I could not do so now. I didn't know what to say, but something was expected so I said it was alright, but how could I know whether it was or not?

If I felt able to speak on her behalf, she continued, would I ask the Lord Chancellor if she could have free access to me, whoever was eventually my guardian? I nodded, but she would not have been able to see this.

In the silence, only soft footsteps passing in the corridor outside, I heard my mother praying. The last thing she said was, 'Barbara, whatever happens, hold on to your faith.' I paused before answering because I hadn't understood my faith was at risk. I took it for granted that I was a Catholic and why would anyone want me to be something different? Before I could reassure her, my mother's breathing came in short, sharp rasps and I realised she had fallen asleep. There was little sleep for me, turning on the hard, straw mattress throughout the night, counting the dreaded hours through the cries of people struggling to hold on to life itself, never mind sleep.

My mother still slept soundly when I was jolted awake by the bell for early morning prayers. I dressed quickly, helped by a nun who brought me warm water, clean cloths, and the plain, chaste dress and cap my great-aunt had ordered. In the refectory, the sisters stood close by, encouraging me to swallow every mouthful of the bread, eggs, and warm ale they thought I needed to face my day in court. The Abbess herself escorted me through the nunnery gates to the Montagues' waiting coach.

'Be brave, be strong, young Barbara,' she called to me, as the coachman escorted me up the carriage steps. 'Be like your mother.'

It was a day of lies. That ghastly woman, Lady Mary Herbert, told the court her timely intervention with the British Ambassador had only just prevented the Montagues from whisking me off to marry Anthony somewhere outside France.

Even worse, the Montagues had deliberately risked my honour by allowing me to visit Anthony in the house of an unknown woman in La Roule and had disregarded all the rules of respectable behaviour, by sending my cousin and me alone in a post-chaise, from Paris to Cowdray. Had I only imagined my great-aunt travelling with us for the entire journey?

The Herbert woman tried to impress everyone with a story that I had been paraded around London in the Montagues' coach before I was presented to the worshippers of a Catholic church.

I didn't understand why this was so wrong but judging from the murmur that circled the cold walls of the hall, her words had gone down well with the court. The Montagues did have an enormous carriage but so what? It wasn't a crime, just embarrassing. The so-called church was a tiny chapel at the back of the Portuguese embassy. I stared at the woman who claimed to be my aunt and every time she glanced across at me I mouthed the word 'Liar' in her face, until Lord Hardwicke frowned at me and shook his head.

Next on the stand was the Earl of Powis, the one who wanted his mother to look after me. In my mind I had created a monster but he wasn't bad looking for his age. He smiled at me and I couldn't help smiling back before I saw the Montagues glance at each other with alarm. He pushed the religion thing and as I listened to his arguments, I understood why my mother was afraid he might win. No one had told me there were laws against being Catholic in this country and I was almost convinced, like everyone else, that the Montagues had behaved as if there weren't.

This tall man, with a plump face and kind eyes, argued that by raising me as a Catholic, the Montagues had ensured that if he died without having children, I could not inherit the Powis estate, as was my right. It was his duty and the responsibility of the court, to remove me from the influence of the Montagues so that I might be raised in the faith of my country of birth.

He proposed his own mother, Lady Chirbury, take on this responsibility, a woman of impeccable moral standards. If the court did not agree, he would instruct his lawyers to invoke the penal laws of Great Britain against the papist Montague family.

Then it was my turn. The Lord Chancellor asked me to take the stand and I was escorted to face the court. There were no windows, apart from one huge arch at the end of the hall and candles already sputtered on the walls. Through the smoke, I saw the upturned faces of the crowd reflected back at me like rows of moons.

'Lady Barbara Herbert,' Lord Hardwicke said, using a booming voice to make himself sound more important. 'You have the right to state your views but I will make the final decision. Are you ready?'

I nodded, remembering my great-aunt's instructions about behaving well. 'I am sure Lady Chirbury is a kind and respectable woman but I have never met her. The Montagues have cared for me as if I was their own daughter and I want to stay with them. There is no truth in the gossip that I am to be married to my cousin. He is like a brother to me, nothing more.'

Lord Hardwicke raised his eyebrows. 'You are saying, young lady, that adults in this court have shared mere gossip and tittle-tattle?'

I nodded and turned my body slightly to face Lady Mary Herbert. 'My Lord, worse than gossip, they have lied on oath. That woman,' I pointed at Mary, 'is nothing more than a conniving cheat.'

A universal intake of breath and chatter followed my words. Lord Hardwicke thumped his gavel. 'Silence! I have heard enough. I agree with this astute young woman that Lady Mary Herbert is guilty of gross exaggeration and I am surprised the Earl of Powis used her as a witness. However, I find myself convinced by the Earl's arguments. Lord and Lady Montague, I am sorry to say you will have no more contact with Lady Barbara Herbert. This hearing will reconvene in two weeks to decide on the matter of future guardianship. The court is dismissed.'

I sat alone on my bench, as everyone trooped out of the courtroom, heading home to their safe lives and welcoming families. I realised, too late, that I had not argued for my mother, had forgotten to convince the Lord Chancellor that she should be part of my life. I hadn't scanned the crowd to find my great-aunt's face, to mouth my farewell.

There was a tap on my shoulder and a clerk offered his elbow to lead me from the hall. My interim guardians were waiting for me, he whispered. Would I even recognise them? It didn't matter, I decided. I would not speak to them, I would not eat, I would stay in my room and refuse to get dressed. There was nothing more I could do.

CHAPTER 28

1750

MARY

Why was there never any fresh ink? Mary cast down her pen and rang her handbell for Miss Griffiths. However often she explained to her servant that replenishing the inkwell was one of her key duties, it always seemed to be empty.

Anne Griffiths defended herself, her Welsh accent becoming stronger as the red circles on her cheeks burned with indignation. 'Well, my lady, it seems to dry out so quickly. You write so many letters.' This was said with a tone of disapproval.

Mary had returned from London in a mood of great irritation with the world, a mood which had been hard to shift. It was obvious she was unwelcome in Paris, with strangers actually elbowing her in the street and no one leaving their calling cards, but she had no idea why. Whatever the reason, it wasn't fair of her to make Anne the butt of ill humour.

'I'm sorry, Miss Griffiths,' Mary said. 'Please bring me some tea and then go out for more ink. I have two more letters to write today.'

'Another one to Mr Shirley?' Miss Griffiths asked, although it was none of her business.

Mary turned away. 'Never mind who they're for, just bring the tea... please.'

While her maidservant was absent, the sounds of cupboard doors slamming, water boiling and a porcelain cup and saucer crashing onto a tray, drifted through from the kitchen to her small, shabby room, and felt strangely comforting. The window facing Mary's desk looked out onto the rooftops and back windows of the Temple Precinct. As she had reminded that rude Mr Shirley, it wasn't charity: she paid her way like everyone else. But who else would want to live here, even for a pittance?

Anne Griffiths set her tray on a table next to her favourite armchair, one whose silk armrests were now dirty and frayed and the back headrest greasy from her hair. It didn't matter, she only noticed the dirt if she peered and what was the point of looking? She didn't have any visitors.

That Earl, the man she hated but whose name she had the misfortune to share, had treated her with utter rudeness and contempt after the custody hearing, striding past her, his eyes roaming elsewhere. When she had rushed to speak to him, expecting only gratitude and a reward – a considerable reward – for her contribution to his success, he had pretended not to see her.

It wasn't her fault everyone in court had laughed at her evidence. She hadn't received a word of thanks, nothing for her expenses in London or the money she was owed. Travelling back had been exhausting, having to find the cheapest accommodation and transport when she had anticipated having a purse full of money. She itemised her expenses and all the money owed to her by the Herbert estate and sent the same invoice daily to the Earl's agent. She never received a reply.

When Miss Griffiths returned with the ink, her second letter would be to Joseph Gage, suggesting they meet. He had qualities she rarely found in others, mostly his unusual habit of finding her company interesting if not enjoyable. They had spent almost thirty years together, had lived through frightening and exhilarating times. If she could swallow her pride after their last row, then so could he. It was time they were reacquainted.

Joseph suggested meeting at Café Procope, near his home in Saint-Germain-des-Prés. Mary knew the place and its reputation for harbouring an artistic clientele, and imagined that Joseph believed he fitted in, which he didn't. She would humour him, let him preen amongst his friends, trying to show her how much he didn't need her. That was fine, she would play his game, because she needed him, although perhaps not quite in the way he was expecting.

Inside, the café was dark, even darker than the rainy day outside, despite the mirrored walls and chandeliers heavy with burning candles. It was full of men and all eyes tracked her as she made her way to where Joseph sat in a corner with a carafe of wine and two glasses. A waiter hurried over to take her dripping cloak and Mary returned one of her winning smiles.

'Where are all the women?' she asked Joseph, scanning the room for anyone she might owe money.

Joseph bared his teeth in a wolfish grin. 'At home in their salons, flirting with their husband's friends.'

He poured them each a glass of wine and as he concentrated, Mary thought how unfair it was that time had not played tricks on him as it had on her. He suited his well-trimmed grey beard and slightly rounder build, whereas she had to battle with facial hair and an expanding girth every day.

'So, Mary,' he said. 'I was expecting to hear from you. What on earth have you been up to in London?'

She summarised her story, emphasising her generosity in trying to save her niece from an unfortunate marriage, how hard she had worked to help the Earl of Powis in his duty to the family, 'but since I returned, hardly anyone in Paris will speak to me,' Mary concluded.

Joseph shook his head, smiling to himself, his attention caught by a torrent of rain thrashing at the window.

'What are you laughing at?' Mary asked. 'What's so funny?'

'Only you, my dear, only you would think it wise to humiliate the richest and most influential Jacobite family in Paris, criticise the Catholic faith and accuse others of having inappropriate morals and think you could get away with it. You are a Catholic and from a Jacobite family; you pretend to have a title from the exiled Jacobite king; you are in debt to nearly everyone... and let's not discuss your own reputation for living with me, unmarried, for most of your adult life. Why on earth did you do it?'

Mary sipped her wine. 'I did it for money, Joseph,' she whispered. 'I am owed so much by the Earl of Powis and was promised more. I didn't think... I didn't think people here would find out.'

Joseph tipped his head back and laughed, a sharp bark that lacked any humour. 'Oh, Mary, everyone knows. The people in this district, they're not aristocrats but many are Jacobite sympathisers and it's all they've talked about for months. I've had to work very hard to pretend I've never met you.'

Mary became aware that all conversation in the café had

stopped and the men stared at her, some with interest, others with obvious dislike.

'Am I safe here?'

Joseph glanced around the room. 'I'd say not, but as long as I'm with you, no one will dare lay a finger on you. When we've finished here, I'll walk you home.'

Mary held out her glass for a refill. 'I need to be paid. That's why I'm here.'

'And you want me to encourage the person who owes you this money?'

'I want all of my expenses and my inheritance, backdated to the day my father died. The man's name is James Shirley, he's the Earl of Powis' agent in Paris.'

The rain had stopped. Outside the window, the wet streets shone, glimmering in a shaft of unexpected sunshine. Shopkeepers carried their goods outside and pedestrians gathered, resuming their day's activities.

'Let's finish this,' Joseph said, upending the carafe, 'and find somewhere to play cards. On the way, you can tell me where I'm likely to find him. Is it just a scare you want, or shall I play a bit rougher?'

She lifted her chin and drained her glass. 'Start with a scare; we'll keep the rest in reserve.'

Joseph snapped his fingers and a waiter hurried over with Mary's cape. Seeing Joseph was leaving, everyone turned back to their drinks and kept their gaze safely fixed on the marble tabletops.

Mary hooked her arm through Joseph's elbow. 'I do like you, Joseph,' she said. 'But I can see you're still a bully.'

He pressed her arm against his ribs. 'I like you too, Mary, and I can see you still enjoy revenge. Come on, let's make some money, just like old times.'

Mary thought it would do Joseph no harm to walk to the Tuileries Gardens, where there were many more cafés frequented comfortably by women. It was an easy route, crossing the river by the Pont Royal. The exercise would be good for him.

She would have preferred to meet in the early evening, when café owners lit lamps around the outside tables and the garden became a magic place of laughter, glasses chinking and plants made mysterious by contrasts of light and deep shade. It was one of the disadvantages of having no acquaintances, no one to sit with in the Tuileries, to enjoy together the beauty of sunset falling over her favourite place. She could come alone, but the risk of walking home as an unescorted woman was too great. Tonight, if Joseph had been successful with Shirley, he might offer to accompany her home, allowing them to linger until dusk.

Joseph dropped a bag of coins onto her lap. 'These are your expenses,' he said. 'The rest will follow once the other matter is settled.'

Mary looked up at Joseph, screwing one eye against the sun. 'He took some persuading?' she asked, scanning the crowd for anyone watching before slipping the bag under her gown.

Joseph smiled and showed her his hands, stroking a thumb across his bruised and grazed knuckles. 'Let's say, I had to follow him to his lodgings and help him search for the money, which he claimed he didn't have. He may need to wait a day or two before holding any meetings on behalf of the Earl, since he accidentally hit his head on the edge of the fireplace.'

'Thank you, Joseph. This money will make such a difference. For a start, I'll be able to pay my maid. What was the other matter?'

'Shirley says you won't get your inheritance until the Earl has concluded his business, which means marrying your niece. Did you know about this?'

Mary nodded. 'I knew that's what he was up to. It's a ruse to wipe out his debt to her, but my agreement with him was simply to get her out of the clutches of the Montagues. He's trying to delay paying me... as usual.'

Joseph lifted his eyebrows. 'And you got this agreement in writing?'

'No, I didn't, you already know I didn't, so don't ask. The child is at Oakly Park now, with Powis' mother, so I have fulfilled every part of the bargain. It is only right that I should be paid.'

Joseph shook his head. 'It may be right, but my guess is you won't see a penny. You have been used. I'm not taking on someone as powerful as the Earl of Powis, so don't ask me. You're facing another fight through the courts, Mary.' Joseph turned his face towards her and grinned, shaking his head. 'Another fight through the courts and no money to pay your lawyers. No one will lend you a single livre in Paris, not once the Montagues have spread the word that you have been complicit in the betrothal of a child barely fifteen years old, to a man of forty-eight.'

Joseph could be so infuriating, self-righteous, and smug. Mary struggled to hold her temper in check, forcing down all the hurtful words she could throw back at him, except for the very worst thing, the most wounding accusation, which somehow wormed its way out to be spoken aloud.

'You know all about it, don't you, Joseph, exploiting a young woman for her money. At least the Earl won't kill Barbara. You live every day hiding under stones because the Caryll family will never forget, or forgive, so don't lecture me about my behaviour.'

Joseph stared, gripping one of his wrists with his free hand. She knew he wanted to strike her and enjoyed the prickling sensation of fear arising from her stomach and thighs. Her words had hurt him. Good.

He gazed around at the groups of women seated at nearby tables before replying, his lips fixed into a tight line over his teeth. 'Catherine Caryll was thirty when I married her and what happened was not my fault. You, on the other hand, have colluded to secure a child bride for a man old enough to be her father. Think about her wedding night, Mary. You ought to be ashamed of yourself.'

Joseph threw some coins onto the table before striding away, his cloak swinging around his shoulders. He turned back, as if changing his mind and bent over, hissing into her face. 'Don't trouble the exiled Jacobite king with any more requests to confer on you the title of Duchess. He will not reply to you, nor will anyone else in this city, including me. You are finished in decent society. You are finished in Paris.'

CHAPTER 29

1750

HENRIETTA

Another summer in Chelsea, one she had not expected to see. Henrietta and John had taken rooms in one of the new streets spreading out towards the Thames from the Royal Hospital. Care from the nuns, whenever her health was in decline, combined with fresher air in Chelsea, meant that Henrietta was surviving but there was no question of recovery. John was occupied at Ranelagh Gardens and lived with Henrietta in Chelsea whenever he could but during the winter season, he had to find rented rooms in London.

With sadness, they had let their beloved house in Great North Street and John had lodgings near the theatre at Covent Garden. Parties and dinners with friends belonged in the past but John still found friendship and business contacts through the Beefsteak Club.

Her daughter, now fifteen, lived with Lady Chirbury at Oakly Park. Henrietta had not seen Barbara since last year, the night before the first custody hearing. It was impossible for her to travel to Shropshire, even if she was welcome and that was unlikely. It was no surprise when the Earl of Powis won the second hearing, especially as he used her older brother James as an unexpected witness.

She was glad not to have been present, to hear their joint condemnation of the Catholic faith and the Montague family. She wished she'd been even nastier to James when they lived together as children with Granny and Grandpa Webb. He was already a bully by then and sadly, had grown into the image of his father, arrogant and vengeful. Her husband said that religious converts were always zealots but she thought this was too forgiving.

It was John who visited Barbara between the hearings, bearing a letter from Henrietta, when the child was briefly residing with their friends. The child had agreed to see him, but kept him waiting for hours. John handed over the letter from her mother and they exchanged a few words. There was little else to report except that the child was pale but otherwise healthy. She guessed John kept the worst from her, to stop her worrying but what else was there but worry, imagining the fear endured by a child who had lost everything that was safe and familiar, with no inkling of what was to come. She felt her daughter's distress but it was still embarrassing to learn that Barbara was refusing to dress or even speak to her hosts.

When she was abandoned at Odstock at seventeen, she'd had some preparation for marriage and Amelia was with her. With hindsight, Granny Webb had tried to make sure she would be cared for, at least until the wedding. Henrietta regretted being so ungrateful.

She felt well enough to walk as far as the gardens of the Royal Hospital and rested on a stone bench, shaded underneath a spreading chestnut tree. She caught her breath, listening to insects busying themselves with the rue and lavender planted in the garden close by. She recovered enough to control her gasps and could breathe in the air, the scent of herbs drifting towards her.

The letter John had carried to her daughter was regrettable. The girl had not replied, of course she hadn't. Henrietta knew she had written too much detail about her own health and it had been a mistake to share her fears about John being left alone after her death.

She should never have burdened her daughter with such worries when the child carried so much pain of her own. What mother would do that? Her aunt, Lady Montague, would never have made such a mistake.

A man approached, his tread heavy on the gravel paths. He paused to look around and when he spotted her, waved and stepped over the box hedging, walking straight through the plants to reach her more quickly. It was Corbyn Morris. Henrietta's stomach turned over. Why would he rush to find her, unless it was bad news of Barbara?

Morris stopped sharply, clipping his heels together and gave a minimal bow before removing his hat. He dropped onto a bench opposite, close enough for them to talk but far enough to avoid an accusation of impropriety. Henrietta was glad to see two nearby gardeners had stopped work to scratch their foreheads and stare.

'I've found you at last, Lady Beard,' Morris said, panting. 'Your landlady told me I might find you here. You are a creature of habit it seems.'

'Is my daughter well? What news is there?'

'When I last saw her, she had settled at Oakly Park and seemed amenable to the company of Lady Chirbury.'

'Since my child is not ill or unhappy, I have no other reason to wish to speak to you, unless you have brought news of the Earl's intention to pay his arrears to me and my daughter.'

Morris gave a short, sharp bark of surprise. 'You have great foresight, Lady Beard. The Earl intends to honour his debt to your daughter by marrying her. In that way, he will owe her nothing but she will have the honour of becoming his Countess. As for *your* settlement, we'll see your husband in court.'

Henrietta gasped. How blind she had been. This was the Earl's intention all along, to separate Barbara from the family who loved and protected her and give the child to his mother, alone, vulnerable, and easily persuaded into a betrothal. 'Barbara is only fifteen,' Henrietta whispered, licking her dry lips. 'She is too young to marry but when she does, it must be to a man closer to her in age.'

Morris shook his head. 'The girl is old enough to express her own opinions. We don't need your consent but it would help our cause if you gave your blessing. The Earl needs a speedy resolution.'

Henrietta felt dizzy, feeling the world slipping away from beneath her hands, even as she clutched the rough edge of her seat. Powis would have his way whatever she said, whatever she tried to do. Her only option was to gain some influence, while it was still possible.

She listened to the scraping sound of the gardeners raking up the browned heads of fallen roses but beyond Morris' heavy breathing, there was silence. No voices rang out in laughter or even ordinary conversation, not a single bird rustled amongst the branches above. There were things she wanted for Barbara, things she believed must happen, left unsaid in the long, wasted hours of sickness. She must try to remember everything.

Henrietta paused. 'I give my consent with three conditions,' she said. 'If Barbara agrees to marry, I must be recognised as the

Countess' mother and allowed free access to her. Secondly, she must truly understand that she has a choice of guardian and can ask for another hearing at the Chancery Court. Finally, she must be allowed to practice a religion of her choice, without discrimination.'

Morris stood and swung his cloak around his shoulders, rescuing his hat from the bench. 'Thank you, Lady Beard. I will hurry now to inform the Earl. He wishes to propose to your daughter as soon as possible and begin preparations for the wedding.'

'Do not forget my conditions, Mr Morris,' Henrietta called after him. 'I will send Lord Powis a copy through my solicitor and will write to my daughter with an explanation.'

'Send any letters to your daughter through me,' Morris replied, calling over his shoulder.

'I will not,' Henrietta shouted back. 'John will carry them to her.'

Exhausted, Henrietta fell sideways onto the bench. Breathing was only possible in short bursts. The air felt dense, too thick to swallow and her tongue stuck to the roof of her mouth. She sat up, resting on her hands to stop them trembling and leaned forward, feeling a wisp of breeze touch her brow. At last, her pounding heart slowed and she could breathe again, deep, rasping gulps of air that filled whatever capacity remained in her obstructed chest.

There was a crunching sound. A young man approached, pushing along gravel paths a heavy wheeled device that was between a sedan chair and a carriage. Despite the heat of the day, the man conveyed in the chair was covered in a blanket. Only his yellow face and a pair of clawed hands were visible.

'Would you mind if I leave this gentleman next to you?' the young man asked Henrietta. 'There is no other shade at this end of the garden. I will sit over here.' He gestured to the newly vacated bench.

The patient, a man of extreme old age, stared up into the branches of the tree, as if fascinated by the dancing shadows. His skin was paper thin and marked by brown and purple lesions. Only a few wisps of hair covered his naked scalp.

'How old is this man?' Henrietta asked the carer. 'He looks as if he is close to leaving this world.'

The young man, dressed in a form of military uniform, frowned. 'He can hear you, my lady, but to answer your question, we think he's well over ninety. No one can be sure.'

'I'm so sorry,' Henrietta replied. 'That was thoughtless of me.'

They sat in silence, listening to the insects. Henrietta glanced at her aged companion, thinking how unfair it was that he had lived through many years he didn't want and she, like her own mother, would have so few. She decided to walk a little further to the pleasure gardens, where John would be rehearsing with the cast from Drury Lane.

'I wish I had one of those,' Henrietta nodded towards the wheeled chair. 'I need someone to push me around.'

The young man stood and bowed. 'Please don't leave on our account,' he said.

Henrietta smiled to reassure him. 'Not at all, my husband is rehearsing over there,' she waved in the direction of Ranelagh Gardens, 'and I hope to catch him before the evening performance.'

'Ah, what a delight,' her companion replied. 'On summer evenings like this, we leave the windows open so the veterans can hear the music. It seems to calm them. Many suffer terrors from their military campaigns. We can heal their bodies but their minds remain fractured forever.'

'You are doing a wonderful job,' Henrietta replied. 'My

husband and his friends often sing for charitable causes. I will speak to him about your patients and see if a private performance can be arranged.'

'Who is your husband, if I may ask?'

Henrietta straightened her back. 'He's John Beard, the tenor.'

The young man bowed again, as if he were in John's presence. 'Everyone has heard of John Beard,' he said, his fine, unshaven skin blushing a deep pink. 'We would be honoured if he would pay us a visit.'

'If I ever reach Ranelagh Gardens,' Henrietta said, lightening her words with a laugh, 'I will ask him.'

John and his companions were rehearsing in the Rotunda, where it was cool, although the performance tonight would be outdoors. Henrietta weaved her way through a multitude of servants carrying lamps and chairs to the lawn in front of the outdoor stage, smelling the tantalising aroma of onions frying as street vendors began to prepare for the throng of visitors expected after dark.

She found a solitary chair left behind inside the main auditorium of the rotunda, unable to face the climb up to the balcony where there was always seating. John saw her arrive and touched his nose in greeting before finishing his song, accompanied by a small orchestra. John often complained that the challenge of the summer season was to learn so many new popular songs, which were rarely repeated the following year. She had heard him practise this one at home, an ode written to celebrate the birthday of Frederick, the Prince of Wales. It was essential that it was note-perfect, every single time, and John would not stop rehearsing until he was confident.

After three more renditions, a welcome chance for the sweat on Henrietta's skin to dry and for her breathing to recover its pace, John came to find her, mopping his brow.

'My darling,' he said, lowering his head to kiss her. 'You should not have walked all the way here.' He glanced around, looking for another seat. 'Come on outside,' he said, offering her his elbow. 'Let's go and sit in the new Chinese pavilion. There's plenty of shade and we'll find somewhere we can be together.'

They progressed at Henrietta's pace to the pavilion, where several young couples were taking advantage of the privacy. She tried to avoid staring but it was hard not to look, to feel envy for their youth and hope. Her fury at the conspiracy which had snared her daughter, who might never, ever feel the quality of love Henrietta shared with John, burst from her in a flood of words snarled by ugly tears.

'Barbara is being forced to marry,' Henrietta cried. 'I had no choice but to give my consent. They have trapped her and they have trapped me.'

John wrapped his arms around his wife, holding her in a tight embrace, while her sobs subsided. 'Slow down, and tell me everything,' he whispered.

Henrietta repeated the details of her meeting with Corbyn Morris, pausing to breathe whenever fresh tears erupted.

She felt John's chin scratch across the top of her cap, as he shook his head. 'It was deliberate... he made sure he would catch you alone. If I see that man, I will kill him. They have made sure that everyone who cared for Barbara has lost control of her. I'm proud of the conditions you set, that took courage. We will make sure our lawyer and friend is made aware of these.'

Henrietta shook her head, wiping a smear of slime from her top lip with the back of her hand. 'He is helpless, as are we. The only person with any influence in this situation is Barbara herself. We must help her. She must know her rights, understand her own power. If I write to her, will you take the letter to Wiltshire?'

'Of course; I am free the night after next. That gives you all day tomorrow to compose your letter, since I do not want you to even think of attempting to start it tonight. If you will excuse me abandoning you for a moment, sweetheart, I will hail that sedan chair over there, the one just depositing a noble guest, and ask him to take you home. I will be late, as always and expect you to be deeply asleep when I slip in beside you.'

CHAPTER 30

1750

BARBARA

I don't even know her first name because she expected me to call her Lady Chirbury from the start but in private, I call her the Dowager. My memories of coming here are hazy, because at some point during that second hearing in Westminster Hall, my mind soared up into the rafters and I sat up there on a beam, looking down on the men and their wigs, surrounding the Lord Chancellor and the husk they thought was me.

My mother's brother was called as a witness and I do remember noticing that he had a beaky nose, a bit like hers. He and the Earl of Powis spun a tale about my background, a girl locked up in convents, kept away from her family, while a secret papal cabal performed evil deeds around me.

That might have been more exciting than the boring life I'd actually led. It was true that I felt like a prisoner in the convent but isn't that how children feel in every boarding school? Even Anthony thought he was locked up at Eton. The judge believed their stories and I was handed over to the old bat, the Earl's mother, like a parcel. When we left the court, I was still up in the eaves and had to be led away, as if I were blind or deaf.

The Dowager is immensely proud of Oakly Park, a house built for her by her son. It's nowhere near as grand as Cowdray, the greatest house I've ever lived in, with its wide courtyard, tall, twisty, chimneys and deep windows. If you look back towards this place from the garden, it's boxy, without elegance, like a house a child would draw. I haven't made these comments out loud, it would only upset the Dowager. So far, she's been on my side.

I tried not to speak to her at first and kept to my room but when I'd only been here a couple of weeks, she burst through the door, shouting at me that she was short of a hand for her card game, tossing a new dress onto the bed, one made to fit me from a dark-blue silk.

The next thing a maid appeared and rushed me into dressing, pinning up my hair, and then I was placed at the Dowager's card table, surrounded by old ladies, clones of Lady Chirbury in their dress, hair, and powdery smell.

The Dowager didn't know that I was well-acquainted with the elderly and their ways, through playing cards with my great-grandmother, Granny Webb, and her ancient friends, women who often had to be woken up to play their next hand. She also didn't know that I almost always won at card games. I saw the glances between them and enjoyed their discomfort.

Now, I spend almost every day gambling with the Dowager, either with her friends or just the two of us, as she tries to learn from me. I've never met anyone so competitive, not even Anthony. So much for the Earl's plan to keep me safe from corruption.

She called him Henry Arthur, her son the Earl, always using both names, as if she was trying not to mix him up with someone else. He visited regularly but mostly spoke to his mother. I always left the room when he was announced and in case he tried to greet me by kissing my hand, I smeared both of them in oil of cloves, so that he would get a shock when he leaned over. Mostly, he ignored me and I haven't bothered with the oil of cloves again because the Dowager complained about the smell.

No one seemed troubled that I wasn't going to school and the question of my problematic faith never came up. The Dowager was not a regular at the local church, although we did call on the cleric and his wife about a charitable committee she pretends to be interested in, but only when she isn't playing cards. All that fuss in court had been for nothing. The autumn came and went, Christmas passed, followed by a bitterly cold winter, where we stayed by the fire, played cards, drank sweetened tea, and ate cake.

Things started to change as my fifteenth birthday approached. I knew all about monthly bleeds, that was one of the few advantages of living with other girls at boarding school, so I wasn't shocked to find blood on my shift one morning but the event seemed to throw the rest of the household into a panic.

I told my maidservant to bring me cloths but she had lived for so long with an old lady, they were unprepared for a newly bleeding girl. I had to stay in bed until the maid brought me a few of her own spare cloths. Once I was washed and dressed, the Dowager called me into her morning parlour. We sat side by side at her fire while a servant poured us coffee, which I hated.

'I'm so sorry, my dear,' she said. 'I thought you must have started years before and had your own supplies. It was remiss of me not to ask your great-aunt but the two families are not speaking to each other.'

'Fourteen isn't late,' I said. 'Many of the girls at school didn't start till then.'

The Dowager shivered as if troubled by an unpleasant thought. 'School... what a waste of time for girls. I only had a governess until I was ten and what harm has that done me?'

You might be better at cards, I thought, but knew not to say anything, another tough lesson from living with other girls in a dormitory. 'I have wondered what has become of my education,' I asked. 'I'm happy to have a governess, if that would suit you better.'

The Dowager lifted her eyebrows and gave a small screech. 'A governess! That is not what he has planned for you.'

I lowered my eyes, in case my next question was too intrusive. 'I assume you mean your son. Since he went to so much trouble to bring me into your care, am I to be your lifelong companion? If he doesn't marry and produce an heir, I understand I will inherit. I'm guessing that's why I'm here, to become part of the Herbert family and learn your ways, even change my faith if necessary.'

The Dowager gave another screech and I realised this was a laugh, something I hadn't heard before. 'Nonsense, girl, he intends to marry you, once you are fifteen. You will be the Countess of Powis and your children will inherit.'

I couldn't speak, couldn't find a single word to convey the shock. I was to marry an old man. My stomach dropped and I had the sensation of my scalp lifting from my head. Then I was floating and wrapping myself around the chandelier, looking down on my own rigid body.

The Dowager misinterpreted my silence and plunged on. 'Don't worry, he won't touch you until you're eighteen, he has promised me. Anyway, there's no need... he has plenty of other women. He wants a wife and heirs, that's all.'

A month after my birthday, John Beard came. I liked John, ever since we spent that summer in Lille when I was a child, but I have never quite forgiven him for taking me back to the convent when it had felt as if we were a family. I guessed the Dowager's wish to boast to her friends about meeting the famous tenor overrode her son's instructions and she let him stay.

We endured her company in the library until John, in his calm and gentle manner, asked if he could have some time alone with me. I was surprised when she agreed, giggling like a young girl in the presence of a suitor, and said she would ask a maidservant to bring us refreshments, since our guest had travelled so far.

'How is my mother?' I asked. 'Is she able to visit me herself?'

John shook his head and produced a letter from inside his coat. 'She cannot travel, I'm afraid, but we recently heard about the Earl's intentions and she was desperate to speak to you. Her thoughts are in this letter.'

I took the letter from his outstretched hand. 'It seems I must marry the Earl of Powis.'

John bared his teeth as if the thought disgusted him. 'No one can force you, Barbara. Whatever they threaten, you cannot be made to marry against your wishes.'

'What shall I do, John?' I pleaded.

'You must make up your own mind. If what he is offering is acceptable to you, then agree. A marriage to Lord Powis would return to you all the rights and privileges of your birth. But I must tell you he has another reason for marrying you. As his wife, you would lose all right to the money the Herbert family has denied you from birth. For myself, I would prefer you to marry someone you love, at a time that is right for you but I am not willing to direct your life, unlike others.'

'If I refuse him, what will become of me?'

John stroked his moustache between a finger and thumb.

'You will not be abandoned. The Herbert family will threaten you with a convent but the Montagues will always have you back. Don't forget there is also the entire Webb clan, who would welcome you. Your mother will not live long, I'm afraid, and our lives are split between Chelsea and my lodgings in the city, but we will do whatever we can to help.'

I sat alone in the library after John left, hoping that the Dowager wouldn't intrude and question me. The room smelt of leather from the covers of new books that would never be opened. I liked that everything was clean and worked properly at Oakly; the fireplaces didn't smoke, the windows opened and there were enough earth closets for everyone, with fresh cloths and bowls of scented water replaced several times a day. If I said yes to the Earl, this house would be mine and the Dowager would have to curtsy to me.

My mother's letter had many crossings out, as if she had struggled to string all her muddled, contradictory thoughts into some sort of order. Once again, she spelled out her sorrow at giving me up, how she would do it differently if given a second chance. I felt only impatience. We couldn't change the fact that she had left me without a mother, abandoning me to great-grandparents, a couple so old they had to send me away to a boarding school when I could hardly say my own name. I was the one who had suffered but only her distress seemed to matter.

She admitted giving her reluctant consent to a marriage between me and the Earl of Powis, but only if it was my choice. Why had she been asked to give her consent? Henrietta Beard was nothing to do with me, other than through the accident of birth. More followed about how important it was that she was recognised as my mother, if I would please ask for this and invite her to visit when her health allowed. Wouldn't I have to forgive her first, otherwise what would cosy mother and daughter chats mean? At the moment, I didn't want them. I didn't need them.

The next bit was about marriage itself, my mother coyly trying to say what the Dowager had expressed more bluntly, that I wasn't to be forced into the act until I was ready. I knew all about wedding nights, the older girls at school had spared no details until a nun overheard and they were beaten with wooden paddles until they bled. I was never beaten at school, protected by the Abbess being my great-aunt for some of my time there. The nuns were wary of me and the girls didn't like me, thinking I was a favourite, so I hadn't found it any sort of advantage. I had no fears of a wedding night. Every married woman goes through it and most seem to survive, so what was the problem?

The third thing on my mother's mind was her fear for my faith. She stressed that I had the right to insist on remaining a Catholic and could not be forced to change, even after marriage. The little I knew of my mother, I understood how much her faith meant to her but that was about her, not me. In this household, faith meant little, apart from token adherence and I found I wasn't missing it.

I dropped my mother's letter onto the floor, where it slipped across the highly polished floorboards and slipped under a side table. My mother had no insight at all into my life. She didn't know me and nor did any of the others, not the Montagues, the Herberts, the Lord Chancellor or John Beard. The Earl of Powis wanted me as his wife, simply to meet his own ends, without any idea who he was marrying. What was to stop me doing the same? I had lived without love for so long, it would be no hardship to continue.

Other women may not be so fortunate but a certain type of aristocratic woman can live the life she chooses. I had seen this with my great-aunt, the Viscountess Montague. As the Countess of Powis, with a new background of wealth and respect, no one could control me, and no one would direct me, especially not him. The answer was perfectly clear: I would say yes.

CHAPTER 31

1751

HENRIETTA

On the day before Barbara's wedding in late March, Henrietta still held out hope that an invitation would come. There must have been some confusion about their address, with all the upheaval of leaving their home and John finding lodgings in Russell Street. Weeks spent in the convalescent nunnery meant giving up the wasteful expense of rooms in Chelsea.

Whenever she was discharged, new rooms were easily found but this meant frequent changes of address. She had been diligent about letting Barbara know whenever their residence changed but her daughter had never replied.

'We shall still go,' Henrietta said to John at dinner. 'They cannot turn us away. I am her mother.'

'Henrietta, the wedding is in Bath. We might travel all that way for nothing, even if we make it in time. I don't share your confidence that they will admit us.'

'John, I must be there, even if I have to stand outside and all

I see is my daughter arrive and leave. What if our invitation has got lost and we're expected?'

'Of course, my darling, we will go, if you feel strong enough but it's not a good time for me to leave London. I'm singing at the Prince of Wales' funeral on the first of April and then at the funeral service for Thomas Coram at the Foundling Hospital, on the third. We're right in the middle of rehearsals.'

'You never expected us to be invited, did you, John?'

'I had half an eye on the date but as time has gone on, my hopes for you did start to fade. I think Handel will understand if I miss tomorrow night's rehearsal as long as he can rely on me being there for the performance. It's not me he has to worry about, I'm already note-perfect. Should we leave tonight?'

The determination which only moments before had given Henrietta a brief surge of energy seeped from her limbs and she felt overcome with exhaustion. 'I am weary, John,' she said, 'but I will sleep during the journey. If we travel in our best clothes, we might arrive in time. The worst that can happen is we wait around Bath Abbey for hours. We have to be there.'

John leaned across the table and wrapped her hands in his. 'I'll go out and find a post-chaise, if you can be dressed and ready to leave as soon as I return. Don't risk your health, Henrietta. I will understand if you cannot face the journey and so will Barbara.'

Henrietta shook her head. 'I will go, John, however I feel. We must have been invited, I am sure of it. We cannot let her down.'

The carriage dropped them outside the abbey. Guests were already gathering, talking, and laughing in groups and Henrietta and John hovered, uncertain whether to go inside. An older woman argued with a man nearby and Henrietta overheard their row.

The woman's voice rose. 'I am Lady Mary Herbert, a cousin of the groom and the bride's aunt. I helped make this fortuitous match happen. You cannot turn me away.'

The unfortunate man, clearly one of the groom's men, pretended to scan his list of guests, as if there had been some oversight. 'I'm sorry, Lady Herbert, but your name is not on this list.'

'The Duchesse d'Herbert to you, young man,' Mary shrieked. 'I have travelled all the way from Paris, at great expense. You must admit me!'

At a signal, the floundering groomsman was joined by three other men, one of whom was Henrietta's younger brother. She turned her back, so as not to be noticed, as Mary Herbert was dragged across the grass by her armpits and dumped into the street beyond the precinct.

'Quick, let's sneak in,' she whispered to John, 'while they're fighting off Lady Mary.'

John linked arms with his wife and they walked as fast as Henrietta could manage towards the entrance. They looked back to see the three men still struggling to restrain a woman at least twenty years their senior.

'Who on earth was that?' John asked.

'That must be Barbara's aunt, the poisonous old bitch who started this whole thing,' Henrietta replied. 'If it wasn't for her interference, my daughter would still be living with the Montagues. She doesn't know me, we've never met, but I wouldn't be able to hold my tongue if we were introduced.'

'A good idea to slip inside while they're distracted,' John replied. 'If anyone challenges us, I hope we're on the guest list, but I suspect not.'

They were forced to walk all the way down the aisle, the

seats further back already occupied. Everyone stopped talking to stare, whether at their shabby clothes or at John Beard, the royal tenor. Henrietta felt horribly conspicuous and recognised no one. At the front, an elderly woman dressed in ostentatious finery, blocked their path.

'And who are you?' she sniffed.

This must be the Dowager Lady Chirbury, Henrietta thought, taking note of the full mother-of-the-groom regalia.

'I am the bride's mother,' Henrietta said. 'This is John Beard. You have already met, I believe.'

Henrietta heard the sound of the choir swell, announcing the bride's imminent arrival. Lady Chirbury peered at John, then beckoned to the groom, an older man pacing by the altar, with his best man at his side. Barbara's future husband shifted to glare at Henrietta over his shoulder, then whispered something to the younger man on his left.

Earl Waldegrave, Henrietta's older brother, spun around, his face twisted and swollen with fury. 'You are not invited,' he hissed. 'How dare you turn up like this. You must leave at once.'

James Waldegrave grasped Henrietta's elbow and steered her to the side aisle at the edge of the central pews, forcing her through latecomers towards the entrance, thrusting at her back with his free hand. She could no longer see her husband.

Her brother pushed her out through the church doors and she staggered against the wall, gasping for breath. Hurrying behind his wife, John caught James by the seams of his expensive wedding coat and threw him against one of the stone carved figures guarding the entrance. Henrietta heard the sound of fist hitting bone, then John dragged her brother up from where he had dropped to the ground, tossing him back through the church door onto the flagstones, like a sack of vegetables.

'Now go and finish your best man duties, if you can,' John

called out, and turned back to Henrietta, wiping his hands on his cravat as if he had touched something unclean. 'My darling, are you alright? he asked, helping her to stand.

'That was magnificent,' Henrietta whispered, straightening her robe. 'I didn't know you had that in you.'

John grinned. 'All actors learn to fight, whether on stage or in the bars around the theatre. It's essential training for the job.'

Henrietta put her hand on John's arm. 'She's here. Look... it's the Powis carriage.'

A group of men had gathered at the church doors, their brows lowering with threat but seeing the bride stepping down from her carriage, they hesitated. They could not risk spoiling her ladyship's entrance or their master's wrath.

'Shall we leave?' Henrietta hissed. 'They'll attack you as soon as she's inside.'

'No, wait,' John said, straightening his back and adjusting his wig. 'I will sing for her... listen to this.'

Henrietta held her breath. John's voice soared, welcoming her beautiful daughter. The child stepped carefully down the long path, almost tripping on the hem of her dress, supported by Lord Hardwicke, the High Chancellor, a man who had sacrificed her daughter to lies and deceit and now led the girl into the arms of a stranger. The choir inside stopped singing, pealing bells fell silent, the gathered citizens of Bath paused in their chatter. Even the gang waiting for their chance to teach John a lesson, flung the church doors wide for everyone inside to hear the tenor John Beard sing an aria last heard at a royal wedding.

At the words, *'This is the day which the Lord has made,'* Barbara paused, lifted her veil, and stared at her mother and stepfather but her gaze was unfocused. At the high arched doorway, she stopped to adjust her bridal gown before turning again, seeing her mother but with eyes that were blank. With that final glance, Barbara continued on her way to become the Countess of Powis.

As the church doors closed behind her daughter, John tugged on Henrietta's arm. 'If you can manage, my darling, we should run for it.'

Four months later, Henrietta and John made their way to Edward Webb's office in Grey's Inn. Edward met them at the door, his face bright with good news but Henrietta allowed him to fuss with chairs and for the clerk to bring refreshments, even though she would have been happy for him to blurt out whatever it was, without this ceremony. But Edward needed the performance and she owed him this.

'I'm afraid we've made no progress on the arrears,' Edward began, 'but the Earl of Powis has offered to purchase your jointure for a one-off payment of two thousand, two hundred pounds. He wants a written agreement that all debts are cleared and no further payments will be due.'

John gave a low whistle. 'That is a lot of money, Henrietta, and will cover everything we owe. We could have a fresh start, without litigation dragging us down.'

'But there is so much owed to me,' Henrietta argued. 'There have been years without payment of my jointure.'

'If I may interrupt,' Edward said, 'as your lawyer, I would recommend you accept. I can understand you want everything you are owed but to continue fighting will only mean years of further litigation, with no guarantee of success. In fact, I cannot quite believe the Earl's change of heart.'

Henrietta smiled and looked at John. 'This is my daughter's doing. As the Countess, she is learning where her power lies. I am proud of her.'

'I think my wife is saying that we agree,' John said. 'Am I correct, my dear?'

Henrietta paused, seeking a moment to clear her head. It was hard to accept that her marriage settlement had been a fantasy, concocted by old men in too much of a hurry. Her entire life had been lived in its shadow and to be relieved of the burden would indeed be a relief, both for her and for John.

'Yes,' Henrietta nodded. 'I agree.'

The lawyer pushed his back against his chair and raised his eyebrows. 'Thank goodness for that!'

Turning to his clerk, Edward instructed that a bank account be opened for John that very day and the money transferred at once. 'Let's act quickly, before the Earl changes his mind,' He grinned.

Every penny was spent within six weeks, and the account closed but this only brought Henrietta pleasure, knowing that every tradesperson owed money had been paid, her cousin Edward Webb and Amelia were owed nothing and they had enough put by for lean times. Only once the burden was gone, did Henrietta fully appreciate how John had been dragged into meetings and court appearances at the expense of his career, simply because he was her husband. He could now fill his diary with engagements, without worry.

There was one meeting that John was determined to have, even though Henrietta tried to persuade him that it wasn't worth it. He arranged to meet Corbyn Morris one last time in April, at the Tennis Court Coffee House. He returned after his evening performance and slipped into bed, turning away from her, even though she could tell he wasn't asleep.

She sat up and wrapped her arms around her knees.

Glancing at John, she saw his eyes were open, staring into the dark.

'Did you sort it out?' she asked. 'Whatever it was you needed to talk to him about?'

'You were right, it was pointless,' he whispered. 'It has needled me for so long, that man accusing me of being of low birth. I wanted him to apologise.'

'And did he?'

'Of course not. In fact, he made it worse by saying we weren't invited to the wedding because we wouldn't have fitted in, not because of your poor relationship with your family. The Earl of Powis decided we wouldn't know how to mix with the other guests.'

Henrietta sighed. 'That was cruel. It's not true, John, and you know it. You mingle freely with men from all levels of society at the Beefsteak Club and are highly regarded by the royal family. I doubt if the king would even recognise the Earl of Powis but he knows who you are.'

'I asked about the promise he made, for you to be properly recognised as the Countess' mother, your right to see Barbara whenever you choose.'

Henrietta gave a snort of derision and rested her cheek on her knee, facing him. 'I can imagine his reply to that.'

'He claimed to have put the matter before the Earl and your daughter but it was not a priority for either of them. They plan to travel in Europe soon and will decide on your access when they return.'

Henrietta reached out for John's hand. 'Thank you for trying but don't waste any more time on Morris. My daughter knows I want to see her but the feeling is not returned. I have accepted this. Any blame lies with me.'

John stretched out an arm and she fell into his embrace, her head resting against his shoulder. She could smell his sweat and greasepaint left in the creases of his neck. He kissed her, slowly at first and then with growing passion, before his free hand found her breast.

'Are you well enough?' she heard him whisper.

∾

In the days when she had enough health to walk into the countryside from their old house in New North Street, John and Henrietta had been curious about a new building on Lamb's Conduit Fields. At the Beefsteak Club, members talked about the Foundling Hospital charity set up by the sea captain Thomas Coram. These were the very buildings seen on their walks. Many members petitioned the club to give support to this deserving cause and John was keen to become involved, since his friend, the artist William Hogarth, was a governor and Handel sponsored a yearly benefit concert for the charity. John's enthusiasm was infectious, so she chose not to remind him that their youthful indiscretion had led to her being ejected from the original working party. Prompting his memory might only have made him angry and resentful.

John agreed to sing Handel's *Messiah* for the fund raising concerts, refusing to accept a fee. Like the rest of London society, Henrietta would have hated to miss these evenings, but she had the unique privilege of attending as John's wife.

She wasn't proud of wanting to be seen, her status acknowledged by the aristocratic women who had once belittled her, but the pain of exclusion from her daughter's wedding and hearing Corbyn Morris' harsh words repeated by John, made her determined to attend on both dates in May, despite her failing health. She would rest for days beforehand, to harvest every ounce of strength.

The wealthy patrons assembled in the newly completed

Court room, to view Hogarth's latest paintings. These select guests were entertained by a chamber orchestra and served mouthfuls of tempting food, accompanied by glasses of red wine. John was rehearsing, so Henrietta tried to mingle, reaching out for some wine as a waiter swept past, carrying a tray, giving her something to occupy her empty hands. She knew no one, and the voices around her roared. Scanning the edge of the room, she searched for a seat.

'Henrietta!' a voice rang out through the babble and she turned around to see an elderly woman patting the seat next to her.

It was Frances Byron, her nemesis from Great Marlborough Street. Desperate to halt the room from spinning, Henrietta forced a smile through taut lips and sat down. When she was able to focus on her companion, she wondered how aged Frances seemed, before remembering her former neighbour was at least fifteen years her senior.

'So lovely to see you,' Frances said, peering over a pair of pince-nez spectacles. 'You are thin, though. I hope you're well?'

'Well enough,' Henrietta replied, hoping she hadn't sounded brusque. 'Thank you for spotting me, I needed to rest.'

'That's why they squeeze these sofas around the edge of the room,' Frances replied, her voice carrying an edge of pride. 'For the elderly amongst us, and the infirm of course. I have influence on these matters, since my son is a governor.'

'Are you still involved with the Foundling Hospital?' Henrietta asked. 'I remember you were a leading light on the original committee.'

'It's wonderful to see how the whole project is coming together but I'm no longer taking an active role. Your husband makes an important contribution, raising funds. When you have recovered your strength, Henrietta, why don't you consider joining the women's committee?'

'Lady Byron–' Henrietta started to speak but was interrupted.

'It's Lady Hay, actually. I married Sir Thomas over ten years ago.'

'I do apologise,' Henrietta continued, 'but it was you who threw me off the committee. Don't you remember?'

Frances widened her eyes. 'I did no such thing, Henrietta. You must be mistaken.'

Henrietta scraped her bottom lip with her front teeth. Was this conversation even worth pursuing? Deciding to plough on, Henrietta said, 'I'm afraid it's true, Frances. You accused me of all sorts of things because I was John's lover, even though I was an adult and a widow. You *did* ask me to step down from the committee.'

Frances frowned. 'I do remember something occurred between us but once you and John Beard were married, I would have looked kindly on a request to rejoin. It takes two people to mend a fence, Henrietta. Is there any chance you could introduce me to your husband tonight? We did so love hearing him sing at Ranelagh last summer. Such a wonderful evening with the masquerade and fireworks. Sir Thomas was quite taken with it all.'

All of these people, every single one of them, Henrietta thought, would have refused to meet John earlier in his career but now he was famous, with friends like David Garrick and William Hogarth, they all wanted a part of him. It was infuriating.

She had wasted enough time pandering to this woman. There was so much she could say and she relished the thought of Lady Hay's reaction to a dose of scathing wit – but John's future lay with the patronage of women like this, not forgetting their husbands. She could not destroy his future.

Pushing herself to stand from the low sofa, she held out a

hand to her enemy. 'Well, Frances, I'm glad we had this chat and sorted things out between us. I'm afraid John will have to take me home after the performance; my health is not good.'

Frances' lips twisted in a parody of sorrow and she gripped Henrietta's hand, pulling her so close Henrietta could see face powder trapped in the deep pouches under Frances' eyes. 'I was sorry to hear about your daughter, what happened at the Chancery Court. Life is hard for women, is it not?'

'Please do not waste your sympathies,' Henrietta replied, struggling to release her hand from the older woman's grip. 'My daughter is the Countess of Powis and has few regrets.'

Henrietta slowly edged her way around the room, pausing to balance against furniture, desperate for the outdoors and fresh air. 'If you wealthy women have sympathy to spare,' she muttered aloud, 'save it for those abandoned children and their distraught mothers, those we are trying to help tonight.' Nearby guests turned and stared, their conversation falling silent. Henrietta threw them a wide smile and set off in search of John.

CHAPTER 32

1751

BARBARA

I don't remember much about the wedding but the months beforehand are fixed in my mind, much like images from a child's scrapbook.

Henry visited Oakly more often and sought me out, instead of his mother, but we did have to endure her presence as a chaperone during our awkward conversations in the library or morning room. We both struggled to find a topic where there was any common interest but this wasn't surprising given that he was old enough to be my father, or even my grandfather.

He tried to interest me in politics, telling me that my uncle James was tipped to be prime minister one day, or he explained how the estate worked or about his career in the army, but it soon became obvious that I didn't understand what he was talking about.

It was easier once he proposed marriage in his matter of fact way and I had agreed, because then we could talk about the wedding. The Dowager came up with the guest list and two months before the date, the three of us gathered around the small table in the library, cosy with logs burning in the grate and warm chocolate with sugar to drink.

I scanned the list and asked, 'I can't see anyone here I know. Where are my family, my mother, or the Montagues?'

A look passed between Henry and the Dowager. 'My darling, we can't ask the Montagues because they are still refusing any contact from us. The rest of your family are Catholics and it would be rude to make them sit through the Anglican wedding service. As for your mother and Mr Beard... we thought it was for the best if they didn't come. They will feel out of place and the expense of outfits, overnight accommodation, a gift, will place a financial burden on them.'

'There's also the question of your mother's health and John Beard's schedule,' the Dowager interrupted, her head tilted to one side in a feint of concern.

'So there will be no one there for me?'

She emitted her ridiculous screech of laughter. 'Goodness me, Barbara, we will all be there for you and your new husband will stand at your side. Your mother's brothers will also be present. The Earl Waldegrave will be Henry Arthur's best man.'

'Well that does fill me with confidence,' I snorted, 'having those two uncles present. Who will give me away?'

Henry's cheeks coloured and I was pleased to see his discomfort. 'We thought we'd ask the High Chancellor.'

I emitted a long parody of a sigh. 'I suppose he may as well finish the job, since he was happy to give me away to strangers in the Chancery Court.'

'My darling, I understand how you feel about what happened to you in court but I felt I had no choice,' Henry replied. 'It possibly could have been handled better but I hope I can make it up to you, throughout our life together.'

You certainly will, I thought, but instead I said, 'I want my mother and John Beard there. Why don't you ask him to sing for the congregation and then my mother can be a guest?'

Henry shook his head. 'Believe me, I had thought of that, but I have to take her brothers' feelings into account. Is there anyone else you can think of who could be invited?'

I shook my head. They knew I had no friends, so it was safe to make this offer, one that sounded generous but was empty. As they talked on about guests and food and venues, I stared out of the window. It was almost dark, being late January and the sun dipping over the frosty landscape made Oakly Park seem almost beautiful.

The Dowager had tried to find me some friends but she had no idea that a fifteen year old has nothing in common with young women in their twenties with babies. From the kitchen, I often heard the young maids laughing but if I crept down to listen, they always spotted me and stopped talking, dropping me a curtsy. I had to pretend to be looking for something, before slipping away.

Henry noticed my attention had drifted and stood up, offering me his arm. 'Come on, Barbara, let's walk before dark. I'm stifling in here.'

Walking in the grounds was the only way we could escape from his mother, who had an aversion to outdoors. I didn't know how to be with him. I had tried being grown-up but he seemed to prefer a girlish coquette, so that was the persona I adopted most often. A flirting little girl, with a sprinkling of moody adolescent, got me my own way over most things, including a trip to Paris with the Dowager to have our wedding outfits made by Mr de La Frenai himself.

Sometimes, Henry took my hand as we walked and once, we sneaked into a copse of trees for a kiss but I really didn't like the smell of him up close. He reminded me too much of great-grandfather Webb.

Henry and I walked briskly through the icy grounds and at the highest point, we looked back at the house, the windows growing brighter as the dusk encroached.

'We should turn back,' he said, 'before they send the dogs out to search for us. About the wedding,' he hesitated, his eyes scanning the frozen earth around his boots. 'Your mother and Mr Beard cannot come. My mind is made up. You will have noticed I give in to all your wishes and that is the husband you can expect me to be, for all the time we are together, God willing. On this one matter only, I will not change my mind.'

I nodded and turned sharply on my heel, setting off at such a pace he had to run to catch up. We walked in silence, Henry settling for an angry adolescent as his future wife, because in that moment, there was no other person I could be.

I do remember preparing for the wedding. My maids treated me like a princess through the long hours until two o'clock, when the household carriage was expected. It would be arrayed in white and pink spring flowers, fresh from the greenhouses.

I lay back in a tub of warm water, allowing my hair to float around me, and enjoyed an unfamiliar tingling sensation through every part of my body when a maidservant massaged my scalp.

Wrapped in sheets, my dripping hair was combed out, then fresh hot water arrived, carried by men from the household and the estate, between them struggling to manage the buckets and slopping water onto the floorboards. Afterwards, the maids smoothed my skin with scented oils and my nails were clipped on both my hands and feet. I was led from the damp, steamy bedroom that had been mine since I arrived at Oakly Park, to my bridal chamber, where a door led to Henry's dressing room and his adjoining bedroom. There was another door to my personal dressing room, where my intimate toilette could be hidden from my husband's prying eyes.

My wedding robe waited, hanging from a wooden mannequin, but first my hair had to be dried in front of a roaring fire, both servants brushing so that warm air reached every strand. I was placed in front of the dressing table mirror, still in my morning robe, and watched the girls' expressions turn fierce with concentration as they pinned up my hair with lace and a new thread of pearls. In front of a full-length mirror, they dressed me layer by layer, first my new shift of almost translucent linen, then my silk petticoat of the palest, most iridescent grey, the threads of my embroidered stomacher tugged across my back and finally the robe itself.

On the day I collected my wedding gown, Mr de La Frenai had made sure to be in the shop himself and at the sight of me, he seemed to be distressed. He wrapped my gown into a silk parcel, tying the ribbons too fiercely and wiping tears away from his eyes with his thumbs before handing the package to our servant. The Dowager snapped at me to ignore him and I wondered what she had seen, what had made her so angry.

The girls also cried when they stood back to admire their work. My gown was of grey, silvered silk, embroidered with green and blue flowers. Lace frilled upwards from the scooped neckline, allowing only a tantalising glimpse of my small breasts and the short sleeves were studded at the hem with beads of jet. From underneath the sleeves, layers of lace from Lille folded to my elbows. Across the stomacher, jet beads stretched in lines across the fabric, drawing the eye down to the tightly fitted waist, where the skirt split and pulled around to the back, the fabric falling in pleats down my back and legs. Underneath, I wore only a little padding at my hips to make sure the skirt moved correctly as I walked. I stared in shock at my image. This was no bride, this was a child dressing up as a bride. That must be why my dressmaker had wept.

I did not weep, too careful of my lightly applied make-up, designed to make my already fresh face appear even more youthful. My rouged lips and cheeks resembled those of a doll. I was placed on a chair in front of a side table, sipping at a glass of wine and picking at some food brought by my maids, concerned that it would be hours before I ate again. I gave them the ribbons and silk wrapping from my La Frenai gown and they left me alone to wait by the fire.

Staring into the flames and listening to the gentle shifting of the logs, I escaped into a daydream which carried me through the day. The last detail I remember properly was the bridal horses looking ridiculous because someone had tied pink ribbons into their forelocks.

I heard John's voice and thought I saw my mother at the end of a long tunnel. It was cold in the abbey church and I shivered, leaning against Henry's elbow as words murmured around me. Someone nudged me to say my responses and then too many people kissed me. Dried flower petals were thrown into the air, touching my cheek and I raised my face to watch them swirl down like snowflakes. There was a smell of roasted meat but I felt too sick to eat, a buzzing silence while men spoke, and clapping so loud it hurt my ears. Henry shouted into my face, clicking his fingers, before leading me onto the floor where he gripped me tightly around the waist and whipped me around to music that faded then thundered. I heard the Dowager's voice, shouting at him that he'd had enough to drink.

Finally, the long day ended and Henry carried me upstairs, tossing me onto my bridal bed. The maids stripped me of my finery, moving my weightless limbs as if I were a puppet, before helping me into my night shift, the fine silk smooth against my bare skin. Giggling, the maids drew the embroidered hangings around the bed frame, then shushed each other, but they were wrong to imagine what would happen next, because Henry would not come back. He had promised me and he was a man of his word, whatever else he might be. Besides, he had another woman, or many other women and would have his pick if he needed to satisfy his lust. All I had to face was a deep sleep, and that had never been more welcome.

CHAPTER 33

1752

MARY

What sort of world was it when a young man treated a woman of rank in such an appalling way? She was the bride's aunt, the woman responsible for bringing the couple together but because her name wasn't on a so-called list, she had been spoken to rudely and actually manhandled. It was perfectly obvious that her invitation had got lost between Wiltshire and Paris! In her day, it would have been enough for a man like that to recognise her bearing, her natural dignity, and admit her to the wedding, fearing repercussions against him for making a mistake.

There would be repercussions alright, as soon as she had drafted this letter. The Earl of Powis had replied to the last letter from her lawyer, claiming she owed the Herbert estate over three hundred thousand pounds because of her financial misjudgement and he would deduct her paltry claim from this sum. He was mistaken if he thought she could be threatened. Where was his evidence?

She totted up all the expenses from her wasted trip to Bath, along with her invoice for everything she was owed and sealed the document. If only she could charge for her inconvenience, squeezed into the cheapest public coaches, forced into the bowels of the cross-channel boat with vomiting adults, screaming children and even animals. She wasn't sure which had smelled the worst, the animals, or the human seafarers.

Mary had been home for several months, stuck in her dark rooms at the back of the Temple Precinct. Paris society had been stubbornly unforgiving of her betrayal but she hated that Joseph was right. There was no one to visit and no one dropped off their cards. Everyone seemed to know the Montagues or the Webbs and were terrified they too would be ostracised if they included the Duchess d'Herbert in their social gatherings. Worse, those she owed money, far too many of them, who might once have gently pressed their claim when they met her at the opera or at dinner, now pursued her through their lawyers with vindictive enthusiasm. Luckily the Grand Prior ruled his state within a state with a strict adherence to rules of entry. She was not the only debtor hiding within its walls, protected by guards.

Pursuing financial claims against others was her only occupation and one that gave her great pleasure. It was fun to upset the heirs of bankers and investors who had tricked her in the past, young men and women who tried to claim it was none of their business. They could not be held responsible, they pleaded, for mistaken advice given by relatives they had never even heard of. But it *was* their business and for as long as she lived, Mary would make sure the deception was never forgotten. The Earl of Powis should have checked the history of the family he had inveigled his way into. The Herberts were exceptionally long-lived.

There was a tap at the door and Anne entered backwards carrying a tray with their morning coffee. Miss Griffiths had become 'Anne' in the months since her humiliation in Bath and she had become 'Mary.' This new configuration of their relationship had been one of drift rather than choice but in her isolation, Mary found it helped to have one companion and friend. She had lived with her Aunt Anne for most of her adult life, and it was somehow comforting to find another Anne for her elder years and certainly made it easier to remember the woman's name.

Anne poured their coffee, the rich smell bringing the promise of comfort, along with the scent of small lemon cakes, fresh from the kitchen. Mary had known real poverty in Spain, where even the basics of life had escaped her, burdened with an elderly aunt and let down by her father. They weren't poor now, reaping the benefits of her foresight by investing in a lead mine in Brittany, almost twenty years ago. If anyone would deign to speak to her, she ought to be reaping a little more respect.

A small but reliable income, and paying almost no rent, allowed her to employ a new housemaid, so Anne had time to play cards, walk with her in the nearby Tuileries, or even just sit by a fire on dark, wet afternoons. With her failing eyesight, Mary had also hired a young man for a few hours each week to help with her correspondence.

Anne passed Mary the cream and sugar and both served themselves generously.

'I thought we might take a stroll, once we're finished, since it's a lovely day outside,' she said.

'You wouldn't think so in here,' Mary grumbled.

Anne glanced around, as if the gloom was something she

had only just noticed. 'That's why we should go out, find a café and eat some ice cream. It's almost summer.'

Mary scraped cake crumbs from her lips with her little finger before reaching for another. 'I want to show you something first.' She pushed herself to stand, pausing to gain her balance against the arm of her chair and swayed towards a sideboard. Reaching inside, she retrieved a lacquered box.

'These belonged to Mary, Queen of Scots,' she said, watching for Anne's reaction. 'They've been in my family for about two hundred years.'

Mary tipped the jewels into her palm from a small bag of purple velvet, frayed at the edges and smeared with dust and cobwebs. She trickled the rosary beads between her fingers.

'And what is that other piece?' Anne asked, looking up at Mary from under her eyebrows.

'That's a relic of the true cross,' Mary said, holding it up to catch the light from a single sunbeam flickering through the window.

'My goodness,' Anne said. 'How did you inherit these? I thought you weren't on good terms with your family.'

Mary hesitated, remembering the day she had slipped the bag into her petticoat shortly after her father died. Her brother obviously didn't want them, since he had left the bag behind when he searched their father's rooms himself. Only Mary knew what they were, how rare and important, so why shouldn't she keep them?

'They were a gift from Mary Queen of Scots to my ancestor, the first Earl of Pembroke. They've been handed down through the family,' Mary said, neatly skirting the matter of how she became the beneficiary.

Anne blew out slowly, after taking a long intake of breath. 'I know it's a long way off, Mary, but who will inherit these after you?'

Mary sniffed and chewed her lip. 'It has to be Barbara, my niece, although I regret being forced to honour her in this way, after I've been treated so badly.'

'Is there anyone else more deserving?' Anne asked.

Mary thought of her Aunt Anne, with her fierce Jacobite loyalties. Who would she have wanted to receive these gifts? The answer came to her, as if her aunt had prodded her in the back.

'I had another aunt called Winifred, the Countess of Nithsdale. She lived at the Jacobite court in Rome, was governess to Prince Charles. Her husband fought with the Jacobite army at Preston... that's a place in the north of England. I believe they had a son who inherited the family estate in Scotland. I think my Aunt Anne said he had children. It is that family who deserve these.'

'You must put that in your will, Mary. Barbara is your only close relative and she will be your executor but if I'm spared for a few years more, once you have sadly left this world, I will personally make sure that your Scottish family inherit these precious relics. When you look down from heaven, you'll see me worrying at the Countess of Powis like a terrier chasing a rat.'

Mary laughed. 'I'd enjoy that, except I won't be in heaven. I'll ask my lawyer to draft a new will, making you responsible for their safe delivery. Come on, let's go out, before we lose the best part of the day.'

'I'll call the maid to bring our outdoor things,' Anne said. 'While we're walking, you must tell me everything about your family history. It sounds fascinating.'

'Don't expect me to talk about Wales,' Mary said, fastening her cloak. 'My father loved it there, but I've never been and it's too late now.'

CHAPTER 34

1753

HENRIETTA

This small room with its bare white walls was now her only home. She would never leave. Their precious house in New North Street was gone, the neat rooms in Chelsea returned to their landlady for the use of another summer season performer.

She listened to the sounds of the nursing order; nuns' voices echoing from far away but also close to her door, sharp cries from other patients, seeking relief from their pain, the ordinary background noise of buckets and scraping plates. Here, life was lived right next to death. Her time would be soon.

Henrietta wished to see her daughter but had accepted this would not happen, it was expecting too much. Parents forgive children but the opposite is rarely true. She had not forgiven her father for his neglect of her as a child and then his outright, public rejection of her as an adult. As for her grandparents, her forgiveness of them was not complete either. She had been so lucky to find John Beard, to be truly loved. That was more than most women ever had in a lifetime.

It would soon be time for her wasted body to be washed and then a nun would try to help her swallow a few mouthfuls of broth, but days had passed since she had eaten anything. Sometimes the priest came, to talk about her fears, but she had none. She would have liked to live longer with John but was not afraid of what came next.

After his evening concert, John often visited the convent and would lie next to her, holding her in his arms but careful of putting pressure on her thin bones. He would tell her about the performance, who had been in the audience, who he spoke to, all the precious moments of his life. When she tried to talk about living after her death, how he must not be afraid to marry again, he would silence her with a kiss.

They had already planned her funeral at St Pancras Old Church, where she would be buried alongside the Webb family. Of course, John would sing. He said his heart would break but he was such a professional, Henrietta knew his distress would vanish in that moment. They enjoyed deciding who would be invited and who would be turned away at the door of the church, her brothers, and Lady Mary Herbert right at the top of the unwelcome list.

The nun finished her tasks and Henrietta felt the room darken, although it was still daylight outside. Her breathing became more difficult, long gaps between each breath, every one rasping and shallow. It was hard to swallow.

Henrietta listened and beyond her open door came the faint sound of vespers. She could no longer see clearly but a dark shape flickered in the doorway, then she felt the mattress dip as someone very light sat on the edge of her bed. The visitor took her hand and brushed the skin with her thumb. It hurt, but Henrietta didn't want it to stop.

A female voice whispered, 'Mother?'

Henrietta made the effort to clear her throat. 'Barbara, is it you?'

'It is me, your daughter. The Abbess sent for me. I came at once.'

'Barbara,' Henrietta sighed, 'are you happy?'

'I am not happy, because you are leaving me, but I'm often content, which is enough.'

Henrietta squeezed Barbara's hand. 'You have no regrets?'

'None at all,' Barbara said. 'I am in control of my own life, at last.'

'Will you have babies?' Henrietta asked.

The mattress moved in tandem with her daughter reaching over her body. There was the sound of water being squeezed from a cloth, a damp sensation across her brow.

'I will try,' Barbara replied. 'Henry is keen, of course. We are waiting until I am older.'

Henrietta nodded. 'I like to think of grandchildren.'

It was dark. There was no pain. Her daughter was still with her, the pressure of Barbara's hand light on her fingers. There was one thing left to say. She must remember, find the words.

'Barbara?'

'Yes, Mother?'

'Be kind to John.'

CHAPTER 35

1755

BARBARA

I have a baby boy we've called George, born only a few weeks after my twentieth birthday. I am pleased with him, especially now he smiles at me, but Henry is behaving as if I've given him the greatest gift. He's like a puppy, fawning over me and the child, spending hours in our newly decorated and very expensive nursery and employing an army of nursemaids to help. I have refused a wet nurse, and Henry watches me feed our child, his eyes misting with tears, as if I am a painting of the Virgin Mary.

One thing I insisted upon was a proper midwife, not the strange woman recommended by the Dowager's friends. Henry always listens to me over the Dowager, since I pushed her out of all matters of household management. I'm better at it than her, especially the accounts, and everyone has noticed.

I wish my mother was here. I'd like her to see my baby and tell me all about having me at seventeen. I wasn't ready for a child at that age and I'm not really ready now. That's probably what mothers are for, once you're an adult, to give you help but only when you ask for it.

John has been to see the baby, invited by Henry. He talks for hours about my mother, sharing everything I should have known. I had no idea she liked cats and spent too much money on fine dresses and shoes. He always refuses to stay for dinner, although Henry would love to boast that he had welcomed the great singer to his table.

The world is changing, too late for Henrietta and too late for my husband. Henry tolerates John as a visitor because everyone in his social circle is joining the Beefsteak Club. Our titled friends, even royalty, can't get enough of actors, painters, and singers these days.

Everyone knows John Beard and has heard my mother's story, so the members always refuse my husband's requests to join. The same is true of the governors of the Foundling Hospital. They don't want Henry to be one of them, no matter how hard he pleads.

He feels the rejection but I don't sympathise and he's stopped talking about it. Now we're a married couple with a child, it makes no sense, what he did to me. All he had to do was wait a few years, court me properly and ask me to be his wife. He thinks I'll forgive him but I won't.

We bought tickets to hear John sing at the Foundling Hospital benefit concert days before my mother died. He showed not a sign of his torment. It was the same at my mother's funeral, John sang as if my mother was there, facing him from the congregation, encouraging him. At the reception after the funeral service, John reminded my husband that he had sung at the door of our wedding and I was pleased to see Henry redden with shame.

I've never admitted that I have no memory of that day, except hearing John's voice carry me into the church.

I wasn't heartbroken at my mother's funeral, although other people expected it of me. I was glad to be with her when she died but I didn't know her well enough to love her.

She was a stranger to me, but not to the Webbs, who turned out in force at her funeral, bearing their sadness at her mistreatment by them. I tried to meet as many as I could, my mother's remaining aunts, her only uncle, and her cousins and listened carefully to their stories. Henrietta was loved by her mother's family but the Waldegraves didn't even try to attend. That was no surprise but it was a puzzle when the Montagues were absent. Perhaps they are still bitter and cannot face my husband.

I haven't thought much about anyone's experience of the Chancery Court hearings except my own but now I am a mother, I think about how they must have felt to be accused of mistreating a child. Such awful things were said about them and their religion, perhaps their bitterness may never heal. They probably regard my marriage as a betrayal but I will try to see them, once the baby is weaned.

In the churchyard, I was introduced to Amelia, my mother's oldest friend, and reminded that she was present at my birth at Hendon Manor. Amelia is a Webb too, married to Edward, my mother's distant cousin and lawyer. I have invited her to visit us today, at Powis House, the Herbert family home in London, built by my grandfather. It is no distance from her home in Red Lion Square.

I settled on the informal morning room to meet Amelia, trying to avoid overwhelming her with the grandeur of the rest of the house. The room has a pleasant light through tall windows and overlooks the garden, but since it was September and the baby was in a crib by my side, the maids lit a fire, making the room feel warm and inviting. I felt nervous, pacing between the writing desk and the armchairs until a tap on the door announced Amelia's arrival.

'Mrs Edward Webb,' the maid announced. 'Shall I take the baby? I think he needs his cloth changed.'

With five nursemaids travelling with us to London, there was some competition over tasks. 'Thank you, Miriam,' I said, casting a wide smile at Amelia. 'Bring him back afterwards: a clean cloth always seems to make him hungry. Besides, I want to show him off to Mrs Webb.'

Amelia took a seat on one side of the fire and looked around. 'I have no memory of this room. Much of the house was closed off when I stayed here with your mother, just after her wedding. I do remember the hall. Who could forget those floor tiles and the decoration on the ceiling?'

I sat down opposite her, next to the empty crib. 'My mother was here, with you?' I said.

Amelia nodded. 'Your father borrowed it from his older brother to show Henrietta the sights of London but then he disappeared. Your uncle threw us out, sent us packing to Hendon Manor.'

To my own ears, I sounded like a parrot, repeating Amelia's words. 'My father disappeared, straight after their wedding? What on earth was he thinking? My uncle then sent you away, to a place where you were strangers. Oh, poor Henrietta... poor you. How did you manage? You were no more than children.'

'Henrietta was seventeen, I was fifteen,' Amelia said. 'Hendon Manor was in a poor, neglected state and the staff were used to living there alone. We weren't welcome, especially me, with my French ways, which have all but disappeared, by the way.'

The maid returned with the sweet-smelling baby and I passed him to Amelia to hold. Of course, she said he was perfect but she has four of her own, so perhaps was being generous. I opened my nursing bodice and reached out for George, enjoying the sensation of him nuzzling, as he searched for my breast.

'How was the birth?' Amelia asked.

'I'm told it was unremarkable but that was the midwife's opinion, not mine. A first birth cannot be unremarkable. No one told me what to expect.'

'Your mother gave birth easily too, it must run in the family. She did complain a lot, well, yelled and swore actually. She used language I'd never heard her use before.'

We were interrupted again by a maid bringing us hot chocolate and cake. In the silence, as our cups and plates were laid out, our cake served, our drinks poured, the baby's snuffling and gulping sounds grew, too loud for someone so tiny.

I sipped at my chocolate before asking, 'Did she look after me herself?'

'Of course,' Amelia said, 'but we had a nurse living with us at the time. A woman called Alice Douglas. She was a great help to your mother.'

There was so much to learn. Who was this Alice who had cared for me? Where was she now? Such detail is passed down in families, mother to child, the rich heritage of each individual's past. This is what I was missing, not through neglect but because no one had thought it mattered enough to ask Henrietta.

Amelia noticed my distraction and changed the topic. 'How are you coping, Barbara?' she asked, her tone enquiring and gentle. 'It's a lot of responsibility for a woman of your age, being a Countess.'

On safer ground, I shared the routine of my days, running the household, caring for my child, staying out of the way of the

Dowager. I confided that I wanted only one more baby, hoping that Amelia would not take offence. 'Once that baby is weaned,' I concluded, 'I'll think about charity work. Because of John's influence, I might try to help the women's committee at the Foundling Hospital.'

'Oh my goodness,' Amelia interrupted. 'Your mother was part of that group, from the very start. Even before she met John.'

I gasped, shaking my head in confusion. I had always assumed my mother's interest arose from John and his friends.

'I am sorry, my dear,' Amelia continued. 'This is too much. If you would like, I will come again. Now that my children are older, I have plenty of time to tell you everything you might wish to know and many things you'd prefer not to. For now, let's talk about other things. I hear that your husband is selling Hendon Manor?'

'Yes,' I said. 'He's negotiating a sale with John's friend, David Garrick.'

Amelia laughed. 'I wonder what your grandfather or your ghastly uncle, Lord Montgomery, would have made of that? An actor will be Lord of Hendon Manor.'

'He could be, indeed, if he chooses to live there. It's a relief, don't you think, to live in a time where it is possible for a man, or woman, to be judged on their worth, not their birth.'

Amelia stared into the fire, deep in thought, then turned back to me, as if she judged it safe to say her next words. 'I was born into the servant class, Barbara. What you say is true only if you have enough money. We are lucky that both our husbands have more than enough. Our time is indeed one where talent speaks more than money or class but the poor will never be judged on their worth, only what they lack.'

I swallowed, afraid of having said something stupid, but

seeing Amelia's smile, I knew that this older woman, my mother's friend, would be good for me. Whoever my mother had been, and in time I would know, she had made wise choices in her companions. I would try to follow her example.

THE END

Also by Morag Edwards

The Jacobite's Wife

The Jacobites' Plight

AFTERWORD

All the characters in this novel lived real lives, apart from Amelia, who is my own creation. The important events happened as described but some details have been modified to suit my purpose as the author. The personalities of these characters, their motives, ambitions and conversations, are entirely fictional.

For those who are curious, this is how their lives ended:

Barbara Herbert, Countess of Powis (1735-1786)

Barbara had one more child, a daughter, whom she named Henrietta. As executor of Mary Herbert's will, she was keen to avoid inheriting any of Mary's debts. After all beneficiaries were paid, Barbara was left with a small profit, which helped to cover her gambling debts. In 1775, Miss Anne Griffiths came to London and with Barbara, travelled to Terregles House in Dumfries to hand over Mary Queen of Scots rosary beads and crucifix to Lady Winifred Maxwell, the granddaughter of Winifred, Countess of Nithsdale. Barbara and Henry's son George never married and the estate passed to their daughter

Henrietta, whose husband Edward Clive, 2nd Baron Clive, was created the Earl of Powis in 1804.

Lady Mary Herbert (1686-1775)

True to her word, Mary lived to be eighty-nine. She was finally made a Jacobite Duchess by the exiled King James III in 1759 and in her will was referred to as, 'My Lady Marie Herbert, Duchesse d'Herbert et de Powis.' On the death of James III, the Old Pretender, she continued writing regularly to his son, the exiled King Charles III.

Joseph Gage died in 1768 and despite their differences, he named Mary as the executor of his will. The Spanish government rescinded her mining concession in 1767 on the grounds that she had allowed her one remaining Spanish mine to fall into disrepair.

For the rest of her life, Mary used litigation to pursue those she believed had wronged her and finally won her case against the Earl of Powis in the House of Lords in 1776, with an award of £3,859 and a lifetime pension. While Mary struggled with social and family relationships throughout her life, she had a better understanding of her servants. She left money to all her servants and a generous legacy to Miss Anne Griffiths.

John Beard (1715-1791)

John Beard married again in 1759 to John Rich's daughter Charlotte and became deputy manager of Covent Garden under his father-in-law. Following John Rich's death in 1761, John became manager until 1767.

In the 1766 hearing in the House of Lords, when Lady Mary Herbert brought legal proceedings against the Earl of Powis, John forgave the Earl enough to give evidence in his favour. He sang for Handel until the composer's death in 1759 and continued for many years afterwards to sing the roles composed specifically for him.

John was president of the Beefsteak Club when the Prince of Wales, later King George IV, was admitted as a member. In 1760, he was elected a governor of the Foundling Hospital charity. King George III created for John the unique position of *Vocal Performer in Extraordinary to his Majesty* in 1764. Inheriting a fortune from his wife's family, he and Charlotte built a fine villa in Hampton, where they lived in retirement close to many of their friends, including David Garrick. John and Charlotte had no children of their own but they brought up children from Charlotte's previous marriage and two nieces, following the death of Charlotte's sister.

It has recently been discovered that the priest who conducted John and Henrietta's marriage ceremony was not licensed, so they were not, in fact, legally married. Luckily, this was unknown to them at the time.

ACKNOWLEDGEMENTS

I am indebted to the enthusiasm and energy of the wonderful team at Bloodhound Books, for bringing *The Jacobite's Heir* to publication. Particular thanks are owed to Betsy Reavley, Director and Founder, for recognising that *The Jacobite's Heir* would bring the Jacobite trilogy to a satisfying conclusion. Clare Law has been a remarkable editor, catching my many errors and anachronisms and gently suggesting when something is not quite working. A heartfelt thank you to Tara Lyons, Editorial and Production Manager, for her exceptional organisational skills in meeting deadlines but also her kindness and flexibility. Hannah Deuce, Social Media and Marketing Executive, has been outstanding, as ever, in using her professional insight and energy to market this book. Thanks also to Shirley Khan for her eagle-eyed proofreading, and to Lexi Curtis for her great work with social media and publicity. Thank you all for your support and dedication.

About the Author

Morag Edwards spent over thirty years as an educational psychologist and uses her knowledge of child development to shape fictional characters in both her historical and contemporary fiction. She has an MA in creative writing from the University of Manchester's Centre for New Writing and is an active member of Leicester Writers' Club.

The Jacobite's Wife was Morag's debut novel and the first in a planned trilogy. The second novel in the series, *The Jacobite's Plight*, was published in 2024. *The Jacobite's Heir* brings the trilogy to a close.

Morag also writes contemporary domestic-suspense fiction under the author name Isobel Ross and her novel *Crash* was published by Bloodhound Books in 2024.

Morag has self-published two works. The first is *Broken,* a domestic suspense novel. The second is a hybrid memoir, using the author name Isobel Ross, *Almost Boys: The Psychology of Co-ed Boarding in the 1960s.*

A Note from the Publisher

Thank you for reading this book. If you enjoyed it please do consider leaving a review on Amazon to help others find it too.

We hate typos. All of our books have been rigorously edited and proofread, but sometimes mistakes do slip through. If you have spotted a typo, please do let us know and we can get it amended within hours.

info@bloodhoundbooks.com

www.ingramcontent.com/pod-product-compliance
Ingram Content Group UK Ltd.
Pitfield, Milton Keynes, MK11 3LW, UK
UKHW040843161025
8419UKWH00031B/453